40 Grade Code

BOOK ONE

The Sandy Krave Saga

To my friend Marcello
Thanks for your support
All the best
Robert de Vinn

Robert de Vinn

40 Grade Code

ISBN: 9791220091879

TABLE OF CONTENTS

PROLOGUE

In the year 2166, the world is no longer the same. Outbreaks of pandemics and wars between the big powers of the world have ensured a massive change. All countries and states of the world realigned into four major regions for technological relevance and the chance of survival. As time went on, battles raged between humanity and recurrent pandemics, which ravaged the world relentlessly from the beginning of the twenty-second century.

The new regions of the world, the West Federation; Oceania Liberation; the Underworld; and Afrasia, are each run independently of one another, having a self-sufficient economy, with rarely any form of trade between them. Everything from the peoples' way of life to the currency in use is different from one to the next. For ordinary people, contact with people from outside their region remains minimal. Each region is kept on lockdown while they strive to become richer and more powerful than their rivals.

This is how the balance has been maintained for decades past, but once again, the world is about to experience a ground-shaking event that will reset the dynamic of power on a global level.

Global domination plans by rich men of the Oceania continent and alliances with Underworld mercenaries, traitors, and spies, both in Afrasia and West Federation, are destabilising intercontinental security.

The saga begins in the vast region of Afrasia with a certain mission assigned to Special Agent Sandy Krave, who would soon be overwhelmed by several frantic events that would change her life.

Sandy Krave is one of the few special agents of Afrasia to obtain the highest recognition of elite combats: the 40 Grade Code.

PART I - Girkland, Afrasia

MISSION IN THE UNDERWORLD

Sandy Krave & Special Agent Will Burne
Meet and Join Forces

Chapters One through Seven

"The meeting of two personalities is like the contact of two chemical substances: if there is any reaction, both are transformed."

–C.G. Jung

Girkland, Afrasia: 2166, May 01

The metal door of the special practice room loomed large before the tall, white-haired, green-eyed, ebony combatant, Sandy Krave, who was dressed in a tight-fitting training suit that matched the dark colour of her skin. She had just completed the +8 difficulty training with an AI-generated opposition, and she had won—albeit narrowly. The training had pitted her against twenty-five combat avatars and required her to use a great deal of her mental strength, fast hands, and superb vision to ensure victory over the level eight computer. She had completed that training not long ago, and she was already back for another session. Naturally, she wanted to take on the avatars again and win convincingly this time. That was the way of the 40 Grade Code, the creed which special military officers in Afrasia were mandated to follow. They must never be satisfied with simply a *good* performance; they must strive to be better.

"No way you'll start slipping up, Sandy," she muttered to herself. "Keep training hard. Hard!"

The nature of her job demanded perpetual excellence, and Sandy stayed true to it by constantly remaining at the top of her game—never relenting, never relaxing. She had previously completed all the levels in this training machine, also called tramach, but she did not mind doing all the levels again to keep herself as fit as a fiddle. She had first learnt this high level of discipline from Adha Long, her guardian. Adha was the high-ranking officer in the service who had raised Sandy after some gruesome accident had claimed her parents' lives.

She still remembered the pain and shock that had coursed through her system when Adha revealed to her that he was not her true father on her eighteenth birthday.

"Your parents died in an unfortunate accident," Adha had told her in his signature gentle voice.

Sandy Krave shook her head to clear the disturbing thoughts of her parents dying, then she stepped forward and placed her thumb on the door handle. She saw a blue light blink twice as the hi-tech knob attempted to verify her fingerprints. There was a flash of green a few seconds later, and the door gave way automatically with a sharp *click*. Sandy walked into the practice room as all the lights, which had been off earlier, began to click on. Within a few seconds, Sandy was bathed in the bright warm, white light from hundreds of bulbs fixed in arrays, high above on the ceiling of the training room.

"Please wait for step-two verification," the metallic voice of an AI, which was modelled after a male Afrasian voice, resounded around the room.

Sandy Krave waited on the spot while she stared in the vacant space in front of her. When the verification was complete, a huge screen would pop up in the vacant space before her, and she would then be able to access the console of the training segment.

"Step-two verification complete," the AI voice came again.

The widescreen slowly appeared before her, with various options for the available training regimen. Sandy walked up to the screen and flicked through the options. Of course, she could decide to take on the +9 difficulty, but she was not satisfied with her lowly score on the +8 guys, so she decided she would have another go at it and obtain a much better score.

Sandy clicked on the difficulty she wanted, and she heard the computer telling her to wait for another moment while her option was being processed.

"Processing complete, step into the red area for the iris scan."

Sandy rolled her eyes, wondering why the techs had made the training machines so hard to access. She understood that security and privacy were vital, but she still felt the whole verification process could be reduced to one or two steps. They could combine the fingerprint verification with the iris scan at the door, just as it had been in the old tramachs. She would speak to Colonel Randall about it. These countless verification steps took away the drive to train multiple times.

The training screen finally came up, and Sandy instantly slapped on the electronic wristband that would cause her avatar to appear on the screen in front of her AI enemies, just like being in the Underworld reality. Next, she slipped on the special headphones and picked up the weapons she had selected: a laser gun and a thermo-shield that she could swirl around her to ward off the shots of her adversaries, who were all armed with F15 firearms and electro-swords.

"Training starts in three, two, one… Now!"

While the training was still loading, Sandy checked out the battleground map; it was mountainous terrain, similar to the massive highlands abundant in the western part of the Afrasian continent.

The sound of an F15 round crashing into her armour jolted her to awareness. She could not face all the enemy combatants at once. She had to use the terrain to her advantage; the caves and crevices of the mountain, the rocky slopes were—

Buzz!

The loud buzzing sound that filled her ears just then had nothing to do with her current training session. Instead, it was an alert from outside the training room notifying her that she had an important call on her smartphone, which she had placed in the wall pouch outside. Sandy tried to block out the distracting buzz and concentrate on slaying the Underworld enemies scattered around her, but the buzz came louder still, jarring her nerves.

"Dammit," Sandy cursed as she yanked off the training devices strapped on her body and dropped them beside the screen. She knew that she would have to take all those time-wasting verification tests again.

Sandy stamped her foot on the floor and walked out of the training room, annoyed that her training session had been disturbed and not so sure she would get to continue again.

"I'll continue," Sandy reassured herself as she walked to the wall pouch where she had placed her phone. She retrieved her phone and stared at the caller ID, displayed in a tiny blue font across the screen.

Owen Briggs.

Sandy sighed. Owen calling means something big was about to happen. Maybe a high-profile job or something that only she could handle at the moment.

"Hey, Sandy. I've been calling since, forever," Owen's high-pitched voice floated into her ears.

"Was training in the special," Sandy replied.

"Oh, I thought you broke all the levels?" Owen asked.

"Ah, yes," Sandy said as she set her back against the wall. "The techies are working on something new. I have to keep myself busy 'til they come up with something."

"Chuck it somewhere; the time has come for some real action."

I knew it, Sandy thought. The fact that Owen called meant there was a mission somewhere that needed the attention of one of the best Special Agents in Afrasia.

"What's the story?" she asked Owen.

"Switch to secure-two," he instructed her.

Secure-two was one of the lines on which only very vital missions were discussed.

"Done," Sandy said, after hitting on the right part of her screen and seeing the green tick, confirming that she was on a secure line.

"Great, I am on my way to the Rig. I'm bringing someone very important with me. Can you make it in ten minutes?" Owen asked. "I will like you to hear the details from him."

Sandy did a quick mental calculation. The Rig was about five minutes away if she used the fly lanes. "I'll make it."

"Great," Owen said. "This is big, Sandy. It's intercontinental. You will get the details when you get your ass down here."

"Alright," Sandy said. The line went off, and she dropped her phone in the breast pocket of her training suit.

She was wrong when she said she was going to continue training after the call. She had to get her ass to the Rig, as Owen had said. There was a big mission waiting for her.

… … …

Fly Lane Station: Girkland, Afrasia

Two men sat in folding chairs under the shade pavilion provided by the large waiting area at the fly lane station closest to the Rig. The men were engaged in a relaxed conversation as they sipped chilled Viva, the soft drink brand that was the most popular in Afrasia. One of the men was Owen Briggs, Sandy Krave's business partner. It was he who sourced for special missions and high-paying jobs for the sharpshooting lady. Briggs' attire was a corporate outfit that included a sparkling white shirt, a black jacket, and well-starched trousers of the same colour. His hair was trimmed low, and he had sharp eyes that made him a powerful observer of any situation in which he found himself. His quick eyes watched as people walked in and out of the fly lane station.

"Tell me again, why we are about to use this lady you call Sandy?" the bespectacled man beside the Owen Briggs demanded. "We could have contacted Martinez. He is familiar with how things work on the international scene and would not be bamboozled by anything in a kind of delicate mission like this one."

Owen Briggs shook his head. "From the combat point of view, Sandy is anyone's match in this business. She is that good. She is better than Martinez in stealth missions, and even Martinez knows this. Sandy is unrivalled in terms of combat experience."

"It's fine. It does not matter who does the job. I just want it done," Briggs said, and he leaned back in his chair. He raised the glass of Viva to his lips, savouring the sweet taste as he looked around, enjoying the view of the fly lane station and the Rig that was close to it. The Rig was a big, beautiful park at the heart of Girkland, the capital of Afrasia, which had big private booths that could accommodate individuals who wanted to engage in private talks without the fear of hidden mikes picking up their conversations. Sandy and Owen often conducted their business at the Rig, not because they were into anything illegal, but because they wanted to keep the details of their business engagements and the information about Sandy's missions secret.

When Sandy eventually arrived, they would switch to the private coaches and discuss the business at hand.

The sight of Sandy making her way across the park in a fly car made Owen sit up. He no longer slouched as he did before she arrived.

"Hello, Owen," she said, pulling off her shades and settling in the seat opposite them.

"Hi, Sandy. Shall we proceed to the private room?" Briggs said. The others agreed and got up to follow him.

The coaches were designed for relaxation, and now that they were inside, they could discuss private details without being overheard. Owen waved Sandy into a seat and began to speak at once.

"This gentleman beside me is Doctor Kean; he is the head of a giant corporation that has reaches in Oceania and the Western Federation. Doctor Kean, this is Sandy Krave, the finest combatant among all the special agents in Afrasia."

Dr Kean regarded Sandy as if looking for something in her appearance that validated Owen's assertion that she was at the top end of the Afrasian special agents in terms of skill. He offered his hand, and Sandy grabbed it in a firm handshake.

"Pleased to meet you, Dr Kean," Sandy said, with a cold smile on her pretty face.

"My pleasure," Dr Kean replied. "Now, to the business. I am not familiar with you. When I told Briggs to get his finest agent here, I was expecting Martinez or Jon Kong. I am, however, hopeful that you will justify Mr Briggs' confidence in you by executing this mission without issues."

"Details, doctor," Sandy said as she leaned back in her seat. "Give me the details of the job."

Dr Kean fished a flat device out of his hip pocket and pressed a button on it. Instantly, an image was projected on the wall of the booth opposite Sandy. She saw the image of a square-faced woman with thin lips and large brown eyes.

"Do you know this woman?" Dr Kean asked Sandy.

Sandy peered at the picture again. That face was hugely familiar, but she could not quite place exactly where she had seen that face before, which was a little strange because Sandy possessed an extremely solid memory. Names, faces, figures were easily saved and retrieved in her head, even though advanced technology these days made it unnecessary to keep so many things in mind. With two clicks on her phone, she could access vast databases that could provide answers to whatever questions she had.

"I am certain I have seen her before, but I can't place where I… Oh, wait. That's May Lay."

"Correct," Dr Kean beamed. "That indeed is May Lay, the wife of George Lay."

Little wonder I didn't recognise her face instantly, Sandy thought. May Lay and her rich, powerful husband were on the other side of the world, in faraway Oceania Liberation. Since the Great Uprising, when contacts with any kingdom outside Afrasia had been banned, Sandy had not seen or heard anything about May Lay. In the days before the Great Uprising, May was a very popular figure. She had travelled around with her husband on philanthropic missions to the more impoverished regions of the world. She distributed food and other palliatives in areas struck by natural disasters and war. Thirty years of limited access to external information, and the fact that May had aged considerably, ensured the delay in Sandy's recognition of the good woman.

"What about her?" Sandy asked, hoping Dr Kean would hit the nail straight on the head and tell her exactly what had to be done. Being an ex-military officer, she was used to straight-to-the-point debriefing backed up with files to refer to for more information, but Dr Kean was here talking in trickles and dribbles, like someone eager to maintain suspense.

"Yesterday at 21:00, I received notice that May had been kidnapped on her way to a fundraising event outside her home continent," Dr Kean revealed. "She was in an armoured copter with at least ten guards escorting her, yet she was somehow taken away by some gunmen."

Sandy sat there waiting for Dr Kean to continue speaking while she pondered who could have masterminded the kidnapping of Lady May Lay.

"I did a little digging around and a little pushing for info here and there, and I was able to get useful details about how the operation was carried out, but the main focus here is the perpetrator. Who was behind the abduction of May Lay? That's the question here," Dr Kean said, "and I have the answer."

The image of May Lay that was projected on the wall instantly vanished as Dr Kean tapped his device. In its place came the face of a middle-aged Caucasian man with a clean-shaven head and hairless face. Without needing to rack her brain at all, Sandy recognised the face before her. Jain Lester, international criminal, terrorist, and the brain behind countless high-profile robberies across the four continents of the New World. He reigned supreme in the Underworld, where the heads of cities were powerless to stop him.

"I'm not surprised," Sandy said. "Lester has been quite the threat to global peace the last few years."

"Absolutely," Dr Kean affirmed. "Now, this is something massive. Lester kidnapping May is about the worst international crime since the robbery of the West Bank."

Where do I come into all this? Sandy thought. *Surely this man doesn't want me to go after Jain Lester and save May Lay.*

"I have a plan to save May, and it involves you," Dr Kean said.

Sandy looked at Owen Briggs to confirm he was listening to the madness that was proceeding from the doctor's mouth; she saw that Owen wore a determined look on his face, and he seemed to be taking Dr Kean's words seriously.

"You want me to go all the way to Oceania Liberation, or somewhere in the Underworld wherever May Lay is being held, and get her out, just like that?" Sandy queried, dumbfounded.

The corners of Dr Kean's mouth lifted in a small smile. He ran his hands through his curly brown hair as he spoke. "I know it's not that easy; I know, and that is why I have made arrangements with an equally brilliant stealth combatant from the West Federation to partner with you on this mission."

Sandy rose to her feet abruptly. "Owen Briggs should have told you I only do solo missions since I left active service. I don't work with no Westies or anybody for that matter. I work alone."

"The plan I have here is for two combatants," Dr Kean said. "Will you change your mind if I give you a transfer hit of one million fusia upfront and pay double that after you succeed in the mission?"

Sandy's eyes grew wide. One-fucking-million fusia was more money than she had ever made in her life. Now, she could make three million if she and a certain Westie could successfully get past some toughies in the Underworld and get May Lay out of bondage.

"Well, yeah, I'll do it for that," Sandy answered.

"Great," Owen Briggs said with a deep sigh. "I was afraid you would turn it down."

Owen knew that Sandy routinely turned down private jobs whenever she didn't like something about the job, but three million was more than enough money to make a person ignore one or two odd conditions.

"One question for you, though, Dr Kean," Sandy said. "Isn't this mission odd? Why are you paying this huge sum of money to get May Lay out of Lester's nest? Why not just leave it to Oceania Liberation's government or May's husband? What's in it for you?"

"That's more than one question," Dr Kean chuckled. "But I'll answer you all the same. The reason I'm paying so much is because I'm closer to her than anyone in the government, and I care about her just as much as her husband. May Roseline Lay is my elder sister."

… … …

Miklos, Afrasia

The sun was high up in the sky when Will Burne stepped out of the cab that had conveyed him from the secret underground terminal, which was the alternate entry point to the Afrasian city of Miklos. He tossed a wad of yellow bills to the driver, and the man instantly pocketed them.

"Watch out for the Feds," the driver cautioned as he revved his vehicle and zoomed off.

"Thank you," Burne muttered as he pulled his hooded green jacket tighter and began to head towards the three-storey building where Dr Kean had asked him to wait.

Will's footsteps on the paved floor were brisk as he could not wait to get out of the streets and meet Dr Kean. As he walked on, his mind flicked to the events that had brought him from the temperate weather of the West Federation down to the hot region of Afrasia.

He had just executed the arrest of a kidnapping kingpin in Nothë, one of the largest states in the West Federation. His superiors had granted him the requisite refresher leave that he was usually given after completing major jobs. In one of the quiet neighbourhoods in Nothë, he had been in his little house when he received a call from an unknown number. The caller tracker on his phone did not give him any clues as to who was calling. That was rather strange.

"Will Burne speaking, who's this?" he had said.

"I am Dr Kean. Are you in a place where you can view a mail without getting another pair of eyes on it?"

"Yeah, sure. I'm in my crib," Will replied.

"Awesome, I'll send you a mail with a couple of attachments. Please go through those files. There's a number in the first file; call me if you are interested."

How did he get my number and mail?

The attachments had contained quite a lot of information, but the highlight of everything was the enormous amount of money this Dr Kean was offering to pay. And that's if he chose to help him save the woman whose picture was included as one of the attachments to the mail. For that obscene sum, Will knew he would not hesitate to go down to hell and duel with Lucifer.

And 2.7 million westons. That was crazy money.

Will Burne had grown up with one life lesson: if something sounded too good to be true, then it probably was. So, after going through all the materials sent to him, he first verified every little detail in the mail. He did backwards searches until he was satisfied that there was nothing foul at play, for now. After that, he grabbed his phone and placed a call to the number in the mail.

The raspy voice of a mother shouting to her child to hurry up and not make them late brought Will back to reality. He was now a few hundred metres from the front area of the meeting point.

"Joe, come on, we are going to miss the bus," the hapless woman said to her young child, who seemed disinterested in catching the bus because he was more interested in staring at Will's white face.

Will turned his face away from the little boy's line of sight and focused on getting to where he was headed. It was obvious that white faces were scarce in Afrasia. Miklos had the highest number of non-Afrasian citizens, yet the population of whites was still negligible; and, it had been that way ever since those intercontinental restrictions had come after the Great Uprising. The last of the great upheavals that had coursed through the entire Old World had culminated in a total change. From the spate of pandemic outbreaks, natural disasters, and nuclear wars that marked the end of the Old World, the surviving humans had regrouped themselves into new continents. They had ensured that no migration occurred between continents except in very rare cases.

"Westie," the little boy screamed. "Mama, look at that Wes…"

The boy's cry blended into a muffled grunt as his mother clamped her hand over his mouth and began to drag him away from Will. He pulled his hood tighter over his head and walked even faster toward his target location. As he neared the building, Will pulled his mobile phone out of his pocket and dialled Dr Kean's number.

"I'm approaching the meeting point. Where are you?" Will asked.

"Pass by the left side of the building and walk down; you will find us in a van parked by the road," the voice of Dr Kean boomed from the speaker of Will's phone.

It only took a second for it to register what the doctor had just said to him. "Us? What do you mean us?"

"I'm not alone, Agent Burne. This is more than a one-gun mission."

… … …

Will Burne craned his neck as Dr Kean brought his debriefing to a close. In the immense lab, which the clean-shaven man who Dr Kean had referred to as Owen Briggs had driven them to, the bespectacled doctor had talked about where exactly May Lay was being held in the Underworld. He went on to lay out plans for how Will and Sandy Krave, the dark lady in the room with them, were going to launch the offensive that would rescue the woman in captivity.

"It's a nice plan, needs more work, but it's a solid foundation," Will said, rising to his feet and stretching his arms. "Do we get out of the Underworld with the same submarine?"

"Yes," Dr Kean said, "it will remain there after you get off. So you will meet it there when you guys get back. Any other questions?"

"You said you would provide us with tech coordination and continuous info from here, using a screen transmitter? So, it would seem that our lives are in your hands?" Sandy asked.

"I understand that an error on my part would put the mission in jeopardy, and that is why I will be extra careful. The lives of the two of you, and my sister, are too important for me to toy with," Dr Kean said. "I can't trust the task of monitoring the mission and providing direction to anyone else."

"When do we leave for the Underworld?" Will asked.

"Tomorrow morning," the doctor answered. "We will do a mock test of the operation this evening. I will communicate the location of the training to you by 16:00."

The room fell into silence as Dr Kean peered through his lenses at Will and Sandy to see if they were on the same page as him.

"In the absence of questions, the debriefing is over," Dr Kean said. "Agent Burne, you should spend some time discussing tactics with Agent Krave before training this evening. I am sure you can work out something more sophisticated than the basic framework I have provided. I will take my leave now; when you are done formulating things with her, there's a cab outside that will take you to your lodging until it's time for our training this evening."

Will wiped his sweaty forehead with a hanky. "I hope someone won't see me and be eager to call the Feds on a Westie."

"No, no," Dr Kean said. "There are a good number of Westies around here. You might get stares from kids, but nothing serious. This is still the only safe zone for foreigners in the whole of Afrasia, and that is one of the reasons I brought the team down here to meet you. The other reason is that it's easy to get out of this continent through this city. We will easily get you onboard an airship heading to The Last Wall. There, you will board the submarine that will take you to the Underworld."

"It's good then," Will said. "This is my first time in Afrasia, and tomorrow, I'll be touching down in the Underworld. Some mission this will be."

"Mr Briggs, shall we give the agents the chance to talk and bring up some more solid ideas on how to breach the defence set up by Lester's men?" Dr Kean said.

"Certainly," Owen Briggs replied, then he turned to Sandy, "we are pulling this off, right?"

"Depends on this Westie right here, but yes, I'll do my best," Sandy said, with a little smile lighting up her face.

Perhaps it was the way her teeth flashed brightly or the dimples that appeared on her cheeks as she smiled; Will couldn't say, but he found himself feeling something for the dark lady in front of him, something he had not felt in months, or maybe years—a deep feeling of attraction.

He had not been seriously taken by any lady since he split with Jennifer, his high school sweetheart, when she could no longer cope with the risky demands of his job.

"Will, sweetheart, you have made enough out of this job. Why not quit and go into something less dangerous?" Jennifer had asked him one night, after a passionate round of mind-blowing sex.

"I… I can't leave now, Jenny," Will had replied. "I have more than three missions lined up. Maybe when I finish those."

"We both know you will get other missions before you finish the ones you have now," Jenny said as she took her head off his chest and stared straight into his eyes. "Will, I want you to stop. Do it for me."

Will had not stopped. He couldn't. This job was the only thing he was highly skilled at, and he was passionate in his pursuit, which almost always pitched him against the most violent and the most dangerous fellows in the West Federation. Will could not imagine doing anything else, apart from going after the big-time criminals that were too powerful for the cops to handle. He wasn't sure he could fit into normal civilian life, and he was not ready to find out. Jenny was a sweet girl, but he had to let her go when she kept telling him she couldn't bear the thought of him getting killed. It was just as well that she had left him too, because he had been growing concerned about her becoming a victim of his job. Those big, bad guys he kept attacking might have hurt her, eventually. Staying apart was the best thing for her.

"Hey, Westie," Sandy called, jolting Will out of his reminiscence.

"Yes, Afrasian," Will replied.

"What took you away like that?" she demanded.

"What do you mean?"

"Hey, I have been calling you for some time now," Sandy said. "Is this how you lose concentration? I think I should start giving more thought to the dangers involved in this mission rather than the money, since it doesn't look like my partner can stay focused enough to cover my ass."

Will let out a throaty laugh. "Come off it. Maybe if you had called me Burne instead of Westie, I would have heard you."

"But you are a Westie, aren't you?" Sandy said. "Why don't you want to get called what you are?"

"Westie is not exactly an endearing term," Will said as he walked away from the spot he had been standing and surveyed the big lab, which was full of vials, glass tubes, and giant metallic cylinders.

"We are partners in this mission, not old chums, so I'll call you Westie if I like," Sandy said defiantly, but there was a hint of a smile on her face as she spoke. "Alright, Burne, it is."

Will opened one of the windows of the lab and looked out into the sunny sky. "What do you think of this mission, Sandy?"

Sandy flicked an errant lock of white hair from her face before she replied, "I think we are both fools, knowingly walking into a death trap, but the money is enough recompense. For all we know, Dr Kean might have underestimated the numerical strength of the Underworld mercenaries guarding the crypt May Lay is in."

"I agree," Will said. "It's risky business, but I won't forgive myself if I turn down that kind of money. I have been in greater danger for much less."

At that moment, Will's heart softened toward Sandy. He found himself intrigued by her. Unlike Jennifer, this was a woman who understood and embraced danger, not one who feared it.

………

Mondh, Underworld

"Approaching the drop point. Get ready to exit." The captain of the submarine, which was taking Will Burne and Sandy Krave to their destination, had made the announcement as the vessel nosed deeper into the waterfront of Mondh, the desolate part of the Underworld territory where Lester's men were holding May Lay, gradually bringing to a close the ten-hour journey that had stretched from the airship terminal at The Last Wall, down to this place.

Sandy rubbed her gloved palms together as she anticipated the mission she and Burne were about to get into. Yesterday, they had gone through two training drills that were modelled after the approach they would employ in attacking the restraint facility where May Lay was being held. During the drills, she had gained a huge level of confidence in the abilities of her partner. Any doubts or uncertainties she previously had about his combat skills were allayed when they trained together. He was good, really good. And he was damned attractive too.

Sandy remembered that moment when they were shooting at targets, and he was able to strike down two targets with one bullet. The little smile that had flicked on his face had somehow touched a chord of affection in her. She had experienced an overwhelming desire to reach up and flick the errant lock of hair dangling before his eyes, off his face. She could not remember when she had felt such an intense desire and deep connection with a man.

"He's a partner on this job, a teammate," Sandy muttered to herself. "You must treat him as that."

Forcing herself to think less about Will Burne's handsome face and well-built frame, Sandy checked the twin F15 guns that she liked to use in gunfights, ensuring that they were holstered correctly. Next, she adjusted her night-vision lenses; and after that, she grabbed her backpack, which contained other materials that they would need to get May Lay out of the clutches of Jain Lester and his army of bandits.

"Get ready to exit the vessel," the voice of the captain came again.

Sandy turned to look behind her, hoping Will was getting ready to get off the submarine just like she was.

"Burne?" she called when she didn't see him.

There was no response to her call either.

"Burne?" she called again, a little louder this time. Still no answer from him. Sandy wondered where he was. Why did he have to hole himself up somewhere when they were so close to dropping off?

Sandy was just about to call the captain's attention to make another announcement over the radio so that Burne might hear, wherever he was, and start heading back, when just then, Will appeared from one of the enclosed parts in the interior of the submarine. He was fully kitted in the black tactical outfit intended as their combat uniform for the mission. His weapons were holstered, and his night-vision lenses were fixed; he looked decidedly battle-ready.

"Where did you disappear off to?" she asked him.

"I went to check something out."

"You didn't hear the captain's announcement?"

"Sure, I heard it the first time," Will said.

The grave voice of the captain boomed within the submarine once more. "Get ready to evacuate the ship in three, two, one, now!"

They were both standing on the hatch when the captain uttered the word "now." There was a sharp beep from the hatch, and in the next moment, both combatants were ejected from the submarine with blinding speed. Flying through the air, they landed on the dry ground almost immediately and quickly scrambled to their feet. Sandy turned behind her to see the submarine slowly receding into the river.

Sandy flicked open the cover of a narrow, long, flat device strapped to her forearm. Nothing was showing on the device's screen for a long while, as Sandy waited patiently for something to come up.

"Check your vidcom," Sandy finally said to Will. "Mine seems to have been broken when we landed."

"They aren't so fragile," Will said as he pushed his damp hair backwards. "I remember the last one I used on a certain peacekeeping mission some years back was so strongly made that it took bullets and did not break."

Will flicked open his own vidcom, and in a matter of seconds, the face of Dr Kean was visible on the screen.

"At least we have one working," Sandy said as she closed her faulty vidcom and got close to Will to see Dr Kean's face more clearly.

"I am glad you got to the edge of the Underworld in good time," Dr Kean said as he fiddled with his glasses. "You know what to do next; head straight down the road that you see, go on for three clicks. I will be here to give directions in case you get anything wrong."

"Alright," Will said and immediately started down the road that Dr Kean was talking about. "We are still some distance from the site of action. I can't wait to go at those Underworld beasts."

Sandy chuckled and kept level with Will as he walked in the direction indicated by the doctor. In the pitch-black darkness of the night, the night-vision lenses illuminated their path, showing them the road and its winding shape. Sandy understood the apathy that Will appeared to feel for the people of the Underworld. It was common knowledge that the Underworld had the highest number of terrorists and bandits of all the continents in the New World. No less than seventy-five per cent of the world's most prominent criminal cases were committed in this lawless continent.

The brisk walk down the road reminded Sandy of her first special mission. She had been in the Afrasian military for years and was a celebrated combatant. Then came her first special mission, assigned by her superiors. She went after a cult of deadly martial artists who kidnapped little boys and turned them into cold-blooded killers. The secluded temple where the cult perpetrated their malicious activities was far away from Girkland, so she had to be flown to the nearest airstrip. Then she would find her way to the temple in the dark with the aid of special goggles, just as she was doing now.

"That's it, guys," Dr Kean announced to them from the device, bringing Sandy back to the present. "You will now take a left turn off the road and follow a narrow path, all the way down until you get to a big, gated house. That is where May is."

"Okay, what's the estimated distance to that place?" Will asked.

"Less than two clicks. From this point on, you should be prepared for anything. You could come under fire at any moment. Be careful."

"Got it," Will said. "Come on, Sandy. Let's go kick some bandit ass."

He broke into a jog, and she kept up with him. Both combatants had unholstered their F15 firearms, ready to engage should any hostile party bring a gunfight. They jogged down the path, guided by their night-vision lenses, getting closer to their target with each passing minute.

When the big apartment, which Dr Kean told them about, came into sight, Will and Sandy exchanged glances. They both knew it was time to execute those complex moves they had gone through during their drills. It was time for them to truly kick some bandit ass. They split up, just as they had planned, with Sandy taking a left while Will would head towards the back entrance. The plan was for Sandy to cause a distraction and draw some of the guards to her, giving Will the opportunity to enter the facility and get May out with less resistance from Lester's men.

Will stealthily made his way towards the back part of the big house. He was careful not to make any sound with his combat boots, knowing that the worst thing that could happen in this precarious moment was for Lester's bandits to become aware of his presence on this side of the house.

Slowly, he padded on, listening for sounds of footsteps or voices of men conversing, but he heard nothing. He kept moving forward until he got to the back of the house. He found the back gate and heaved a sigh of relief. He was at least one step closer to getting his hands on May Lay and getting her out.

"Krave, are you in position?" Will whispered to the small microphone taped to the collar of his tactical shirt.

"Affirmative," Sandy replied. "You?"

"Ten-four, I'm in position," Will said. "When are you moving in?"

"Right away," she replied.

"Copy that." Will remained in position while he waited to hear Sandy's feedback. When she had drawn the attention of Lester's men, he would then go in and get May. There would definitely be fewer men inside at that point.

There was a loud gunshot at the other end of the house. It sounded distinctly like the roaring of an F15 gun without a silencer. Sandy had fired the distracting shot. It was only a matter of time before a good number of the men inside would troop out to face whatever danger was coming to them, while he would go in with less resistance to get May out.

"Burne?" Sandy's voice came through the receiver on his left ear.

"Yes, Krave. Should I go in?" he asked her.

"Something is wrong," Sandy replied. "The house seems to have fewer guards than Dr Kean led us to believe."

"What do you mean?"

"There has been no reaction to the shot I fired. Dr Kean gave us the impression the house was bursting with guards. At least some of the men should have come out to check who fired a shot outside. But there's no one."

"I'll take that as great news if there are few men. It means we have less work to do to get May out of this damned house. I'm going in."

Will raced over to the back gate, flipped open the passcode panel on the wall, and quickly punched in the code that Dr Kean had revealed during the debriefing, which he had also written in the file he gave to Will and Sandy. Will held his breath as he waited for the console to process the code. A few moments later, the gate finally swung open with a slight creaking sound.

Will drew in a steady breath as he walked past the gate with his firearm at the ready. He continuously looked left and right, watching for any movement from his adversaries. He walked further into the big compound.

"Burne? Are you inside?" Sandy asked.

"Affirmative," he replied in a whisper. "I am approaching the front entrance of the house."

"Have you encountered anybody yet?"

"Negative," Will breathed.

Will began to carefully approach the entrance to the large house, on high alert, not to be fooled by the fact that he was yet to see any enemies. He was close to the front door of the house when he finally saw someone. A man was sitting on the floor with his back against the wall; his head hung at an unnatural angle. Cautiously, Will rushed over to examine the guard, and his suspicions were instantly confirmed. The guard was dead.

"Krave, there's a problem," Will growled into the mike. "I think someone might have gotten here before us."

"How the hell did that happen?"

"I don't know," Will said as he kicked open the front door of the house. "I really don't know. I just hope May Lay is safe."

Even as Will said those words, he knew the probability of it was slim to none. It was wishful thinking. If anybody had attacked the house, then their target was mostly likely May Lay. What he didn't know was if the people who had attacked this place were good guys or baddies who wanted to get their hands on the handsome ransom that May Lay would fetch them.

Will's heart started beating wildly in his chest as he saw two other guards on the floor in a pool of blood. This wasn't good. Not good at all. Little wonder no one had responded to Sandy's shot outside. They were all dead, every last one of them.

Will pushed open the door to the house and let himself in. The room he entered was lit by two bright neon lamps hung at each end of the room. Will pulled his night-vision lenses off and looked around for the door that would lead to the part of the house where May was, as he had seen in the little map provided by Dr Kean.

Will found the door to his left and quickly raced over to kick it open. But, unfortunately, right behind the door was the body of another dead guard.

"Dammit," Will breathed. The chances of May still being in the house was getting slimmer by the minute.

He thought of opening his vidcom and telling Dr Kean what was going on but decided against it. Instead, he would first confirm if May had been taken from the house before speaking to him.

"Talk to me, Burne," Sandy's voice suddenly materialised into his ear. "What is happening in there? Should I come in?"

"There's fucking nothing to come in for. All of Lester's men have been gunned down, and I am more than certain that May Lay has been taken away from here. I'm going in to confirm, though."

"Alright," Sandy sighed.

By now, Will had passed a confusing maze of rooms, and he was finally at the door of the room where May was supposed to be. He pushed the door open and walked inside. The room was sufficiently lit by a low-hanging chandelier of bright red neon bulbs. There was a chair in the middle of the room with a figure sitting in it. The figure's head was bowed, and its hands and legs were bound.

A dummy. A mockery by those who had gotten to her first before he came along.

As strongly as Will felt that the figure in the chair was not May or even human at all, he still walked closer to confirm. As he walked closer, he began to smell blood and the stench of unwashed human flesh.

Certainly, May Lay was taken not so very long ago. The smell was still in the air.

Will finally stood next to the figure at the centre of the room and gently lifted the hood off its head. An uncontrollable gasp escaped his lips as he found himself staring first at the long and matted hair of a woman; then, in a flash, he was peering into May Lay's bloodied face. Her mouth was gagged; eyes wide, she was shaking her head violently as if she desperately wanted to say something.

Will went behind her to loosen the piece of cloth that secured her mouth; and, he had started to loosen the pieces of cloth binding her hands when he heard her whisper to him.

"It's a trap," May's muffled voice was low and cracked.

"What did you just say?" Will asked. He took a pause from untying the cloth that was binding her wrist to the arm of the chair and walked forward to face her. "A trap?"

"You have fallen into their trap," May said. "This is exactly what they wanted."

"What are you talking about? I don't understand…"

Will did not complete his statement; because at that moment, he began to hear the loud zooms of vehicle engines outside and the whirring of copters coming in all directions towards the house. He left May for a moment and briskly walked to the window to see what was going on out there, but he was unable to see anything. Then he remembered that Sandy was still outside. She had to know what was going on.

"Krave, what the hell is happening?" Will bellowed into the mike.

Will did not hear anything from Sandy for quite some time; all he continued to hear was the alarming sounds of approaching vehicles and advanced military aircraft.

"Are you there, Krave? Talk to me. What's going on?"

"I don't know," Sandy's voice finally came through in a loud whisper. "I think we're about to be surrounded. Get out of there. Fast!"

… … …

Mondh, Underworld

Sandy Krave rhythmically clenched and unclenched her gloved fist as she tried to remember where they had deviated from the plan Dr Kean had given them. Why had things turned out so bad? Why was the house littered with the bodies of dead men? Why were copters hovering over the house, bathing the entire perimeter with piercing red lights? Why were vans driving into the area filled with armed men? How did it all end up this way?

"Burne, get your ass down here fast," Sandy whispered into her mike. "An armed unit is coming into the house. I can't take them on. My cover cannot hold against fierce firepower."

"Alright, I'm already headed out. I'm almost out of the house now. I'm with May Lay," Will responded.

"She's alive?" Sandy enquired, surprised.

"Badly beat up, but she will live if we can escape this," Will said.

Sandy squeezed her fist hard. She did not want this mission to be her last. No, it would not be. She watched as another copter landed in front of the house.

"Go, go, get them here," Sandy heard the command issued to the armed men dropping from the copters.

Sandy bent her frame lower behind the little bush in which she was hiding. She wished Burne would make haste and get out of the house quickly, so they could set about making their escape.

Moments passed, and Sandy still saw no sign of Burne. She knew that he had not been killed. She would have heard the gunshot. Had he been captured? Sandy felt a strange sense of dread. If Burne were captured, then she stood little chance of getting away from these men, whoever they were. If Burne were captured, she was going to—

"Krave," Will's whisper suddenly cut into her thoughts.

Sandy heaved a sigh of relief at the sound of Will's voice. She was glad he had somehow manoeuvred his way out of the building. She turned to see him carrying a body over his shoulder.

"How did you get out?" she whispered back to him.

"I couldn't take the back gate. So I had to dig my way out, through the wall."

"Good thinking. The area is covered," Sandy whispered rapidly to him. "We will have to go slowly and not attract any attention. Have you informed Dr Kean of the development? He might have an alternative plan to get us out of here, faster."

"Kean is a fucking bastard," Burne said, a little too loudly. "I will kill him with my bare hands when I get hold of him. I have thrown the fucking vidcom away."

"I've got them!" a voice boomed behind them.

Sandy and Will quickly exchanged glances as they wasted no time in drawing their firearms. A loud shout came from within the house as the men who had gone inside began to rush out.

"Run!" Will cried as copters began to fire in their direction.

Sandy and Will were returning fire as they ran wildly through the bushy terrain that faced the house. The roars of blazing guns and the cries of their adversaries who were getting hit filled the air.

"Left, turn left! We cannot go back to the submarine!" Will said as he continued to fire.

Sandy turned in the direction Will was going, trusting that he seemed to know something about the situation that she did not. He had promised to kill Dr Kean when he saw him next. Does that mean Kean had set them up?

Will led the way through a bushy path. He was doing a good job of bearing May's weight and still steering them away from danger. But, behind them, Sandy could hear the sound of booted feet in hot pursuit as Lester's men came after them.

"Do you know where this path leads?" Sandy asked Will as they ran on, evading occasional gunfire from the men behind them.

"Damned if I know," Will replied. "If we get lucky, it might lead to somewhere we can hide our heads 'til we lose these bastards."

Sandy turned and fired a shot into the darkness behind her. Unfortunately, she could not see very far behind her, despite her night-vision lenses being on. However, as she ran down the unknown path with Will, she realised that their situation was not as hopeless as it had earlier seemed. If they could keep ahead of those chasing them until they got into a terrain where they could hide and kill stealthily, then they might be able to escape with their lives.

Sandy and Will kept up the race for their lives for a few more minutes before they finally burst through the bush and found themselves on the bank of a flowing river. Relieved, Will set May on the bank by the river.

"I knew we were going to escape," Will said, panting from all the hard running and the weight of the woman on his shoulders. "Fuck Kean. Fuck them, all."

Having said that, Will raced forward and dived into the river. Sandy jumped in after him, feeling a sense of calm for the first time since Will told her the guards in Lester's house were all dead.

… … …

It was still early in the morning. The faint outline of the moon was yet visible in the clear blue sky. In a copse not far from the river they had dived into last night, Will sat with his back against the trunk of a tree, turning his big knife in his hands and listening to the song of a lonely bird. He watched as May and Sandy were talking about the events that had brought them to this point when they should ideally be back to The Last Wall by now. Will would not forget the raw anger that had coursed through him when May had revealed to them that she was an only child; she had no brother named Kean.

Why? What did Kean intend to achieve by lying and sending them on a mission that he knew was bound to fail? That was the question that had been on his mind since May's big revelation. He could not fathom any answer to it.

Now, he listened as May explained the situation.

"President Morgan and my husband, George, have always been desperate to gain more power for Oceania Liberation. They were not content with the landmass and the natural resources in the lands that they had. They wanted more, and the only way that was possible was to wage a war against other continents," May explained.

"I knew about it, and I always tried my best to dissuade my husband from having a hand in something that would bring death to thousands of people. He is a wealthy man, which I believe you know, and has always been renowned around the world for being a philanthropist. What I did not know about him was that he wanted the things he did. More than the immense wealth he possessed, he wanted political power. I suppose—"

"How did all of that get to involve us? You said it was a trap when I ungagged you in that room?" Will asked. He was less interested in the long stories the woman seemed eager to narrate. What he wanted to know was who had set them up and why. He supposed the woman was trying to explain the why with her story, but it was starting to get long-winded.

"George and Morgan struck up a deal with the Underworld. They were going to be allies in a war against West Federation and Afrasia, and they were going to share the loot of their victory in an agreed manner. I got this information only by chance. After my initial refusal to agree with his war-mongering desires, he became hostile and hid things from me. I did not know his hatred for me had grown to the point of using me as a mere pawn in his glory-seeking game."

May bent her head and began to cry while Sandy put her arms around her hunched shoulders to comfort her.

Will turned the piece of information May had revealed in his mind in the same manner he turned his knife. It was easy to see how the lines connected at this point. Dr Kean was working for George Lay and President Morgan of Oceania Liberation. Since they wanted a war against West Federation and Afrasia, and they wanted to assign blame for starting the war, why not get two very prominent agents from the two continents involved in an ugly situation with the wife of the richest man in Oceania Liberation? Dr Kean had told them that Jain Lester had abducted May, but Will was sure that the news would not be presented that way in Oceania Liberation. Instead, the abduction would most likely be linked to either West Federation or Afrasia, and the subsequent arrest of Sandy and Will would be enough to spark global outrage. To make things even worse, the schemers would kill May Lay, and that would give President Morgan a chance to declare hostilities on the home continents of the agents in question.

Will stopped turning the knife and gripped the handle tight. Morgan had failed. George had failed. That bastard Kean had failed, too. He and Sandy had escaped with their lives, and May was also alive.

By now, May had stopped sobbing and was muttering some words to herself. Sandy stood up from beside her and walked over to where Will sat. "Have you figured out a way out of here?"

"Not yet. We are in the middle of nowhere," Will said. "We can't go back into the mainland of Mondh. I'm still thinking of a realistic place we can head to."

"We have to warn our people back home," Sandy mused as she fiddled with her white hair. "If George Lay could have come up with a dark plan like this, not minding the death of his wife of many years, then we can be sure that he would try another plan to get what he wants."

"True that," Will said. "I will get us out of here soon."

"I believe you," Sandy said, and she turned to walk back to where May sat.

Will thought deeply about their situation. They had weapons to stave off attacks from their enemies, but they did not know how to get out of this place yet, or where they should head.

Could they head back to Last Wall without getting into the hands of the seamen from the Underworld? Was that not the only option they had?

Will thought about what to do with May Lay. She would never be safe in Oceania Liberation again. She would have to stay in West Federation or Afrasia for the rest of her days. He watched the woman shivering slightly, even though she was wearing a big dry jacket from Sandy. The icy coldness of the river must have chilled her down to the bone.

"Krave, we are going to make for The Last Wall this night. We have to get out of here and return to Miklos," Will said. "I will make us floatable rafts. That's the only way I believe we can get out of here."

"I'm sure those baddies will be waiting for us," Sandy said. "We will be ready for them."

Will jerked his head in agreement. Looking at Sandy with her beautiful ebony skin, which contrasted with her flowing white hair, Will felt another surge of passion. He suddenly realised that since the first time he saw her in that lab back in Miklos, the feeling of intense passion had not diminished by any bit. Spending the whole of yesterday with her, passing through all sorts of dangerous situations together, had only increased the intensity of those feelings.

Maybe when they were out of danger, he might get the chance to explore his feelings for her and perhaps even get her to open up to him; because he clearly saw the way she looked at him sometimes, and he knew enough about women to recognise the ones that fancied him.

Will drew his F15 and rubbed it tenderly. If they could get past the men who were likely waiting for them on the waters of Mondh, then he would make it a duty to spend some time having fun with Sandy if she didn't mind. But he had to stay alive until then.

… … …

On a Raft: Escape from the Underworld

In the pitch darkness that currently reigned in Mondh, a large inflatable raft slowly glided its way across the surface of the vast body of water that linked the Underworld with The Last Wall. On the raft were three persons: Will Burne; Sandy Krave; and May Lay, all seated in deep silence as they tried to get away from their enemies without attracting any attention. Now, they were halfway to their destination, and Sandy knew that as long the night remained dark and moonless and they made no unnecessary noise, they had a good chance of escaping from the Underworld seamen.

Sandy rubbed her sleepy eyes as the raft floated over the calm waves of the sea. For the past few hours, they had been on the waters, paddling hard and doing everything they could to stay out of the line of Underworld seaman; now Sandy felt her body needed some rest. However, that had to wait until they were completely safe. As things stood, they had to remain alert.

The night-vision lenses allowed Sandy and Will to see clearly ahead, but May could hardly see anything in the thick darkness. Fortunately for them, the night-vision lenses gave them the advantage to navigate their simple craft away from the reaches of the enemy. Their Navigate Master, the special navigation app on their vidcoms, would have really come in handy to help Will sail towards The Last Wall. Unfortunately, the vidcom had stopped working the previous night when they had narrowly escaped from the clutches of the Underworld mercenaries. There was no doubt Dr Kean had intentionally cut them off.

"You okay?" Sandy leaned close to ask May in a whisper.

"I'm fine," May whispered back. "Where are we headed?"

"The Last Wall," Sandy said.

From The Last Wall, they would look for a means of transportation back into Afrasian cities. From there, they would go after Dr Kean and expose the conspirators that wanted to bring a war to Afrasia and West Federation. Sandy tried to imagine herself pressing the muzzle of her plasma pistol against Dr Kean's forehead while he spilt everything about the conspiracy plan into a recorder held by Will. She imagined the fear it would bring to his eyes. It would make her feel good to see Kean begging for his life; that might be some recompense for all the trouble he had put them through.

"Oh, shit!" Will groaned in front of them and instantly scrambled to his feet.

Sandy moved away from May and made for where Will now stood.

"What's wrong, Will?" Sandy asked in a lowered voice.

"Underworld ship," Will said, pointing towards the direction he was facing.

Sandy let out a groan of her own when she saw the huge vessel with the Underworld flag attached to its hull. Sandy could see at least two cannons mounted on the ship. Finally, their fragile bit of luck had run out. It wasn't just any Underworld ship—it was a warship.

"Paddle left!" Will whispered his order.

It makes sense, Sandy thought, as she began to paddle the raft away from the danger zone they were in at the moment. If they could paddle hard enough to the left, they would temporarily be out of range of the cannons on the ship.

"Have they seen us?" May asked.

"I suppose they have," Will replied. "They surely have night lenses and sensors. So we must assume they are staring at our asses on their screens, right as we speak."

"If they can see us," May began, "why are they not shooting—"

The roar of a cannon releasing its missile cut through the silence of the night, and in the next moment, there was a massive explosion as the missile hit the spot where the raft had been just a few moments ago. Splashes of water, as well as bits of fire, flew into the air. Sandy felt her heart beginning to slam within her chest. That missile must not hit them. They would be dead meat in the blink of an eye.

"That was a warning shot," a metallic voice floated into Sandy's ears. "You cannot escape. Surrender now."

Sandy and Will exchanged worried glances. They stood little chance of surviving if they continued to paddle away from the ship on their tiny raft, but they had no chance of staying alive if they just gave up. They would use them for their devious plans and eventually eliminate them at the end of it all.

"We fight, right?" Sandy enquired, determination in her voice.

"Damn those bastards! If we have to go down, we go down fighting, like proper soldiers."

"Great," Sandy said. "Engage them while I gently pad—"

The cannon roared again, and another missile hit the area a few feet from the raft. This shot was closer to home. It caught the edge of the raft and set it on fire. The impact of the blast threw May off balance, and she almost tumbled into the water, if not for Will's quick reaction. Sandy busied herself with putting out the fire that was burning on the edge of the raft.

"We have you locked down," the voice from the warship threatened again. "Surrender now!"

"Shoot the blinking light!" Will said as he helped May back into a sitting position on the raft.

Sandy knew that the red blinking light was the warship's device to track their movement; if she could break it with her F15 rifle, then they would be off their radar until those baddies came up with something else to track them. As Sandy dropped the paddle and grabbed her gun, another shot from the cannon slammed into the water, perilously close to the raft.

It's clear that they don't want to kill us, Sandy thought. She wondered how long they would continue to threaten them with blasts from their cannons or if they would run out of patience.

Sandy steadied herself and fired the first shot with the F15 rifle. Unfortunately, the shot failed to hit the warship.

"Out of fucking range!" Sandy cursed. "They can hit us, but we can't get them. We have to make a run for it."

"You think that's the best we can do?"

"Yeah, we have nothing else to do. We can leverage on the fact that they are not shooting to kill at the moment," Sandy said. "If we can beat them to the bend ahead, then we might just make it out of this alive."

"Let's do something first, before we run," Will said thoughtfully.

"What?"

"We'll paddle close to them, get within range, and hit that damned red light," Will said. "As long as that light keeps blinking, we are cooked. It's only a matter of time before they get tired of wilfully missing target."

Sandy gave a nod of acknowledgement. Will Burne had not ceased to impress her since this mission began. His ability to think fast was something she really admired.

"Let's hit them together," Sandy suggested. "I'll take out the red light, and you fire at any of the men on the ship that you see. That'll reduce the chances that they hit us with their sidearms when they realise we didn't come to surrender."

"Right," Will said as he began to row the raft towards the warship armed with blasting cannons waiting ahead.

At this point, there were no more shots fired from the ship. Sandy figured the mercenaries on the ship had probably assumed they were ready to surrender, just like she'd hoped. Sandy took a deep breath as the raft began to get within the range an F15 rifle could do some damage to the ship. Her fingers twitched in anticipation. This was the moment that would determine their fate for the rest of the night.

"Now!" Will called, suddenly.

He dropped the paddle and jumped to his feet beside Sandy. They both drew their F15 rifles and took aim.

"Fire!" Sandy yelled and began to hit the ship's tracking light with shot after shot from her rifle.

Will was following suit, firing in the same determined manner at the thugs standing on deck, knowing both of which would otherwise be a problem to the trio if they did not eliminate them. It took a minute to register that they had not come to surrender, as the men on board did not immediately return fire. Chaos ensued as they scrambled to take cover.

May was hunkered down behind them, attempting to take cover from the return fire.

The shootout didn't last long, and the baddies weren't as good a shot as Will. Their bullets whizzed past the little raft, hitting the water with the sound of a *plunk!* In less than two minutes of active shooting, the part of the ship that Sandy and Will were shooting at exploded.

"Yesss!" Sandy roared in delight. She quickly holstered her rifle and leapt at Will, wrapping her arms around him in an emotional embrace.

She did not know why that felt like the right thing to do. They had just weathered a great storm together, and the relief of escaping death was just too much for her to handle alone.

Will embraced her tightly and patted her on the back as they remained in each other's arms.

"Yes, we did it," he whispered against her flowing white hair.

"You are going to pay for this!" the voice from the warship roared. Gone was the cockiness in the speaker's tone, suggesting that the party on the craft was currently trapped. Now, all Sandy heard in that voice was anger: the anger from a predator that had missed prey belonging to his superior.

"You are magnificent!" May said, overjoyed. "Are we out of danger?"

"Our odds of getting away are greater than ever," Sandy said as she broke the hug with Will and went for the paddle.

"Worst case scenario is they start firing at random," Will said. "Yet the danger of blind shooting cannot compare with when they could see us."

True that Sandy thought. They could breathe a little easier with the knowledge that they were safe for the night.

… … …

The Last Wall: Afrasia-Underworld Border

Will followed Sandy's lead as the trio travelled to the airship terminal, where they would find the appropriate airship to convey them back to Girkland in the heart of Afrasia. The main complex of the terminal loomed ahead: a skyscraper that contrasted with smaller buildings surrounding it. Will knew that under normal circumstances, he would not have needed Sandy's help to locate the airship they needed to board; he was used to always being in the lead, and he had a keen sense of direction that made him able to find his way around places. Now, he was too tired to remember the route he and Sandy had passed through when they arrived at The Last Wall two days ago. It was quite unusual for him to forget things like that, but the fatigue of paddling and manoeuvring the raft took its toll on him. He was certain that he would grab some sleep while on the airship en route to Girkland.

The three walked towards the terminal with tired limbs and empty bellies. The last thing they ate was a bunch of berries they had found on the island they stayed on before starting their voyage with the raft. Will did not want to think about how many hours ago that was.

"Can we get something to eat around here?" Will voiced his thoughts when his stomach did not stop rumbling.

"I could do with a bite as well," May said. Her voice was a little shaky. It was clear that her exposure to the extreme cold over the past two days did not sit well with her ageing body.

"There's food in the complex," Sandy said reassuringly. "We'll get there soon."

They were inside the big complex within a few minutes. Will remembered how impressed he had been with the beautiful interior of the complex and how well organised the throngs of people were in each compartment of the complex as they went about their business; now, he was too hungry to care.

Sandy led them into an elevator, then selected the twelfth floor. When they got out, Sandy pointed to an open door about two hundred metres away.

"The terminal restaurant is over there," she said. "Go and grab something to eat while I get us the tickets for the next airship."

"I don't know if Kean gave you some cash, but I have nothing here," Will revealed. "How do I get the food without money?"

Sandy dipped a hand into her hip pocket and brought out some yellow notes that Will knew to be the colour of the legal tender in Afrasia. "The restaurant is pay-after-the-meal, but that's ten fusia, enough to get three plates of food, just in case."

Will grabbed the money and led May into the dining area while Sandy went the other way. The restaurant was substantial and had hundreds of tables with attractive covers carefully draped over them. Colourful bulbs hung from the ceiling, and the waiters were smartly dressed and looked efficient.

"I always like to sit at a table by the window," Will said to May. "Do you mind, ma'am?"

"Oh, well. As long as it doesn't make the waiter take too long to get to us," May said with a slight chuckle.

Will and May headed for the nearest table that was beside a window. When they took their seat, Will found the electronic menu on the table. He stared at the food list on offer, but he didn't recognise anything on the menu. Afrasian and West Federation meals were nothing alike.

"Are you familiar with any of these?" Will asked May, gesturing at the e-menu.

"No," May replied honestly. "I don't know any of them. Should we try this Taboujca fries, or perhaps call one of the waiters to ask which foods might be the best choice for non-Afrasians?"

"I'll ask Sandy," Will said.

Will tapped the little device that was perched on his ear to switch it on, then he spoke into the tiny mike pinned to his shirt.

"Hey, Sandy," he said gently.

There was no response. Will spoke again, but Sandy said nothing. Since Will did not hear any background noise, he knew that Sandy's com device was not switched on.

"Couldn't reach her," Will told May. "You think Taboujca fries will be nice?"

"Just a feeling," she replied with a shrug. "Right now, I feel like I could eat just about anything."

"We'll take that, then," Will said and instantly clicked Taboujca fries on the e-menu. When the option for the number of plates came up, he selected three.

"Your order will be delivered in two minutes, thirty-seven seconds," a robotic voice announced.

"Can't wait for much longer," Will said as he leaned back in his seat.

After two minutes, a sharp-looking waiter came with the large square tray of Taboujca fries Will had ordered. Will stared at the meal, trying to identify it by its appearance among West Federation meals. Will could not compare it to any meal on his home continent, but the fries smelled heavenly and looked just fine. He hoped they tasted just as well.

"Where are you?" Sandy's voice sounded in Will's ear just as he was about to lift the fork to his mouth. She was speaking through the com device.

Will lifted his eyes and saw Sandy at the threshold, looking around, trying to find where he and May were seated.

Dammit, she's beautiful, he thought.

Her features were attractive and exotic. The combination of dark skin, white hair, and green eyes were something Will found extremely alluring. He wondered if many Afrasians looked like this, or Sandy was just of different physical stock to most people around here.

"Look straight ahead of you," Will replied. "We are next to the window at your 12 o'clock."

"Okay," Sandy said, and the com device clicked off.

Will finally took his first bite of the Taboujca fries and found the taste immensely satisfactory.

"It's nice," he said to May, "really nice."

"Yeah, it could be worse," she said.

Sandy arrived at the table and wasted no time in joining them. "You ordered Taboujca? Well, not a bad choice. There are—"

That was as far as she got before a gunshot rang out and the glass window beside their table exploded. As the glass shattered, the whole restaurant erupted in a state of panic.

"Get down!" the fellow who fired roared. He was dressed like one of the security officers at the complex, except he wore a face mask. "Everybody on the ground!"

The masked man was not the only one who was armed; Will noticed as he went down that four other masked gunmen were dressed as security officers of the terminal.

"Stay down, and we won't hurt you," the man who had spoken earlier said. "We have only come for some specific people; we will get them and go and leave the rest of you alone."

From his bent position, Will could see two of the men headed in his direction were armed with pistols. Had Underworld thugs followed them to Afrasia? He looked to his left and saw Sandy covering May Lay.

"Sandy," he whispered. "They are coming for us."

"Yeah, I can see that," she replied. "I'll take the bastard in front."

"Now!" Will shouted, and they both rolled in opposite directions. Will went to the right and Sandy to the left. Instantly, their F15 guns began to blaze. The gunmen, who were moving towards the table occupied by Will and his companions, were easily cut down by the speed and precision of the shots fired by the two special agents. There was an instant outbreak of chaos in the restaurant, as people who had earlier complied with the instructions to stay down suddenly took to their heels and began to run in different directions.

"Shoot them, dammit!" the gunman at the centre, who looked like he was the leader of the gang, bellowed.

The remaining men began to fire wildly at Will and Sandy, not caring if they hit innocent people in the process. Will turned a table on its side and hid behind it as plates of steak smashed on the floor. He started firing at the gunmen from there while making sure he did not shoot any of the scared diners running helter-skelter in a bid to find safety.

The sound of gunfire and people shouting filled the large room. Will squinted his left eye as he took careful aim at another gunman and cut him down with a single shot. Will saw that Sandy was doing just as well as he was. She was, without a doubt, a highly-skilled sharpshooter.

After a long gunfight, Will and Sandy had finally cut down nearly all their adversaries, which left only the leader. He was hiding behind the serving counter, spraying his machine gun in their direction at varying intervals. By now, the impeccable arrangement of tables in the restaurant was turned upside down, scattered by blazing guns and running feet.

Will peeked from behind a table and saw the leader was no longer standing with his gun or firing at the moment. Was he reloading his gun? Will decided to take the opportunity to attack him. He raced towards the counter, ready with his gun, in case the gunman stood up abruptly and tried to shoot him. Will was almost to the counter when the fellow leapt out and jumped at him. Will tried to fire, but the man was quick to kick his gun away, following up with a round kick that struck the side of Will's mouth.

"I've got him!" Sandy screamed from behind.

Will took the hint and threw himself onto the floor, just as Sandy's firearm cracked the shot. The leader groaned in pain as the bullet caught him in the shoulder, throwing him slightly off balance. But, he recovered almost immediately. Then, clutching his shoulder, he made for the exit of the restaurant. Sandy fired again, but this time her shot went narrowly wide, hitting the door frame instead of their fleeing adversary. Sandy aimed to shoot a third time, but she relented when she saw that the fellow had gone.

Will rose to his feet just as Sandy hurried over to where he was.

"Are you okay?" she asked.

"Yeah, sure," he said. "I just took a solid whack on the face. Nothing serious. I—"

Will stopped when he noticed a cut on his side, just below his ribs. He had not noticed the injury during the fight. The mad rush of adrenaline had blocked out the pain earlier, but now he was beginning to feel it.

"I'll be fine," Will said. He grabbed a napkin lying on the floor, not far old, and pressed it to the surface of the wound to stop the bleeding.

Will and Sandy hurried over to where May had hunkered behind a chair.

"I think it's me they want," she said. "Just go without me. They will stop chasing you if I'm not there."

"No way," Sandy said as she bent beside May. "We will keep you safe. We are in this together."

"Yeah, we won't leave you," Will said.

The blaring of sirens began to sound downstairs. Without a doubt, Afrasian cops had gotten wind of the shooting in the terminal.

"Why don't we check the faces of those criminals before the cops get here?" Sandy said. "From their facial structures, we can determine if they are from the Underworld or wherever."

"Terrific idea," Will said. He rushed over to where a gunman lay in a heap, to the left of him. Will pulled off his mask and stared at the dead man's darkish face and closed eyes.

"Afrasian here," Will declared.

Sandy hurried over to join him. When she saw the face of the dead gunman, a gasp escaped her lips.

"What?" Will asked. "Sandy, are you okay?"

"I know him. He is… He *was* on my team, in one of the last missions I did for the Afrasian army," Sandy said.

"The Underworld has infiltrated the Afrasian army with spies and double agents?" Will mused aloud.

"The question is, who can we trust at the moment?" Sandy said and heaved a long sigh. "I think we have to rethink our travel to Girkland."

"What do you have in mind?"

"We should head to somewhere that I am positive we can truly be safe," Sandy said.

Will looked at his side to see if the bleeding had stopped. Blood was still seeping out of his black outfit. He would need more napkins. Sandy had said she would get them somewhere safe; he hoped she was right about that.

"However, before we go to this safe place, we need information that will help us avoid approaching the wrong people for assistance," Sandy added. "There is only one way we can get that."

"How?" May asked.

"What information are we talking about?" Will asked a salient question of his own.

"Okay, this is what I have in mind," Sandy said as she started to lay out everything they needed and how they were going to set about getting their hands on it.

Will listened to her calm, measured voice while the wailing sirens from outside began to sound closer. *Quite a brilliant idea*, he thought, when she finished speaking.

… … …

PART 2 - Xio Chan, Afrasia

THE RISE OF AN INTERCONTINENTAL CONSPIRACY

Sandy's Intel and Reminiscence in Her Safehouse

Chapters Eight through Eighteen

"When the whole world is silent, even one voice becomes powerful."

–Malala Yousafzai

Kim Koom County, Afrasia: 2166, May 07

It was noon when Will and Sandy alighted from the coach of the bullet train that had taken them from their drop point at the airship terminal at Mukt. For the first time in the last few days, they were going somewhere without May Lay. They had agreed that she would be safer on the super-speed train. All she had to do was remain in the luxury coach that they had all been in until the train got to its final destination, then she would drop and wait for them in a nearby restaurant. Will gave her his com device and a quick lesson on how to speak into it without attracting any attention.

The decision to let May remain on the train did not sit too well with Will after all the efforts they had put into keeping her safe, but Sandy maintained that it was the only option they had. She argued that they could not take her to their current destination with the high probability of getting involved in a gunfight.

"She's safe in here," Sandy had said to Will when they were still debating the issue.

"And at the restaurant, she's going to stay alone? How safe is that?" he asked. "Are we sure the baddies won't just swoop in on her when they see we are not there to protect her?"

"We won't be away for that long," Sandy countered. "Besides, we will give her the com device. If something happens, say those fellows abduct her at the restaurant, she can tell us, and we will track them."

Now, Will and Sandy were making their way through a narrow path that cut across a wide area of tall grasses as they headed towards the SIL building in that area. SILs were *Special Information Laboratories* belonging to the central government of Afrasia, which only approved data entry officers, data analysts, and security operatives were allowed on the premises. Sandy had told Will that SILs were the only places in Afrasia to access the classified information they needed.

"Sounds like it won't be an easy place to get into," Will had said when Sandy gave him the details on the train about the SIL they wanted to infiltrate.

"You're right," Sandy had replied as she munched a candy. "SILs are always difficult to get into, but I have been in this particular SIL two or three times before."

"I'm sure it's not legal to break into a facility of the Afrasian government," Will grinned. "It's odd because you certainly don't look like a lawbreaker, occasional or otherwise."

Sandy chuckled and looked at him innocently. "I sometimes break the rules for the greater good. We all do at one point or another. Doesn't mean it's right to break rules, but…"

A gentle ticking sound close by brought Will back to the present. The sound was coming from the smart digiwatch strapped to Sandy's wrist. She clicked something on the small screen of the watch, and the ticking sound immediately went off. Will looked far ahead of him and saw that the SIL was now in sight, even though they were still a good distance from the building. The SIL was a big cylindrical-shaped building situated on a wide expanse of mowed land around it. There were numerous security operatives outside the building, walking around in what appeared to be a coordinated manner as they surveyed the surroundings.

"Don't tell me we are going in that way," Will said as he pointed in the direction of the building.

He could not see how they could attempt to enter the building in broad daylight when so many guards were around there. They would surely be caught if they tried that.

Sandy chuckled. "No, we are not. Come with me."

Sandy led the way to the left, and Will followed closely, observing their terrain as he walked behind her. They were still hiking through tall grasses, but now they seemed to be on a slightly higher ground than the point where the SIL was built.

"Load your freeze," Sandy said suddenly. "We are getting close to the action."

Freeze was the term used among special agents for specially designed bullets that rendered targets unconscious rather than take their lives. Dr Kean had provided Will and Sandy with rounds of freeze along with real bullets before they set out for their mission in the Underworld.

Will retrieved a round of freeze from his pocket and jammed it into his F15 rifle. Sandy did the same and also keyed the silencer into the mouth of her rifle.

"You ready for this, Burne?"

"Bring it on, Krave," Will replied.

His side still hurt where he had been wounded in the shootout at the Afrasian-Underworld border, but he had patched it up nicely and didn't think it was going to make him fare worse in their current stealth mission. If Sandy was ready, he was ready too. While Will was thinking about this, Sandy dropped to her knees and began to run her hands in circles through the tall grass.

"What are you doing?" he finally asked after a few moments, when he did not understand what she was trying to do. Was she looking for something?

"I'm trying to get… Oh, yeah. I found it," Sandy said and instantly pulled up a metal lid.

"A tunnel?"

"Smart guy," Sandy said as she swung her legs into the hole beneath her. A few seconds later, she had vanished down into the tunnel.

Will immediately went into the tunnel after her. Like most tunnels Will had been in, it was low and dark. The air was dank and barely breathable, but Will kept moving forward, following Sandy's lead. They stepped lightly as possible, being cautious not to make sounds that might travel to the other end of the tunnel and alert the guards to their arrival.

The cramped, long tunnel took about ten minutes of slow, hunched-over walking to get them to the end of the tunnel. Finally, Sandy signalled with an upward movement of her forefinger that they had to climb up to get out of the tunnel. Will jerked his head twice in quick succession to show that he understood what she meant.

Sandy led the way up the wall as she started slipping her feet into the holes that had been strategically designed into specific parts of the tunnel wall. She climbed so quickly and adeptly that Will struggled to keep pace with her fast hands and feet. Will did not know what exactly to expect on the other side. He feared that they might climb out and immediately fall into the hands of waiting guards at the other end, but he reassured himself with the thought that Sandy knew what she was doing. If she had breached the tough defence of this place two times on her own before, then surely, they had every chance to succeed.

Sandy was the first to poke her head out after pushing another lid aside at the top of the tunnel. She looked left and right before she signalled to Will the all-clear. Will climbed out of the tunnel a few seconds after Sandy had lifted herself out. They both looked around, trying to be certain that they were not walking into the hands of the guards.

Will noticed they were now in a room with shiny, silver-metallic walls and bright light bulbs high up; this place was possibly inside the building he had seen earlier.

"Are we inside the SIL?" Will whispered to Sandy.

She nodded and immediately pointed towards a door almost opposite them, signalling it as the next place they had to go. They started towards the door, and when they got there, Sandy quickly punched a button at the centre of the metal door. Instantly, a holographic display of numbers and symbols popped up, right in front of them. Sandy stepped forward and began quickly tapping numbers and symbols. Will's quick eyes picked up the first six characters of the code: 9^#12&. After that, he could no longer keep up with the speed at which Sandy punched the code. Will's eyes widened as she continued inputting code, the length of the code growing by the second.

When Sandy was done, there was a deep hum as the security system evaluated Sandy's entry. Then, the door clicked open after a moment, and they stepped in, Sandy taking the lead while Will covered her from behind. "How did you know the code?" Will asked.

"I don't," Sandy replied, "it's a standard cheat code for hackers, designed to override the system without tipping anyone off to our presence. It's rather lengthy, but I've long since memorized it, and it's come in handy countless times."

In the new room they stepped into, giant computer systems were placed haphazardly on rows of tables occupying nearly the entire room. The systems looked quite old; they seemed like the supercomputers that were much in vogue in the 2090s but had now been phased out because of the emergence of more efficient devices. As soon as they got into the room, Sandy turned and released a couple of quick shots into two of the room's upper corners. Will saw that she had disabled the cameras monitoring the room.

"Are we really going to get the information we need from these old systems?" Will asked.

"No," Sandy replied. "These computers are no longer in use. They've been wiped. We have to go further down to get what we need. Oh…"

Will stood by, expecting Sandy to make the next move. He had his F15 on the ready; he would not hesitate to knock down any guard he saw. He turned back to Sandy and saw that she no longer appeared confident as she had been earlier; a confused look was on her face.

"What's wrong?" Will enquired.

"I don't know. The whole place has been remodelled," Sandy said. "There used to be a door over there, where I could get into the labs without being seen."

Will wiped his sweaty forehead with a single swipe of his forefinger. "Maybe they found out that someone has been coming in to access their systems."

"Come on," Sandy said. "There's another way."

Will followed Sandy as she headed to the right. He continued looking left, right, and behind them to ensure there was no one watching them. They got to another door with a console panel similar to the one that Sandy opened earlier. Just like the first time, Sandy called up the holographic screen with a press button affixed to the door. She began to input the code, but Will couldn't clearly see the code as she punched it in this time because Sandy's body was blocking his line of sight. As he was looking over his shoulder to make sure no one was sneaking up on them from behind, the door unlocked with a *click,* signalling that Sandy was done.

Sandy held a finger to her lips and motioned for Will to get down into a crouching position. They both crouched by the side of the door, waiting.

"Jazim, is that you?" they heard a voice on the other side ask.

Will curled his finger around the trigger of his rifle as he began to hear the sound of approaching footsteps from the other side.

"Jazim?" the voice came again.

The voice had barely finished calling out to Jazim when the door swung open as someone pulled it from the other side. Will saw the black trousers first; then he saw the green shirt and brown face. It was one of the guards. He had probably been standing close to the door when it clicked and had been curious to see who was there. Will's eyes quickly went to the pistol holstered at the guard's waist. It was a ray gun, which could bore a huge hole through a target at close range.

Will wasted no time in pulling the trigger; the freeze bullet caught the guard in the stomach. He didn't fall instantly; he stared wide-eyed in shock at the duo crouched before him, then he staggered backwards. He opened his mouth to speak, but words refused to flow from his mouth. Will knew that one of the first body functions that the freeze disabled was speech. It was designed that way to prevent human targets from giving off cries of alarm. The guard would wake up in a few hours with a very hazy memory of what had happened to him—if he remembered at all. In a few more seconds, the dark guard fell backwards. He was just about to come crashing down when Sandy scrambled forward and grabbed him by the under the arms, lowering him to the ground quietly.

"There are people on the other side," Sandy whispered. "We have to be discreet. Cover me. I'll be done in a minute."

Will nodded as he remained in a crouched position. Sandy stealthily went on into the room while Will covered her from behind. Will saw that this room was about three times bigger than the one packed with the old-model supercomputers. There were far more computers in this room, and all the ones Will could see were new engines. He could also see a large number of operators working on many of the systems.

Sandy was already on her way to a big computer not far from the door. Will watched as she sneaked quietly to the system and began to tap the supercomputer's screen with speed. Will took his eyes off her to look for guards or officials who might have noticed that one of the computers was being used by an outsider. But, for now, nobody had noticed anything.

He continued watching them for any signs they had noticed, and every minute that went by, he felt more and more anxious to get out of there. *You have spent more than one fucking minute!* Will screamed in his head when he saw Sandy still tapping on the computer.

Will felt worse when he noticed a guard tilting his head sideways as if he were receiving a message from his com device while he was simultaneously walking in Sandy's direction as she worked on the computer.

"Damn it!" Will growled under his breath. He ran his eyes around the room again. There were probably a hundred guards here, baring the ones he could not see from where he was. He and Sandy would stand little chance of escaping if they were found out right here in this hall.

Sandy! Will roared in his head. What the hell was taking her so long?

The guard was still approaching her desk, shouldering his way through clusters of officials and fellow guards, as he made his way towards the back end of the hall where their operation was being carried out.

Forty seconds!

That was it. According to Will's calculations, the guard would be close enough to Sandy's desk in forty seconds to notice her, and by then, it would be too late for her to leave without another exchange of fire.

"Fuck!" Will cursed. He would have to shoot the guard; that was the only solution. He hoped that he and Sandy would be able to slip away undetected when the guard finally dropped to the floor unconscious.

Will raised his gun and aimed quickly. He coiled his finger around the trigger, and… The guard suddenly turned away from Sandy and headed to his right.

Will let out a breath he did not realise he had been holding. That was damned close. Almost immediately, Sandy moved away from the computer and quietly slipped back towards Will.

They both sneaked out of the room and gently closed the door behind them, exhaling loudly.

"What took you so long?" Will asked. "You had me really tensed up in there."

"Took me longer than I expected to copy what I needed," Sandy said. "I could barely breathe, too. Thank goodness, we are getting out of here without any—"

The sudden blaring from the nearby alarms swallowed the rest of her response. Approaching footsteps alerted Will and Sandy that something was wrong.

"Quick! To the tunnel!" Sandy yelled as she broke into a run.

Will quickly ran after her, and together they raced through the passageway they had passed through earlier until they returned to the storeroom with abandoned systems.

"You don't think it's something else?" Will said as they ran back in the direction of the tunnel. "Maybe it's not us they are chasing."

The sound of gunshots from behind them rubbished that line of thought. Just as Will and Sandy got to the entrance of the room with old computers, a group of guards rushed in from the back door and began to fire at them heavily. "Run!" Sandy cried.

Will raced forward, matching her quick strides as he wondered what had happened. How did the guards detect their activity? Perhaps someone noticed the unconscious guard or the computer's anti-virus program had picked up that Sandy had copied vital information?

Will got to the tunnel first and pushed the lid aside; he stepped to one side to allow Sandy to go in while covering her. He fired two quick shots at the first guard that appeared within his sight. Then, he shot his freeze bullets at two more guards before Sandy screamed at him to get into the tunnel.

A bullet whizzed dangerously close to Will's ear. That propelled him to abandon his gunfight with the swarming guards and to leap into the safety offered by the dark tunnel. But, before he went down the tunnel, he unstrapped a gas grenade hung on his waistband and tossed it at his adversaries. That would keep them away for a while.

He looked back over his shoulder, satisfied that they were not following them, at least for the moment, and continued moving on.

As Will climbed down, deeper into darkness, he wondered if the guards were going to be tenacious enough to chase him and Sandy properly. He was not sure about that. But, one thing was certain: Sandy would never be able to use the tunnel to gain access to this SIL ever again.

… … …

Sandy Krave's Bunker: Xio Chan, Afrasia

Sandy felt a sense of calm as she led Will Burne and May Lay into the large living room in her private safehouse. In this place, she felt untouchable, invincible to the forces that were against her. This was her personal bunker, hewn out of a large mountainous rock close to River Tov's bank in the little Afrasian village called Xio Chan. The nearest city to that place was Mukt, and it was about thirty-five kilometres away.

The safehouse was given to her by Adha Long, her guardian. He had given it to her the day she earned her last badge at the 40 Grades training camp, which was over a decade ago. She had since made the safehouse a true home to Tilda herself. It was where she hid herself away whenever she wanted to escape from the world.

Sandy's mind flicked to how she and Will had escaped from the special information lab at Kim Koom county by the barest of margins. The guards had followed them down the tunnel, but the two, in top physical condition, were able to outrun the guards to the grassland bordering the building without being caught. They had returned to Mukt to board a train to the last station, where May had been waiting for them.

"Quite a lovely place you have here, Ms Krave," May said to Sandy regarding her bunker.

Sandy had been glad to see that May had kept out of trouble when she and Will had been at the SIL. They met her at the restaurant near the station; she was eating a local dish while she watched a sports game on the tube when they got there.

"Thank you," Sandy answered with a smile.

Will seemed fascinated with the framed works of art hung in various parts of the living room. He went from one to another, peering into the frames as if he wanted to see beyond what the physical eyes could make out from the frame.

"Are you a fan of Ahima?" Sandy asked when she noticed that he showed a special interest in the painting of one of the most celebrated artists in Afrasia.

"Ahima?" Will intoned. "Is that her name?"

"Ahima Botha, that's the name of the artist, not the girl in the drawing," Sandy explained.

"It's beautiful," Will said as he walked away from the painting.

In his eyes, Sandy had read the conclusion to that statement: *Just like you.* She could see that he liked her. In the past few days they had spent together, going through varying degrees of danger, she could tell that the feelings between them had grown. They had developed from mere teammates to the kind of comradeship that was forged by watching each other's backs and covering each other's asses.

There's more, Sandy confessed to herself. She was attracted to Will Burne's handsome face and strong hands. She remembered staring at him as he gripped his F15 rifle on one occasion and wondering how it would be to have his hands gripping her tits in the same manner. She thought about having his fingers coiled around her nipples, just as he coiled his index finger around the trigger…

"Let me show you the rooms," Sandy said suddenly, snapping herself back to reality.

She took Will into one of the two rooms in the bunker, and he sat down on the bed.

"Goodness me," Will said as he ran his hand over the soft, bouncy bed. "Can't remember the last time I slept in something this comfy."

A light chuckle escaped Sandy's lips. "Enjoy it while it lasts."

Will bent down to unlace his boots. The look on his face told Sandy that he couldn't wait to kick them off. She stared at her own boots, caked in mud from the ocean shores of the Underworld, and soot from the tunnel at the SIL in Kim Koom County. She needed to kick her boots off as well. The past few days had been crazy, with the number of deadly situations they had been in.

"I'll leave you to rest," Sandy said as she started towards the door. "Let me attend to May."

… … …

The last of the warm water streamed down from the showerhead jets onto the ebony skin of Sandy Krave as she turned off the tap. She grabbed her towel and began to wipe the moisture off her body slowly. She felt all her body aches evaporating as she stood there in the bathroom, towelling off wetness from her dark skin.

After a few moments, she stepped out of the bathroom, having slipped into a comfy nightdress. The hot shower had done a lot of good to her body. It left her feeling very relaxed and soothed. She walked into her room and found May sleeping soundly on the large-size smart bed. The woman had taken a shower earlier to wash off the grime that had stuck to her body in the course of the wild events over the last few days.

Sandy tried to imagine how difficult this whole situation was for May. From being an internationally recognised business owner and philanthropist to scurrying for safety in a gunfight between spies and special agents. From living in one of the most luxurious mansions on the globe to sharing a bed with a trained killer in the middle of nowhere. She wondered what it meant for one's husband to have a hand in one's abduction. Surely, May was going through a lot.

Sandy slipped into bed beside May and instantly felt her smart bed reconfiguring itself to match her body temperature underneath her back. Sandy's lips curled into a big smile as she remembered the last time she had been on this same bed with someone of the same sex. It was during the sexual awakening process of the 40 Grade ritual.

The memory had remained in her head because it was the first time in her adult life that she was sexually exposed to another woman's body. She remembered that night when she and Amisha Son were paired in the one-on-one sexual activity of the ritual that was reserved exclusively for the most elite fighters in the Afrasian army. A week before the ritual, she had been asked if she wanted a man or a woman to be paired with. She had chosen to go with someone of the same sex because she wanted to be more dominant during the 40 Grade ritual. She knew how domineering men could be in bed; she wanted a situation where she would be on equal footing with her partner. Also, she wanted to use it as a means to explore the experience of being with a woman.

Amisha's ancestry could be traced to India and Korea. She stood at five feet, seven inches, much shorter than Sandy. She had long black hair, a smooth, beautiful face, and a petite body. She looked like the complete physical opposite of Sandy, who was tall, dark, and curvy in just the right places.

The process of the 40 Grade sexual awakening was steeped in complexity. The essence of the ritual was for the participants to engage in intense sexual activities that would later reinvigorate them for the coming months. The sexual energy created and absorbed during the ritual was usually channelled into a vital mission ahead. It served as a game in the sense that whichever one dominated the other would be adjudged by superior officers observing the game (on big screens in a conference room) as the winner of that session. It was called 40 Grades because an elite fighter had to engage in forty such games before leaving the Special Agent Academy.

Sandy Krave could still remember in great detail how she and Amisha had both went to bed, bathed in oils and aromatic perfumes. She had expected to dominate Amisha in bed by making her moan and scream with pleasure as she licked and played with the erogenous zones of her body.

When they got into bed, the first thing they did was lock their lips together in a hot, passionate kiss. They tightened their arms around each other's bodies as they deepened the kiss, exploring the depths of each other's mouths. Sandy found the experience of kissing another woman quite strange but no less pleasurable than kissing men. After they had been kissing for several minutes, Amisha stretched her body across the bed. Sandy attempted to please her by going straight to her nipples and delivering sharp flicks with her tongue. While Sandy sucked Amisha's nipples, she slowly took her fingers to Amisha's clitoris and began to rub it gently. She squeezed Amisha's perky breast with one hand, rolling her tongue around the nipple while she pressed her fingers against Amisha's swelling clitoris with the other. Next, she slowly inched her middle finger toward her opening as she massaged her folds.

Am I doing something wrong? Damn you, Amisha. Moan!

There was no sound from the little lady. She lay there on her back, staring at Sandy like she wasn't doing anything at all to her body. Sandy grew more concerned about her performance as she continued to suck Amisha's nipples without a positive result.

After that, Sandy let her mouth run all the way down Amisha's belly, down the region that contained her pubic hair until she got her lips against Amisha's swollen clit.

Sandy began to flick Amisha's clitoris with her tongue while sliding a finger into her wet vagina. There was a slight whimper from the small woman, but she quickly recovered her stoic composure and refused to give off any more sound, no matter how much Sandy tried to please her.

Sandy was clearly frustrated with what was happening. She knew that Amisha was winning already if things continued this way.

"Let me try," Amisha whispered.

Instantly, Sandy knew she had to agree. She was going to show Amisha that she could resist pleasure as well.

"Yeah, let's see what you can do," Sandy replied casually, as she rolled off her fellow officer to lie on the bed.

The first thing Amisha did was lean towards Sandy's head and rolled her serpentine tongue against the interior of her ear. Sandy did not know why she found that little act arousing, but it really did arouse her. She felt a rush of moisture between her thighs. The next thing she felt was Amisha's tiny finger circling around her pussy until it nestled in a surprisingly odd place: her perineum. Amisha began to rub that spot between her vulva and her anus.

"Whaha ohhh!"

Sandy attempted to scream, *What are you doing?* But what came out of her mouth was a loud moan that echoed around the room.

Amisha now leaned against Sandy's pussy and began to roll her tongue against the sides of her vulva. It was insanely pleasurable. Sandy reached for her own boobs and began to squeeze them out of intense pleasure as Amisha did crazy and wonderful things to her honeypot with her tongue and fingers.

By the time Amisha began to drive her finger into Sandy's cunt, she was visibly shaking and moaning uncontrollably. Amisha had driven her body to the heights of pleasure. Sandy, a fierce competitor who always wanted to win every challenge, agreed she had lost the 40 Grade challenge to Amisha. What she got in return was a massive climax that made her body shudder in the wildest sensation of pleasure…

May stirred next to her on the mattress, turning to face the other side in her sleep. That little stirring motion jolted Sandy out of her deep reminiscence. It had been so long since she had thought about that particular 40 Grade session with Amisha. After that, she had engaged in many sexual awakening rituals, taking on different men and women as it caught her fancy to choose. After that, she had won most of her 40 Grade games, but none were as memorable as that mind-blowing encounter with Amisha Son.

Sandy suddenly noticed a pool of moisture between her legs as she lay there beside May Lay. Dear goodness, she was really wet. Crazily horny. Her mind flitted to the standard control thought that she had taught herself to use when she needed to put her sexual desire in check. Yet, as she tried to purge her mind of sexual thoughts, she grew hornier. Desire coursed through her body in a way she hadn't experienced in a long time.

She knew the cause of this seemingly untameable desire. She wanted him, and she knew he wanted her.

… … …

Sandy's Desire: Xio Chan, Afrasia

Sandy swung her curvy body out of bed while taking care not to wake May. She tiptoed to the door and pulled it open, letting herself out of the room as silently as possible. She walked towards Will Burne's door with her mind made up on one thing: she would determine how much Will wanted her.

She turned the knob of his door and found it unlocked. *Wasn't that a good sign?* she asked herself. She took a deep breath; then knocked on the door.

"Sandy?" Will's voice came from the other side of the door. It didn't sound like a sleepy voice to Sandy.

"Yeah, it's me," she said.

"Come on in."

Sandy opened the door, stepped inside, and closed the door behind her. She stood just in front of the door staring at Will, who was clad only in boxer shorts as he sat on the edge of the bed. Will had switched off the bright bulb and had left only a dimly lit bulb in the corner of the room. In the dim lighting, Sandy could clearly make out the broadness of Will's chest, and she wondered how it would feel to have her breasts pressed against that broad chest.

"You uh… Forget something?" Will stuttered.

It was obvious he was getting turned on by the revealing nightdress Sandy had chosen to put on. She could see his erection straining against the fabric of his shorts.

Sandy walked over to where he sat and slipped off her nightdress, letting it drop to the ground in a loud rustle. She heard a gasp of wonder from Will as he saw her big boobs springing free. She cat-walked towards him, completely nude. Will rose to his feet and rushed forward to meet her halfway. He circled his arms around her, pulling her into a passionate embrace. Sandy felt her boobs rubbing against Will's broad chest, and she remembered she had wished for exactly that a few moments ago.

"Mmmm," a sigh of contentment escaped Sandy's lips as Will's hands snaked down her back to grab her naked ass. Sandy parted her lips to accommodate Will's probing tongue, and they instantly began to move their tongues together in desperate need to taste each other. They kissed for a long time, savouring the sweetness in each other's lips as they moved their hands over each other's bodies. Finally, Sandy let her hand slip down Will's body until it cupped his erect penis, which was pushing furiously against the material of his boxers.

"I want to feel you inside me. Right now," Sandy whispered directly into Will's ear, and as she spoke those words, she felt him shudder and his dick growing even more in length and in girth as it made its way down the leg of his boxers.

Sandy smiled as Will grabbed her up and proceeded to lay her on the bed. The anticipation reminded her of the night she had with Amisha, and she thought of the mind-blowing sexual pleasure that Amisha Son had delivered to her body with her tongue and fingers. As Will bent down to remove his shorts, Sandy caught sight of his big cock standing firm, ready for action. *He wants me just as much as I want him.* She felt a rush of electricity in her pussy as she grew wetter, and her clit throbbed that much harder at the thought.

Sandy propped herself up and bent her head until her face was directly in front of his cock. She reached out with her hand and grabbed his erection. *Damn, but he would more than satisfy her!* His cock was throbbing as she held it, as if it were also feeling impatient to slip into her moist pussy. Looking into Will's eyes, Sandy parted her lips and took his cock in her mouth.

"Fuck!" Will growled, rolling his eyes back in immense pleasure as Sandy began to swirl her tongue around the sensitive tip of his penis.

Sandy teased him for a few more moments before she began to move her mouth swiftly up and down his erection, taking him deeper with each movement. She continued sucking his cock, harder and faster, taking him deeper into her throat until Will's penis began to pulse more rapidly. Sandy knew what that meant. He was edging towards the bliss of releasing his seed.

"Okay, okay," Will said. Then, stopping the climax, he pushed her away as he pulled his cock out of Sandy's warm mouth. "Time to make you scream the roof down."

Sandy leaned back on the bed as Will climbed in beside her, staying upright on his knees. He pushed her legs apart, anticipating the moment he could penetrate her wet pussy. Sandy shuddered with pleasure as Will rubbed the tip of his penis against the mouth of her slippery, wet folds. Her waist jerked upwards, her back arching as Will teased her, rubbing his dick against the entrance of her ready pussy while he worked her swollen clit with his thumb.

"Now, Will," Sandy whimpered. "I can't wait any longer to have you inside me." Will rubbed his dick against her pussy one last time before he slid it all the way to the hilt, deep inside her.

"Ohhhh," a wild gasp floated from Sandy's lips as Will's rigid cock slid into her.

He went in slowly at first, maintaining a slower, rhythmic pattern as he went in and out of her pussy. Sandy wrapped her legs around him as she wanted to feel him deeper inside of her. After a few minutes of slow strokes, Will started to thrust a little faster. Sandy moved her waist upwards in unison with him to meet his fast strokes. Moans flowed uncontrollably out of her mouth as Will's probing dick hit the walls deep inside her, stimulating her sensitive G-spot. She could see galaxies of stars exploding behind her lidded eyes as she screamed out in pleasure.

Will was thrusting faster still, pushing harder and deeper with every movement; at this point, he was groaning as loudly as Sandy was moaning.

He felt her pussy tighten around him one last time as she reached full climax, giving him the green light to blow his load. "I'm fucking cumming," Will grunted as he slammed his dick deep into Sandy one last time before he pulled out and unloaded his seed on her big, beautiful breasts.

Will collapsed on the bed beside Sandy, truly spent from their round of passion. They both lay on the bed for a few moments, panting hard as they had both pushed the limits of their bodies to experience intense pleasure. After that, they put their arms around each other and headed to the bathroom to clean up. As they moved on, Sandy could feel Will's semi-turgid cock pressing up against her buttcheek. She allowed herself a small, knowing smile; she knew that they would be doing more than just cleaning themselves up in the bathroom.

… … …

Who Can Sandy Trust?

It was already late in the morning before Will Burne stirred from the deep sleep he had drifted into after the demanding entanglement with Sandy. He held his arm over his eyes as he waited for his eyes to adjust to the bright light from the rolling bulbs high up on the ceiling. His eyes roved under the shade provided by his arm, and before long, they landed on a digital clock hung on the wall directly opposite the bed. The time was 10:57.

Pain shot through Will's lower back as he drew himself upright. Truly, he and Sandy had gone hard on each other over the night. He stared silently at the space beside him, where she had settled when they finally crashed onto the bed together after returning from the bathroom.

"Dammit," Will muttered as he swung his legs off the soft bed. His head was becoming clearer by the minute, and he began to think of the events of last night. It was indeed the most intense sexual encounter he had experienced in quite a long time. Jenny, and the plethora of other women he had gone to bed with at one time or another in his life, did not in any way come close to the mind-blowing sessions of sexual expression he and Sandy had been engaged in throughout the night.

Will checked the area near the bed, looking for where he had shed his clothes before he and Sandy got things started. He felt a terrible growl in his belly. Was he hungry, or did ravenous come close to how he truly felt? He could not remember the last time he had woken up this late. His time in the West Federation Elite Corps meant he had been trained to wake up at the break of dawn, to be able to snap out of sleep whether he was in the sweet comfort of the most luxurious e-bed or on a cold hard floor in the middle of nowhere. However, his biological alarm system had failed this morning, no thanks to Sandy Krave's heroics in bed! There were times last night when he found it hard to believe that the same battle-hardened agent, who was that amazing in bed, was the same person.

Will finally found his brown boxer shorts, as well as the black leather pants and jacket, which was the uniform that Dr Kean had given to him and Sandy for their botched mission in the Underworld. It felt like a lifetime ago that he had been in that abandoned lab, listening to Dr Kean's verbose debriefing while trying his best to keep his eyes off Sandy's shapely figure. So much time had passed, and so many things had happened.

"Bastard Kean," Will muttered. He still had not forgotten his resolve to track down the doctor and make him pay for the danger he had put them in. Once they had cleared everything before them, he would take the time to hunt down Kean and mete out any due punishment he deemed appropriate. He had no doubts that Sandy would be interested in that.

Will kicked his legs into the shorts, feeling more aware of the constant twanging in his belly. He supposed he had burned quite a lot of energy last night. He really needed to get a bite of something. Will walked towards the bed to check the bedspread for notes or anything Sandy might have dropped, but he found nothing. A smile tugged at his lips as he tried to think of Sandy slipping away from the room, padding along gently, trying hard not to wake him.

Glancing around the room, Will wondered if Sandy had ever kept a man in there before. He did not know why the thought irritated him so much, but it truly did. He was not one to get all emotionally attached to a woman after a fling, which was very much what had happened between him and Sandy last night, yet the thought of Sandy having been with a man in this same room peeved him. He felt something he had not felt in a very long time: jealousy. If he could remember clearly, the last time he had been filled with such emotion was when he chanced on a flirty chat between one of his exes, Sharon, and a rich fellow in one of the big corporations in the West Federation.

As Will looked around, his eyes were suddenly magnetized to a small pile on the little table at the other end of the room. He quickly dashed over to the table and checked out the pile. It contained a tube of toothpaste, a bar of soap, and some other toiletries. The urge to give his body a nice scrub temporarily superseded his need to feed his stomach. He took the pile under his arm and headed for the bathroom attached to the room, which he and Sandy had used for cleaning up—and for even more steamy bouts of passion.

"Okay, boy, time to get these things out of your head," he said to himself as he started towards the bathroom. "It's just a fling, okay? Damn it; she probably feels that way too."

Despite the things Will said to himself, he could not successfully block out the fresh images of the two of them pleasuring each other. His mind kept flitting to that moment when he and Sandy stood facing each other with their lips locked and one of Sandy's shapely legs raised to his shoulder while he drove in and out of her with…

"Stop it!" Will growled to himself, especially the part of himself controlling such memories as last night. He did not like how all his thoughts seemed to be in only one direction ever since he woke up. It made him feel a certain kind of vulnerability that he did not like in the least.

Will did his absolute best to shower without Sandy Krave's naked body popping up in his head; then, he ambled out of the bathroom when he was done. He returned to the room, feeling lighter and a lot better. He looked around and saw that all he had were his pants and jacket from last night. He slipped into them and headed straight for the door. He felt ready for the world. He was also ready to wolf down a chunk of whatever Afrasian meal Sandy had to offer. But, more importantly, he felt ready to face Sandy Krave, the woman who had dominated his thoughts not only since last night but also since the very first time he had seen her in that debriefing room. Sandy Krave, the woman with whom he had bonded in a way that was so special and so different from the female West Federation agents he had paired with at one time or another.

Will Burne turned the knob of the door and stepped out into the little passageway. He thrust his hands into his hip pockets and began to stride forward as if nothing in the whole wide world bothered him.

… … …

Sandy was clicking the keys on the screen of her minicomputer when she heard the sound of approaching footsteps coming in the direction of the living room where she was seated. *That must be Will*, she thought. Finally, he had snapped out of his deep sleep. Sandy set her computer down on the table before her just as she heard Will's gentle knock on the door.

"Come in, Will," Sandy said.

After she had spoken, she saw Will striding into the room. He was dressed in the uniform that Dr Kean had given them and looked as handsome as ever. From a distance, Sandy could detect a hint of the distinct fragrance of the bathing soap she usually stocked in her bunker.

"Hello, Sandy," Will said huskily as he eased himself onto a stool.

"Hi," she replied, flashing him a smile. "Didn't know you were a heavy sleeper."

Will shook his head, "Oh, not me. Today was just, you know, different."

"I know," Sandy giggled.

"Have you started checking the files?" Will asked, pointing a finger in the direction of Sandy's computer.

"Not at all," she replied. "I wasn't going to do it without you around. And maybe May, if she is interested."

It makes sense that May would be interested in knowing about the people who posed a threat to her safety, Sandy thought. Sandy wondered what surprises awaited them in the files obtained from the SIL. She knew one thing for sure; they had enemies within Afrasia. People who were working with both the Underworld and Oceania Liberation while residing in Afrasia.

"Where's May?" Will asked as he gently rubbed his forehead.

"She's in my study going through some books and pictures," Sandy said. "I hope she finds something in there to hold her interest. Most of my books are not here."

At the moment, Will's only interest was the low rumbling in his belly.

"Are you a man of books, Burne?" Sandy asked.

"No man worth his salt abhors reading," Will replied. "I certainly find joy in reading, and I spend time nourishing my mind when I'm not dodging bullets, on a mission, or training."

Sandy fixed her eyes on Will as he spoke. As she stared at him, her mind threatened to flicker back to the events of last night and how they had been locked in each other's arms. She wondered what he thought of last night.

"Sandy?"

Sandy jolted back to reality. "Oh, sorry. What did you say?"

"I asked if I could get something to eat," Will said.

"Oh, definitely," Sandy said. "I'll get you some cereal and a cup of Khanke."

"What's Khanke?" Will asked, his brows inching upward.

"It's a kind of whipped cream mixed with Afrasian honey and some other things," Sandy told him. "You'll like it. At least, May found it delicious."

Sandy rose from her seat to fix cereal with Khanke for Will. She watched as Will ravenously attacked the bowl of breakfast. The way he scarfed it down, one would think it was a meal he ate regularly.

"Thank you," Will said when he was done. "I enjoyed it, as you said."

He rose from his seat, packed the bowl and cup, and asked where to take them. Sandy took the utensils from him and went to the kitchen.

"Now I'm ready to shoot down Underworld rogues; bring them on!" Will said to Sandy when she returned, and they both burst into laughter.

"Speaking about shooting," Sandy said. "I have a tramach in here. It's the closest thing to shooting those bastards in reality."

"I'm ready when you are," Will replied. "When will we check the files?"

"Let's do it now," Sandy said. "We'll go to the study and check the contents with May."

Will nodded his head in agreement, so Sandy led the way towards her study. She had her minicomputer in her hand as she led Will out of the small living room to the study. She noticed that Will was not moving as fast because he observed the paintings and other works of art lining the walls of the passageway they were walking through. The paintings of Ahima Botha, the carvings of Vadu Radi, and other works of Afrasian art seemed to hold Will spellbound as they slowly progressed towards the study.

"Beautiful," Sandy heard Will mutter.

She turned to check what had made him utter that word. It was the painting of a part-black, part-yellow naked female body lying on the flag of Afrasia. It was one of Botha's more recognisable paintings.

"Yes, it is," Sandy said.

After a few more pauses along the way, Sandy and Will got to the study, where they found May thumbing through a thick volume whose author Sandy could not recollect at that moment.

"Good morning, May," Will greeted her.

"Top of the morning to you, Burne," May said. There was a smile on the older woman's face, and Sandy could not help thinking for a moment that May was aware of what had happened between her and Will last night. Perhaps she had woken up in the middle of the night and noticed Sandy was no longer next to her. Of course, it was not even out of the question that the wild moans had roused her in the middle of the night, either.

Sandy had no regrets about last night. It was all her conception, and she knew Will was willing. It had been so long since she practised the 40 Grade ritual, and she found Will Burne to be the perfect man in the current circumstances. At least to partner her in the ritual and to recharge her batteries. If anything, she had a revitalized body, bursting with energy as her gain for the events of the last night.

Sandy set her computer down on a small table and turned to face May. "Will and I are about to check the files we got from the SIL. Are you interested in seeing them?"

"Definitely," May said as she closed the large book in front of her. Sandy saw the cover and recognised the book as one of the strategy books in her collection. A book which she never really liked.

Sandy eased into a seat behind the desk and began to click the keys on her computer.

"Find file X3," Sandy voiced to her minicomputer.

"Repeat voice command for confirmation," the AI from the computer responded.

"Find file X3," Sandy repeated.

Momentarily, the file Sandy had copied from the SIL at Kim Koom county popped up on the screen. It was a record of phone conversations made in secure calls from Afrasia to Ocean Liberation and vice versa, as saved by mobile service providers. It was a piece of information that Sandy could not have obtained elsewhere without causing some eyebrows to be raised.

"Switch to space screen," Sandy commanded.

The display on the screen of Sandy's computer instantly became projected in a bigger and clearer form, in the space right in front of them. After that, Sandy began to scroll through the call records, checking the details attached. There were hundreds of calls, just on the first page that Sandy opened.

"What do we do with all these details?" May asked as she stared into the rows of logged calls.

"We are looking for saboteurs, for officials of Afrasia who are aware of what Oceania Liberation is planning to do and who are supporting them. We need to know which people we have to steer clear of for the moment," Will explained.

"Tough work," May said.

"I won't be listening to the calls one after the other if that's what you think," Sandy told May. "I'll run a program that will transcribe the calls and search for some keywords I'll input right now. If there is anything incriminating here, which I'm sure there will be, the program will sniff it out."

Sandy spent the next few moments punching in words she thought could lead them to what they were looking for. When she was done, she craned her neck and waited for the program to give out the information they wanted to see. After about thirty seconds, the program returned a list of ten calls that contained at least one of the keywords that Sandy had inputted.

"Here we go," Will breathed.

Sandy felt her hands become a little shaky as she tried to click open the call at the top of the list to see the transcribed conversation. Which top Afrasian official was working with the enemy? Were there more than one? Sandy remembered that fellow they had gunned down at the terminal restaurant at The Last Wall. He was one of the men who had been on her team during her last mission with the imperial army, and he had joined forces with the bad guys before he met his doom. How many others were like him in Afrasia? Cops, military officers, corporate officers; who could they trust with the truth of the situation?

Sandy clicked on the file and was instantly confronted with a surge of anger and disappointment.

This message has been deleted.

"No… no!" Sandy cried as she tried an alternative way to open the file. The response was the same.

She tried the next two calls after it and found the same annoying message.

"Damn it!" Will cursed as he clenched his fists and stamped a foot on the ground.

Not to leave anything to chance, Sandy checked each of the seven remaining call records on the list. None gave a different result. Somehow, they had all been deleted.

Sandy was perplexed. It was not the first time she was digging in such records, but she had never encountered something like this before.

"It means," Sandy began, with her head resting against her palm, "we wasted our time and risked our lives for nothing by going to the SIL."

Sandy felt a hand drop on her shoulder. It was Will's hand, in a comforting gesture.

"It's good we tried that out," Will said. "At least, now we know that the people we are up against mean business."

He's right, Sandy thought. They were up against some guys who knew how to clean their tracks, not leaving even the slightest trace of their activities behind.

"We will get them," Will assured.

This time, Sandy did not share his optimism. They did not even know who to go after, except maybe Dr Kean, who certainly would no longer be in Afrasia.

Owen Briggs.

The name of her business partner dropped in her mind. She had known him for so long she was certain he was not aware of Dr Kean's scheme. They would go see Briggs and find out what he knows.

… … …

Sandy Krave Challenges Will Burne

Will Burne could not stop wondering how Sandy Krave could afford such a luxurious bunker. Did special agents in Afrasia receive so much better pay than those in the West Federation, or had Sandy acquired the bunker by other means? Will was following Sandy again as she took him on a tour of the bunker. She wanted him to see her armoury and training machines.

Will wanted to ask her if all special agents in Afrasia owned similar structures, but something about the question did not seem right to him; so, he kept his mouth shut, only nodding at appropriate times as Sandy pointed to this and that. He was particularly interested in the artwork lining the wall, and he had seen enough to determine that Botha was a genius. Her works were, in Will's not-so-expert eyes, exceedingly brilliant.

They finally arrived at Sandy's armoury, which was a glass structure, but Will could not see inside because the glass was not transparent. Sandy stepped before the door and stood still as her irises were scanned. The door swung open after verification was complete.

"There is an alphanumeric passcode option in case anyone else needs to access the armoury," Sandy said as she led the way into the small room. "The passcode is Y-D-N-A-S-6-9."

Ydnas.

It was a very simple code, Will thought. Ydnas was "Sandy" backwards. But, 69?

"I understand the nominal part of the code, but the numeric part is a little unclear," Will said with a mocking, puzzled look.

Sandy giggled. "It is what it is."

Now, Will's attention was magnetized by the impressive rows of offensive and defensive weapons in Sandy's armoury. The room itself was not big, but it housed a vast array of weapons. Will moved closer and examined the different models of ray guns, laser guns, old-model rifles, blasting pistols, electro-swords, and thermo-shields.

"Do all agents have armouries like this?" The very question Will had tried his best not to ask the other time simply tumbled out of his mouth as he struggled to wrap his head about the source of funding behind such a huge collection of weapons.

"No," Sandy said. "The agency did not provide these. I got these weapons and everything in this bunker as gifts."

"I see," Will muttered as he wrapped his hand around the hilt of an electro-sword, and he swung it left and right. The buzz of the weapon as it cut through the air gave Will a big thrill. Electro-swords were his speciality. He remembered his early days in the agency; nobody could touch him when it came to electro-swords. Certain fellows in those early days were faster with guns and had better accuracy, but Will reigned supreme with electro-swords. It took some time before he began to pay more attention to his shooting.

Will set the sword back in its place and proceeded to examine the thermo-shields. He lifted one of the shields, noticing that it felt lighter than the brands of thermo-shields available in the West Federation. Obviously, a more lightweight defensive weapon was more desirable in battle, especially if it offered almost the same protection from F15 bullets and other guns.

She got all these as gifts, Will mused as he placed the shield back in its position. Most likely a rich suitor or a powerful superior who…

"Let's go see the tramach," Sandy said, cutting into Will's stream of thought.

"Alright," Will said.

Sandy and Will exited the armoury, taking a left turn towards a metal door. Sandy stepped in front of the door for another iris scan while pressing on the door with her thumb to verify her fingerprint.

"Verification complete; welcome, Agent Krave," the AI voice prompt boomed from behind the door. The giant metal door swung open with ease, and Sandy and Will went in.

The tramach was a simplified version of the type Will was familiar with. A medium-sized screen, with different options for training types, slowly came into his view. Sandy walked to the screen and browsed through the difficulty options, as well as training duration.

"How about we pair up and take on a band of Underworld soldiers?" Sandy said, with her eyes still fixed on the screen. "We can check to see who killed the most at the end of the training."

"Is that a challenge?" Will asked. There was a half-smile on his lips as he cracked his knuckles.

"Something like that," Sandy turned to face him, winking after she had spoken.

"Good," he muttered as he stepped closer so that he was directly behind Sandy. "Winner gets what?"

"Well, let's say the winner gets the bragging rights," Sandy replied as she selected the +8 difficulty.

"Nah, I'm thinking the stakes should be higher," Will whispered. "Let's go with something more interesting, more exciting, more…"

Will's speech was left incomplete as Sandy turned and placed a finger on his lips. Sandy leaned upward as she took her finger off and planted a kiss on his lips. With a little sigh, Will let his hands circle Sandy's waist and parted his lips to receive her kiss. It felt so natural, so good, having Sandy in his arms. He had a deep, unshakeable feeling that this was the woman for him, and he would do well to cling to her. Will and Sandy kissed on with a passionate fervour that matched the kisses of last night. Will had always maintained a policy of keeping himself emotionally aloof with female partners whenever he was on a mission. That message had been drilled into him and all the other boys in his class throughout their days in the West Federation Military Academy. His superior (after he was selected to be in the Elite Corps), Agent J. Moore, had always told him the same thing.

"When you are taking on an enemy," he would say again and again, "Never go with an unclear head. Forget every other thing and concentrate on the enemy. Getting attached to a fellow agent is the easiest way to get your head messed up and your priorities distorted."

Will pushed everything about Moore and his continuous advice out of his mind and concentrated on the beautiful woman who was stirring in his arms as their lips and tongues moved in unison. After a short while, Sandy pulled out of the kiss and returned her attention briefly to the waiting screen of the tramach.

"Winner gets a head from the loser," Sandy said.

"Great! Now, I'm pumped to slay those Underworld fellows," Will said. "Let's get on with it."

Sandy set the duration to half an hour and picked a maze-like scene for the simulation. After that, she passed Will a thermo-shield and an F15 rifle, the same weapons she chose for herself. Then they both fixed electronic bands on their wrists that would enable their avatars to show on the medium-sized screen so that they could commence with the simulated combat.

"Are you ready now, Will?" Sandy asked as she flexed her digits in anticipation of the combat ahead.

"Let's do it," Will said.

He was not sure how tough the +8 difficulty of this training machine would be, but he reckoned it would be on par with the tough levels in the West Federation versions. He would beat Sandy. It was not going to be easy because he knew she was familiar with this tramach, and he was aware of the fact that she was a good shot with terrific precision, but he was certain that he would prevail. He looked into Sandy's ebony face and thought she, too, was probably thinking of how she was going to beat him.

Sandy hit the start button, and instantly, the Underworld soldiers began to rush towards their avatars on the screen. Will found the controls about the same as the one he was used to, so no problem there; Sandy didn't have as much advantage as he had thought. Will's quick eyes instantly picked a spot where he thought would be a safe zone for him to fire from, and he began to move his avatar in that direction. It took him a moment to realize that Sandy was headed for the same spot.

"No, not there!" Sandy groaned. "Go somewhere else."

"That's the first challenge," Will said, not willing to concede that sweet spot to Sandy. "Let's see who gets there first."

The two avatars sped towards the spot. The race took less than a minute, and to Will's surprise, Sandy's avatar came up top. Will began checking the map for another spot while he noticed the Underworld soldiers steadily approaching. When he saw one of them taking aim with his rifle, Will controlled his avatar to kneel behind the thermo-shield, protecting it from gunfire.

Finally, Will found another spot on the map that was just as suitable for attack and defence. He wasted no time in running towards it. Now, he and Sandy were in place to launch attacks on the approaching soldiers. Will opened fire against the onrushing enemies just as he heard the sound of Sandy's gun blazing as she, too, began to cut down the Underworld enemies.

Will kept his eyes on the ticking clock. He checked the number of Underworld enemies he had killed and saw he was three behind Sandy. It must have been when he was trying to get another spot to take cover; she had pulled ahead of him. He had to catch up. Will took a moment to inhale deeply before he began to unleash fire on their adversaries with renewed energy.

Fifteen minutes down the clock, Will noticed as he darted a glance in the direction of the timer. They had spent half the duration of the training, and Sandy was still ahead, although he had cut her lead down to two. Sandy screamed as she fired round after round at the approaching enemies; she seemed determined to win this clash.

One of the soldiers on the screen aimed at Sandy's avatar and began to fire with intent. This forced Sandy into defence as she had to duck her avatar to hide behind the protective cover provided by the thermo-shield. Will took the opportunity to cut down other enemy avatars. Perhaps the Underworld soldier would pin Sandy's avatar down for a long while, and he would be able to gain a healthy lead over her going into the final five minutes of the contest.

Sandy refused to be subdued for long. When he attempted to reload, she took the opportunity to rise from behind her thermo-shield and knock him down with two quick shots.

Three minutes. Will did not stop firing. He no longer bothered to check Sandy's score because the few precious seconds it would take to do that might end up costing him a victory. The two agents spent the last few minutes hitting the Underworld enemies hard.

Will found himself breathing hard when the timer finally gave off the buzzing sound, signifying the end of the training session. He had really exerted himself. His eyes quickly went to the score table, and he was amused to find that he and Sandy had finished with the exact same score: 225 kills apiece.

“So, it’s a tie,” Sandy said as she unstrapped the electronic band attached to her wrist. Her voice was uneven as well. She was panting. “No winner.”

“We are both winners,” Will grinned as he dropped the thermo-shield.

They were going to take turns pleasing each other. His mind instantly drifted back to the numeric part of the passcode for Sandy’s armoury.

69.

Yeah, they might not need to take turns after all.

… … …

Mukt, Afrasia

Sandy and Will alighted from the self-driving vehicle that brought them from Sandy's bunker at Xio Chan. Sandy had programmed the car to park close to the bullet train station at Mukt. She told Will before they left the bunker that she wanted to pick up some clothes she had ordered for him and May, and she wanted to use the opportunity to show him more places in Afrasia.

"That was what I was doing when you came into the living room this morning," Sandy told Will. "I mean, ordering those wears."

Will was thankful that he would have something to wear, apart from the jacket and pants that Dr Kean had given to him as the uniform for the mission. He straightened his jacket and looked around the station, which was not busy. Only a few people were walking around at that time of the day. Will wondered why he had yet to see a large population of Afrasians standing at any of the places he had been in the continent. From Girkland to Miklos, and now Mukt, he wondered if it was the outbreaks of disease that had happened in mid-century that had made people around here keep distance from each other when they could.

Sandy locked the car door with a quick jab of her thumb, and she started towards the station. Will watched admiringly as Sandy's white hair fluttered in the afternoon breeze, and she walked briskly towards the store's package pick-up area. Will had been intrigued when Sandy explained this delivery system to him. The online store would pack the items bought into a special box that, once taken to the delivery point, could not be opened or even moved by anyone, except the person whose fingerprint matched the little sensor on the box. Even if some rogue or bandits hijacked the box before the owner got to it, they would never be able to get it open. It made sense that Sandy would pay for this kind of delivery since she would not want the items she bought to be delivered to her bunker directly; she would prefer to keep her bunker's location secret.

Sandy got to where the box had been dropped on a special magnetic platform erected to hold such boxes. She placed her thumb on the sensor, and immediately, she could carry it off the metal platform. Will kept his eyes peeled for happenings on the street. He saw two teenage girls staring at him. Apparently, his Caucasian features were not ones they saw every day. Seeing the girls looking at him as if he were a three-horned beast from the depths of the dark world made him chuckle. Intercontinental travels were still not prevalent in current times, so those girls might have been seeing a non-Afrasian for the first time in their lives.

Will wondered if there were any positive aspects to the crazy ban on intercontinental travel between the world's major continents. Why would governments want to keep the continents in isolation, denying them the experience and richness of diverse cultures and lifestyles? Outbreaks of disease were no longer the problem; neither was it war, since no continent was at war with another, for the time being at least.

Will heard the back door of the car swing open, then a gentle thud, as Sandy dropped the box into the backseat. He turned to see her pushing a lock of hair away from her face.

"Are we heading back to the bunker?" Will asked.

"Let's take a little ride around the city," Sandy said. "I promised to show you around Afrasia, and I haven't done that yet."

Will was about to pull the car door open when he heard a loud smashing sound perilously close to where he was standing. A missile came from out of nowhere and embedded into the side of Sandy's car. Will's survival instinct kicked in, and he jumped over the car's hood to get to the safety offered by the other side of the vehicle.

"Was that a stray bullet?" Sandy asked as she, too, ducked beside Will on the other side of the car.

"I'm not sure what to call it yet," Will replied. The shot had only missed him by a few inches, which was not enough to determine if it was indeed meant for him. However, Will knew it was plausible enough that one or more of those guys they had faced off with at the terminal in Last Wall could be back to get them.

Another shot smashed into the car's window, sending shards of glass flying, which instantly lent credence to Will's line of thought. Those baddies were back for more action, and Will knew that he and Sandy were good enough to give them more than they bargained for.

Will pulled out the ray pistol he had stuck in the band of his pants. He never went anywhere without a gun, never. Sandy, too, unholstered her firearm. Will signalled to Sandy with his eyes that he would attack from the front of the car while she should hit the baddies from the area around the boot. It was a simple strategy they intended to employ. Will would fire into the air from his position while Sandy would raise her head enough to watch for return fire and narrow down a location.

Will fired in the direction he believed the bad guys were shooting from. He heard a loud crash, a testament to the fact that he had hit something. It was no surprise that the street had quickly emptied of people. The few people who had been on the street before the shooting started had quickly dispersed. There was return fire from their adversaries across the street.

"I've got them," Sandy replied, "ten o'clock."

Sandy began firing at the bad guys with an intensity even greater than when she and Will had been training. A loud outcry from across the street told Will that Sandy had hit one of those guys. He rose from his crouched position to fire shots at the thugs, who were shooting from what looked like a warehouse. From what he could see, there were about six of them, each wielding a type of firearm Will was not familiar with. Their bullets were heavy, and those guns seemed to be quite effective from this range, although the body of Sandy's car bore the brunt of the shots.

Will picked out the fellow who seemed to be the best shot among them and fired at him. The fellow yelped as he was struck on the arm and fell backwards. In the distance, the wailing of sirens could be heard growing increasingly louder as Afrasian cops sped in their direction. The attackers instantly bounded away, with two taking off in different directions while the others jumped into a waiting blue van.

"After them!" Sandy screamed.

If they could catch one of those guys, they had a chance to determine where exactly those guys were working from, who they worked for, and what they intended to achieve. Sandy jumped into the driver's seat, and Will rushed into the backseat. The Afrasian cops were getting closer, and the last thing Will wanted was to be found at the scene. He would have to start answering a lot of questions, beginning from what he was doing in Afrasia in the first place.

Sandy turned the ignition and began giving directions to the car as it sped along the road. Will looked through the back window and saw that the cops were not yet in sight. Excellent, they stood a good chance of getting away unseen by the cops as they chased the guys who had attacked them. Will was about to return his attention to the front when he noticed a bright green vehicle with colourful blinking lights mounted to it tailing them.

Will retrieved his gun from his waistband and leaned out through the window to fire at the bright green target. He aimed carefully, firing at the front tires of the vehicle. He was not shooting to kill, but just to disable the vehicle. After a few shots, the car veered off the road with the two tires in the front blown out.

Will heaved a huge sigh as he watched the cops scrambling out of the car. Now, he and Sandy could concentrate on chasing the bad guys.

… … …

About Adha Long: The Guardian King

Will and Sandy sat in silence as they rode back to the bunker. Their expectations of finding out who was behind the attack had failed. They had lost the van during the chase. When the van had made a sudden left turn, Sandy's car had slammed into a pole, attempting to make the same turn. Before Sandy could manually get her car away from the pole it had rammed into, the van they were chasing was out of sight. An attempt to continue chasing the van using the tracking device attached to Sandy's car proved abortive as the tracking screen no longer showed.

"Lucky bastards," Sandy whispered again as the car zoomed up the highway connecting Mukt to Xio Chan.

She could not believe that those guys had slipped away from their grasp. Catching just one of them alive would have made so many things clear, but now she had to wait for another chance. Sandy glanced sideways, taking her eyes off the road briefly to observe Will's profile. His jaw was taut; Sandy could tell that he, too, was displeased their attackers had slipped away when they had those guys within their grasp.

Sandy returned her attention to the road as the car breezed past a huge sign that said, "Welcome to Xio Chan." She never knew that such a minor accident could render her car's auto-drive and tracking functions useless. What if it belonged to an individual who could not drive herself? Sandy shook her head in disappointment. Techies should be doing so much better.

"Still pissed that those guys got away?" Sandy asked, without looking at him this time.

"I was thinking of ways to get them to talk," Will replied. "It's a shame we couldn't get any of them."

Sandy nodded in agreement. "I'm thinking of calling Adha. He might be able to make sense of all this."

"Who is Adha?" Will asked.

Sandy thought she noticed a certain edge to Will's voice as he asked that question. He sounded like a jealous high-school boyfriend. Sandy chuckled at the thought of this.

"Adha Long, he was my guardian," Sandy explained. "My parents died in an accident when I was young. He and my father were in the same unit in the military service, although Adha was far higher in ranking. Adha took me in as his child when I became an orphan. He is the only family I have known."

"Oh, I'm sorry," Will said. Sandy thought he looked quite shocked to learn that her parents were deceased.

"Yeah, it's fine," she replied. "It's always tough growing up in a highly militarized world. There were shootings and bombings almost every day when I was young. I don't know how I would have survived that harsh era if not for Adha."

Thinking of the positives, though, being without parents had not limited her career in any way. She was unsure she would have come that far in the Afrasian military if her parents were alive. It was their death that pushed her never to relent, to keep going, to squeeze enough out of her career because she did not know when her time would be up. This approach to life had helped her become one of the finest agents in the agency.

"So Adha has access to more information than you do?" Will asked. "Is he in active service?"

"No," Sandy said. "He's retired now. After the Maharaj himself and his deputy, he was the third most powerful man in Afrasia in the last government. Adha still wields enough power and influence 'til today. He's stinking rich too. I know you were wondering who could have gifted me that armoury and the whole bunker. Well, Adha did."

"Wow," Will said in genuine amazement.

"I'm sure you have heard of him before now," Sandy said as she turned off the highway onto the path down the familiar dirt road leading to her bunker.

"I have only ever heard the name from you," Will said, shaking his head slightly.

"Few people knew him as Adha Long outside Afrasia. Even on this continent, many people do not know him by that name. He is better known as Adi Kalim," Sandy revealed.

She smiled as she noticed a lift in his brows, which signified that name registered in his memory, one way or another.

"The Fiery Eagle?" Will intoned.

"Yeah," Sandy affirmed. Adha had earned that name during the Intercontinental Wars when he was in the Air Force. He earned his legendary reputation by bombing enemy aircraft. He was so quick and efficient that he became known and respected by all, even among those warring with what would eventually become Afrasia after some years.

"Oh, yes, I am familiar with Adi Kalim," Will said. "I heard so much about him from our teachers at the academy. One of them used to show us a picture of Adi smiling as he prepared to step into his fighter jet. So the great Adi Kalim is your guardian. How wonderful."

"Yeah, he was really famous back then," Sandy said as she remembered those days when her guardian was the recipient of honours nearly every few months. She loved going to all the big awards ceremonies with him, and there were many. "I believe that was what formed the decision of the last Maharaj to make him the military director of Afrasia during his reign."

By now, Sandy could see the area near her bunker in the distance. She wondered what May was up to during their absence. Perhaps she was lost in sadness, thinking about how her husband of many years dared to put her life on the line to achieve his selfish aspirations. Sandy tried to put herself in May's shoes: how would she deal with a situation where her husband was willing to use her as a pawn in an intercontinental political chess game?

Sandy parked her high-tech automobile outside the gated entrance to the innocent-looking structure under which Sandy's bunker was built. Sandy jogged over to the gate and opened her eyes a little wider for her irises to be scanned. Here, there were no passwords or alternative means of entry. Only Sandy could enter this bunker. Not even her guardian, Adha Long, could get inside without her knowledge.

Sandy recalled the scientific paper she had read over three weeks ago about the potential damage that iris scanners could do to the eyes over the years. A week later, she had read a counter paper stating emphatically that iris scanners were as harmless to the eyes as fingerprint sensors were to the hand. The second paper detailed that the research for the first paper had been conducted on two obsolete brands of iris scanners…

Shaking her head and sweeping the thoughts of the articles away, Sandy walked back to the car and got in beside Will. He was running his hands over his pistol while staring off into the space ahead of him. Sandy thought he looked lost. Like something had occupied his mind so profoundly that he could not get himself out of it at that moment to notice what was going on around him. Sandy drove through the open gate and down the slope that led to the entrance of her bunker.

In the next few minutes of walking, and in Sandy's case, unlocking doors here and there with her eyes, they finally got back to the small living room of the bunker. Will went to his room to get changed while Sandy checked on May, to find she had busied herself reading the entire time they were away.

"How was the tour of the city?" May asked. She had been aware that Sandy wanted to take Will to a few places in the city. Sandy had offered to take her along, but May preferred the company of books and the safety of the bunker instead.

"We could not go around as we wanted," Sandy revealed to May before she gave a brief description of how they were attacked. She went on to say how they held their ground and gave the thugs a harrowing chase until the minor accident that let them escape.

"How lovely would it have been if you had gotten one of them?" May said. "By now, we would know who we were up against."

"There is one other way we can get some of the information we need," Sandy said. She heard the door as it was pushed open, then she saw Will come striding in. He was wearing a navy blue jacket with a hood at the top; it was one of the new outfits she had gotten for him. The hood on it would make it easier for him to hide his non-Afrasian features whenever they went somewhere.

"It fits to a T. Thanks, Sandy," Will said to her.

"Glad to help," she replied. "Which reminds me," she said as she walked out of the room. She came back after about a minute, holding two clothing bags, one in each hand. "And these are for you, May."

The woman examined the range of wears that Sandy had bought for her, then she thanked Sandy for her generosity and quick thinking. Sandy's response was a gentle smile.

"You started to say there is another way for us to get the information we need?" May prompted Sandy.

"Oh, yes," Sandy said, tucking her flowing white hair behind her ear. "I will make a call or initiate a facetime with my guardian, Adha Long, and ask him for help. I really don't like to bother him with anything, but the current situation demands that I engage his help."

Sandy instantly noticed a sudden change in May's countenance when she mentioned her guardian's name. It was different from the flicker of recognition that had been on Will's face when Sandy told him Adha Long was the same person as the famous bomber, Adi Kalim. The look on May's face gave Sandy an entirely different impression. How did May know Adha? Few people outside Afrasia knew him by that name. So what was the connection between May and her guardian?

Sandy decided to hold her peace for the moment and not ask May how she knew her guardian's real name. Perhaps when she was alone with May, she would ask. She had a feeling that the response she would get from May would shock her.

"You think he can help?" May enquired. She had regained her poise.

"I believe so."

"I'll leave you and Will to it then," May said. "I've been up for some time. I would like to take a nap."

Not long after that, May got up from her seat and left the study. Will and Sandy exchanged glances.

"I think she's hiding something," Will mused not long after the lady exited the study.

"You better believe it," Sandy replied.

… … …

Sandy Contacts Adha

Will sat beside Sandy in front of her notebook computer as the ebony agent and her illustrious guardian conversed. He comprehended most of what they talked about, although Adha sometimes switched to Afrasian military codes to pass his message. Sandy had told Adha that he, Will, could be trusted. It had been a while since Will had seen someone staunchly insist that he was on the good side.

Will stared at the moving image of Adha on the space screen in front of him. He had understandably changed from the lean-faced, handsome fellow with a sharp crew cut whose picture Will's teacher had proudly shown the class that day. Adha was now bald, with his thick moustache and beard having as much grey hair as black. Will guessed he was in his mid-fifties, but he was still good-looking.

"What did you say happened to the files you copied from the SIL?" Adha asked.

"The transcripts won't display. It keeps saying the message has been deleted," Sandy replied.

"That's strange. Someone is clearly trying hard to cover their tracks," Adha muttered. "I'll put some feelers out and tell you what I get. Is that fine?"

"Yes, thank you," Sandy said.

"And keep off the SILs for now. I heard they have been rigged with blasters. You attempt to get in there without the appropriate authorisation, and you might just end up getting blasted to kingdom come."

Now, that was a scary thought, Will mused. In the West Federation, the location of such things as the SILs was virtually unknown except to the highest government officials…

"Just call me if you need anything else," Adha concluded.

Will darted a quick glance at his watch and found that it was broken. He tried to remember what could have caused that. Perhaps it happened when he and Sandy were engaged in the shootout with those Underworld agents in the streets of Mukt.

"So that's it," Sandy said with a shrug as the space screen with Adha's face vanished. "He promised to get back to me when he gets something, and knowing how connected he is, I'm sure it won't take long before he calls back."

"We'll wait then," Will said.

"Did you notice…" she trailed off.

"What?" Will urged Sandy when she seemed unwilling to complete her question.

Sandy looked in the direction of the door before she continued. "Did you see the look on Adha's face when I mentioned that May was with me?"

Will had not noticed anything; he was not sure he had been paying close attention to Adha's face at that moment.

"No, I don't think I was looking at him at that point. What did you see?"

Sandy told Will she had seen a look of mild surprise on Adha's face, but he had done a better job of masking the expression than May.

"Then there is indeed a connection between the two?" Will offered.

"Definitely," Sandy said. "I'll find out more about it later. But, for now, we prioritize our mission, which is to stop George Lay and whoever's with him from starting an intercontinental war."

"Yeah, that's right," Will said. "You know, I have an idea."

"Shoot," Sandy replied.

"Why don't you place a call to that man who was with us during Kean's debriefing? We might be able to get something valuable from him. Like how to find Kean or something," Will said.

The mass of white hair on Sandy's head bounced as she nodded in agreement. "I thought of that when we couldn't access the transcript files this morning. So, yeah, I'll call him now."

Sandy retrieved her smartphone from her pocket and quickly searched for Owen Brigg's contact number. She dialled up his secure line first, but he did not pick up the call. So after another try, she called his other number. This time, the call was picked up on the second ring.

"Hello?" a tired female voice said.

Who was this? Sandy wondered. To the best of her knowledge, Owen Briggs lived alone.

"Uh…Hello. Can I speak with Owen Briggs, please?"

"Who am I speaking with?" the lady on the other end demanded.

Sandy thought about whether to reveal her true identity or not. Telling this lady who she was would make Owen more interested in taking her call, but it wasn't the best practice to reveal who she was to random people.

"Judy Morgan, I handle one of Owen's investments," Sandy said. "So, can I speak to—"

"Owen is missing," the woman declared.

"Oh, what happened?" Sandy blurted out.

"He went out almost a week ago to see one of his clients, and he has not returned since. It's so unlike him."

"I'm sorry about that," Sandy said. "I hope he returns home safe, very soon."

"Thank you," the woman said. "The cops are on the case."

Sandy ended the call and turned to see Will pacing around the room. He had been listening intently to the conversation she had with the woman on Briggs' phone.

"I'll bet it was Kean," Will said. "Surely he has something to do with it."

Sandy instantly saw what he meant. It was possible that Kean had abducted or killed Owen Briggs when she and Will were in the Underworld. She knew that Owen would have called her, if he could, to ask how the mission went.

"Oh no," Sandy held a hand to her face as she tried to keep herself calm. She attempted to keep her thoughts positive, to assume that Owen was still alive.

"We are up against some really bad people," Will muttered. "I'm sorry about Owen."

"I have a feeling he's not dead yet," Sandy said. "I'll hunt down Kean and find out Owen's location if I have to torture it out of him."

And if he's dead? Sandy asked herself. She will make Kean pay with his life if Owen is dead. She would not—

A loud buzz from Sandy's computer cut into her thoughts. She walked over to her PC and saw Adha was calling back.

"That Adha?" Will asked from where he stood.

"Yeah," Sandy replied. "I guess he has something already."

"That's damned fast," Will said as he drew closer.

Sandy accepted Adha's request for facetime, and she switched to the space screen.

"Hey, Sandy," Adha said as his face appeared on the screen. "I've got something for you."

"Okay, I'm listening," Sandy said as she bent forward slightly.

"I just found that three top-ranking officials of the current government are working with some people in Oceania Liberation. They plan to form a coalition to usurp the Afrasian government with military force and install a new government that would be less rigid in terms of intercontinental relations. The identities of those people are not yet clear, but one name that has been suggested is Matt Gold."

Sandy was not surprised. Matt Gold was widely known to be dangerously ambitious, the exact kind of man who would not mind bringing war to his people just to attain a higher leadership position.

"Based on the intelligence with me here, I can tell you that they have allies in the Underworld, and I suppose that explains what happened to umm… Mrs Lay. These guys are trying to spark a war to cause a change of government in Afrasia," Adha revealed. He paused to sip from a glass of Viva on his table.

"What do we do now?" Sandy asked. More than anything, she needed a sense of direction. She wanted to be clear about the next step to take.

"Well, Matt Gold is being investigated, so there isn't much to do for now. The main threat now lies in the West Federation," Adha said.

At the mention of his home continent, Sandy noticed Will jolt to attention.

"Are you sure that fellow is a good guy, Sandy? I wouldn't want to reveal our strategies to the enemy," Adha asked in a special Afrasian lingo that was beyond Will's grasp.

"He's a victim of this intercontinental conspiracy, just like me," Sandy replied in a similar language. "He's not one of the bad guys."

"Alright," Adha said with a gentle nod. "Intel says some Underworld soldiers have been assigned to take explosives over to the West Federation, with the help of some corrupt locals. They plan to bomb key cities like San Mateo and Hringund—"

"Hringund!" Will growled as he leapt to his feet.

"Will, what's wrong?" Sandy asked, briefly taking her eyes off the image of her guardian on the space screen.

"That's where my family lives," Will revealed. He was pacing around again, with his hands thrust in his pocket, understandably agitated.

"We'll stop them," Sandy assured him, then she turned back to Adha. "Can you make arrangements for us to get to the West Federation?"

"Yes, I can," he said. "Promise me you'll be careful."

"I promise."

"Good," Adha said. "Now. If you want, I can send you extra backup. Simons and Walker are more than efficient with guns, and they are just as good with hand-to-hand combat. I can call Jon Kong, too, if you prefer a fellow agent."

Sandy was not sure she wanted more soldiers to join them. She felt comfortable fighting alongside Will Burne. She knew that things would get tough in the West Federation, but she was sure she and Will would do just fine.

… … …

On a Bullet Train to Zhen Baodu, Afrasia

Hringund is in danger.

Will could not stop turning those words around in his mind as he sat in the last row of the bullet train from Mukt to the secret airship terminal, per Adha's arrangements. Will adjusted his hoodie, drawing it well over his head in a bid to keep his straight hair and Caucasian face out of sight. Where he sat in the last row, Sandy was not seated beside him this time. She and May were in a different coach entirely, although he and Sandy continued to communicate with whispers using their com devices.

The passengers beside Will were a young Afrasian couple, maybe twenty or slightly less. Will noticed how they leaned close to each other, whispering and exchanging quick kisses when they thought no one was looking. Will guessed they were confident in doing this because they were in the back row where they could not easily be seen, and the sound of their kisses couldn't be heard as well because of the flick intended to keep the people on the train entertained.

Will concentrated his attention on checking suspicious activity on the train. He kept his eye out for people moving from their seats around the coach. He was ready to defend himself if any Underworld spies tried to attack and had no doubt Sandy was doing the same in the other coach.

The bullet train sped eastward, flashing past buildings of different shapes and sizes. Will watched as the Afrasian landscape flashed by, and he concluded that this part of Afrasia was just as beautiful as where he had grown up in West Federation cities.

"Burne, can you hear me?" Sandy's voice suddenly floated through the com device.

"Affirmative," Will replied. "What's happening?"

"There's this big guy who keeps looking at May and me," Sandy said. "I suspect he's up to something."

In his mind, Will could imagine Sandy taking glances towards the big fellow as she spoke into her com. She was probably also looking around for the big dude's accomplices.

"I don't think there's a problem," Will replied. "If he's a spy and he's dumb enough to let you catch him staring at you multiple times, then I can only say he's no good, and he would be pretty easy to handle. My guess is he's not a spy at all. The guys that we have to watch out for are the ones who make it look as if they don't give a rat's behind about us."

"You are probably right," Sandy said with a sigh. "But this guy looks like… Will, excuse me for a moment."

"Alright," Will murmured. As soon as Sandy's voice was no longer filling his ears, he became aware of a different kind of sound coming from his right side. The kids beside him had taken their quiet romance to another level. The girl was now seated on the boy's lap, and they were kissing nonstop while the girl was grinding her bum against the boy's crotch. The girl's soft moan was what Will had heard after he finished speaking with Sandy.

Will pondered for a brief moment if he should tell them to fucking get a hold of themselves and wait until they were somewhere private before doing what they had to do. But, even as he thought of it, the idea made him smile. It was none of his business what they did since he could see that they weren't minors.

"You are right," Sandy's sounded again from the com device. "He just came around to compliment me and to ask if he could sit next to us, beautiful ladies."

Will figured that he could have heard some of Sandy's conversation with the big fella had Sandy not switched off her com device. He had left his on for the sake of easy communication, and he wondered why she wasn't doing the same. He had to buzz her first to speak with her, and her com device was turned off.

"Told you," Will said.

"Is there anything suspicious going on over there?" Sandy asked him.

"Negative," Will replied. "How close are we to our destination?"

"We're almost there," Sandy said. "We'll get off the train in thirty to thirty-five minutes, and then from there, it will take a few minutes to get ourselves down to the airship terminal."

"Great, can't wait to get there," Will said.

He wanted to get to the West Federation as quickly as possible. He had to do everything in his power to stop the bombers who were planning to wreak havoc in the cities of the West Federation. His mother and two of his siblings lived in Hringund. He couldn't let anything bad happen to that city, or any city in the West Federation, for that matter.

Will wondered why George Lay and the people who worked with him were so bent on forcing the different world regions into one big, united state where similar thinking leaders would now rule the old regions. They did not hold the interest of the common people in their hearts; they were mainly trying to amass power for themselves. This lust for power was so crazy that George didn't even mind using his longtime wife as a tool to spark a war. It was just as bad that people in Afrasia and the West Federation worked for these ruthless people. He couldn't wait for this damned train to stop so he could head for his region.

Going by the speed of this bullet train, Will thought*, their destination must be quite far away for Sandy to have said that it would take them about thirty minutes to get there.* Will looked at the young couple beside him and saw the girl sleeping with her head on the boy's shoulder. Will looked away and began to whistle a Jody tune.

Minutes flew by as Will kept his eyes alternating between the lovely views of Afrasia outside the train and monitoring suspicious movements in the coach. Sometimes his eyes would stray to the movies on show, but he soon got bored because they usually lacked much action to keep his attention. Also, he sometimes didn't understand what the actors said because they spoke in the deep Afrasian tongue that was foreign to people who weren't from this region. It was the same advanced Afrasian Adha had spoken to Sandy when he didn't want him to understand what they were talking about.

"Next station in five minutes," the AI voice prompt that had welcomed them into the train announced.

"That's our drop," Sandy added. "Get ready."

Will pulled himself upright and rubbed his palms together. Now they were getting closer to those Underworld bastards. He remembered the stories his father told him of a time when trains were still controlled by two men sitting in the first compartment of the train, pulling and pushing levers. That was when ticketing officers always moved around in coaches to check tickets when it was time for people to get off the train. All that had since changed. The entire process was more automated and sophisticated than it had been in decades past. No one could get on a train with a fake ticket or sneak aboard the train and run from one coach to another to escape the ticketing officers as his dad had spoken about.

Will let his hand drop to his waistband and ran it slowly over the laser pistol he had slipped in there. He would not be caught unawares if any Underworld agents were waiting for them at the next train station. An F15 rifle or electro-sword would have been too conspicuous to carry with him onto the train; the laser pistol was just perfect.

He stared outside the window, and he noticed that the structures were no longer flashing by as quickly as before. The train was reducing its speed because they were close to the station.

"Zhen Baodu passengers depart at the next stop," an AI voice announced.

Two other people in the coach began getting their things together to get off the train. Will was already prepared to disembark. He jerked himself to his feet and stepped away from the young couple beside him.

"I'm getting off now," Will said to Sandy over the com device as the train rolled to a stop.

"Yeah, May and I are approaching the exit door," Sandy told him. "See you outside."

Will strode towards the exit door, which was now wide open, and he promptly stepped out. Outside the train stood a group of Afrasian cops holding thick black batons, with guns holstered to their waist.

"Have you gotten off?" Will asked Sandy. "There are cops here."

"Oh shit!" Sandy whispered. "No cops on this side. They do random checks. Damn it!"

Will tried not to let anxiety overwhelm him as he walked towards the line of cops ahead of him. Different thoughts ran through his mind as he slowly walked towards the policemen. He was a full-blooded Westian without the temporary permit to allow people from other regions to step foot in Afrasia. Will knew that the temporary permit was so hard to obtain that many people travelling into Afrasia from other regions mostly preferred to sneak into the city. He knew because he had tried to get it the first time he wanted to visit Afrasia.

By now, Will was in front of the cops. One of them, a short fellow with powerful-looking arms, stepped forward and stretched his hand to Will.

"Your papers, sir?" the officer demanded. "And please, pull back the hood."

"Will, just stay calm," Sandy said to him through the com device. "They will arrest you for not having the right papers and for carrying a firearm, but I'll be able to get you out before night-time. I'll place a call to Adha right away."

"Uh, yes, one moment," he said; he turned away and appeared as though he were looking through his pockets to buy him some time. Will quickly thought about his options: allow the cops to arrest him and waste precious time in a cell or attempt to escape from the cops at great risk to his life. He could get killed or wounded. The first option definitely came across as the less risky, but Will was not a man to shy away from danger. He didn't fancy the idea of sitting in a cell at the Afrasian Police Station while bombers from the Underworld were getting closer to their target.

"Where are you?" Will whispered quickly to Sandy. "I'll join you pretty soon."

"Will, please don't endanger your life. You cannot outrun these guys. They will shoot—"

"I am waiting for your papers, sir," the officer said, his tone becoming aggressive. The Afrasian Police Force did not mess around.

Will pretended to feel the pocket on his chest for his documents, and when he saw that the officer wasn't expecting a move, he swung his body forward in one fluid motion and struck the cop square on the forehead. The cop staggered and began to fall backwards, but Will was quick to react. He leapt forward and grabbed the falling officer by the collar, and then he turned him around swiftly. In a flash, he was holding his laser pistol to the officer's temple.

"Drop your guns, or I'll blow his brains out!" Will barked at the other Afrasian cops, who were all pointing their guns at him. "Drop your fucking guns! I'm not joking here!" Again, will roared, and this time, the cops obeyed.

Inwardly, Will heaved a deep sigh of relief. His audacious plan had just worked. He had quickly settled for this idea because he really didn't fancy Sandy's suggestion of letting himself be captured by the cops without putting up a fight. Who knows how long it would've taken Adha Long to get the cops to release him? Now, all he had to do was continue using the officer as a human shield until he got to wherever Sandy was. Then, once he got in the car, he would let the officer go. That was exactly what he would do. He had to save Hringund and the whole of the West Federation.

… … …

Zhen Baodu, Afrasia

The drive from Zhen Baodu to the airship terminal took ten minutes, as Sandy had said. She had taken a good part of the time she spent driving to look at the rear-view mirror, half expecting to see vehicles belonging to Afrasian cops giving them a hot chase. She was quite surprised that the cops had not even attempted to follow them, but she was glad the chase hadn't happened. It meant she didn't have to run at breakneck speed and make evasive moves to avoid being caught.

She was quite impressed with the little trick that Will pulled on the cops. It was very clever of him. She had just resigned herself to the fact that the cops would take him away for a few hours at least. It would have set them back in their journey to the West Federation, but Sandy had assumed it was a better option than for Will to take on the cops at great risk to his existence. Thankfully, he had come up with something better, and they were right on schedule for the long journey to the West Federation.

Sandy parked her car outside a large wooden structure, and she deftly unfastened her seat belt.

"We're here," she announced to her companions.

"This place is an airship terminal?" May asked.

Sandy chuckled. She had reacted the same way when Adha brought her here the first time. This entire area didn't look like a perfect environment to build a terminal. Even the wooden fence did nothing to give the impression that something important was in the vicinity.

"Yeah, it is," Sandy said as she eased out of the car. May and Will also stepped out.

"Now what?" Will asked as they stood a few moments by the car without moving towards the wooden structure.

"We wait for Adha to let us in," Sandy said. "He's on the other side already."

Sandy noticed the uneasy look that crept up onto May's face when she mentioned Adha. She made a promise to herself to get to the root of this, whatever it was. How was May connected to her guardian?

Something was unclear to her about those two, and it bothered her. She had to know the connection between them.

After a few more moments of waiting, the wooden fence began to slide sideways, revealing a path for them to pass. On the other side, Sandy could see her mentor balancing a top hat on his head as he got out of his car. Immediately, she led Will and May towards him. As the three of them drew closer to where Adha stood with several armed men standing sentry around him, Sandy remembered what her guardian had said about getting extra hands to support them in executing this mission. She had told him on the phone that he shouldn't bother, but she wasn't so sure he was convinced.

"My child," Adha said when Sandy got close enough to hear him. He held his arms out for her embrace, and Sandy wasted no time in rushing forward to hug her guardian.

She felt safe in his arms, a feeling that had developed from her childhood anytime she was lonely or scared, and he would hold her to his chest and give her gentle pats on the head, stroking her hair while telling her that everything was going to be just fine. After a short while, Sandy drew out of the embrace and let her eyes run over her guardian again. He looked younger than he actually was.

"Good morning, Mr Kalim," Will said. "It's so nice to see you in person after hearing about you for so long."

"Who's he?" Adha asked Sandy in a whisper. "He looks like the guy that was with you when we were talking on facetime."

"Yes, that's him. He's the West Federation agent who is working with me, at least in this situation," Sandy explained. "This is Agent Will Burne."

"Hello, Agent Burne," Adha said, turning to face Will. "I'm pleased to meet you. Sandy has told me you are on our side. I hope you aren't working for the enemy."

"No, sir," Will replied quickly.

"Who's the lady?" Adha asked, turning back to Sandy.

Sandy could barely keep her surprise out of her face. Why was her guardian pretending not to know May? She had mentioned that May was with him when they were facetiming back in her bunker. So why was he trying to make it seem like he had never seen the woman before? Even though May's fame had gone down considerably after the regions were separated, it was still hard for anyone to claim not to know who she was.

"That is May Lay, wife of the famous George Lay," Sandy said. "I told you she was with me. I really didn't want to leave her by herself at the bunker."

"Dear me, of course, I should have known," Adha said, his mouth widening into a smile. "How are you, Lady May? And how are you coping with the Afrasian climate? I understand that Oceania Liberation is a lot colder."

"I suppose the weather has become much less important since gunmen have been popping up left and right, playing shooting games around me," May replied. "I don't know what would have become of me if not for Ms Krave and her partner, Mr Burne, here."

"You are safe here," Adha said. "Nobody will shoot at you or anything."

"I'm glad to know that," May responded.

"Sandy, Burne, meet Walker and Simons," Adha said, indicating two buff guys who were armed with F15 rifles standing close to Adha's car.

"Father, I told you, I'll be just fine with Agent Burne," Sandy protested. She really didn't think they needed extra hands on this mission. She had come to understand Will and the way he operated during missions, but these guys, what did she know about their strengths and abilities?

"Never underestimate the strength in numbers," Adha admonished his ward. "They are not lousy shots if that's what you are thinking. And I have been careful to pick men who are adaptable in combat. Also, I can vouch for their loyalty."

Whenever her guardian talked this way, it was almost impossible to refuse whatever he wanted. Sandy could see that he clearly wanted her to take those guys with her and Will to offer extra protection.

"It's fine then," Sandy replied with a shrug. She chuckled as she wondered what Will thought of having other guys with them on this mission. Would he see them as threats to her attention that has been thus far undivided? Sandy pushed that thought out of her mind almost immediately. It was hard to think of Will being jealous over something trivial when his home continent was in danger. No doubt, all his thoughts at the moment would be all about saving Hringund.

"Also," Adha said. "I have made arrangements with a man I trust in the West Federation to receive you from the airship terminal when you get there. He'll also provide the necessary lodging before the big showdown against the bombers."

How typical of him, Sandy thought fondly. He always wanted everything planned out and carefully put in order.

"That's fine," Sandy said. "Thank you for everything."

"It is you who deserves to be commended for keeping the world peace intact so far," Adha said.

I—and Will Burne.

Without Will, Sandy did not know if she would have been as successful on the mission all by herself. She remembered her retort to Dr Kean that she liked to work alone, and she wasn't interested in working with a Westie. Now, the Westie was her partner and friend. They had bonded after going through so many dangerous moments together in the short time they had known each other.

"The airship is waiting," Adha announced. "Let's get to it."

The three followed Adha as he led the way across the lush green field. After the party had walked for a few metres, Adha pulled a device from his hip pocket and clicked on it. Instantly, the field before them expanded, gaping open to reveal a terminal with two airships lying side by side.

"That's your ride," Adha said, nodding in the direction of the one on the left. "I'll monitor the mission from here."

Sandy hugged her guardian again, and she promised him that she would be careful. After that, Sandy turned to May and said goodbye.

"Be safe," May whispered in a voice that betrayed her emotion. "I owe you both a lot. I don't think I have thanked you enough for saving me in the Underworld and for helping me stay alive since then."

"It's alright, ma'am," Sandy said. "Just stay here 'til we get back."

May nodded. "I will."

After saying her goodbyes to May and Adha, she and Will moved towards the airship. It was similar to the ship that had taken them from the Last Wall to the interior of Afrasia. Behind them, Simons and Walker whispered something to each other and had a little laugh.

Sandy stepped into the airship with Will right behind her. She found a seat conveniently close to the cockpit and eased herself into it while she watched the pilot taping some pop-ups on the dashboard in front of him.

"I like to sit by the window and watch the skyline as the airship moves," Will said.

"I'd rather catch some sleep ahead of the mission in front of us," Sandy replied.

Will shrugged and took the window seat of the same row she sat. Sandy marvelled at how she had grown to enjoy having him nearby in the little time that they had spent together. She wondered what would happen when they had completed the mission before them, and it was time for Will Burne to return to his home continent. It was even possible that he wouldn't return to Afrasia at all after this mission.

Sandy jerked upright suddenly as she remembered something vital had escaped her mind while with her guardian downstairs. She had intended to ask him to help her locate the whereabouts of Dr Kean. She and Will would track him when they were done with the bombers from the Underworld who wanted to bring the West Federation down to her knees. Well, tracking Dr Kean was one thing that could bring Will back to Afrasia after their current mission. Sandy decided to send Adha a blitzmail. She googled Dr Kean's profile and downloaded a picture of him from one of the dozens on his company's website. She wrote a few words, asking Adha to help her sniff out where this man was at the moment. She also attached his picture to the text.

"Initiating take-off. We will be airborne in thirty seconds," the AI pilot of the airship announced.

Sandy tapped on the auto-harness button beside her, which instantly strapped on her seatbelt, securing her to the seat as the airship began its ascent into the morning sky. Just then, her phone buzzed. She checked it and saw that it was a reply from Adha already.

I'll check into it. By the time you land in the West Federation, I will send you any information I find regarding his location. Have an enjoyable flight, my child.

… … …

The Airship Terminal, West Federation

Will jumped to his feet as the airship halted at the terminal in a part of the West Federation that didn't look familiar to him. He had spent the entire flight staring out the airship window as it nosed through the clouds at the great heights. Sometimes he would take glances in Sandy's direction, only to see her still sleeping in her seat. He had looked behind him on one or two occasions to see what Walker and Simons were up to. He noticed that Walker was mostly preoccupied with the mobile device in his hands while Simons was running his fingers up and down the blade of a big knife.

Will didn't mind having them around. Although they were yet to warm to him and Sandy, he had no doubts that they would all be fine together. He believed they would be able to achieve the objective of the current mission, which was to prevent the large-scale bombing that was about to happen in the West Federation.

Presently, Will grabbed the backpack that contained his other military gear, as well as his weapons. He looked in Sandy's direction and saw she was also getting to her feet. Behind him, he could hear the sound of footsteps, indicating Simons and Walker were approaching.

"Are you ready?" Will asked Sandy.

"I don't think we're going to see any action just yet," Sandy replied. "We need more intel about the location of the bombers."

"Yeah, that's right," Will said.

"It's time to exit the airship," the AI pilot announced. "Have a successful mission."

Will Burne chuckled as he wondered how the AI pilot had known they were going on a mission. He waited a moment for the airship door to slide open, and then he made his way out with Sandy and the other soldiers. Just ahead of the airship was a blue van with a long-haired fellow leaning on it.

That's the man Adha Long spoke about, Will thought. He looked around him, trying to see if anything about this place could give him a clue what part of the West Federation this was. The sparse vegetation suggested the northern part of the continent, but he wasn't so sure, given the direction the airship had taken during their flight.

"Hi, guys," the man said as soon as Will and his party got close to him. "I'm John Croft. Sir Kalim asked me to pick you up here."

The moment John Croft spoke, Will detected the unmistakable San Matean accent that he had.

"What part of the West Federation is this? It doesn't look familiar," Will said to Croft.

"You are from here?"

Will thought that should have been obvious from his skin colour and hair type, but it was true that Westians weren't the only Caucasians in the world today. Oceania Liberation and even parts of the Underworld had people who could be classified as white.

"Yeah, Hringund, precisely," Will said as he clambered into the van. He pointed Sandy in the direction of the vacant front seat.

"Hringund? I go there almost every week," Croft said. "Nice little city with so much artistic brilliance on display, everywhere you look."

Will smiled as memories of his beloved city floated into his mind. Hringund was the West Federation's foremost city of art. It was because he had grown up in a city that placed so much value on artwork that had made him appreciate the priceless works of Ahima Botha in Sandy's bunker.

"And this place is on the outskirts of Gaulvan, just east of Wilnck," Croft informed Will. After that, Croft opened the door of the driver's seat and slid in.

Will had never been to the eastern cities like Wilnck and Gaulvan before now. Little wonder he couldn't determine the exact location when he looked around the area. His assumption that they were in the northern part of the West Federation was even wrong.

"Select driving options," an AI voice prompted from within the van.

"Manual," John Croft replied. "I don't know why this software can't just remember my preferred option; confounded thing drives me nuts with asking."

"You don't like auto-drive?" Sandy asked from within the car.

"I like to be in control," Croft told her. "I mean, I don't believe we should just sit back and let technology do everything."

As much as Will thought Croft had a point, he also believed one should not hesitate to make use of technology for one's convenience. The van roared to life and began to move down the narrow road that led away from the small terminal. Will continued to look around him as the van sped down the road. There were only sparse bushes around, with no buildings or architectural structures in sight.

Will grew bored of staring at bushes after a while, and he decided to break the ice with Simons and Walker. He reckoned they had to understand each other in some way since they were soon going to be fighting on the same side against Underworld terrorists.

"So, what's your favourite weapon?" Will asked Walker, who was seated closest to him of the two soldiers.

Walker looked up, staying silent for quite some time, then he answered, "Used to be Rubov shotguns."

"Rubov?" Will intoned. "Never heard of them."

Walker shrugged and chuckled, "Oh, I haven't seen one in ten years, but Rubovs are the best firearm I have ever used since I've been in service. It's a real shame our government has stopped importing them from Oceania Liberation."

Will knew that there was a time when Oceania Liberation exported their highly-rated weapons to other regions. However, arms trading had stopped long ago as each region attempted to be self-reliant in every sector.

"Which weapon do you prefer now?" Will asked.

"F15," Walker replied. "I mean, it's easy to carry, and it has an excellent range."

"Good choice," Will said. "What about you, Simons?"

Simons raised the big knife in his hands and waved it left and right. "I can't go anywhere without this baby. Fuck F15s, I'm alright with this."

Will and the two soldiers at the rear of the van continued to talk about weapons, comparing those available internationally and those exclusive to each region. They went on like this until the van rolled to a halt in an area that didn't look any different from where they had landed. All Will could see were sparse bushes stretching as far as his eyes could see. There were no buildings in sight. For a moment, he wondered if they had actually arrived at their lodging accommodations or the van had a mechanical fault.

John Croft stepped out of the van, announcing that they had arrived at their destination. That answered that question.

"Is it me, or does this place look like it's missing the actual lodging?" Sandy asked. "Croft, are you sure this is where we are supposed to be?"

"Yeah, I'm sure," Croft replied. "Just come with me."

Will swung his body out of the van, landing on his feet. Looking around, he noticed he was standing in the middle of the narrow road that went on and on into the horizon. *This is quite a strange place,* Will thought. He never realized there were such incredible stretches of lush, green land in the West Federation before now.

Croft led them away from the narrow road and took them through some bushes. Some of the bushes rose high enough to reach Will's chest, in some instances. Finally, after walking for a few minutes, they found a glass board about three feet off the ground. Croft crouched and punched in a code on the glass screen.

"Awaiting confirmation," a female AI voice said. "Please wait."

They only waited a few seconds before the AI declared that the confirmation process was complete. Additionally, a green light flashed on the white screen. Without further delay, doors opened in the grass, allowing a chamber-like structure to emerge from under the white screen. After the elevator was fully above ground, the doors slid open to reveal a well-lit interior, which had enough space for three people. Will, Sandy, and Walker stepped into the chamber first, leaving Croft and Simons outside.

"When the SmartEl stops, just step out and wait for us there," Croft told them.

SmartEl?

Will had never heard that term before, and he wasn't familiar with this type of underground elevator. The door of the SmartEl snapped shut complete with a *ding!* after Croft had spoken, and the elevator began a swift descent almost immediately. The SmartEl stopped moving downwards in a blink, and Will walked out of the elevator into a spacious room. The lobby was as brightly lit as the interior of the SmartEl. Will looked around and saw a passageway leading out of the big room. There were desks and chairs arranged in order at one end of the room, with a glass screen on the wall. That side looked like a high school classroom. Will, Sandy, and Walker stepped to the side of the SmartEl to wait for Croft and Simons.

The SmartEl returned shortly with Croft and Simons stepping out. The fair-haired fellow stepped forward and began to show the soldiers around the underground building. It was indeed styled differently from Sandy's sleek one at Xio Chan back in Afrasia. Croft showed them all the rooms, with each of them picking one that suited them. Will was careful to choose a room next to Sandy, just in case they needed to discuss or see each other without the knowledge of the other two. After picking their rooms, Croft showed them where they could find food, supplies, and other necessities.

"Did you see that part of the central room with the glass screen?" Croft asked them.

"Yeah," Will replied.

"That's where you will receive instructions from Sir Long," Croft told them. "If you need anything, I'll be the one to get things for you, even if it means going out to the nearest city to get it."

Croft left them shortly after that. Will turned to Sandy and asked her what she thought about this place.

"Nowhere near my bunker in terms of comfort," she said with a chuckle. "But it's just fine, given the circumstances."

"That's true," Will said as he started towards the room he had chosen.

He pushed the door open, seeing a decent-sized bed in the corner of the room with a table and chairs at the centre. An old ceiling fan rotated above them on the elevated ceiling as Will glanced opposite the bed to see a door leading to the bathroom. Will walked over to the chair and eased into it, relaxing his body after the not-so-comfortable van ride.

Will pulled the laser pistol from his waistband and placed it on the table. He rubbed his forehead as he leaned back in the chair, thinking of the events of the past few hours. He couldn't wait for Adha to get back to them with the info about the exact location of the bombers. He wasn't exactly sure how long it would take them to get to those Underworld terrorists and take them down. The only thing he was sure of was he would do whatever it took to save the West Federation from the criminals bent on disrupting the waters of global peace.

… … …

PART 3 - The Terminal, West Federation

A CLANDESTINE JOURNEY

Will's Home Ground: No One Is Safe

Chapters Nineteen through Twenty-Nine

"Extinction is the rule. Survival is the exception."

–Carl Sagan

In a Secret Bunker, West Federation: 2166, May 17

It was the second day of their stay in the bunker. The remainder of their first day had been uneventful as they had waited in vain for Adha to get back to them with the intel they needed to carry on with their mission. Finally, after hearing nothing from Adha, they had all gone to sleep in their respective rooms. The night found Sandy tossing and turning about on her mattress as she thought about what the future held for them all.

Earlier today, Will had shown up in her room to suggest something.

"I was thinking; we all should train together in the training machine," Will had said.

"Shouldn't we be reserving our energies for the task ahead? Who knows when Adha could ring us up and tell us we have to move," Sandy countered.

"Umm, I don't think we can head out that quickly," Will said. "What we are expecting is info on where the bombers are currently and how soon we can hit them. We can't go out just yet. We need to know where we are attacking so we can make plans and all that."

"You're right."

"Yeah, so I'll go tell Simons and Walker about the idea. Training together will help us understand their approach to combat and present us with their strengths and weaknesses," Will said.

"Alright," Sandy had replied. "How soon do we start?"

"As soon as we're all free."

Will had left her room immediately afterwords to tell Walker and Simons. It didn't take long before they started the training, and it turned out to be more interesting than Sandy had expected. They had first paired up, with Sandy picking Will as her partner while Simons remained with Walker, and they had attacked a virtual camp of Oceania Liberation soldiers. Sandy and Will had picked F15 rifles as their preferred weapon, but the weapons of their rivals weren't common ones. Simons had chosen a knife, while Walker had selected an unfamiliar shotgun that he called a Rubolov, or Rubov, whatever that meant.

The first training session went to Simons and Walker. While Sandy and Will had fought beside each other multiple times in reality, they had only spent a single session together in a tramach. And on that occasion, they had been competing against each other in an attempt to outscore each other. With the fluid way Simons and Walker wiped out the opposition, they easily outscored Sandy and Will by 11 kills.

"Let's go again," Will said after the AI voice declared Team Dexter, which consisted of Simons and his man, the winner. "This time, we switch partners. What do you think?"

"Sounds good," Sandy said.

"The hell, man, I need a few seconds to catch my breath," Walker said, still panting.

For the second round, Will paired up with Simons, the knifeman, while Walker and Sandy got together and began discussing tactics.

"Your Rubolov has great range, right?" Sandy said to Walker.

"It's Rubov," Walker replied. "And yes, its range hits distance shots far cleaner than the F15."

"Great," Sandy said. "Handle the enemies at the rear flank, and I'll take care of the vanguard."

"Okay, sounds like a plan," Walker replied.

The second session soon commenced with Will and Simons gaining an early lead, but by the conclusion, Sandy's team had caught up, and they won by three kills.

"So, I end up on the losing side two times in a row? Incredible stuff," Will muttered. "You guys are really good."

"How about one last session where we play as a single team, and we see who records the most kills singlehandedly?" Simons suggested.

"Ah, finally, now is my time to shine," Will said as he adjusted the strap on his hand.

Sandy smiled softly as she saw the determined look on Will's face. He was desperate to put an end to his losing streak. It was interesting to see that competitive streak in him. Even when it was just a game, it was clear he didn't enjoy losing.

The third session began with Will racing into an early lead, and he didn't relent for the entire duration of the training. There were times when Sandy took her eyes off the screen to watch the muscles of his arms bulging as he fired at the virtual enemies. Not even Simons, with his long-ranged Rubov, could deny Will Burne victory this time. Sandy struggled to fight off the urge to walk up to him and plant a kiss on his lips. She really liked this man.

Now, they had retired to their rooms after the exhaustive training sessions were concluded. True to Will's words, Sandy now felt like she knew a few things about Walker and Simons and their approach to combat. At this point, she could go into the field and fight next to them without any misunderstanding.

Sandy was currently in the bathroom, scrubbing off the sweat that clung to her skin with a bar of soap and some water. As she bathed, her mind drifted to the day when she and Will had curled around each other in the bathroom, giving each other indescribable pleasure. The thought caused her nipples to instantly grow taut, while she also became distinctly aware of the small pool of moisture running down her thighs, having nothing to do with her bath.

Focus on the mission, Sandy.

She really had to get her mind off Will Burne. They were just partners on this mission, nothing more. She had no doubt he would leave Afrasia immediately after settling everything regarding this mammoth intercontinental conspiracy. They had no business together beyond the events that had brought them together. It was quite possible he had other women in his life, or he just didn't feel like getting emotionally attached to anyone at the moment. She had taken a hint from the fact that he had never made a move towards her. Really, the only time they had talked about what had happened between them in the bunker was the morning after, when she had called him a heavy sleeper.

Sandy stepped out of the bathroom in time to hear a loud knock on her door.

"Who is it?" Sandy demanded.

"It's Will," he replied. "Adha has something for us in the main room."

"Oh, okay," Sandy said. "I'll put something on and join you in a minute."

Hastily, Sandy rummaged through her backpack and retrieved the black-on-black jacket and pants that she liked to wear. Then, she shoved her feet into some slippers and hurried out of the room. On her way to the main room, she saw Simons stepping out of his room while tying his long hair into a red band. Together, they jogged into the main room, where Will and Walker were already seated. Adha's face was already visible on the glass screen. Sandy quickly eased her butt into a seat while Simons walked to one of the desks at the front to sit.

"I'm glad to see you all," Adha began. "I have just gotten the intel I requested regarding the location of the bombers. Unfortunately, the techies I put on the job failed to provide anything yesterday, and that's why you didn't hear from me until now."

Sandy adjusted her sitting position as she waited for her guardian to reveal what he had found. She peered at the glass screen, watching as Adha took his face from the camera for a while. It looked like a message had dropped in his mobile device or something.

"Yeah, so, what we have at the moment is a group of the bombers are already in the West Federation, waiting for the first shipment of bombs to arrive. Their present location is North Lembria. Are you familiar with that city, Agent Burne?"

"Yes, sir," Will replied. "It's a known nest for criminals of different sorts. So I'm not surprised those guys are hiding there."

"The plan at the moment is to wait for the explosives to arrive at the border of the West Federation. I will alert the right people about the explosives and the ones who are bringing them in. The bombers are the ones you will go after. By dawn tomorrow, I will provide you with more details on where they are in North Lembria. They have been moving around a lot, possibly trying to cover their tracks, but we will get them and make them talk so we can find out who is responsible for this mess."

Adha spoke for a few more minutes, during which he asked them if they were comfortable in the lodging and if there was anything they needed.

"My child," Adha said, turning his attention exclusively to Sandy. "The information you requested about the person who got you into this situation will be forwarded to your device."

"Thank you," Sandy replied with a smile. Finally, she would know where Kean was. She could tuck that info away until after they dealt with the bombers.

Adha said goodbye to the group, and when they had replied with their own goodbyes, the General's face disappeared from the glass screen.

"Whew," Simons muttered. "So, we have more waiting. It's fine."

Sandy returned to her room to check if Adha had forwarded the message to her phone. She tapped the screen to open her phone and saw that she had a blitzmail from him. She opened it and saw a picture of Dr Kean sitting next to George Lay and President R. Morgan, the leader of Oceania Liberation. The short text under the picture confirmed that Dr Kean was residing in Oceania Liberation at the moment. He was staying at an apartment in one of the presidential estates in the region.

Fucking Bastard.

She didn't care if he slept in the same room with President Morgan. She and Will would go after him and make him pay. They would find a way.

Sandy eased to her feet with her smartphone still in her hand. She would head over to Will's room to tell him what her guardian had just sent her. She slipped her phone in her breast pocket and adjusted her jacket. As she strode towards the door, she felt the same sexual excitement she had felt earlier in the bathroom beginning to stir again. Her nipples were straining against the sleeveless vest she wore under her jacket. She marvelled at how the mere thought of being alone with Will was setting her body on fire.

That's enough, Sandy. You are just going to tell him what you learned about Dr Kean's whereabouts, nothing more.

Sandy continued walking toward his door, assuring herself that all she would do in his room was speak about Dr Kean and wherever he was in Oceania Liberation.

Will's voice was sleepy when he answered her knock on his door.

"Sandy?"

"Yeah, it's me," she answered. "Can I come in?"

She turned the knob and pushed the door open. She found him sitting on the bed and stifling a yawn. It truly looked like he had been taking a nap before she knocked.

"Sit," he said, waving to the vacant chair.

This was just the second time Sandy was entering Will's room. The first time had been when John Croft had taken them around the bunker. She walked over to the chair and made herself comfortable.

"Adha just sent me a blitzmail about the current location of Kean," Sandy began.

Every remaining atom of sleepiness immediately cleared from Will's face as soon as he heard the name, "Kean." Sandy thought she heard him whisper *that bastard*, but she wasn't sure.

"Where is he?" Will asked. "Let me guess, the Underworld?"

"No, he's in Oceania Liberation."

"I knew he wouldn't stay in Afrasia," said Will. "We'll go after him when all this is over, right?"

"Yeah, of course," Sandy said. "Here is the blitzmail Adha sent. There is a picture attached."

Sandy walked over to hand him her device. He took it from her and peered at the picture of Dr Kean with his powerful friend.

"Whether he dines with the president or whoever he likes, we are going to hunt him down," Will said.

Definitely, there was no way Kean would get away with this.

"Umm, I just remembered something," Will said as he handed Sandy her phone.

"What's that?" asked Sandy.

"You owe me a head," Will said in an immature manner that made Sandy burst into laughter.

"I don't know what you're talking about," Sandy said innocently, still laughing.

"Come on, you shouldn't forget things like that," Will said with a chuckle. "We had this session at the tramach, and we said the loser was going to give the winner a head."

"Well, I didn't lose," Sandy said with a shrug.

"I didn't lose, either," Will countered. "Are we just going to let the game count for nothing?"

Sandy flipped her white hair out of her face, crouching in front of Will. "What exactly do you have in mind?"

"Since the game ended in a draw, I think we should take turns giving each other head or do it at the same time. That's what I think," Will said.

Sandy remained silent for a moment, feigning as though she were thinking about the idea. She kept her face passive, although deep within her, the urge to get down with Will was growing stronger by the minute. Sandy shrugged as if she didn't mind one way or the other.

"Let's do it," she said.

She had barely finished her statement before Will lunged forward and wrapped his arms around her. The wetness between Sandy's thighs surged as she felt Will's hot breath against her neck. The way his hands firmly encircled her waist, she could feel his desire. He wanted her.

Sandy parted her lips, welcoming Will's hungry kiss. She let her hands run up and down his firm chest as they began kissing fervently. A soft moan escaped her lips as Will's fingers went under her jacket and began to rub her aching tits. The slow circular motion that he was making around her areola was driving her crazy. She didn't know why these little touches drove her out of her mind, but that was exactly what was happening at the moment.

Sandy and Will kissed and explored each other's erogenous zones as their bodies entwined. It was Will's turn to moan when Sandy cupped his hard penis in her hands. She slipped a hand into his pants, deep into his boxer shorts, and began to stroke his turgid shaft.

"Oh, Sandy," Will gasped. "I want you."

Taking the lead, Sandy gently pushed Will onto his back, then straddled him. Next, she took off her jacket and vest, all in one upward movement. After that, she kicked off the black pants she had on, leaving her green panties, already moist with her wetness. While she was undressing, Will, too, was busy shedding the few articles of clothing he had on his body.

Before long, Will had only his boxer shorts on, while Sandy's green panties served as the only thing keeping her from being completely nude. Will took a moment to roll out from under Sandy to rush over to the door and lock it. Sandy knew it was highly unlikely that Croft or one of the other guys would come here without knocking, but nothing was impossible.

Will hurried back to the bed after he had locked the door. Beads of sweat were already clinging to his sculpted chest. Sandy moved her leg over a little to allow Will to get back underneath her. She leaned forward and kissed his nipples, then continued to kiss his body until she got to the edge of his shorts. Without wasting time, Will fixed his thumbs into the waistband of the shorts and pulled them down to reveal his throbbing member.

Sandy took off her panties and turned so her mouth could easily get to Will's lower body and that he, too, could bury his face between her legs. They were in the 69 position. Sandy bent her neck to take Will's hard rod in her mouth, but she stopped short as she felt the warm touch of Will's tongue against her swollen, wet clit. She jerked her waist as she felt an electrifying surge of pleasure jolt through her entire body. She couldn't even explain what she had just felt.

Forcing herself to welcome the shiver that had just racked her body, she refocused her attention on Will's cock, and took it into her mouth as she had intended to just moments ago. She took his penis halfway into her mouth while making sure her tongue was drawing tiny, teasing, irregular shapes around his tip. The sharp groan that escaped Will's lips thrilled her. This was what they both wanted: to make each other shiver with pleasure. She had a very good idea of how this encounter would end.

… … …

A Shocking Morning: Secret Bunker, West Federation

The first thing Will became aware of when he snapped out of his sleep was the fact that Sandy's head was no longer on his chest. They had fallen asleep that way, with Sandy placing her head of long white hair on his bare chest after they had cleaned up together in the bathroom. Now, Will realized as he stretched his body, Sandy had left the room. This was the second time it had happened.

Will tried to pull himself to a sitting position quickly, but the pain he felt in his back made him move a little slower. He realized that the training sessions with the team, and the pleasure sessions with Sandy, had taken their toll on his body. A grunt escaped his lips as he swung his body upwards.

He picked up his vest and boxer shorts and quickly put them back on. He walked over to his backpack to retrieve his black uniform. He wanted to go outside and sit in the main room for a while. He found that staying in his room reminded him of the steamy encounter that had just taken place between him and the ebony beauty. Sometimes, he wished he had met her before he joined the military. Thoughts of willing his life to the West Federation government would never have entered his head.

There were times when he wondered what Sandy thought about him. Did she feel anything for him, or was this pure sex with no strings whatsoever attached? What would happen when they finished with their current mission? He knew the answer to that question, but he couldn't bring himself to admit it. However, it was the truth. He and Sandy would go their separate ways after they had completely killed off the waves of conflict in the erstwhile calm sea of global peace. Sandy Krave was the kind of career woman who would not let a man slow her down in her work. As much as he desired to have a special relationship with her, something special beyond fucking the energy out of each other when they were both horny, she wasn't going to entertain such a thought. Who knows? She might draw away and deny him any further sexual advances. No, he wouldn't let that happen.

By now, Will had slipped into his black shirt, and he was heading towards the door. The fleeting scent of Sandy still clung to his nostrils even though she had left the room quite some time ago. Will opened the door and stepped into the passageway. He was impressed by the—

A massive explosion suddenly rocked Will's world and filled his ears, putting an abrupt end to his train of thought. Will ducked and placed his body against the wall. He could feel the floor and wall behind him still vibrating from the impact.

What the hell was that?

Another explosion rocked the bunker shortly after. Will was already making his way towards the main room when the second one happened. The force of the explosion threw Will off his feet, sending him crashing against the door of one of the rooms. Unfortunately, the door wasn't latched, so Will tumbled through the door and landed flat on his back.

Will kept his head down, wondering who was trying to blow them away. Had the Underworld bombers found out about them? With a loud groan, Will scrambled back to his feet. Probably, the more sensible thing to do was to stay down to avoid being hit, but Will didn't like the way he was isolated. He also wanted to check on Sandy and find out what Simons and Walker were up to. Together, they would be able to figure a way out of this problem.

As Will got back on his feet, he realised that a large splinter of wood had torn his pants and pierced him in the thigh. Will pulled out the bit of wood and threw it away. His heart was beating rapidly as he wondered who was responsible for the attack they were facing. If the attack continued, it was only a matter of time before the entire bunker collapsed on top of them from the sheer force of the explosions.

Will emerged from the empty room he'd tumbled into, and he raced towards Sandy's room. He really hoped nothing had happened to her.

"Sandy, are you okay?" he called from outside her room, barely managing to keep himself from rushing in to check on her.

"Yeah, I'm fine," Sandy replied immediately from somewhere deep inside her room.

Will let out a breath he didn't know he was holding. He opened the door and rushed in, filled with relief that Sandy was alright. He found her lying on the floor with her arms covering her head.

"Have you heard anything from Simons or Walker?" Will asked as Sandy lifted her face to look at him.

"No," Sandy said. "I just heard the explosions; nothing more."

"We need to find out what's happening," Will said. "Do you want to stay here, or should we check the main room together?"

"Let's both go," Sandy said.

Will and Sandy slowly progressed towards the passageway together, having to brace themselves for the possibility of another explosion. Finally, they arrived at Walker's room to find his door open. Probably, it had been blown open by the massive blasts from nowhere. They checked the room and found Walker on the floor, clutching his left leg and sweating profusely.

"What happened?" asked Will.

"The first damned explosion," Walker spoke. It was clear from his speech that he was in pain. "Took me by surprise. Threw the desk right over, on my calf. Something is definitely broken in there, 'cause I can't fuckin' walk."

Sandy stepped forward and began to tend to Walker's broken leg.

"Where is Simons?" Will asked.

"I don't know. Who the hell is hitting us?"

Will drew his laser pistol and pulled himself upright. "I'll go check the main room, see if I can find out anything. And I'll get Simons and bring him back here, so we can all put our heads together for a—"

BANG!

This explosion was deeper and much louder than the first two. It shook the entire facility, sending light fixtures and ceiling tiles flying from above. Both Sandy and Will were knocked off their feet as Walker shouted in pain. With the way Walker cried out, Will was afraid that his other leg might have taken a hit too. Sandy was the first to get back on her feet. Will groaned his thanks as she reached down and helped him up. Now the room was beginning to crumble. The facility's structure was compromised. Together, Will and Sandy helped Walker to his feet to move him by placing his arms on their shoulders. They made their way to the passageway while Will kept an eye out for Simons.

Who is hitting us?

Their misery was compounded when they got to the main room and found the glass screen shattered into a thousand pieces. Even worse than that was the horrible sight on the opposite wall: a severed head. Pinned to the centre of the wall and still dripping blood was the severed head of their companion, Simons.

Walker let out an ear-piercing scream at the sight of Simons' head nailed to the wall. Will couldn't even utter a sound. Only one thought kept bouncing in his head.

What the hell is going on?

None of them could answer that question yet.

… … …

Sandy's heart was thudding in her chest as she stared at Simons' severed head on the wall. Though she had seen many deaths, this one left her. swallowing gobs of saliva as a chill spread through her body. The horrific sight of Simons' bloody head attached to the wall in such a crude manner repulsed Sandy. Simons' eyes were still open. They stared at what? She could not say. The ear-splitting scream from Walker made it difficult for her to keep her thoughts composed.

"No, buddy, nooo!" Walker roared as he dragged himself forward, despite his wounded leg, towards the wall that held his companion's head.

Sandy shook her head in acute disbelief and sadness. Whoever had done this was heartless and barbaric. She struggled to keep her emotions in check as she watched Walker stand in front of Simons' dripping head, bawling, unashamed, like a little kid. It was a different thing to lose your man to the hot, piercing bullet of an F15 or the slash of an electro-sword across the chest. This was just plain cruel.

Will held a hand over his nose and mouth as he blinked back tears. It was impossible not to be moved by the heart-breaking scene they were all witnessing. The grief was made even worse because they had all bonded through the training sessions together. They had fought, sweated, and trained hard together in the tramach. It was never easy to stare into the empty eyes of someone who had been on your team, knowing they were dead.

Sandy knew that their grief could yet be compounded if they didn't find a way to keep whoever had done this at bay. There was no doubt this brutal attack on Simons and the explosions were coordinated. They would have to remain on their toes if they didn't want to go out the way Simons did.

"It's gonna be okay," Will said to Walker, trying to soothe him as he pulled him away from the sickening sight of his friend's dismembered body part.

Walker leaned against Will and continued sobbing inconsolably. It was easy to see he and Simons were close. Who knows how long they had known each other?

"We have to get out of here," Will turned to address Sandy. "There could be another explosion any minute."

"You are right," Sandy replied. "The front—"

Attention!" a voice boomed from every corner of the main room where they stood. It was a loud, male voice that rang in Sandy's ears. "You are trapped in there. Our men are everywhere around this bunker. You have no other option than to surrender yourselves now."

"Fuck you!" Will growled.

"Who the hell are you?" Sandy roared at the same time as Will.

"We can't surrender!" Will said as he led Walker back to where Sandy stood.

"Yeah, I know!" Sandy said.

Where was the sense in letting the enemy get you that easily? If one had to be caught, it only made sense that the enemy would sweat and bleed for it.

"We can see you in there," the voice announced. "There is no escape. Drop your weapons now and proceed to the front door of the bunker."

"They can see us?" Sandy whispered to Will. "There are cameras, then."

"Yeah, sure," Will said. "So, we blow them out."

"Right."

Sandy and Will cast their expert eyes around the length and breadth of the room, seeking the cameras that could be giving away their position to the enemies outside. Sandy caught one camera placed strategically close to where the now broken glass screen had been. She blew out the camera with a single shot of her laser gun. Will, too, found one above the door that led away from the main room and took it down.

"Now, we're going to kill you!" the voice roared over the speakers. "Get them!"

"Bring it on," Will shrugged with a wry smile on his face.

Sandy was glad that the criminals they were up against had at least grown tired of hitting them with explosives. If things had continued the way they were, she and the others would have stood little chance of getting out of this alive. But, even now, Sandy was not so sure they would be able to hold off the gunmen sent down by the owner of the loud voice on the speakers.

Will drew his laser pistol and held it at the ready. Sandy took up her firearm. They had no choice but to stand their ground and match their enemies, fire for fire. Or… was there another way? An idea dropped in Sandy's head that there might be an emergency exit somewhere at the rear of the bunker, just like hers, back in Afrasia. Sandy began to think of where the rear exit might be. She was unsure if it would be there, but they had to try at least and look for it. That would be their plan. They would hold off their adversaries while looking for a way out of the bunker.

"Will, I think we might be able to get out of here without taking the front door," Sandy said.

"Really? You mean, like an emergency exit somewhere at the back?"

"Yeah, I think so," Sandy said. "There should be, anyway."

"But that guy said his men are all around the bunker," Walker said. His voice was little more than a groan. It was obvious he was in immense pain.

"I don't know; we just have to take the chance," Sandy offered. "We can't let them get hold of us, just like that."

"Yeah, let's go," Will said to Sandy. "I'll help Walker along while you lead the way. If we're lucky, we will find the exit before they come in."

Before they could execute their plan, the door of the SmartEl slid open, and they heard a *crack* as a rifle was fired. Will's hope of getting away before their adversaries arrived was dashed already. Sandy ducked and threw herself behind a desk to take cover. She saw Will bearing Walker's weight as he tried to find a place for the two of them to hide. He was firing at the two masked men who had walked into the main room through the SmartEl.

"Die!" Sandy Krave roared as she fired her laser gun at the two masked guys whose blazing guns were wreaking havoc in the bunker.

One of the guys was struck on the arm, and he was momentarily incapacitated, but his companion maintained a threat. The two men could not keep up with Will and Sandy's strategic shooting from their covered vantage points. In less than five minutes of exchanging gunfire, they were cut down, leaving Sandy and Will to breathe easy for the moment.

"Okay, let's go now," Will called to Sandy. He helped Walker back to his feet, and they headed towards the back door out of the bunker.

Sandy, too, rose from her hiding spot and raced after her companions. She was about rounding a corner when a shot rang out from behind her. She cast a glance over her shoulder and saw that four masked soldiers had now emerged from the SmartEl. A sigh escaped her lips. She and Will still had more shooting to do.

She fired two quick shots at the new guys. She didn't hit any of them, but she managed to prevent them from advancing.

"More of them?" Will called as he shouldered a limping Walker forward.

"Yeah."

"How many?"

"I can see four," Sandy answered. "There could be more."

"Hold them off 'til I set Walker down."

Sandy took a few seconds to watch Will, carefully assisting Walker to a sitting position. She took her eyes off him shortly after and began firing at the advancing enemies. It was difficult for her to take on four guys, but at least she kept them from advancing as quickly as they would have if nobody had been shooting at them. A bullet from one of the enemy soldiers ripped a chunk out of the wall Sandy was hiding behind. For a moment, Sandy was dazed, wondering what would have been if she had not quickly withdrawn her head.

She was relieved when Will finally came up beside her and shook her, with his hands on her shoulder.

"We'll get through this," he reassured her. "We have both been through worse."

"That's true," she nodded.

"Good," Will said. "Now, let's show them who they're dealing with."

They both stood in the hiding spot and watched the masked soldiers approaching cautiously, knowing they could be attacked at any point.

"Those two on the left side are mine," Will whispered.

Sandy swung her arm out of the hiding place, just far enough to aim at the soldiers on the right and fire. Will did the same to the guys on the other side. Sandy's ears were filled with the sound of gunfire from their adversaries' rifles. Nevertheless, she remained focused and fired continuously at her targets. A smile appeared at the corner of her lips when one of the men she aimed at dropped to the ground. The other took cover behind a desk and was occasionally shooting from there. Both of Will's targets were hiding, too, firing their shots from behind desks.

"Go grab some grenades from the armoury," Will ordered. "I'll hold them while you are gone."

"Okay," Sandy said. She dashed down the passageway, heading for the arsenal that was beside the room housing the tramach. She got to the door and was glad there was no security lock on it. She didn't remember John Croft saying anything about a passcode. Sandy pushed the door open and quickly grabbed a handful of grenades. She hooked them on her belt and immediately dashed out of the armoury. From her current position, she could hear rapid gunfire. Will was still holding them back.

Sandy hurried back. Her snow-white hair jiggled as she ran back to the main room. Will had killed one of the enemy soldiers, leaving just two of them. Will nodded at Sandy, and she understood what that meant. He was giving her the go-ahead to throw a grenade. Sandy took a moment to check where the two remaining enemy soldiers were, and when she had seen what she needed, she yanked off the lid and threw the grenade.

Immediately after she threw it, she launched herself into Will's arms to brave the impact of the explosion sure to follow. The explosion was just as ground-shaking as the earlier ones that had rocked the bunker. The good thing about this one was that it tore the two remaining enemies to shreds of meat and dark fabrics. The force of the explosion threw both Will and Sandy to the ground.

"Dammit," Will growled as he scrambled upright and helped Sandy to her feet. "We keep moving. More of them will come, but we will not let them stop us."

He was right, Sandy thought. Although more masked soldiers would still descend into the bunker, for now, they were alone. They had to keep looking for that emergency exit. Whether there would be enemies with guns at the ready waiting for them outside was another issue. The important thing was to get out of the bunker first.

They returned to the position they had been in earlier, with Sandy in the lead while Will came behind, with his arm curled around Walker's body as he helped him forward.

"I'm fucking useless," Walker cried at one point. "I'm slowing you two down, and you know it. Just leave me here and go."

"No way," said Will. "I can't afford to lose two men on the same mission. No, we'll get you to wherever we're going. Don't worry about our pace. The important thing is to make progress."

The echoes of stamping feet from across the room reached Sandy's ears as she and her companions continued to run towards the part of the bunker where her gut told her they would find an exit. More of the enemy soldiers were touching down in the bunker, as confirmed by the footfalls. Sandy took her mind off the numbers of the enemy. For the moment, she was only interested in discovering a way out of the bunker, and she was damned sure they would find it. She was not sure how, but she knew that somehow, they would find a way.

……………

Another Traitor in the West Federation

With wave after wave of enemy soldiers dropping into the bunker to engage Will and his companions in battle, it was by some miracle that they managed to find the exit door. Locating the point exiting the bunker was purely by Sandy's genius, but the task of keeping the enemies off their back had been undertaken collectively. At one point, even Walker, with his broken leg, bore his pain with stiff dignity and joined in shooting at their adversaries.

Now, they were outside the bunker for the first time since they stepped into it the previous day. Will looked around him and saw a stretch of thick bushes. The sky was dark, but the silver light of the moon illuminated their path. This whole thing reminded Will of the time he and Sandy had been chased around the Underworld by armed mercenaries. How powerful were these people? Why does it look like they had infiltrated everywhere already?

Walker's weight was slowing them down, but Will was determined not to leave him to die at the hands of those masked guys. They might not even kill him. They might take him to their camp and torture him until he spills everything he knows. Will did not want to lose Walker the way they had lost Simons just this night. He told himself he would help Walker survive this and get back on his feet eventually.

They were moving through a narrow, straight path that cut through the bushes. Sandy was still in front, and Will, carrying his man, was a few steps behind. Will knew that none of the enemy soldiers would come at them from behind. Sandy had blasted one of the walls leading out of the bunker, leaving a huge pile of debris. That was enough to deter the guys on their trail from coming up from behind them, at least for the moment.

Will was already thinking of where they would go from here. If they got through this long stretch of bushes, they would look for a place to hide their heads until morning. After that, they would find a way to get in touch with John Croft. He would know where they should go next.

"Wait," Sandy said suddenly, holding up her hand.

Will halted his movement and stared at Sandy. "What's wrong?" he asked when she remained silent.

"Those guys are approaching from the front," Sandy revealed. "I can hear their footsteps."

Will listened too and found Sandy was right. Maybe he would have noticed earlier if he was not so lost in thought about where they would go from here. It appeared the voice that had told them the bunker was surrounded was not lying after all.

"Quick, take a left!" Sandy said in a harsh whisper. "They are—"

The sudden barrage of gunshots swallowed the remainder of Sandy's speech. Will struggled to move Walker forward, helping him take the path as Sandy had directed. After a few steps forward, Will realized it was best to duck away from sight rather than continue making themselves an easy target for the enemy. He pulled Walker down to safety from the blazing guns of the men, now behind them.

Will was momentarily separated from Sandy, who was further ahead of him, but he could see her clearly as she ducked behind a row of bushes, away from the men attacking them. Will ran a hand over his face as he began to think of ways to get out of this line of fire.

"Hey!" Sandy called in a hushed tone. "I got one grenade left. Should I launch?"

"Go for it!" Will called back.

Will kept his head down and listened as the explosion took out the enemies on the other side. Now that they were out of grenades, they had to get out of here as quickly as possible. It would be pretty tough for them if more enemies came at them, and there were no grenades to help them tilt the fight in their favour.

"All clear," Sandy announced after taking a peek from where she had taken cover.

"Great, let's get going," Will answered. He helped Walker back to his feet.

"Bastards!" a voice growled from behind them. Will turned swiftly and saw a masked soldier with his rifle held at the ready. His black jacket was burnt at the shoulders and around his chest. Will guessed he had just survived the wild blast of the grenade.

Will had always been known in the agency for his quick reflexes and ability to hit a clean shot when there wasn't much time to aim, but he was not quick enough to prevent this masked soldier from firing off a shot. Will's laser went off just milliseconds after the enemy's shot rang out. Walker's loud groan of pain was like a punch to Will's gut. The shot had clipped his shoulder. He slipped off Will's arm, crashing to the ground. Will's first shot had gone wide, but he made no mistake with the second. The missile from his laser gun struck the enemy soldier square in the forehead and sent him tumbling backwards.

He held his gun steady, ready to fire at the soldier again if he made any moves, but the fellow remained motionless on the ground. Then, when he was convinced that the bandit was dead, he returned his attention to Walker. Sandy was already beside Walker before Will could get a look at him.

"Is he alright?" he asked as he knelt and peered at their companion, who was bleeding copiously from the shoulder.

"He's breathing," Sandy said, brushing a hand over Walker's slowly heaving chest.

Will shook his head, frustrated. Walker would be a lot tougher to carry through the bushes now that he'd been shot. Will wasn't sure if there were more of the masked men coming after them. It was odd that they were yet to unravel the mystery behind the bombing of their bunker and the subsequent attacks. He knew it was linked to George Lay and his fellow conspirators, but he was interested in knowing who was coordinating the attack here in the West Federation. Was it someone he knew? Will tried to think of top men in the West Federation military who were corrupt enough to be involved in this, but he couldn't single out anyone. This was unprecedented. He wasn't sure he knew anyone in the West Federation so determined to make the region become unified with other regions.

"What do we do now?" Sandy asked.

"I don't want to just leave him," Will said. "I think we can still get him to safety with us."

"Or, get us all killed?"

"I think we have repelled enough attacks to survive the night," Will said. "No one is coming after us, as far as we can see."

"That's until the next mercenary, or whatever they are, shows up with their guns spitting bullets at us," Sandy said. "We need to be mobile in this situation. It's unfortunate that Walker is down."

It really was unfortunate. They would be better off putting a lot of distance between them and the squad of masked soldiers. Now, they were not making progress at all.

"Okay," Will breathed. "We'll stay here and watch out for those guys. I'll think of how we can reach John Croft."

"I have his contact here."

"You do?" Will said.

"Yeah. Remember when he told us we could speak to him if we needed anything?" Sandy said. "I took his number before he left the bunker. I mean, how the hell were we supposed to let him know if someone needed something if none of us had his number?"

"That's great! I have been thinking so hard about a way to reach him. I didn't know you had his number," Will said. "Dial him up."

Will watched as Sandy tapped the call option on the screen of her phone. She handed the phone to Will when it started ringing. Will scanned the area around them with his eyes as he waited for Croft to answer the call. His mind was boiling with different thoughts. What if Croft didn't answer? He could be away from his phone or something. Will knew they had to get away from this area as quickly as possible, and they needed Croft to get them out of there. Who knew what the Underworld rogues had up their sleeves next? There could be more of them approaching at any moment.

"Is he not answering?" Sandy asked.

"He hasn't answered," Will replied.

He started to wonder what they would do if they couldn't reach John Croft. It was tough to think of them wandering aimlessly, without a specific destination in mind.

"We could call Adha," Sandy offered. "I'm sure he knows someone else that can help us."

"Good idea," Will muttered. "But, let me try Croft one more time."

After he dialled, the ringing continued again. Will was glad they had the option of calling Adha for help. It didn't look like John Croft was going to answer this call.

"Hello?" a voice suddenly broke into the other end of the call. "Is this Sandy Krave?"

The voice sounded very much like Croft's. Will was pleasantly surprised that the man had answered the call.

"Hi, it's Burne," Will said quickly. "We have been attacked. We are outside the bunker, as I speak."

"You were attacked? How?" Croft asked. The sleepy edge that had been in his voice earlier had now vanished. Will could imagine Croft sitting up with his eyes wide open after he had just heard that the bunker's defence had been breached.

Will gave a summary of the night's events, starting from the explosion to the sight of Simons' head pinned to the wall, followed by the shootout with the enemy soldiers.

"Bloody hell!" Croft growled. "Where are you, right now?"

"We are in a bush, close to the emergency exit of the bunker."

"Alright, just stand down; stay there! I'll drive down and get you from there."

"Thanks, man," Will breathed, then he turned to Sandy. "He's coming to get us."

Sandy nodded, keeping her eyes fixed on Walker. Will handed Sandy's phone back, then joined her in staring at their companion lying on the ground. Sandy had patched up the bullet wound on his shoulder with a strip of cloth. It was a good thing he had stopped bleeding, but Walker would be better off receiving proper medical treatment as soon as possible.

Will cocked his head sharply as he heard a sudden rustle of leaves some distance away. He looked towards the direction he presumed the sounds were coming from and saw two masked soldiers sneaking their way.

"I thought we were done for the night," Will whispered. But apparently, they had more shooting to do. Will could only hope that he and Sandy would come out topside in this do-or-die shooting session.

……… ……

They were walking down the narrow path leading away from the bunker as directed by John Croft, who was waiting for them in his vehicle. Just moments after Will fired a shot from his laser gun into the gut of the last enemy soldier standing, a call had come in from Croft telling them he was in his truck, driving towards their position.

"I'll be there in five minutes," Croft had said. "Just follow the path; you will arrive at a road on a slope. That's where I'll pick you up."

Sandy cast a glance in Will's direction. She could see he was straining under Walker's weight. She truly wanted to help, but she knew it was more than she could handle. The continuous shooting and running she had indulged on this night alone had left her feeling drained. All she wanted to do now was get to Croft's truck and get a little rest. She was too tired for anything else.

The moon shone brilliantly through the leaves on the branches high above them, allowing them to see far ahead of them. Sandy thought of typing a message to Adha to inform him of the current situation, but she was too tired. She could feel fatigue spreading throughout her entire body, making every step she took pure torture. The promise of safety and comfort Croft's truck held was what drove her forward, despite the incredible exhaustion she felt.

Now that they were under attack, their chances of getting their hands on the bombers that wanted to destroy Hringund seemed damn near impossible. These people meant serious business. She imagined President Morgan, George Lay, and their army of conspirators talking about their plan to thwart the attack on the West Federation cities. She wondered how those people had known she and Will would be at the bunker.

The appearance of the road that Croft had talked about far ahead of them filled Sandy with fresh energy. She kept pace with Will as he jogged towards their destination. Sandy pulled her phone from her pocket and compared the time on the call log with the time showing at the top of her screen. It had been almost ten minutes since that conversation with Croft. It was possible he would be there already, waiting for them to emerge from the bush.

Sandy kept her eyes focused on the road ahead. They were close to being safely away from the roaring guns of the masked soldiers. Just hours ago, she and the others had been engaged in mock training sessions in the tramach, not knowing how much actual fighting they would have to do by the end of the day. That thought about their time in the tramach brought back heart-breaking memories of Simons and how he had been brutally murdered in the main room of the bunker. She shuddered as she thought about him and the cold-blooded way someone had pinned his head to the wall. He had been full of life when they were competing in the tramach earlier today. Now, his life was snuffed out, forever.

Sandy wondered how someone had managed to behead Simons and nail his head to the wall under their noses. She and the others had no idea that it was even happening. It didn't make any sense to her. Could it be that Simons had met his grisly end *after* he had gone outside his room to check on the first explosion? Maybe one of those masked guys had sneaked up on him from behind and sliced his head clean off his neck.

"Almost there," Will grunted.

Sandy was not sure if he was addressing her or Walker. They kept up with each other's jogging pace as they got closer to the road ahead. Sandy promised herself to get some proper shuteye after getting into Croft's truck. She would try to understand the mysterious events of this night when she had gotten enough sleep. She would also reach out to Adha and let him know one of his trusted men was down, and the second had been knocked out of service by enemy fire.

Briefly, Sandy wondered what would have been if just she and Will had undertaken this mission. There was a chance they would be in a better situation than this because she and Will were already used to fighting by each other's side. There wouldn't be the burden of Walker's severely injured body, which was currently preventing them from moving as fast as they could. On the other hand, without Simons and Walker on this mission, it was possible the masked men could have shot either her or Will. Anything was possible. It was hard for Sandy to imagine trying to help bear Will's weight if he were seriously wounded.

Sandy and Will emerged at the road, panting hard. Although it didn't seem like the masked soldiers were actively coming after them, they were desperate to get away from the bush and go somewhere safe for the night. Sandy stifled a chuckle. The bunker was supposed to be the safest place to stay in this part of the West Federation. It would be difficult for her to feel relaxed, wherever Croft took them from here. Yes, she needed to calm her mind with a good dose of sleep, but she would definitely keep her firearm within reach. She was not going to be caught unaware again.

Sandy saw a container truck parked a few yards away when they emerged. She had no doubt it was John Croft's. She started towards the truck, glad she had made it here in one piece. The driver's door swung open when Sandy got closer to the truck, and Croft jumped out. In the bright silver moonlight, his face looked whiter than normal.

"Thank goodness you escaped," Croft said as he unlocked the door of the container. "You'll have to stay back here. The front seat is filled with some equipment I haven't had time to transfer to the back."

"Okay, it's fine," Sandy said as she climbed in. She didn't mind staying in this container, as long as it meant she would be safe from the masked wolves that had descended upon them back at the bunker. The interior of the container was lit by two bright bulbs. Sandy saw two window-like openings and smiled. It would be more comfortable for her to hit the sack right here than in a seat anyway. Behind her, Will helped Walker into the container.

Sandy was about perching her ass on the smooth floor of the container when she caught the whiff of a strange smell. It was powerful, overwhelming, and she had not perceived anything like it before. It stung her nostrils and made her cough.

"It's a fucking trap. That's Arblow!" Will roared suddenly. "Sandy, get out now!"

Sandy had no idea what an Arblow was or why Will was suddenly telling her to get out of the container. She tried to enquire what he was talking about, but the smell overpowered her will to speak. She let out a gasp and tried to talk, but words refused to flow from her mouth. Sandy saw Will clasp a hand over his nose and beckon to her.

Will started pulling her from the container, but just then, someone struck him from behind. At this point, Sandy was not sure she was seeing things clearly, because her vision was getting more distorted by the minute. She blinked rapidly, struggling to steel herself against the growing effects of the gas.

Get out now!

Sandy tried to force herself to move out of the container, but she stumbled and fell. The world was swimming before her. She knew she was feeling the effects of the gas. Arblow, or whatever Will had called it. She held her hands out towards the opening of the container, wishing Will would grab her hand and pull her away from this rapid descent into darkness, into oblivion. Sandy had been here before, and she knew she was slipping into unconsciousness.

Will's warm hand did not encircle hers or pull her out of the dark cavern she was falling into. Instead, the last thing she heard before she was totally engulfed in darkness was the word: *bastard.*

Will rolled haphazardly down the slope by the side of the road, struggling to get his hands around something that he could hold onto. As he tumbled down through the tangle of bushes, pain and guilt gnawed at his heart. He had not done enough to protect Sandy and Walker. If he had been alert enough, he would have saved them from spending too many seconds in that container filled with Arblow. Neither had he been quick enough to prevent John Croft from delivering the kick that caught him on the neck and sent him sailing down this slope.

Bastard! John Croft is a double-crossing bastard!

Will felt the wind rush out of his chest as he slammed against the ground with a sickening thud. He lay on the grass for a while, groaning and cursing in his head as he sucked wind and waited for his air to come back. From where he was lying, he could hear an engine roaring to life. That was it. Croft was driving off.

Will scrambled back to his feet, ignoring the searing pain he felt in his left thigh. He knew he could not get back up the slope in time to see the truck driving away. Angry, he slammed his fist into his palm.

Simons was dead, Walker was wounded, and now, Sandy was taken from him in this gross manner.

Are you going to just let this happen?

There was nothing he could do about it at the moment. He had not foreseen that Croft was a traitor. At least, that solved the mystery of how the masked soldiers had found them at the bunker. It was crazy to think about because he remembered clearly that Adha Long had called Croft a trusted man. Now, the man to which he had entrusted his ward's life had betrayed his trust.

Another thought dropped in Will's mind as he began to limp back up the slope. He tried to dismiss it and focus on his leg. Something must have struck him in the thigh when he was tumbling down the slope. Will tried to push the thought away, but it refused to budge.

"It's impossible," Will muttered.

Or was it? Could it be that Adha—*Sandy's* Adha, someone she had trusted—had a hand in this international conspiracy? Will thought it was unlikely, but he knew anything was indeed possible. After the shocker Croft had given him tonight, he wasn't going to be so quick to trust anybody anymore.

If a man as powerful as the great Adi Kalim was involved, he would not want anything bad to happen to Sandy anyway. Would he? He had seen how much the man cared about Sandy. It was doubtful he would approve of what John-fucking-Croft had just done. Will grit his teeth as he imagined himself grabbing Croft by the throat and squeezing—hard. He would kill that bastard the next time their paths crossed, that's for sure. More than killing Croft, Will longed to find Sandy and save her. For now, he was weak, battered, defeated; but by morning, he would have the strength to go after Croft and save Sandy.

… … …

Outskirts of Gaulvan, West Federation

Dawn found Will rolling out from under a parked car outside a cottage along the road. He had passed the night beneath the car. It was not the most comfortable of places to sleep, but Will had experienced worse. He had thought of knocking on the cottage door to plead for a chance to rest his head inside, but he had decided against that. He didn't feel he deserved the luxury of sleeping in a bed after what had happened last night. He had let his companions down. *It could have been worse,* Will thought. He, too, could have been caught in the container with Sandy and Walker, and there would be no hope of thwarting the enemy if that had happened.

Will rubbed his eyes as he pulled himself upright beside the green car. Ideas on what to do next were swirling in his head, but the one he found most useful was contacting Adha to tell him what happened to their mission. He would tell him to track Sandy using her phone. The challenge right now was to find Adha's number.

Will's attention was drawn by an older woman peeping at him from a window. He stretched his arms and started walking. The challenge of getting the great Adi Kalim's number was not so hard. All he had to do was contact his techie friends in the agency to get the number. His mind went to Fred Black, one of the brightest guys in the technology department. There was no information in the world that Fred could not dig up. All Will needed was a phone to reach Fred. If Fred was not available, Will knew two or three other guys who were just as skilful.

As Will walked down the road, he ran his hand through his hair and thought of what Sandy might be going through at the moment.

I hope she's alright.

Will was not willing to entertain the thought that Croft could have killed Sandy. Thinking about that would make him lose his mind. Instead, he forced himself to think positive and retain the hope that Sandy and even Walker would be fine. Only Simons was gone.

The day was getting brighter by the minute. Will thrust his hands in his pockets as he looked around him for a car that might be going somewhere, anywhere. He didn't care where. He just wanted someone to take him out of here. He would use the opportunity to get on a phone and call Fred or anyone else who might get him through to Adi Kalim.

Will let his hand drop to his waistband and felt his laser gun. He wished he had been quick to draw his gun when Croft had attacked him, but the raw shock of catching that whiff of Arblow dulled his reflexes. And the fear of Sandy having already climbed into the container and taking the sleep-inducing fumes into her lungs had left him unprepared for what happened next. Will had been able to detect the gas early because he and his team had once used it on a mission to hunt rebels in the southern part of the region.

Will saw a car approaching, and he began to wave it down. As the vehicle neared, Will noticed that the driver, a girl with fringy brown hair, was locking lips with another girl beside her. Obviously, the car was on auto-drive. Will stopped waving because he knew it was useless. Nobody in the car even noticed him.

For a moment, Will wondered if it would be a good idea to look for a way out of this part of Gaulvan so he could return to the capital, San Mateo, which was where he worked. Maybe he could check on his family in Hringund and see to it that they were fine. Yet, he knew he had to start tracking Croft as quickly as possible too. He wanted to know where the fellow was so he could hunt him down and save his companions. He wanted nothing more at the moment.

Another car drove down the road. It was an old, black vehicle that looked like it was manufactured two decades back. Will waved at the car, and he was pleased when the driver pulled up beside him and waved him in. The person behind the wheel was an ageing woman that somehow looked exactly like the woman he had seen earlier today when he got out from under the car where he had slept.

"Thank you," Will said, settling into the seat beside the woman.

"You're welcome," the woman said, keeping her hands on the wheel, a sign that the auto-drive feature was not activated. "Have you been standing there a long time?"

"Well, yeah," Will said, wondering why she had said that.

"Not surprised," she replied. "You look like someone who has been in a gunfight. You know those tough military guys we see on our screens in combat movies? Like Nick Ferran and Jack Pope. Yeah, you look just like one of them."

She was chuckling as she mentioned the best action movie stars of that time, so Will guessed that she had absolutely no idea how close to reality her words were.

"Excuse me, ma'am, can I use your phone for a minute? I need to make a very important call."

"You seem to have a lot of needs, young man," the woman said with a laugh that revealed a dimple on her chin. She switched her engine to auto-drive on her car's dashboard and began to rummage through her bag. "Just a second. Okay, here you go."

Will thanked the lady and quickly dialled up Fred Black's number.

"Hello?"

"Fred, this is William Burne from WFSIA," Will said quickly.

"Oh, Will. What's up? Where are you, man?"

"Somewhere in Gaulvan," Will replied. "Fred, I need you to get me someone's contact."

"Okay, sure," Fred said in a relaxed tone that gave the impression that whatever Will had to say was going to be a walk in the park.

"Can you get me Adi Kalim's number?" Will asked.

"Kalim? The Fiery Eagle?"

"Yes," Will replied. "I need it, urgently."

"That's not something you'll find in the public domain," Fred said. "But I'll get it in two minutes."

"Oh, that's great," Will said. "Thanks, man."

The line went dead as Fred ended the call. Will took a moment to hand the phone back to the woman, but she motioned to him to drop it in the small compartment between his seat and hers, probably so he would be able to monitor the message he was expecting. After that, Will leaned back in the seat and waited for Fred to get the number to him. He looked outside the window, watching the bushes lining the side of the road. There were so few structures around here. He remembered Croft had said this place was the outskirts of Gaulvan. He was sure there would be more buildings and structures in the interior of the city. He had never been in the city before, but he knew it would be similar to other cities he was familiar with in the West Federation.

Will reached out to check the time on the phone and saw that it had been over two minutes since the call with Fred. Perhaps, getting Kalim's number was proving a lot trickier than Fred had anticipated.

"Where are you headed, Ferran?" The woman beside Will said suddenly. "I'll be home pretty soon. Where should I drop you?"

Dammit, Fred. Send the number!

"Umm… Drop me when you get to your place," Will said. "I'll find my way around from there."

"Okay," the woman said while keeping her attention on the road ahead. Judging from what he had seen, the lady did not like using the auto-drive feature. Will could not comprehend why anyone would bother to go through the stress of handling the wheel when the technology was there.

Will grew more alarmed that Fred had not sent the number when the car began to slow down. He could see a small, cream-coloured house just ahead that he guessed was the woman's house. Why was Fred taking so long? He wondered what this woman's reaction would be if he told her he wanted to stick around for a while. He really needed to get Kalim's number and tell him what was going on. It was very important for him to track Sandy's phone and tell him her location.

The car rolled to a halt outside the house Will had been watching slowly creep closer since earlier, and still no message from—

Buzz!

The smartphone suddenly vibrated in the compartment where Will had dropped it. He quickly peered at the screen, hopeful it was a message from Fred and not something else. It was indeed a message from Fred. Will grabbed the phone and stared at the twelve-digit number that Fred had sent. Within the minute, he had committed it to memory. He did not forget to delete the message when he was sure he had accurately memorized it.

"Thank you very much, ma'am; you have been a blessing," Will said.

"You're welcome," the lady said.

"I'm sorry for causing further problems, but do you know where the closest hotel might be?"

"Oh, not sure, but I can check that here."

She tapped her phone screen a few times, then she turned her attention back to Will, "It's about a ten-minute walk from here. You'll go straight down the road and take the second turn to the left. You'll see the building from there. It's painted green. Really easy to locate."

"Thanks again," Will said before he alighted. The idea of going to a hotel had dropped in his mind while he was thinking of alternative plans if Fred could not get Adi Kalim's contact info in good time. If hotels in Gaulvan were like those in San Mateo, he could get a room with a phone without paying westons. Instead, he could pay through his electronic bills' wallet.

Will adjusted his soiled shirt as he began walking down the road to where the lady had directed him. The morning sun was peeking out from behind a lump of white cloud. The street was coming alive as people began to emerge from here and there. Will thought about what he had to do as he made his way towards the hotel. He would spend a few hours at the hotel to collect his thoughts and freshen up. The events of last night had shaken him up pretty badly. The shock of losing all three of his companions was still there. First, he had to calm his body with a long, hot shower; then, he would reach out to Adi Kalim and maybe eat something spicy for breakfast.

His stomach rumbled at the thought of food. He was so fucking hungry. Will moved his hand to his laser gun again. He would need that firearm to hunt down Croft. His thoughts strayed to the army of Underworld bombers making their way to North Lembria. That's who he thought they would be squaring up against in this region; he never suspected Croft would be the problem.

Be ready, John Croft. I'm coming for you.

… … …

Who Can Be Trusted in the West Federation?

Will stepped out of the shower feeling a lot better than he had felt in hours. He finally had the calm, composed feeling he had wanted to attain before placing the call to Kalim. He wanted to be able to approach the conversation with nerves that were soothed. Now, he felt ready to give Kalim the unfortunate news about his beloved ward. He knew the man would feel terrible about the situation, but the good thing was, there was a solution. All Kalim had to do was help him keep track of Sandy's location by using her phone.

Will's mind flicked to the drama that had unfolded when he got to this hotel. The receptionist had told him that they could not take him because he had no cash on him.

"But I have e-bills," Will had protested.

"I'm sorry, sir, but we only take cash here. It's westons or nothing."

"That's freaking crazy," Will snapped. "The law says you can't decline virtual bills as means of payment. Isn't that an electronic bill machine over there?"

"Yes, but—"

Another staff member interfered at that point, and after some minutes, Will was allowed to pay using e-bills. While entering the details of his account on the machine, he had mistakenly typed in Adi Kalim's number. It took the receptionist to tell him that something was wrong with his e-bill account number. Will went on to pay for a room that had a phone after rectifying his mistake.

Presently, Will eased himself onto the bed and dragged the stand next to his bed closer. He picked up the phone and punched in Kalim's number. Will heaved a sigh as he waited for him to answer.

"Hello, this is the office of the former special adviser to the Maharaj; who is on the line?" a female voice said.

"It's Will Burne," Will said. "I would like to speak with Mr Kalim."

"Will Burne? Okay. Oh, I'm sorry, Mr Burne, I just checked the schedule. Mr Kalim does not have an appointment with you."

"Hey, listen. Tell him it's about Sandy, and it's really important that we talk."

There was silence for almost a minute, and Will had to check the phone's screen to see if the call was still connected.

"Hello?" The voice Will heard this time was in no way feminine.

"Is this Mr Kalim?" Will enquired.

"Yes, what is the problem?"

"Umm, sir, our bunker was attacked last night," Will revealed. "Simons was killed, and Walker was injured. Sandy and I got away, and we took Walker with us, but Croft betrayed us. He knocked out Sandy and Walker with gas, and he took them with him. I don't know what he plans to do with them, but I know he doesn't mean well."

"What the hell! Where were you when all that was happening?" Kalim roared.

Will suddenly felt relieved that this was a phone conversation. He did not want to imagine standing before Kalim, telling him that Croft had abducted his lovely ward.

"I tried to stop him, but it all happened so fast, and I did not expect what happened because you had already vouched for his loyalty."

"Shut up!" Kalim roared. "You are fucking incompetent."

"The situation can be rectified, sir," Will said, ignoring the insult. He guessed he deserved the tongue lashing from Kalim. He, too, knew he should have done better to stop Croft. "If you can give me Sandy's location by tracking her phone, I promise to get her back."

"I'm not going to trust you with my daughter again," Kalim said. "I am going to do the tracking and send men I *know* I can trust over there to get her out. So don't you go an inch near her, ever again!"

"With all due respect, sir, it was one of your trusted men that caused this problem," Will said. "At least, you know which side I'm on. Can you say the same for the men you are sending?"

"Get off my phone, you incompetent piece of shit!"

Will remained still as the phone went dead. Adi Kalim would not send him Sandy's location. As much as he understood the man was angry with him for letting Sandy slip away, Will thought it made sense that Kalim would trust him to right this wrong. He was in the best position to save Sandy because he was in Gaulvan, where he believed Sandy was being kept. He didn't think Croft would have taken her out of the city; she had to be here somewhere. How long would it take Kalim to get men down to the West Federation? Or did he plan to use his loyal men who were already in this region? After what John Croft had just done, how could Kalim bear to entrust Sandy's life into the hands of these "trusted" men?

Will buried his face in his palm for a moment; then, he began to type a message. Dozens of thoughts swarmed his head as he continuously tapped the screen of the phone. He could not allow Sandy to just be at Croft's mercy until Kalim's men came around. No, he had to do something.

Every minute that we spend waiting counts. Send me the location, sir. I promise to get her back in one piece.

That was the message Will typed up, and after he had read it twice, he sent it to Kalim. He was not sure if that would convince the man, but he just had to try. A knock on the door of his room drove his attention from thoughts of Sandy and her guardian.

"Who's there?"

"Your clothes are ready, sir."

"Drop the pack right there; I'll pick it up," Will said.

Will waited a moment before he opened his hotel door and grabbed the pack that held his washed and ironed clothes. Now, he would grab a bite to calm his growling belly while waiting for Kalim to respond. He really hoped the man would send him the details he needed. He could not bear the thought of Sandy being held captive by that treacherous bastard, John Croft.

Will was putting on his shirt when he heard the message notification from the phone on the stand. He rushed over to see what it was. It was a message from Kalim, and it was not the dignified response befitting of someone of his class.

Fuck off, Agent Burne.

What a response. It was clear how painful Sandy's abduction was to him, but was this necessary? It did not have to be this way. Will brightened as another idea formed in his head. He tapped on the phone's screen a few times and held it to his left ear.

"Hello, Fred. I'm sorry to bother you, but I need your help again."

……………

The first thing Sandy noticed when she opened her eyes was she was hanging upside down. She knew that feeling of having her long white hair flowing in the wrong direction, having the floor appear like the top, of having her body in a state that resembled floating in the air. She had been in a similar position before as part of her 40 Grade training.

The bright natural rays of light that flowed into the room through the open window revealed it was morning. Sandy blinked twice as she tried to clear the fogginess in her head. She had no idea why she was in this tiny room, hanging from the damned ceiling. The last thing she remembered was getting in the container with Walker and Will…

The memories of the night before rushed into her head at that point. She remembered the arrival at the bunker, the address by Adha, the steamy bout of passion she had with Will, and then—the explosion.

"Walker?" Sandy called softly. She remembered now that he had been wounded yesterday and had been with her in the container. What about Will? She was unsure what had happened, but she remembered he had not gotten in with her. Instead, he was telling her to get off the truck before she blacked out. Where was Will? Where was Walker? She remembered that Will had yelled at one point that something was a trap. Did that mean Croft was responsible for what happened at the bunker? Or was it someone else? So many thoughts bouncing around in her head, coupled with her body's unnatural position, led her to develop a headache.

What the hell is going on?

Sandy had no idea how to get herself out of her situation because she had yet to understand the circumstances. She turned her head left and right, hoping to see somebody around. To her left, Walker was hanging the same way she was. His eyes were closed, and Sandy thought he looked unnaturally still.

"Walker!" Sandy called again, a lot louder this time. She received no response to her call.

Just then, the sound of a door opening filtered into Sandy's ears. She turned her neck but was unable to see who had opened the door. She could hear the pounding of boots against the floor.

"I told you she'd be awake," a voice announced from behind Sandy.

Knowing she couldn't see who was talking at the moment, she kept her eyes fixed straight ahead of her. Her heart was beating fast as she tried hard not to panic. Before she could think any more about who might be behind her, someone appeared before her. It was Croft. He had a dark smile on his face, and a cigar hung on his lips.

"Hello, Sandy," he said, with his smile growing wider.

"Croft, what's going on here?"

"Is it not clear enough? You are hanging from the ceiling, soon to be deployed for a bombing mission. Your teammate, Walker, did not survive his injuries. He's dead."

Sandy felt a stab of pain in her heart. They had lost both Simons and Walker to this mission. All of that, because of this bastard, Croft.

"Where's Burne?" Sandy asked.

"I knew you were going to ask. I saw that you two had something serious going for you. Unfortunately for you, he's probably dead, too, from a broken neck. I don't think he survived the height he fell from," Croft said with a shrug.

"Adha will skin you alive when he finds you!" Sandy growled. The thought of Will being dead in a hole somewhere clogged her heart with pain, making it difficult for her to speak, as much as she wanted to.

"Don't worry about me," Croft said with a nasty smile. "You should worry about getting caught as you lead the bombing squad from North Lembria to the various sites of action. That's what I want to use you for."

"I will never be a party to terrorism!"

"It's not your choice, my dear Sandy," Croft said as he dug his hand in his pocket and brought out a vial. As he began to wave it in her face, she could see that it contained light blue liquid. "It's not your choice at all."

It all felt like a rotten nightmare, like a scene from a horror movie. Sandy did her best to remain calm, but it was hard not to give in to fear when you didn't know what to expect.

"I have a little surprise for you," said Croft. He beckoned to someone behind Sandy.

A masked man soon entered Sandy's line of sight. He stood beside Croft and awaited further instruction.

"Remove your mask," Croft ordered.

The masked fellow bent his head and pulled his mask off. Sandy found herself staring into a face she had never expected to see again… Simons.

… … …

Gaulvan, West Federation

Fred had delivered again. Will had sought his help to get Sandy's location, and the techie had just called him back with the exact whereabouts of his snowy-haired friend and colleague. Now, Will was getting ready to go after John Croft and get his friends back. Fred had confirmed that Croft was no longer on the move. He had parked his truck outside a big warehouse, somewhere on the outskirts of Gaulvan, and had remained inside for hours. Croft was less than two hours' drive from where Will was.

Will cracked his knuckles as he thought of getting his hands on Croft. He was going to shoot him in the balls, smash his face, do all sorts of things to make that bastard cry out in pain. He wondered if Kalim's new set of trusted men had yet arrived in the West Federation. It was indeed possible that Kalim already had men on the ground in this continent, and he would deploy them with a simple phone call. Will was determined not to bother enquiring if there were going to be a rescue party or not; all he knew was that he had to get Sandy and Walker out of the vile grasp of Croft.

The thought of Croft hurting Sandy or even killing her filtered into Will's head, but he quickly pushed it off. He had to remain positive. Sandy could not die. If there were anyone on this mission that was indispensable, it was her. No, Adi Kalim would destroy anyone who dared to even think of killing Sandy. And he, Will Burne, would not let anyone get away with hurting or killing Sandy. But he must not let that happen!

Will ran a hand over the muzzle of his laser gun as he thought of a plan to get Sandy from Croft. He wondered if he should involve the West Federation police for a seamless rescue operation, but he feared for the stooges among them, men who had the enemy's interest at heart. He could not bear to entrust Sandy's life to the cops. He would have to do this alone. Or…

His mind drifted to Agent Blackwell, one of his trusted colleagues. Maybe it would not be such a bad idea to reach out to Blackwell and try to get him to execute the mission with him. A quick calculation told him it would take quite some time for Blackwell to get down there from San Mateo to help rescue Sandy. There was no time for delay. He would have to go after Croft alone and get Sandy back immediately. Waiting was not an option. He could only relax after he had gotten

Sandy back, safe and sound, from the bastard who had snatched her away from him. Will knew that his mind would not be settled, even if Kalim's men got to her first.

Will slipped his laser gun under his waistband and started towards the door. He removed the key from the door and headed towards the reception desk. He felt ready to take on whatever accomplices Croft had with him.

"I'm checking out," Will said as he dropped his key on the counter. The lady on duty was not the same one who had tried to deny him a room.

The receptionist thanked Will and implored him to use the hotel again whenever he was in that part of the city. Will jerked his head in a nod as he walked towards the front door. He was bursting with combative energy, the same that had helped him prevail as a soldier in previous battles. He could not wait to get to the part of Gaulvan where Fred had told him Croft was.

Will stepped out the front glass door of the hotel and headed to the taxi service that ran beside the hotel. He got a taxi and headed to where Croft was. He took his seat and drummed his fingers on his thigh as the driver gunned the taxi. A part of him still debated whether it would have been better to have contacted the cops or have some sort of backup. Did he know what lay in stock for him at the warehouse? Maybe the place was bursting with enemy soldiers, and going there would be like walking into a damned death trap.

"There's no fucking going back now," Will muttered.

"Did you say something now?" the driver asked.

"Not to you," Will told him as he rubbed his palms together. He needed to push aside every thought of a plan B. Instead, he should be directing all his thoughts towards getting to that warehouse, finding his way in, and getting Sandy out of there.

Will leaned against the headrest as he leaned back into his seat. From the blinking digital timepiece on the car's dashboard, he could see they were still well over an hour from the warehouse where Sandy was.

What if she has been transported away from there before my arrival?

Will looked outside the car window and saw buildings flashing by. He would get to the warehouse first and do his best to get Sandy out of there. If she's moved before he gets there, he will continue to track her with Fred's help. The important thing was to get her out of Croft's hold as quickly as possible. It was quite unfortunate that none of them had suspected Croft of being capable of pulling off something as sinister as this. There had been no reason to suspect him, as Adi Kalim himself recommended him.

Will mentally ran through all the enemies he had to tackle: from John Croft to the bombers in North Lembria who planned to set certain cities in this continent ablaze; to Dr Kean; to the principal enemies; to the likes of George Lay and President Morgan of Oceania Liberation. There were so many adversaries to fight, and priorities were shifting with the passing of events. For now, Will just hoped he could get Sandy back, and then together, they would agree on the next course of action. He would understand if she was not able to continue in this fight against their powerful enemies. He would ensure that he stopped the bombers from destroying his home continent.

Will let his eyes stray to the timer on the dashboard and saw that they were now forty-five minutes away from the warehouse. He heaved a deep sigh, steeling himself for the tough task ahead. Whatever happens, he must save his friends. He must save Sandy.

… … …

Sandy's legs could not bear her weight when she tried to get back on her feet. Croft had pressed a lever, releasing the rope binding her legs that held her upside down. She remained on the floor, blinking hard and trying to clear her foggy head. Seeing Croft and Simons standing side by side close to where two masked guards stood at alert threatened to drive Sandy out of her mind. Simons wasn't dead? What was that bloody head they had seen in the bunker? Apparently, it was nothing but a ruse.

After a few moments of feeling the strength returning to her lower limbs, she began to rise again, and this time, she was successful. She got to her feet, trying to keep her legs steady. She saw Croft smiling as she steadied herself. Her hand went to where she always kept her firearm, and she realized she had no weapon on her.

"You didn't expect me to leave weapons on you?" Croft crooned, still smiling. "Don't waste your energy trying to fight me. Keep it for the greater challenges ahead."

Sandy felt like running forward and smashing her fist into his face, but she was too weak to carry out what she so much desired to do. It was hard for her to imagine that just hours ago, she and Will had thought of John Croft as their ticket to freedom from their enemies. But, unbeknownst to them, he was the source of the problem.

"Why did you do this?" Sandy asked, her question directed towards Croft. She remembered he had spoken of Walker succumbing to his injuries. It felt crazy that Walker, who had been fighting beside her just last night, was now dead, and Simons, who she had thought was dead, was now staring at her.

"I was loyal to Kalim for many years," Croft said, walking towards Sandy. "I was one of the men he could stake his life on. But you must know, Sandy, that a man's loyalty has its limits. There are many others like me who have seen the light of the unification attempts and have realized that the people behind these plans are unstoppable. You can't stand against them. So your best bet is to go with the flow, to join them."

Sandy shook her head as if trying to prevent Croft's words from taking root in her mind. She had guessed that the enemy's reach ran deep but hearing it from someone who was a part of that system made the whole picture even scarier. The knowledge that everything she and Will had done so far had done nothing to reduce the influence of their enemies left her feeling sad. Their efforts had not been good enough.

"Their plans are not in the best interest of the people, and you know it," Sandy said.

"People's interest?" Croft laughed. "When has that ever mattered? I am surprised by how naïve your worldview is about this whole thing. The masses will always have it bad. That is just reality…"

As Croft continued to speak, Sandy's mind drifted to what Croft had said earlier when he first came into the room. He told her *she* would lead the bombing team into North Lembria, and he insisted that she would not have a choice. How on earth does he intend to make her do what she would otherwise never engage in? Maybe by threatening her life or by injecting her with a chemical agent that would suppress her will?

"We are giving you the opportunity to join us, now," Croft said. "So many influential people in all different walks of life are unified with us. We are growing in strength every day, and we will continue to keep getting more people on our side."

The way Croft talked, it felt like something deeper was going on, something far more extensive than what she and Will even considered they were fighting against. Thinking about Will gave her a sinking feeling in her chest. It hurt her beyond measure to imagine he was gone, destroyed by the evil conspiracies of the enemy, consumed by forces that he had not even fully grasped.

"What am I supposed to do with you guys?" Sandy asked. She would feign interest and see if it would help her to regain her freedom. She wanted to get out of here and discover the whereabouts of Will—if he were still alive. He *had* to be alive. She was unwilling to accept that Will's body was lying dead in a ditch somewhere on this continent. *No!*

"It's simple," Croft crooned in his slimy voice as he stood before her. "You are going to help us weaken the power of the central government in your region with a series of missions that will be given to you. First, however, you need to join the team of bombers before we're convinced of your willingness to join. Remember, you can't afford to mess with us. You will be killed if you do *anything* contrary to what we expect of you."

Sandy nodded despite the threat and bile rising in her throat. The thought of helping these bastards made her feel sick at her stomach. All she needed was for these guys to give her half a chance of escape, and she would snatch it before they knew what was happening. She wondered what Adha must be thinking now that he had not heard from her team for the past few hours. She knew how restless her guardian could be whenever he was worried about her.

"Alright, I'm ready to join the winning team," Sandy nodded to Croft.

"You will get a wash first," he replied. "Then we will give you something to eat."

Were these guys really so brainless to think she would dump all her values as an Afrasian to join them? She knew that she could not blame them. There were other Afrasians who had consented to become a part of this dark movement.

Sandy's train of thought was interrupted by the sudden emergence of another armed man at the door. He was masked, just like the three others in the room alongside Croft and Simons, as well as those that had attacked Sandy and her colleagues back in the underground bunker. The moment he opened the door, Sandy began to hear the sound of rapid gunfire from outside. Her brows went up as a testament to her shock. *What was going on outside?* The moment he closed the door behind him, the gunshots could no longer be heard. It was clear at once to Sandy that the room was soundproof.

"What are you doing in here?" Croft demanded hotly. "And what the hell is all that noise outside?"

"There's a fellow outside," the masked soldier replied. "He's taking down our men with a laser gun. He's quick and sneaky. We haven't been able to hit him and believe me, we've tried!"

"Have you got an ID on his face?" Croft asked, quickly walking away from Sandy.

"Not yet, sir," the soldier replied. "He's too fast. He ducks before we can get a clear shot of his face. Should we call the base for help? They could send in reinforcements within five minutes, and he might be one of many."

"We'll handle him or them, whichever be the case," Croft replied with confidence, then he turned to the masked guards in the room. "Tie her up and watch her. I will be back soon."

Sandy heaved a sigh as she watched Croft race out of the room, with Simons following him. Sandy swelled with hope. She had a feeling it was Will who had come to save her. He certainly fits the bill of someone who could be very quick on the draw and causing the enemy all sorts of problems. But Croft had told her that Will was dead. Could it be someone else on the rescue mission? She knew Adha could also track her if he wanted, and after not hearing from her for a while, he would be concerned. Sandy was not sure whether to be excited or sad. Even if it were Will, she was not sure he would be able to get her out of here alive with the guards inside here with her, and those she presumed to be standing outside.

"Up with your hands!" one of the guards barked, waving his rifle as he moved closer to her. He planned to tie her up as Croft had instructed. "Turn your back. If you make any funny moves, I will gun you down."

Sandy raised her hands above her head and turned as the guard had ordered. Hundreds of thoughts were swarming in her head. This was a fairly good chance for her to put her escape from this place in her own hands. She had been trained to get out of dangerous situations on her own. Waiting for help was not the kind of thing someone trained in the 40 Grades would do. Sandy decided to swing into action.

When she heard the sound of the guard's boot on the floor within striking distance, she knew he was ready to tie her up with the rope, after which he would press the lever that would make her hang upside down again. Sandy was not going to let that happen without a fight. Suddenly, she swung her leg upward, delivering a front kick to the guard's chest, making him fall backwards and crash to the ground.

She quickly rushed at the fallen guard, hoping to grab his gun, but two shots from the other guards prompted her to freeze in place. In the split-second that Sandy held back, the fallen guard scrambled to his feet, still holding to his gun. Sandy gritted her teeth in frustration as she glowered at the three guards in the room, all with their muzzles levelled at her.

"I told you not to try anything stupid, didn't I?" the guard she had kicked, growled.

Sandy knew he could not shoot her. He didn't have the authority. It seemed Croft and his people had big plans for her.

"Can't remember that," Sandy replied defiantly.

"You think I can't kill you; right now!?" the guard roared.

If he could, he would have done it already, Sandy thought, a smug smile spreading on her face.

"Take it easy, Mitch," one of the other guards appealed to him. "Just tie her up and let the bosses deal with her when they come back."

Sandy glared at Mitch, the guard. She kicked herself for not being able to get his gun. Without a doubt, she would have gunned down the other two and found a way to escape. Now, that hope was dashed already. She had to watch for another chance to strike and attempt to make good use of it. She would ensure she did not fail again. But, for now, she would just allow the guard to tie her up. Or… should she try another tactic?

… … …

Getting Back on Track: Gaulvan, West Federation

Will aimed at yet another of the masked soldiers guarding the warehouse, and his shot forced the criminal to withdraw into his hiding spot. He was in a shed adjacent to the warehouse. Fred had given him this specific location as one of the good positions to take cover while attacking the den of enemies. Will had done a good job of killing some of the warehouse's defenders and ensuring that the others were not able to engage him in open fire, yet his mind was not at ease. He did not know if Sandy was alive or not. This whole gun battle would count for nothing if it turned out she was already dead.

"No way," Will muttered. He did not want to think of that. He would concentrate on holding his position for now while keeping the men at the warehouse pegged back.

He knew that they must be planning to take a back route to attack him or possibly sneaking Sandy out of the warehouse to a secure location. He had planned for that already. It was only a matter of minutes before he would leave this spot and take a more direct approach. This could have been easier for him if he had backup, but he could not trust anyone at the moment. Only himself and Sandy—and maybe Walker—could he genuinely trust. It was a shame that Simons had been killed. Maybe he would be standing side by side with Will, now, as they battled to win this gunfight.

Will suddenly realized no gunshots were coming from the opposite side anymore. Had these guys already taken the initiative to come towards his hideout? He slowly lifted his head to check the situation around him and saw no movement at all from his adversaries. None of them was in sight, anywhere around the warehouse. There was an eerie silence surrounding the whole place.

"Huh. What's going on?" Will mumbled as he kept his grip on his laser gun. He remained on high alert; he did not want to be taken by surprise. A few more minutes of silence convinced Will that the masked soldiers he had been shooting at had withdrawn from the gunfight. He had no idea what they wanted to do, and it left him agitated.

He remained in his hideout for a while, trying to detect if this was a plan to draw him out to a more open spot and shoot him down. He only hoped they were not using the back door to take Sandy out of the warehouse.

"Damn it!" Will whispered. "I need to move, do something!"

He was about to slip out of his hideout to take the direct approach he had previously planned when he heard the door of the warehouse swing open.

"Burne!" A familiar voice called from outside the warehouse.

Will slowly lifted his head and saw it was Croft, holding a pistol against the temple of a man with splatters of blood on his face and black jacket. Will blinked twice, questioning his sanity, as he stared at the face of the man whose head Croft's gun was strategically placed against. It was Simons.

What the hell was going on here?

Simons was dead, Will was certain of it. They all had seen his head spiked to the wall in that bunker.

"Come out now, Will Burne, or I will kill him—for real," Croft said.

Still in his hiding place, Will tried to piece together what he had just seen with prior events, and it still did not make sense. Whose severed head was left dripping with blood while they were still in the bunker? How had these guys been able to snatch Simons away from the bunker with the others completely unaware? Will was glad on the one hand that Simons was still alive, but on the other hand, he was confused by this entire thing. There was a chance that—

"Burne!" Croft yelled. "Come out, now, or I will gun him down right here before your eyes!"

Will weighed his options as he watched the fear in Simons' eyes; he could go out and try to prevent Croft from killing Simons or stay here and try an alternative idea, maybe take a shot at Croft or something. The problem with stepping out of his hiding spot was that he and Simons would both be in danger. On the other hand, staying in the hiding spot would keep Will from any risk of capture.

Without further thought, Will had made his decision. He exhaled through his mouth and scrambled out of the hiding place. He held his laser gun tighter as he walked towards Croft, who was still holding his gun to Simons' head.

"Drop the damned gun, Burne," Croft said. "I will shoot him if you don't do as I say."

"What's all this about?" Will asked. His anger stirred as he got close to Croft, the man whose betrayal had made Will suffer physically and emotionally over the past few hours.

"Drop your gun, and maybe we'll talk," Croft said.

Will did not want to talk. Instead, he wanted to make Croft pay for his treachery. He bent forward a little as if he were going to drop his laser gun on the ground, but in a blink, he changed his stance and fired a shot at his hated adversary. Will had targeted Croft's right eye, but his shot struck Croft on the neck, sending another splatter of blood to Simons' face.

What followed was as bizarre as the earlier events that had left Will scratching his head in confusion. Simons let out a roar as soon as he saw that Will had shot Croft, the man who had just held a gun to his head. Instantly, he drew a rifle tucked under his jacket and aimed it at Will. Two other masked guys rushed out and stood beside Simons, raising their guns as they did so.

Will leapt out of the line of fire just before the first shot rang out. Pain jolted through his ribcage as he landed violently on the ground. He rolled across the lot, taking cover behind a parked car.

Simons shot at me? What the hell? Is this a fucking dream?

The stark reality of the situation set into Will's mind as a shot from one of the other guys smashed the glass windscreen of the car he was hiding behind. He fired two shots in response and was glad when one caught a masked guard on the other side.

One down. Two to go.

There was an exchange of fire on both sides for a few minutes before Simons rushed towards the warehouse entrance, leaving the masked guard to continue the gunfight. It was easy for Will to shoot down his last adversary. Now that the last guard was down, Will started towards the warehouse. He was bent on catching Simons; preferably, he wanted to catch him alive. Will wanted to understand the whole drama that had played out.

Will got to the entrance of the warehouse and pushed the door open carefully. He drew back quickly the moment after he opened the door, anticipating a surprise attack from Simons or one of the other men defending the place, but nothing happened. He waited a few seconds before he determined that the coast was clear for him to progress.

He crossed the threshold and saw the warehouse interior was divided into a passageway, with rows of doors on both sides in which some of the doors hung open. Just as he was wondering which door to open first, two quick shots rang out from further down the passageway. Will gripped his laser gun tighter as he heard the sound of those gunshots. His heart sank as he considered the possibility that it might be Sandy who had just been shot.

Throwing caution to the wind, Will raced towards one of the open doors further down, which he guessed the shots had been fired from. His heartbeat quickened as the fear of the worst-case scenario lodged in his head. He could not bear to lose Sandy, but as things stood, he might have just allowed her to slip away from him forever.

Will bit the inner part of his cheek—hard, drawing blood—as he ran towards the door, a mixture of emotions coursing through him. There was hope, fear, and sadness warring within him, all jostling for space in his heart. Finally, Will got to the door and swung his body frame into it. His peripheral vision caught someone holding a gun, and he quickly reacted by raising his firearm in a like manner.

After blinking a couple of times, Will saw clearly who was holding the gun: Sandy. She was in the same outfit that she'd had on when they were forcefully separated yesterday. With a quick glance, Will saw that she had shot down three guards, all of them in the head. There was no sign of Simons.

Both Will and Sandy lowered their guns and ran to embrace each other; Will was so relieved to finally see Sandy was alright.

"I almost shot you. I thought it was Croft," Sandy said as she held him in a tight embrace, with her head resting on his chest.

"Croft is dead," Will told her. "Did you see Simons?"

"No, he didn't return after he left here with Croft."

Will kissed Sandy on the forehead and ran his hand through her snow-white hair. Thoughts of her being dead had plagued him since Croft snatched her away from him. Now, he was thrilled to have her back.

"How did you free yourself?" Will asked when they broke the hug.

"Long story, I'll tell you later," Sandy asked. "Do you think Simons is hiding somewhere, waiting for us to come out?"

"I'd better not see him anywhere because I would be tempted to blow his brains out," Will said.

They had a lot of things to handle: searching for and questioning Simons; reaching out to Adi Kalim; going after the bombers at North Lembria; and a whole host of other things. But for now, Will preferred to spend this moment with Sandy and be happy about their reunion.

… … …

En Route: North Lembria, West Federation

The bus dashed along the road, taking Sandy and Will closer to North Lembria with every passing minute. Sandy sat in the seat next to Will, watching the romance movie flickering across the screen on the bus with half interest. She noticed Will was staring out through the window, keeping his eyes on the structures that flashed by as the bus moved northward. She knew how much he liked to sit by windows so he could observe the surroundings.

Sandy heaved a sigh as she thought of her experience in the warehouse. She was grateful Will had come for her. It had distracted the enemies and allowed her to use her military intelligence to outsmart the guards at the second attempt. She had promised herself not to fail if she got a second chance to escape, and she had not failed. The moment she came face to face with Will remained etched in her memory. She could not forget the initial desire to shoot, thinking it was Croft who had returned. Then she saw it was Will and couldn't resist the urge to launch herself into his arms.

They had spent quite some time holding on to each other before they made any attempt to find out where Simons had gone. They were not able to find any clues to where he had headed. Will had been disappointed with the way things turned out. They still couldn't crack any details of the real motive behind these people who wanted to unify the regions. Maybe Croft would have been the ideal person to tell them everything they wanted to know, but Will had killed him during the exchange of gunfire. Now, they were limited to the previous information they had.

Sandy chuckled as she remembered how long it had taken her and Will to agree on what they should do next.

"You should probably head back to Afrasia," Will had whispered to her as they sat in a taxi from the warehouse. Sandy was unsure where they were going, but she was sure Will had a place in mind already. "I have a friend who can work up the right papers to get you out of here."

"No," Sandy had countered. "We still have a lot of things to do. Simons is at large; there are still bandits at North Lembria to deal with and every plan of President Morgan and George Lay that we want to destroy."

"This fight is proving beyond us," Will had said, leaning close so the driver would not pick up what he was saying. "You should go back to your life before all this began, and I will attempt to do the same after I have done my bit to stop the bombing these people are planning to carry out."

"I can help with that too. Don't you need me?"

"I don't want you to get hurt," he had replied. "The whole events of the night made me realize that my soul would be scarred forever if something happened to you on this mission. This is my fight now. Let me fight it without bothering about your safety."

Sandy had seen that he genuinely cared about her, that he really wanted her to be safe, but would she have come this far in her career as a special agent if she was someone who played it safe, someone who shied away from where the fight was? No. Maybe she would see the situation differently if Will were no longer fighting against the mechanisms laid down by those who wanted to destroy global peace, but since he was still involved in the fight, she would stick around too and help him fight the battle.

"I want to stay," Sandy had simply said. Will had stared at her long and hard, as if looking at her in this manner would make her change her decision.

After a moment, Will had jerked his head in a nod and said that there was no problem if she wanted to stay.

"We stand a good chance of succeeding if we work together," Will had conceded. "I just want you out of danger's way."

"I was trained to seek danger," Sandy had replied with a smile. She was hungry and tired from the tough physical conditions she had been subjected to from the previous day until that moment, but her spirit was unbroken. She was as willing to fight as the first time Dr Kean had given them the contract to the Underworld.

"Has Adha given you information on where the bombers are?" Sandy had asked. "He said he was going to communicate that to us before those bastards attacked us."

"He hasn't given any info, but with a call or two to some tech guys I know, and with a bit of luck, we would be able to track the prospective bombers."

Will had stopped their taxi outside a hotel, and he told her that was where he had passed the previous night. No sooner had they got to their room, Will grabbed the room's phone and dialled Adha's number, but the call went unanswered. So he tried again, but there was no response still.

"He probably thinks I'm still trying to get your location from him," Will had said.

"Then he should just answer the call and tell you."

"No, he thinks I am incompetent. He feels I shouldn't have let Croft take you away in the first place," Will had informed her, then he went on to tell Sandy about how he had pleaded with Adha regarding her location—to no avail.

"Was this the same room you took the first time?" Sandy had asked.

"No."

"Then I believe the phone number should be different."

"Oh yeah, you're right," Will had said. "Maybe there is something he is busy with. I will send a text telling him that you are alright now."

Presently, Sandy was still staring at the screen showing the romantic movie. She did not know how far away they were from North Lembria, but she knew that they had come quite a long distance. She was in much better condition now. She had showered at the hotel, washing off the grime and blood that had lodged on her skin in the course of the crazy events of the past several hours. She had also eaten a plate of Nutri-carbs, which Will had suggested to her because she was not familiar with any of the foods on offer by the hotel. The food had restored her energy and left her feeling ready to take on the whole world.

Sandy's mind flicked to how they were going to stop the bombers at North Lembria. After working out some details with him, the tech person Will called while in the hotel had given a location after a few minutes. Now, they knew where to go in the city, but they weren't sure how exactly to approach the situation. It was possible that they would limit their activities to spying on the bombers and reporting the situation anonymously to the cops. She wondered how effective the West Federation police force was anyway. It surprised her that no police had shown up during that gun battle at the warehouse. She was certain if that kind of shooting had taken place in Afrasia, the whole place would be besieged by police officers. It appeared security was not so tight in the West Federation, definitely not at the level of her home continent.

She had hoped to speak with Adha when they had access to the phone, but their calls were not answered. Not even after Will had sent a text that Sandy was fine. She hoped nothing serious was wrong at her guardian's place.

May Lay. The name suddenly rang in Sandy's head as the bus moved northwards. It had been so long since Sandy had heard from the woman, and she was curious to know if the lady was alright. *She should be,* Sandy reasoned. May would be safe with Adha.

"We are almost there," Will said to her suddenly. "We will get off soon."

Sandy responded with a simple nod. She knew it was time to forget about other things and focus on the task at hand: to attack the group of bombers waiting for shipments of explosives coming through West Federation's borderlines. With their plans to wreak havoc on major cities on the continent, the safety of millions was at stake. They had to execute this mission perfectly, or there would be fiery consequences.

… … …

There was nobody at the location Fred Black had given them. Will and Sandy eventually settled on a plan of attack against the bombers. They also planned to take one of the fellows alive to drill for more information on how things were in the enemy's camp. Now, as Will peered into the last room of the cottage Fred had directed them to and saw that it was also empty, he realized they were not yet where they needed to be. They had more tracking to do.

"I kind of guessed this was going to happen," Sandy said as she placed a hand against her face in a gesture of exasperation. "Remember, Adha said these guys move around constantly."

"Yeah, that's right," Will replied as he closed the door of the last room.

"How did he even come up with this location in the first place?" Sandy said. "How did he know they were here?"

"You think maybe Fred was wrong? Well, I doubt that. And, I don't know about the technology involved or how he does his tracking," Will said, "but I know Fred is a genius with things like this. They must have moved, as you said."

It was even more disappointing that there was nothing of note left behind that could indicate the next destination of the bombers. When they had seen there was nothing else to do in the cottage, Will led the way out the front door.

"Simons," Sandy said suddenly.

"What about him?"

"He could have warned them we were coming," Sandy said.

"Maybe, maybe not," Will said. "He doesn't know we can find our way down here. Remember, we didn't have any info on the location of the bombers while we were still in the bunker; Kalim promised to send that to us."

"He could have realized we would easily get that from Adha afterwards," Sandy said.

"Yeah, you're probably right," Will conceded.

Dusk is already upon us, Will thought as he stared into the sky. They had not succeeded in getting what they wanted, and it was painful. He needed to get back in touch with Fred. He needed a phone.

"We need to find a store that sells phones," Will said. "I need to communicate constantly with Fred. And, we need a sense of direction."

"That's true," Sandy replied. "What about a place to pass the night?"

"That too," Will said. He had thought about that already. There wasn't much they could do for the rest of the day. They would just find some lodging and make the next move based on the recommendation from Fred. If it were possible, they would also try to reach Adi Kalim again. Will hoped everything was fine at Kalim's place. He hoped May was safe too. After all she had been through, Will did not want her to fall into the hands of the enemy, or worse.

Will asked a male passerby where they could find a store that sold mobile devices. The man could barely keep his eyes off Sandy in the short time of his conversation with Will.

"Walk down that path and take a taxi to Light Gate," the man said, keeping a sideways gaze on Sandy. "It will only cost a few westons."

"Thank you," Will said.

"Damn, she's a beauty," the man muttered as he took one last look at Sandy before slowly walking away.

In a way, it reminded Will of when he arrived in Afrasia to meet Dr Kean, and he had met that little child who stared at him and called him a Westie. Will and Sandy turned and headed down the path the man had pointed out to them. Will did not have any westons on him to pay for the taxi fare, but he knew his e-bills could be used to pay, too.

"Do you think it is such a bad thing that some people are trying to bring the regions together?" Sandy asked suddenly, taking Will by surprise.

"I think it is not about the act itself," Will said after a moment of deliberation. "It is the motive behind the action. George Lay, Morgan and these high-ranking people are cooking up something sinister. They must never be trusted."

"I agree," Sandy said.

"I am not concerned about the politics of it; I have no care which region aligns with the other or which one stays aloof," Will continued. "My problem is entrusting the lives of millions to a man who sees nothing wrong in using his wife in a game of international politics. As for Morgan, his evils are well documented."

By now, they had arrived at the road where they would find the store they sought. It didn't take long before they found a taxi heading towards Light Gate.

"You take e-bills, right?"

"Certainly," the driver replied.

Will had to ask because he had almost been turned away at the hotel in Gaulvan for not having westons to pay. He opened the door for Sandy to enter before he slipped in beside her. The taxi soon began to move down the road. Will could not wait to get his hands on a phone. It would allow him to get vital info from Fred and do a whole host of other things. He wondered if Kalim had seen the message he sent regarding Sandy. It would not be good if the man kept worrying about Sandy when other things needed attention now.

He turned to look at Sandy as she rubbed her fingers together. It was hard to guess what was going on in her mind at that moment. Will remembered the words of the man who had directed them, and a smile tugged at his lips. Sandy was indeed a beauty. Will felt a stirring in his loins as he stared at her ebony face, framed by flowing white hair. He could not wait to get to their destination.

Sandy felt the sexual tension building between them as the evening wore on. She thought of how they held hands in the store when they bought the phone. Will had settled on two sleek devices, one for each of them, and he had paid with his e-bills wallet.

While still at the store, they immediately searched for a place to pass the night and soon found one nearby. Will paid for the room and made enquiries for dinner as well. Now, as they headed into the room, Sandy observed the interior. It was bigger than the one in which they had lodged at Gaulvan. Up above them was a chandelier, which shone blue light. On the wall directly opposite the king-sized bed was a widescreen television.

Sandy was taking off her boots just then. Her feet had been caged in those boots for hours until she removed them at that hotel in Gaulvan where she had freshened up. She started thinking about the attack at the bunker the previous evening and everything that had happened since then. She knew there was more to come, though. They had yet to lay their hands on the bombers on a mission to set the West Federation cities on fire. They needed to get a hold of someone on the enemy's side to get more details, to understand how powerful the forces standing against them were.

It was a little bit unsatisfactory for her, the way John Croft had died so easily in the shootout outside the warehouse. She wanted to make him suffer, to make him spill his guts, to make him pay for drugging her with Arblow and tying her upside down. She hoped things would be a little different with Dr Kean. She hoped she would get to make him pay for involving her in all of this.

Sandy cast a glance in Will's direction and saw he was busy setting up their phones. It was clear he wanted to get through to Fred as quickly as possible. She, too, had to get in touch with Adha. She wanted to convince him that she was fine and find out his situation.

She got up from the bed and went to stand before the mirror in the corner of the room. She stared at her reflection and stifled a smile. Her face had not changed much since she took her first 40 Grade challenge with Amisha. She still remembered how she had been dominated that day. Thinking about that day made Sandy's mind fly to the last time she and Will were together. That was at the bunker…

"What are you thinking about?"

Sandy had been so lost in her erotic thinking she didn't notice when Will came up behind her. Only when he whispered against her neck did she feel his presence. In the seconds that followed, she felt something else from him. She could feel the stiffness of his shaft pressed against the underside of her bottom as he hugged her from behind.

Sandy was about to open her mouth to give a reply, but she decided against it. She knew what she wanted, and it was not a conversation. She wanted to wrap her arms around Will and feel his chest against hers. She wanted to feel his penis throbbing, not against her ass, but against the walls of her vagina as he slowly thrust into her.

"That's pretty wild," Sandy muttered.

"What did you say?" Will asked. His hands were running up and down her hips, gently pulling her closer to him.

Sandy turned to face him before she spoke. "I want to blow you until you scream, then ride you 'til you beg for mercy. I want to dominate you."

A look of surprise flickered on Will's face. Sandy could see that he had not expected her to be so direct in her approach.

"Let's see you do that," he replied with a smile spreading across his face.

Sandy took Will by the hand and led him to the bed, where they both shed their clothes. Will was down to his shorts while Sandy was left with her panties. She gently pushed Will onto the bed, climbing in with him. Her hand slid downwards, inside Will's shorts, cupping his erect member. While she ran her hand over his penis, her lips found Will's for a passionate kiss.

It felt like it had been so long since they had been together this way, but Sandy knew it had been only a couple of days ago. Her body yearned for Will's hands to rove over her body. She wanted him so badly.

Their tongues continued moving together rhythmically, exploring each other's mouths heatedly. Sandy could feel Will's dick swelling even bigger as she stroked it. Another shudder racked her body as she thought of that swollen shaft sliding deep between her legs and hitting all the right spots. She thought of the toe-curling, scream-inducing pleasure that Will had always given her. She wanted that now, but she desired to please him first.

Sandy broke their kiss after a few more moments, and she let her mouth trail down his muscled chest until it curled around his navel. She felt Will jerk a little as her tongue flicked over his navel.

Easy, man. We are just getting started.

She let her mouth continue on its downward journey until she got close to his groin. She could feel Will shuddering even more as she put her lips and tongue to work on his nether region. Sandy wondered what was special about her touches tonight. She had never really known him to be this responsive when they had been together before.

A groan escaped Will's lips when Sandy got her mouth around the tip of his dick. It felt like he had experienced a jolt of electricity through his entire body. Sandy probed deeper, rolling her tongue around the head of his dick. She was tugging at his shaft with her hand while stimulating the tip with her lips and tongue.

"Damn it, you are driving me crazy!"

Sandy smiled. That was what she wanted. She enjoyed feeling his dick pulsing against her lips. After a few more moments of teasing the tip, she took the length of his cock in her mouth and began to suck him. The movement of her mouth on his dick grew sloppier by the minute, drawing grunts from Will as he lay on the bed.

Sandy began to alternate between teasing and sucking, and with that, Will was driven crazy with pleasure; he jerked his waist in tandem with the movements of her mouth on his dick. At one point, Will held her head with his hands and thrust into her mouth a few times. The feeling of receiving his thrust in her mouth made Sandy think of having him thrusting between her legs and getting the right strokes in the right places already. She continued the blowjob until she felt him edging towards ejaculation.

"Do you want me to stop?" she drew back for a second to ask him.

"Don't fucking stop," Will grunted.

Sandy sucked on him until he jerked violently and eventually shot his hot seed into her mouth. It was what she wanted. She wanted to milk him dry.

She watched as he let out an exhausted sigh after he had ejaculated. It was remarkable that his penis had not yet lost its stiffness. It continued to throb as Sandy held it in her hand. Will wanted to wiggle out of Sandy's hold so he could taste her pussy in return, but Sandy was not interested. She did not want him going down on her, doing all those flicks against her clit or lapping at her folds with his tongue. Instead, she wanted to have his penis sliding in and out of her while she held her hands against his hard chest. She wanted to fuck the hell out of him.

Sandy once again prevented Will from rolling away by keeping her hands on his chest. She easily climbed on top of him, sliding her body forward as she straddled him and gently rubbed his erect penis against her vagina, which was still covered by her panties. The panties had already become soaked with her wetness. She was turned on beyond measure.

She quickly pulled off her panties and slipped Will's dick into her swollen, throbbing pussy. She let out a moan of ecstasy as she felt him drive his dick all the way in. This was exactly what she had been looking forward to all evening. She had felt that tension building up between them, and now they were having a serious roll between the sheets.

Will's hands cupped Sandy's breasts as she continued to ride it, bouncing against his groin so hard that her ass was slapping against him. His fingers and thumbs encircled her nipples, pinching them, as she rode him harder and faster still. She began to lose control of the movement of her waist until it felt like the constant pounding was happening all on its own.

Sandy kept her gaze fixed on Will's face. He was enjoying the moment, leaving her to do most of the work. As she stared at his face, she felt a desire to ride him harder, to go faster than this pace that was already incredible. So she did just that, managing to ride him harder, even though she thought she had been going at her fastest pace already.

Moans began to slip out of her mouth as Will's dick continually struck the sensitive spots deep inside her. She pushed his hands away from her tits and grabbed them herself, squeezing hard.

"My turn, time for me to take over," Will announced.

Before Sandy could utter a single word of protest, Will grabbed her waist tightly with both hands and started delivering upward thrusts that did wonderful things deep inside Sandy's vagina. It was her turn to shudder as the walls of her pussy undulated against the probing dick of the man she was riding. No, she was no longer the one in control. Will had taken over this game from her.

Sandy could do very little to move because Will had locked her waist within his firm grip, but she delivered more moans and screams as she felt herself diving into a pool of pleasure. She could feel her toes curling as Will continued with his masterful strokes. It was clear Will was determined to give her a huge orgasm with the way he was thrusting. He was driving her crazy, and she didn't want him to stop. It was everything she had already conceived in her mind before it all began; and more.

… … …

North Lembria, West Federation

Sandy and Will lay side by side on the bed after two passionate rounds of sex. Before now, Will could not remember ever pushing the limits of his body so hard simply because he wanted to make a woman feel good. Sandy was indeed special. Will cast a glance in her direction and saw she was resting with her eyes closed. Or were they slightly open? He couldn't say exactly. She had been that way since after they had cleaned up from their long, sweaty rounds together. It looked like her body needed to sleep, but she was not always so willing to do that.

Will's eyes flicked to the images that were being displayed on the television. It was an action movie that had two gunmen firing at each other. It reminded him of himself and that bastard John Croft. His mind went to Simons, another sneaky fellow who had masked himself as loyal to Adi Kalim. He didn't know if it would be easier for Fred to lead him to Simons or the bombers.

Thinking of Fred reminded Will he had yet to reach out to the tech wizard as he planned. He had been setting up the phone earlier when he looked up and saw Sandy standing in front of the mirror. She had looked so alluring he had abandoned the idea of reaching out to Fred to go over and hold her from behind. The outcome of that decision was about an hour of fulfilled desires and pleasures attained.

Will rolled out from under the sheet. Then, clad only in his shorts, he walked over to the small table where he had left the phones. The time he and Sandy had spent having sex made them forget all about dinner.

"Are you going somewhere?" Sandy asked from the bed, drawing Will's attention momentarily away from the phone.

"In my skivvies? Hell no," Will replied. "I was going to do what we talked about, you know, getting back on with Fred."

"Okay," Sandy said. "Have you set up the other phone?"

Will said that he had, then passed one of the phones to Sandy.

"I like the design, it is… Oh, my goodness!"

At first, Will did not understand why the phone's design had drawn such a loud exclamation from Sandy. Then, he looked at her and realized her gaze was fixed on something else: the television screen on the opposite wall. He spun quickly and was confronted with images and texts that all said the same thing. There had been a big explosion in San Mateo, the capital city of the West Federation.

Will felt a rush of anger, of burning fury. The bombers had already started perpetrating their destructive acts, and there was nothing he could do to stop it. He had to reach out to Fred right away to find out where they were headed before they wreaked havoc on the next city. An image of his city, Hringund, burning, left him scared. He didn't want to lose his family. For now, he could only hope that none of his colleagues were victims of the big explosion. He kept his eyes on the screen for a few more seconds as the camera panned over the casualties: some being moved on stretchers; some with less severe injuries; and those who had burned to death.

Will tore his stinging eyes away from the television screen and furiously inputted Fred Black's number. He dialled the number and was surprised when there was no answer. He tried again. Still no answer. Strange, that was unlike him; he had always answered before. A thought popped into Will's head. What if…? *No!* Will suppressed the thought immediately. He felt certain Fred was fine. Maybe he was just busy with something.

"I got a blitzmail…" Sandy said, more to herself, although Will heard her clearly. "Could be from one of those movie channels about the rental."

Will remained silent while fighting the urge to try Fred's number again. He was quite eager to hear that Fred was okay, but he was sure Fred would call him back when he got to his desk in the office.

"Will!" Sandy called suddenly, breaking into Will's thoughts that were full of growing concern for Fred. "You won't believe what I just got."

"Um… A mail from your superior telling you there is work to do back in Afrasia?" Will guessed.

Sandy shook her head. "No, not that. It's a message from May Lay."

"May?" Will intoned. "What's it about?"

"I don't know yet. It says, 'Go through the documents attached carefully. For your eyes only,' and it has several attachments," Sandy said. "It sounds like something serious, don't you think?"

"Just read the attached documents and spare yourself the suspense," Will said.

"Right," Sandy breathed as she tapped on the phone screen to download the attachments. She had only read for a few seconds by Will's reckoning when she exclaimed, "What…What the hell?"

"What is it?" Will asked, but there was no response from Sandy. Instead, she just handed him the phone for him to see for himself.

It only took Will a few seconds before his eyes connected with the words that had upset Sandy.

My husband killed your parents, and Adi Kalim knew about it.

……………

Sandy was astonished at what she just learned. The only man she had trusted all her life was involved with the one who killed her parents? What other surprises would this mission spring on her?

The bombing had come earlier than expected. Sandy could sense the worry in Will.

The bombing must have distressed him greatly. He was pacing the room all over again, trying to call Fred. Unfortunately, Fred was MIA, and so was everyone else on this mission. Owen was nowhere to be found. Sandy knew the mission was compromised as soon as she found out Owen Briggs was missing. She was faced with many huge, contrasting choices now, and her next move would make a massive difference in the rest of her life and even the entire world.

Sandy didn't know what she felt towards Adha at the moment. He had been the one man she thought she could trust until the day she died. Although she found out late he was not her birth father, he had always given her nothing but love; he seemed like a good man, so it was hard for her to believe otherwise. Could it all have been a lie? Could all the years of love and respect she felt for this man have been deceit? Sandy knew that she needed to face him. She wanted so badly to look into his eyes and hear him tell her May was lying. *No!* May's accusations could not be accurate; she must be mistaken. Sandy placed her hands on the sides of her head, squeezing, overwhelmed with emotions.

"We're going to be okay," Will said as he moved to sit beside Sandy.

"I cannot believe it!" Sandy said to Will, looking straight into his sad eyes.

"I understand how you feel, Sandy." Will wrapped his hands around Sandy and drew her into a tight embrace. They were both overwhelmed with emotion and didn't need any cues before their lips touched once again. In seconds, what started with warm kisses of comfort to each other transformed into hot, steamy passion.

First, it was just lips; then, Will decided to take it a step further. He extended his tongue and wrapped it around Sandy's. He wasn't too quick to go on at this point. For a second, he held back until she joined in, rubbing her tongue on his. It was then that they fervently and passionately became lost in each other. Will's hand started to wander around Sandy's body, one he was beginning to know by heart. As his hands moved down her back, he could picture it in his head. Her skin was as soft as feathers, in contrast to how her hands felt. Sandy's hands were thick, a sign she had experienced a lot of conflicts. Tingles travelled down his spine and to his feet as he knew his hands were travelling ever closer to her ass. Sandy's buttocks were so soft and plump. He couldn't believe how this woman was so perfectly shaped.

He could feel the pressure rising in his shorts. In a few seconds, Will could not wait anymore. His hands moved to Sandy's shirt, which he began to unbutton as quickly as his fingers could move. Her chest was bare underneath, with no bra to keep him from her sweet body. On the second button, he could already see her dark nipple. He wanted to grab it, so he did. Pulling her breast out, he tickled her nipple with his tongue. That had the exact effect he wanted; a moan of pleasure escaped from her lips. Sandy relaxed and enjoyed the attention to her breast; at the moment, she was content with letting him lead. He rushed to unbutton the rest of her top, then gave up and just ripped the shirt off her chest completely, leaving her bare.

Her body was so sexy; he didn't think he could get any harder. Chest against chest now, both returned to kissing, this time more passionately than before. Sandy was the one in a hurry now. Will could hear his trousers rip as she tore them off his body—surprising him with her strength—and in the process, revealing his huge, throbbing cock. A slight smile crossed her face, which turned Will on even more. He loved to think that the thought of his dick made her happy. Sandy reached up and tenderly held his face between her hands and drew him into another kiss. In a split second, Will pushed Sandy down the bed and slammed his dick into her. Repeatedly. Sandy screamed.

"Fuck!" she cursed as he drew his cock in and out of her pussy. He always knew how to fuck her so good; she could not help her screaming. Will leaned down and grabbed her shoulders so he could fuck her harder. "More, baby!" Sandy whispered into his ear.

"Oh, yes!" Will moaned a bit, but aside from that, he was quiet. He was keen on pleasing Sandy; that's all he wanted right now. His hands were on her tits once again, caressing them.

After each reached their climax, the pair heaved a sigh as Will landed beside Sandy on the bed. They quietly lay in each other's arms, relaxed. The sex seemed to have worked, as both had nothing on their minds now but sleep. Silently, they stared into each other's eyes until they fell asleep.

… … …

Will opened his eyes a little earlier than he would have expected himself to. He tried to piece his mind together and have a good read of the environment. The events of the night before played through his mind. He could never seem to get Sandy off his mind. His eyes went to her side of the bed. For the first time on the morning after, Sandy was still lying there, asleep. He could not believe his eyes. She slept so beautifully. He wanted to capture the moment so badly; he did not know when he would enjoy such a luxury again. He turned around to look for his phone on the shelf next to him when it suddenly rang. Loudly.

"Fuck!" Will exclaimed as he picked it up and turned to check Sandy, who was now awake, as expected. Frustrated and slightly angry, he studied the caller ID. It was Fred. A sigh of relief escaped his mouth as he rolled to the edge of the bed, sat up, and answered the call.

“Hello, bud!” Will greeted.

“Will, is this you? Tell me where we met if it is you!” Will was confused at Fred’s intro. He had been so worried about him.

“Indiana. Why—?”

“Listen very carefully. The mission has been compromised. Get out of there! Write this down, then memorize it. 242638. The war is starting now! You are not safe; I am not safe. Go to the Safe Haven. No one is to be trusted. Understand? Don’t trust anyone! Don’t try to contact this… line… and be mi…ndful…” The line went dead.

“Fred?” Will waited a second.

“Fred!” Will was afraid. He had heard an odd sound before the call dropped.

“What’s going on?” Sandy asked, already sitting bolt upright in bed.

“It’s Fred. He sounded like he was in danger, and he also said we were in danger.” Will was damned worried, alright. He didn’t know the next step to take. He wanted to go to San Mateo to check on his colleagues and also Hringund to ensure that his family was safe, but he had to be certain that he would not be in any danger. According to Fred, he was in trouble already. What did he mean by Safe Haven?

“Fred asked us to leave this place and go to the Safe Haven.” Will volunteered more details of the call.

“The Safe Haven? Where’s that?”

“I have no idea. But he said we need to leave here, now.”

“We do. For one, I have to go to Adha to get answers about my parents, see if there’s any truth in what May said.”

“I understand that you do, but the priority now should be getting somewhere safe.”

Sandy stood up and turned on the TV. They needed to know what was going on in the world, especially with the bombers. Overnight, there had been two additional bombings: one in Talgir City and the other in the government home headquarters. According to the news reporter, the Western Federation was shaken by the attack, yet the principal officials meant to protect the people had done nothing.

"This is appalling!" Will said as he turned away from the TV. "Following the surprises we have had in the past few days, I won't be surprised if the whole damn government is in on this plan."

As Will got into the shower in preparation to leave the hotel, Sandy remembered something she had always heard during her 40 Grade training. For every fight, she was always given a location to train. The 40 Grade Code was designed so the participants could train in different battlegrounds they could face in the real world. Something sounded very familiar about the Safe Haven, and Sandy was determined to figure it out.

She turned on her private Nav System and typed in some locations on the map of Afrasia. She tried the word Safe Haven in various ways, and it took her a long while, but she finally found a place named Sav Fehaen. She suddenly remembered why the name sounded so familiar now. She had been curious about that particular course many years ago because she realized a section in the course was inaccessible. Being curious, she had asked her partner why the area was restricted, but she had never gotten any answer. The place was blacked out on the map, but it was named. Will walked out of the bathroom about that time, and Sandy rendered her findings to him.

"Safe Haven. I cracked it. Come, take a look."

Will walked over to Sandy with only a towel draped over his shoulders.

"It must be their secret base, the masterminds of this plan. It's not even marked on the world map. It's called Sav Fehaen."

"How the heck did you figure that out?" Will said, genuinely astonished at how quickly Sandy cracked the case. He'd had utterly no idea what Fred meant by Safe Haven. The pair hurried into their clothes and made their way out of the hotel.

… … …

San Mateo, West Federation

As Will walked down the road, his mind wandered to the events of the last few hours. He had parted ways with Sandy, and he was not happy about it. They disagreed on where to go next. Sandy suggested they return to Afrasia while he wanted to go back home, track down the bombers, and stop their next move. He was also concerned about his colleagues and family. Even if they wanted to return to Afrasia, Owen was nowhere to be found, and according to Fred, the mission had been compromised. Now, he was on his way to San Mateo. He had a lot of things to settle there.

Things were already in havoc in San Mateo. Places were burning, and people were on the streets running to find shelter. Many were injured, and homes were destroyed. Will got to his workplace, and it was already little more than ashes. He placed his hands on his head and was about to turn back when he saw one of his colleagues, Raita Manes. Raita was one of the tech geniuses in the company. She was rushing out of what was left of the building.

"Raita, what happened here?"

"Don't you watch the news? San Mateo has been put up in flames. The bombers attacked from here."

"Right here?"

"Yes. They were members of the Federation."

"Are you saying there were traitors in our midst?"

"Yeah. The word has been out for a while now. Most of us were already suspicious of Gean since you left. What are you doing here? I thought you were on leave."

Gean Davis was the big boss at Will's agency. Many respected the man. Some even took him as a godfather.

"I came back once I heard the news. Is everyone dead?"

"Everyone except Gean. Fucking bastard told everyone bye yesterday and gave us all a raise. I only stepped out to go to my daughter's school; they called me 'cause she was having some issues. I was in awe when I heard the news. I could be gone too."

"Shit!" Will exclaimed as he placed his hand over his mouth in shock. "This conspiracy is beyond anything I ever imagined. I respected agent Davis so much. Never thought he could go against his own."

Many things were running through Will's mind now. Everyone he could run to for help seemed to be dead or missing. Or compromised. Those putting on this show were the influential ones, and it seemed like there was no one left to protect the rights of the people.

As he talked to her, he found out Raita had done a heroic thing inside the building by eliminating bomb materials bearing other continent's names on the tags. The police would be out for an investigation soon enough. Finding bombing materials from another continent would spark a war for sure. The West Federation could take on those continents, but a war would be detrimental to the masses. Just like during the great uprising, many would die.

Just to be certain, Will followed Raita through the rubble to check for any other evidence. When they found none, they headed out. As they walked out to the street, a car pulled up, and Raita jumped into the front passenger's seat.

"Where are you headed?" he asked, curious if he could get a lift.

"Well, I came back here to see if I could find any information about the bombing. It turns out that the bombs are being produced in the Underworld."

"That's not surprising news," Will said with a straight face.

"You know about this?" Raita asked, seemingly unaware of the international conspiracy. Will tried to think fast and decide if she could be trusted or not. It seemed like everyone that had been on the mission with him had been unfaithful and on the wrong side—everyone except Sandy. The mission had been compromised, though. They had not heard from Owen in a very long time.

Raita had been a faithful member of the Federation Agency for years. She was good at her job. She had a family. There was pretty much nothing suspicious about her. Besides, times without number, Raita had shown she was in the game for humanitarian services. He finally decided he could trust her, but he was not about to throw caution completely to the wind. He decided to offer her only a little information. If she proved trustworthy, she would hear the rest as time went on.

"You don't trust me?" Raita seemed to have noticed Will's reluctance in answering her question.

"I do, Raita. It's just… I was on a mission, and it was related to this."

"On a mission outside the Federation? Isn't that against the law or something?"

"I was reluctant to take it at first, but the money offered was more than I could reject. So, where exactly are you headed right now?"

"It's not something I should discuss with you right here," Raita said and indicated Will should get into the car.

… … …

Sandy was hurt when Will agreed to part ways with her. She expected him to fight for her and stay with her and figured when she insisted on going to Afrasia, he would go too. But he did not. After a lot of thought, she decided it was for the best. She was getting too attached. An attachment was very bad for her kind of job. If the 40 Grade training had taught her anything, she had to learn to live alone. That was why she loved to work independently, until three million bucks changed that deal, forcing her with Will. Now, she had powerful feelings for him, feelings she could not deny. She needed to stay away from him for a while so the feelings could go away.

Sandy had to get to Afrasia, but she had travelled to the West Federation illegally, and security at the borders had been tightened since the bombings. In addition, she had no contact with those who sent her here, so she was stranded.

She knew the best way to sneak across borders was through ships. She was already at a depot, standing amid many passengers who looked similar to her. *If Will were here, this would have been harder,* Sandy thought. The guards were checking tickets before sending the passengers onto the ships. Twice, she tried to sneak past them but realized she could not possibly do it. One of the guards seemed to have his eye on her already. She walked back and blended into the crowd. She needed to get in, one way or the other.

"Last call!" the captain announced. "Ship is about to move. All passengers should be on board. This is the last call." Sandy knew she had to act fast, so she rushed to the dock. Great. No one was looking. She ran into the ship after making sure she wouldn't be spotted. After looking into the luggage compartment, she chose one of the cases and climbed inside. The West Federation was next to Afrasia, so the ship should get to the bay in fifteen hours. Sandy braced herself for the ride as the final announcement from the captain sounded. "All aboard." She could hear the guards closing the dock door.

The engine's roar was so loud she had to cover her ears. The ship was on the move. She could put her mind at ease now.

After about three hours of being cramped, Sandy could not bear the noise or heat from the engines anymore. The luggage compartment was too close to the engine room; she had to find a more comfortable place to stay for the remainder of the ride. She lifted the cover off the luggage slightly to check if any guards were around. The coast was clear. She gently moved the lid aside, then stepped out of the crate. Before turning to restore the cover, she heard guards conversing and coming her way. She quickly ducked, going behind the container and knocking over another crate in the process.

"Crazy rats are back again," one of the guards stated. "I thought these docks were disinfected before the journey. I better have a look at this."

Realizing her mistake, she knew she needed to move fast. Without looking, she stood up and ran out the door, thinking she had time to get out before they got there. As she ran out the door, she crashed into the broad chest of one of the guards. Both were startled by the collision, but Sandy got herself together quickly. She needed to run, and she did.

It was too late, though; she could hear the guard over the radio alerting the others to her presence. Every guard on board was now after Sandy. She made sure that none of them got a good glimpse of her face. If she could find the elevator to the main ship, she would comfortably blend into the crowd. Since they didn't know who she was, it would take them a while to find her.

The dock was dark, other than the flashlights the guards shone around as they looked for Sandy.

It didn't take Sandy too much time to realize that she was up against amateurs. Probably just jobless labourers hired for this voyage alone, for very low pay. One of them could simply switch on the overhead light, and she would be revealed. She appreciated the cover darkness afforded her, but she also needed light to find the elevator.

She ran to the wall and started to feel for anything that would help her cause while avoiding the guards' torchlight flashes. She found the light switch first. If she flipped the switch, all the guards would know where she was. She knew she could take them, but she didn't want to take that risk. For all she knew, they could have surprises up their sleeves. So she left the switch and continued to feel on the wall for the elevator button.

One of the guards suddenly regained his senses and ran toward the light switch. Sandy realized this, so she quickened her pace. Once he flipped the switch, she saw the elevator. A sigh of relief escaped her mouth when she realized it was just a few steps away. Before the guards could even run, she was already in the elevator.

"C'mon, be quick." Sandy hurried as she pressed the second-highest button. That should be where the ship crew was. The elevator went up for a bit, and as she left the ground floor, she could feel that familiar sense of rising against gravity. *Ding,* the elevator sounded as she reached the first floor. She was more relaxed now. Only two floors left. *Ding,* as she reached the second floor. Great! Then the elevator suddenly came to a stop.

"Shit," Sandy cursed as she slammed her fist on the elevator door.

She waited, expecting the guards to come for her. She braced herself for a fight. If she had to fight every single guard on the ship, she would. She just had to get to Afrasia. After waiting for several minutes, Sandy sighed her resignation and took a seat on the elevator floor. She realized they were just waiting until the ship docked before they confronted her. *Great tactic, guys,* she thought. She knew the men on the ship were too inexperienced to take her, and they must have realized it too.

…… … …

Hringund, West Federation

The stench attacking Will's nose as he alighted from the car hit him so hard, he had to take a step back. The drive with Raita had been short but very enlightening. Raita had told him about how suspiciously Gean had been acting in the weeks following Will's departure. He would bring strange men inside the company and have long meetings in his office. When Will asked her if she recognised any of the men, she identified May Lay's husband, George, as one. Now, Will was a hundred per cent sure his boss, Gean, had something to do with the international conspiracy. Raita had taken the time to clear away all evidence that the bombs were manufactured on other continents from the bombing site. That would slow down whatever the bombers wished to achieve by their incessant acts. Now, Raita managed to get into the company's database by hacking its security files. She had shown Will pictures of the men Gean was working with, and Will recognised Dr Kean immediately.

"Are you sure this man is working with Gean?" Will asked.

"I am positive. He was around the most often."

The whole situation just confused Will even more. Something fishy was going on, and he was going to find out what. Will also recognised Simons and John Croft. He also tried to call Sandy several times, but her line was not going through. By then, he had stopped trying. Her line was not going through anymore. Will didn't want to be worried, so he encouraged himself, as so much had already been destroyed in San Mateo. The call could be disturbed because of all the bombings. Cell towers might have been hit. He would just try to call her again later.

Raita told Will where they were headed. Gean had spoofed his location on the company's website when he left the day before, but Raita was smarter than he was. She zeroed in on his real location in seconds. She wanted to put a bullet through his head for betraying his men. Will jumped on the plan almost immediately but advised her they should spy on him first before moving in, as they didn't know what they were up against. Raita agreed. Will had expected them to get off at a large building or a hotel, but this stinky place was something else. It was a factory with oil spilt all over. It seemed to be abandoned, but Will was not falling for that trick. In his many years of being a secret agent, he learned things like this often masked secret hideouts for criminals. He walked forward, this time taking the caution to cover his nose with his hands. The pair searched the factory for clues, but the people they were up against were also trained professionals. They left no clues behind, and the pair were no closer to discovering their hideout. Will and Raita would have to use stealth instead of approaching the matter head-on. They left the site after their search came to a futile end.

Will waved to Raita as she dropped him back at the company site. It was getting late now. Will decided to head home. His mother and two siblings lived in Hringund. He had to check on them. As he walked down memory lane, fear and panic swarmed around him. Some buildings were still on fire. Things were not normal here. Many of the displaced people, homeless now and on the streets, were sleeping on the ground. Will was moved almost to tears; this was his home. Because of people's selfish desires, they had caused a lot of suffering. It was unacceptable. They all had to pay dearly. He would double his efforts and ensure that everyone who had a hand in this would not succeed in their plans. As he arrived at his former home, he stood where there should have been a house. All that remained was a pile of ash. A hand of fear gripped his heart, choking him. Where was his family? He tried to reach his mother by phone, but the call went straight to voice mail. He hoped she was safe.

He moved toward the remaining pile of bricks as he spotted one of his childhood toys, his old bike. He couldn't believe she kept it after all these years. His mind went back to his younger years and the days of his childhood. He had left the house when he was just eighteen after being recruited to the Federation for Secret Service. His mother had begged him to stay, but he just couldn't abandon his dream job.

What was worse for his mother was he couldn't tell her why he left or where he was going. After that, he never called her again. It was part of the perks of being a secret agent. He needed to let go of all connections he had outside the agency. It was not a rule, but all the top agents were people without families.

They were fearless and could do anything without worrying about their families. Besides, he took on the most dangerous missions. He was not about to let the news of his death ruin his mother forever. He was content with letting her think he was just a runaway teenager.

Now, some jerks had bombed the only place she had left to call home? Fuck those bastards. For all he knew, his mother could be anywhere by now. She could even be dead; there was no use in trying to find her. He took a moment to stare at his childhood home one last time. Since it had been destroyed, he didn't think he would ever return. Then, for the last time, he paid his final respects to his family and left the site. He had a lot of work to do. But first, he had to find somewhere to sleep.

Will flagged down an AI taxi and headed to his man cave. It had been almost a month since he left. The house was intact, thankfully, although Will knew he could not stay there for very long. He needed to gear up. He had nothing left on him, not even a gun. Will almost hugged his car, "his baby," when he saw it sitting safely in his garage. Robin was like his girlfriend.

He loved the car as much as he loved his job. The vehicle was an AI car, with all the functions electronically controlled by Will's assistant. The Robin was one of the most excellent cars of its time. It was worth a fortune, and that's why Will treated it accordingly. First, he put on his tactical armour and packed a spear. He then grabbed his leather jacket and threw it into the trunk.

He needed to get going, but he wanted to be prepared for anything. In his armour room were many gadgets, including some heavy, dangerous weaponry. Will chose two of his favourites: the Georgian blaster and rifle. The rifle was just like a standard rifle, except it shot lasers. It was extremely quiet, and its rays were invisible. So, whoever you were shooting would never even know what hit them. The Georgian blaster was as powerful as a grenade, yet it was so small it could fit into your pocket. He decided to take a quick shower; he redressed, then got into his car and drove to a neutral place where he could rest peacefully.

The sun's rays bathed Will's light skin as it rose over the horizon, waking him. He had forgotten to put up his sunshades before he went to bed. His phone rang as he was rubbing the sleep from his eyes. Raita was calling him. Why was she calling him so early? Did she have new information?

"Good morning, Raita."

"Will, check the mail I sent to you ASAP." *Click!*

Will scrolled through his phone and saw the blitzmail. It was the last message sent to him that morning.

"I am coming for you," the mail read. Raita indicated it was a forwarded message. Who the fuck sent her that? She called him back almost immediately.

"He took my daughter last night," Raita said, panicked.

"Calm down, Raita; we will get to the bottom of this."

"I discovered some new information yesterday. Gean has taken many of the Federation agents captive. He is working with a man named Simeon Greg. They plan to bomb more locations in the West Federation. Afrasia will be next. I can't seem to access the location, but I believe that if we can locate Gean, we would be able to get our hands on the info and stop the perpetrators before they attack."

"Let's meet up. Our phones could be bugged."

"Great. I'll message you a location."

After Raita hung up, the familiar beep came through almost immediately. Will needed to move.

He entered the location into his Nav System as his tires squealed out of the lot.

"You arrived quickly," Raita said as Will stepped out of his luxurious vehicle. They met up in front of a tall, storied building in San Mateo. There was never a time Will had used the car that it didn't attract stares from passersby; this time was no exception.

"Pretty flashy car for a secret, stealthy mission, don't you think?"

Will looked back at Robin. Although he loved driving it, he saw some sense in what Raita said. The car was just too attractive to hide.

"Alright, I believe we have to settle for your wagon." Raita smiled at Will's disappointment. He never hid the fact that he was proud to own the Robin. It was a good car. They crossed the road and walked into a café. Fortunately, the café wasn't busy; only two tables were occupied. Robot waiters slowly moved around, checking for orders. After checking to see if discussing the matter would be safe there, the pair picked a table at the corner of the café.

"I ran some more checks on that location we got yesterday. It turns out it was once a gold mine. Once the gold rush was over, it was closed down, and the oil factory was built over top of it."

"Are you saying that you think Gean is hiding somewhere down in the mines?"

"Exactly. Look at these." Raita brought out her phone and pressed a button, which immediately brought up some projected images. "Thermal energy should be reduced on the inside of the mine. But, instead, it seems to be increased.

"And, I hacked into San Mateo's security system and found this." She swiped across the screen, flipping to pictures of a car. It was Gean's car. It had been spotted in one particular location in the capital city over five different times. Raita was a genius, and so was Gean. No one would have ever thought that he would be lodged in that part of town. In fact, only the most notorious criminals were known to inhabit that place.

Will and Raita concluded by going over to Gean's place. The ride was a short one. The car was parked in the same spot as in the pictures Raita had found. Raita was careful enough to ensure the traffic camera did not glimpse her car. Anyone could get the information and use it against her. The stench in the area reeked of factory smoke and weed. Many in the area walked the streets in ragged shorts with guns in their hands. The pair stood out of the crowd very quickly, and that drew much attention to them. They should have made better choices with their clothing. Now, they had to find somewhere discreet to watch for Gean without drawing any more attention to themselves.

As if on cue, Gean walked out of a building, looking around before he walked briskly to his car and drove off. Perfect. They left their weapons in the car, just in case the building scanned them for weapons, so it wouldn't trigger the alarm before they could get to the door.

They walked over to the building and tried the outer door. Locked. What else did they expect? That was normal these days. They just needed to figure out the passcode. Fortunately, that was Raita's area of expertise and her job at the Federation. She was good. In seconds, the alarm system was silenced, and the building security shut down. She would restore it when they were on their way out, so Gean would not suspect anything. The interior of the apartment was pretty decent. The living room was arranged like any normal one, with sofas and a flatscreen. They needed to move quickly. One after the other, they searched the rooms until Will found the office. "Over here, Raita," he called to her. She was quick. They knew what they had to do. They needed to extract as much information as they could get from the system. They might not get a second chance. Her hands were fast on the keyboard.

"I haven't been able to breach the firewall. It's hard to crack. I need this passcode."

"A passcode? Can't you find a way to override it?"

"This is the third time I've tried. It's a dead end."

Will slammed his fist on a table. Another dead end. They were this close to stopping the bombings. Why did the firewall need to be so assertive? It was as if the firewall represented yet another brick wall in the neverending series of walls he'd hit on this mission so far. He heaved a sigh and looked around the room. On the far side of the room was a table with files and books. Bingo. There had to be something there. He went over and started searching for anything that could give them a hint.

"We could try some options. His date of birth, his wife's date of birth, his office code?"

They tried all three and many more combinations, but nothing worked.

"Welcome," the AI voice suddenly resounded through the house. Someone had come into the house… It was Gean.

… … …

PART 4 - The Return to Afrasia

IMPRISONMENT AND NEW ALLIANCES

Nothing Is the Same: Evolution or Evil?

Chapters Thirty through Thirty-Eight

"The distinction between past, present, and future is only a stubbornly persistent illusion."

–Albert Einstein

Return to Afrasia: 2166, June 01

The voyage was taking too long. Sandy was beginning to think maybe the boat ran into some technical issues along the way. She thought she must have been in that elevator for two days. Yet, she had only been in there for ten hours. Sandy was asleep when the elevator started quietly rising and stopped at the floor she had planned to go. The sound of the elevator door opening startled her and brought her to her feet. Five hefty men were waiting for her at the door. She quickly realized there was no use in resisting. The cops had matched up with her. Voluntarily, she surrendered her hands for cuffing.

Sandy had no idea if it was hunger or the stress of the past day, but her head ached badly. She had not eaten anything in almost two days. It was beginning to take quite a negative toll on her. Things before her grew blurry and distorted. She had no idea how she could manage being on her feet, though she mustered the strength she had and tried to walk. She hadn't quite made it a few feet when she stumbled and fell to the ground. Before her sight went black, she saw some of the men trying to revive her. They gradually began to blur out of focus before their images finally disappeared into nothingness.

Sandy opened her eyes in jail. Not again! If the past month had taught her anything, it was that she hated being bound. The cell she was in was more like a cage, with a glass door. She tried her absolute best to bang the door off the hinges, even though she knew these jails were break-proof. The doors were adequately reinforced; without an external command, there was no way to unlock them. It was her right to at least one phone call before she was locked up. She should have been allowed that. Sandy wondered why she had not been given her right and determined she would complain to a guard whenever she saw one. She saw many, but they didn't seem to pay any attention to her.

Damned security personnel, breaking the law. Finally, after hours of struggling, she settled down on her cell's tiny bed. There was a small meal waiting beside her. Prison pottage? She would starve to death before she ate such repulsive food. She knew influential people who could order her release or at least move her to better conditions. Her air conditioning was not even constant. It kept turning off and on. She could not stand it in here for long. Her mind wandered to Will. What was he up to now? Had he found the bombers? Was he alive? Was he safe or in a cell just like she was? She should have just listened to him and went with him to San Mateo. Maybe if she had, she would not be in the mess she was in right now.

As Sandy stared at the ceiling of her cell, she started devising a plan for her escape. She knew it was near impossible for that to happen, but she had to try. Prison cells these days were more like traditional homes. They were made with strong glass fibre, and the interior walls were reinforced with titanium. Sandy had a very sharp memory, and since she learned that in her criminal law class, she never forgot it. She remembered the weak spots they had mentioned, too, including the food vent, the toilet, and the air vents. She had never liked criminal law classes. Her mean professor made the experience worse for her. Never did she think those classes would be of any use for her in the future.

Sandy had spent seven waking hours in the cell. She was already planning her escape. They were served meals through a tube by robot AIs. The tubes were made of silicone, easily breakable. She could break the tubes and dig into the air vents with her dinner fork. It was not a foolproof plan, but she could try it. She could also spill some water on her door lock. Everything was made of electricity.

Water contacting the door electronics would give her about half a second of power outage before the auto dryer fixed the problem. If she was quick enough, she could break the door lock. It was also not foolproof, but it was, again, worth the try. Anything that would get her out of that cell was worth the try.

Her mind wandered to Will again. Her mind had been doing a lot of wandering since she left Will. It was frustrating not to be able to take one's mind off a man. His chiselled abs and strong chin played over in her mind, sending shivers down her spine. Oops. Ugh… She was in for it. She wanted to feel his warm breath on her skin, his soft fine hair rubbing against hers, her breasts against his chest. She was mesmerized. She needed to go back to the West Federation. That would be another issue, but she couldn't stand another moment without his lips on hers.

The prison door opened up suddenly, startling her from her thoughts of Will. Surprised, she jumped up from her bed and cautiously walked out the door. In her years of experience, she knew she had to be ready for anything. Slowly, she checked to see if she was walking into a trap. It was too good to be true. It had to be. Why was she suddenly free?

"What the fuck is going on!?" she screamed to the empty hallway. The other prisoners were surprised that she was out, too. From their cells spread down the hall, they yelled at her. Some cursed at her, while others begged her to open their cells and set them free. She didn't have time for that; she needed to make use of the golden opportunity that had just fallen into her lap. She was about to make a run for it when she heard a guard's voice.

"Sandy Krave, you are up for a transfer." A transfer? She hadn't even spent one full day in jail. Why do they want to transfer her? She thought transfers were only for those who applied for it, or the worst, hardened criminals. The guards approached her from both directions. She tried to gauge the situation. Could she take them? She decided to try. She stood still until two of the guards reached her and brought out handcuffs. She looked at one guard as he approached her, and as he did, she drew back her head, standing tall. She quickly bent her head forward, hitting the guard right in the face. He fell to the ground.

The second officer didn't expect the move, but Sandy could see that he was well-trained. He took a swing at her with his stick. She ducked, and in one fluid motion, she hit the floor and raked him to the ground with her foot. By now, the first guard was already back on his feet, and two other guards were running to the rescue. She knew she had no chance of winning the fight, but she had missed a good fight. She needed the adrenaline to feel like herself again. One of the officers took another swing at her. This time, he hit her in the belly. *Great.* She could feel the blood rushing to her brain. She smiled.

"You got to do better than that, officer." She wrestled with him a bit before she managed to pin him down.

"Stand down! We do not want to use force," the telecom resounded throughout the hall.

"Fuck you!" She responded as she took another swing at the officer trying to attack her. She hit him right in the face. One was behind her. *Thud!* Her leg hit his balls. *Great!* Now, she was positive they could not kill her. She was a valuable asset. She decided to use this to her advantage. She started to run.

"Surrender, Sandy Krave! This is the most secure facility in the whole state. You stand no chance."

Try me and see, Sandy thought to herself as she reached the stairwell. She rushed down, but in the middle, she met five officers approaching her. *Turn back*. She went back up, but five more officers were coming down. She looked around. What could she do? There was only one way out. She looked over the railing and down the stairs. There were about five flights of stairs to the ground floor. *Two and a half floors,* she quickly calculated. She could jump down.

The officers looked at her like she was crazy. She really could be mad for the right reason. She smiled and waved at them; then, she jumped over the rails. With accurate calculations, she landed on her hands, tucking her body under and rolling onto the floor. It was madly painful, but she'd had no choice. She looked up and tried to get up. She needed a minute. Maybe deciding to jump down was too crazy a decision, even for her. She struggled to crawl under a desk in the reception area. She felt a little better now. The officers were now in the room with her. There were about twenty surrounding her.

"We've got her," one of the officers spoke into his radio as he cuffed her hands and feet.

… … …

Gean was back home, and Will was still in the tech room with Raita. Their lives were in danger. The door of the tech room was slightly ajar, so Will went to the door and sneaked a careful glance out. Surprisingly, Gene didn't act like he was at all shocked that his security system was left unarmed. That could only mean one thing: he was expecting it. From where he was cautiously peeking out the door, Will could see the Foreign blaster in the man's hand. His face showed he was determined to use it on whoever was in his house. He went straight to one of his rooms, went in, and locked the door. Perfect! This was their chance.

The number Fred gave to him, 242638, had started running through his head. It occurred to him that he had not used that number for anything yet. It had to be those numbers.

"242638."

"What?" Raita asked nervously, expecting that they would have made their way out of the house by then.

"242638. That's the code," Will repeated, being a lot surer the second time. They had to make use of this opportunity.

"What? Are you crazy? You know how ruthless Gean is. He would blow our heads off if he found out we were here."

"We have to try. I have a feeling this will be our only chance."

With a sigh, Raita agreed with him. "You're probably taking us to our deaths, but we'll die anyway if we don't stop those bombers, so no loss."

The code was wrong. "Dammit!" Will shouted unconsciously.

"Wait!" Raita whispered harshly, "There's a number taped on the desk behind the monitor! It looks like an old ID number." Will glanced over and recognized the number as Gean's birth ID number from his files. She typed it in. Wrong again. She typed it backwards. Bingo! Tons of files started to appear on the screen. Raita placed a flash in the system and started copying. They hoped to get all the information copied before they left, but their noise seemed to have attracted Gean. He suddenly appeared at the door and caught them red-handed. He took one shot, hitting Raita square in the chest.

"Oh, no, Raita, no!" Will exclaimed as she slid to the floor, and he ducked behind the computer desk. He quickly put two fingers to her pulse, confirming there was none. "You coward! You killed men who entrusted their lives to you, then you kill Raita, unarmed, in cold blood? I will make sure that I kill you myself!"

A mocking laugh escaped from Gean's mouth.

"You and what army?" he asked, walking around the large room confidently. Will carefully moved from one shield to another without getting caught. The only problem was the space between him and the door. To get to the door, he had to get to Gean first. And, he had no weapon on him, so if he came out, Gean would take a shot. He suddenly wished he'd went back to the car for his Georgian blaster after Raita took down the security system.

One thing kept coming to the forefront of Will's mind: Gean was one of the best marksmen in the Federation. He never missed a target.

It would be impossible for him to avoid Gean's shots. He decided to wait.

"Come on out, Will. I have you cornered. If you—"

Thud!

All Will could make out from that sound was that someone was hit.

"Will?" A familiar voice came from behind the fallen Gean. Will breathed a sigh of relief and rose from his crouched position behind the table.

"Fred!" The two men embraced each other. "How did you get here? I was worried that something bad happened to you when you called me."

"It was Glen. He took us all captive. There are six other men here, besides me."

Gean had taken seven of the Federation's best agents captive. He was strategic enough to pick agents with families or loved ones. These agents would do anything to save their families. The agents were assigned bombing missions and transported to the other two continents: Afrasia and Oceania Liberation.

"Oceania Liberation? I thought the President and George Lay were in on this plan too?"

"Yes, they are, but I think they figured they couldn't trust the Underworld. They're backstabbers, and they know it."

This whole issue was getting way out of control and too confusing to follow. Just then, the bloodstained computer beeped and displayed the word "complete." The files were now in Will's possession. Now that Gean was captured, they could interrogate him to get more information about the missions. Fred could have killed Gean but was smart enough to use just enough force to knock him unconscious. Will smiled at his brilliance. He signalled to Fred, and both men set to work putting Gean in bonds. Now, they would wait until he regained consciousness.

Will settled down to check through the files on the flash drive. The first few files contained details of criminals he already knew. They included pictures of the men and a little bio. He closed the file and clicked on the next. It contained details of the bombing plan. Perfect.

There was a map with red dots indicating the intended bombing locations. The four places that had already been blasted were marked with green dots.

"Perfect. Now, we just have to find out what the next target is," Will said as he went through the files again. Afrasia's map was there too. He clicked on it, and soon, he saw a flashing red dot. It was moving. Someone was on their way to Afrasia. Will's mind flashed to Sandy. He knew she wanted to go back to Afrasia, but he wasn't sure where she was now. She was headed to somewhere named Sav Fehaen. He typed the location into the world map, and a red stop sign showed up. It was not visible on the map. *Shit.* He had to find her and make sure she was safe.

"Looks like he's coming around." Fred's voice snapped Will back to reality. Gean was grunting and trying to move from the chair, but his arms were tied to it. It took him a while to realize what was happening, but once he did, he started to scream and struggle.

"Did you forget what location you chose to keep me in? You specifically said, 'No one will hear your screams here, so don't bother to scream,' right?" Fred said as he walked around Gean. He seemed thin—too thin, almost gaunt—and tired. He must have been in Gean's possession for days. His eyes held great contempt, watching Gean in the chair.

"You would never compromise the mission," Gean said as he calmed down and started laughing at Will and Fred.

"Shut your mouth!" Fred backhanded Gean across the face.

"They are headed for Sedan in Afrasia," Will said.

"Shit! The president is on vacation in Sedan," Fred replied.

"We have to stop the bombing."

The next mission was set. They had the location and needed to move fast. Now, all that was left was killing the traitorous bastard who turned his back on his colleagues. He had to pay for his crimes. With the same gun Gean had used to shoot Raita, Will shot Gean in the arm. Then he shot him in the thigh. He watched as the blood began to flow, and Gean's muffled screams of agony reached a satisfying, all-time high. He didn't want his death to be quick. Gean had to suffer for what he did. That's why he didn't shoot him in the head or the face. He would gradually bleed out while tied to the chair, with no one to help him, the same way he murdered his agents. Will taped his mouth extra tight to ensure no one would hear his muffled calls for help.

Once that was done, they began their search to find a plane or sub to take them back to Afrasia. There were many they could call, many connections they had. The issue was it was unwise to trust anyone, considering what had been happening in the Federation. They would need to go undercover, and Will had the perfect plan for that. He had power over the whole agency, now that Gean had been dealt proper justice. They needed a flight for the mission. Good thing Will now had access to the entire database of the agency. He could easily arrange a flight for them, and that was what he did. They were set to go to Afrasia in three hours.

… … …

New Alliances: Afrasia

Sandy was placed in a transfer truck with another female inmate and five guards. With her hands cuffed to her neck and her feet also confined, she would not have expected so many guards to be placed with her. It was probably to prevent any more stunts like the ones she had pulled previously. The second inmate was sitting opposite her.

"Hey," the inmate said.

It took Sandy a while to answer. A lot was going through her mind. When she finally did, she said, "Hi."

"Keep quiet," one of the guards said. He was tall and hefty. His uniform was more decorated than any of the others. He was probably the boss.

"Would you maybe… wanna get outta here?"

Sandy had heard all kinds of crazy stories about criminals, but she had not seen anything like this before. Even if she wanted to run away, she shouldn't have said it in front of the guards. Now, they had less of a chance of slipping away. She gave a straight look at the lady, who was bent on having her talk.

"You scared of the guards? It's alright. I've handled worse," she said.

Excellent, Sandy thought, *she's nuts.* Even as good an agent as she was, she didn't have such audacity. The guard next to the inmate gave her a good thump on the back.

"Stop talking, or else. I'll gag you," the officer said. This little warning shot did nothing to stop her—she talked even more. She was really in for it, now. The officer gave her another hit. "Don't hit me, you fucking coward!" she screamed back at him as she used her head to headbutt him in the face. She must have been incredible in combat because that one hit completely knocked him out. Now, Sandy realized what she was trying to do. She wasn't slow about it, as she put it all together.

Once the first man was down, they had a better chance of escaping. Although, now the other officers charged at the inmate. Sandy fought one while the inmate fought another. Two down, two to go. The other two officers paged the driver to keep going. They brought out tasers, warning Sandy and her new friend not to come close. No taser could stop her now; she was almost free.

She looked at her new friend, and both smiled at each other as if they were telepathically communicating. They faced the officers and did well to avoid their tasers. In the end, Sandy used the taser to hit her targeted officer, while her friend took out the second one with a knife-hand strike to his neck. When all was said and done, both were breathing heavily and laughing in the back of the truck.

"Pretty nice skills you got there," Sandy commended. Though they had only spent a few minutes together, Sandy already liked her personality. Her friend gave her a nod and a smile.

"Your skills are pretty dope too. I'm Natalie. You?"

"I'm Sandy. It's nice to meet you. We better find the keys to these cuffs and get out of here before one of these guys wakes up."

"Right behind you," she nodded. They searched their holsters and pockets. "Found 'em!" Natalie said as she proudly displayed the keyring she had just found. She helped Sandy out of her cuffs first; then, Sandy did the same for her.

The inmate transport van was designed with tight security, so even though they had defeated the officers, they still had to override the driver's security system. The guards could open the back doors with a security tab, but they needed a password that they couldn't get. In addition, the drivers were trained to keep driving no matter what, except when an officer tells them to stop. So, they had to find another way to make him stop.

Natalie had a plan. Although Sandy was not too happy about it, there was no stopping Natalie. The transfer truck's outer sections were bulletproof, and so was most of the partition between the back of the van and the driver's seat. However, there was a small slot that was not, which was big enough to get a gun through. The van's security system would shut down in the event of an accident to ensure that lives are saved first. Natalie's plan was simple. Shoot the driver through the slot, cause an accident that would override the security system, and get out of the fucking prison.

Sandy took her seat and fastened her seatbelt. With the push of a button, the seats could also turn into strong, individual pods; so, Sandy engaged her pod for added safety. Natalie agreed to do the shooting. She was fast, and she said she could get back into her seat quickly enough. She took one of the officer's guns and fired through the partition slot. One bullet was enough. She hit him right in the head. She was also true to her word of being very quick. In seconds, before everything started flipping, she was belted into her seat and pod protected. The van started to roll, taking several flips before it came to a stop. Both Natalie and Sandy were safe, but the previously unconscious policemen were probably now dead. Once the vehicle stopped, the back doors sprung open. Freedom! Both ladies ran for it.

"Where are you headed?" Natalie asked Sandy.

"I want to check something out, probably in a dangerous place."

"Ohh, the girl likes danger. How'd you get here anyway?" Natalie pointed to the police van. "You look too good to be in police custody."

"I was a stowaway on a ship coming back to Afrasia. You?"

"Well, let's just say that I had a bad drug habit. Can I come with you? I got nowhere else to go. A little combat would take the boredom out of my skin."

Sandy had no business taking a law offender with her on a secret mission. However, she was tempted by her expertise in combat. She didn't know if she could trust Natalie, but she needed help where she was headed. She also didn't know what lay in store for her. After giving it a lot of thought, she decided to give Natalie a chance. Besides, this was a war between the leaders and the masses, and Natalie was not part of the leaders.

"Why not?"

"Great!" Natalie said with a smile on her face. After that, Sandy gave her a brief overview of where she was headed.

"I need to find out if that location is related to what is happening in any way," Sandy said as she rounded up her speech.

"I lived around there once. I know someone that can get us there quick enough. I just need to make a call."

"Be careful what you say on the call though, many cells are bugged now."

Natalie walked up to a stranger and begged to use his phone. He agreed. She made a call, talking to someone for a few minutes. She had waited with Sandy for about ten minutes when someone showed up in a car. Natalie introduced Sandy to its driver.

"This is my brother, Nyman. Nyman, this is a new friend I made today. She's Sandy."

"Thought you were in prison," Nyman asked as the ladies got into the car. Natalie ignored the question.

"I need to get some equipment at my place," Sandy told them.

"But your place is on the other side of town," Natalie complained.

"I can't go unprepared," Sandy replied.

"I know that. That's why I got you covered," she said as she motioned with her hand for Sandy to follow her, then jumped back out of the car. She directed Sandy to the car trunk, and as she opened the trunk, Sandy could see hi-tech gadgets, weapons, armour, and much more of the coolest stuff she had ever set her eyes on. How did a drug addict get her hands on so many gadgets?

"Nyman is a cop," Natalie said as if reading Sandy's mind. "Well, ex-police force." Sandy nodded. She was running out of time. She needed to find Will and be in his arms once more.

It took a ten-hour drive, with many roadblocks, but the trio finally made it to Sav Fehaen. Nyman dropped them off at the final roadblock, and they walked into the forest. They knew that the bush was just a cover for whatever dubious scheme was going on in there. The facility was well hidden. The paths were made so that anyone who wandered into the woods would be led out. Sandy and Nat went off the trail a long way before finding the largest facility they had ever seen. It was heavily guarded too. They needed a plan, and fast.

The facility was heavily ridden with mine traps. Nothing Sandy had not handled before. Skilfully, she moved past the mines without offsetting a single one. Once she was in, she silently knocked out one of the guards and took his clothes. After finishing with the guard, the next step was to get Natalie in. That would be a lot easier than breaking in. She just had to find a weak point in the security system, which would allow her to sneak Natalie in.

There had to be a thousand people working in that place. Apart from the guards, all the workers had neck collars. It didn't take Sandy too long to realize that they were all slaves. *Who enslaves people in this generation?* Sandy thought to herself. They had to do something about it. Later. That would have to be a mission for another time, she promised herself. Besides, she had to deal with this mission for now.

The guards could walk freely in the facility as they were monitoring the workers' activities. This made it easy for Sandy to go through the building without raising questions. Room after room, she kept looking for any information she could uncover or anything she could use. There was a huge central depression, which was most likely where most of the action was happening. She had to check it out. Lost in her thoughts, she wasn't paying attention to where she was headed and bumped into a young man wearing a suit. As she looked up, she could not believe her eyes. Although he had a different haircut, she would always recognise him anywhere. It was Will Burne, standing before her very eyes.

……………

Will and Fred approached their destination in Afrasia. The flight had been extended but comfortable. They spent their time on the plane studying the files they took from Gean's home. There was a lot of information there. They already knew where the bomber was headed and what time he would be there. According to their calculations, they had about one hour to find him once they landed.

"Please keep your seat belts fastened. We've finished our descent, and we're coming in for the landing," the captain's voice announced from the cockpit of the plane. Just then, the ground exploded beneath them. The plane was close to the explosion and took a bad hit. As it crashed, no one on the plane noticed or tried to slow it down because the pilot was out, and Fred and Will were too. The plane crashed into the ground with great force, causing the engine to burst into flames from the impact.

……………

Reunited: Afrasia

Sandy stared into the eyes of Will Burne with surprise and shock over the turn of events. Will barely looked in her direction and walked past her as though he didn't even know who she was. Sandy couldn't help but follow him; she had so many questions running through her mind.

"Will?" called Sandy.

"Good afternoon, ma'am; how may I be of help to you?" replied Will.

"Why are you acting strange? What happened in San Mateo, and how did you get here faster than me?" she asked.

"San Mateo is not so far from Afrasia, you know. It's easy to get here with the right type of transport," replied Will.

"My trip wasn't so great at all. I got arrested by the police while on a ship to Afrasia; I was imprisoned but got transferred to somewhere I still have no idea about. I was placed in a transport van with someone named Natalie, and with her help, we escaped from the van and got here; now we're in search of help and any form of information; but instead, the sight here isn't at all pleasing or comforting," a frustrated Sandy narrated.

"It must have been one hell of an experience. This way: let's get you all cleaned up and settled," Will said, leading her away from the main walkway.

"What about Natalie? I can't leave her out there, just waiting and alone."

"You could always go back for Natalie. Meanwhile, how are you coping with the new upgrades and clone protocols put into place?"

"What upgrades and protocols are you talking about?" Sandy asked, her face scrunched in confusion.

"I'm not surprised by your ignorance of the new system. Almost everyone has had one bad experience or another. Personally, I don't like that my name has been changed from C5001 to Will Burne, and I have been enrolled to start learning his life. According to protocol, once his life form ceases to exist, I will be expected to replace him at all levels of existence."

Now, Sandy was even more confused; what Will was talking about made absolutely no sense. She made a conscious note to enquire about what happened in San Mateo, but first, she needed that freshening up and rest. Maybe once she had some rest, she could make sense of what he was trying to say.

Natalie couldn't wait outside for Sandy forever, so she decided to follow Sandy's trail inside. She got inside and was awed by the beautiful architecture. She saw the slaves and officers; she moved from one passageway to another, trying to find Sandy. She avoided the officers and stayed in less busy passageways. She spotted an officer dressed in white overalls and a helmet; his entire body was covered, and he was pushing a box marked volatile. She followed him until they got to a laboratory where he entered and moved to place the box in front of a man dressed exactly like him, only his helmet had blue stripes, and his face was visible.

He opened the box, took out a flask, and walked to a circular machine to insert the flask into it. Then he typed in some codes and walked away. Moments later, a greenish coloured gas began to fill the glass compartment at that end of the room.

……………

Will walked back into Sandy's room to check on her, allowing Sandy the opportunity to ask him all the questions that had been bothering her.

"Will, I have been wanting to ask you, why are you suddenly so enthusiastic about helping the people we have been fighting all along?" asked Sandy.

"I have not been fighting anyone all along. I've just been programmed to serve the New Order."

"The New Order?"

"Yes, the New Order. It is an uprising that will change everything; it will give stability to everyone and bring calm to all parties involved. The peace everyone has been seeking will finally be achieved. It will serve the greater good."

"I am lost…"

"Don't be lost, Miss Sandy; we have been programmed to replace dead agents; we are to learn their way of life and go out there to live their lives and do as our superiors wish."

Sandy was baffled. He suddenly seemed to be taking sides with George Lay and his cohorts, whereas he fought them all along. What was going on?

… … …

Natalie moved towards the laboratory and attempted to get inside. That's when she realized to gain access to the room, she needed a clearance either from the security room or have a security card. She waited for the officer she had been following to make his way out, then followed him back to the dressing room. She followed him closely into the room, then waited for him to start undressing before she went behind him and held him in a chokehold. She made sure he was lifeless before undressing him and putting on his clothes.

Natalie retrieved his card and hung it on her person as everyone else did. She hid his body behind the lockers, then hid her clothes in his locker. Then, she made her way back to the laboratory and walked in.

No one paid her any attention, so she relaxed. She blended in with the workers but soon realized everyone had a certain duty they were performing, so she grabbed a clipboard and moved to the glass compartment to have a look too, just like everyone else. She dreaded her science classes back in school, but that didn't make her unintelligent about science. There was nothing in the glass compartment, which made her wonder what everyone was staring at.

"It is so small you might need a magnifying lens to see it," she overheard someone say. She walked closer and squinted into the compartment. Then she saw what looked like a dead, half-decayed lizard on the metal table inside the compartment. She looked at her clipboard and saw previous observations. She scribbled blindly on the board as she felt disgusted by the sight before her. She walked away and continued viewing the laboratory. It was spacious and had various glass compartments on the ends. Everyone wore the same apparel, so it was hard to tell anyone apart. The man with the blue striped helmet must have stepped out because no striped helmets were anywhere to be seen.

… … …

After the plane had crashed, Will and Fred were left unconscious, completely unaware of their surroundings. Their burning plane was surrounded by people wearing black fireproof suits with masks covering their faces. The group quickly got to work putting out the fires on the plane, then pulled Will and Fred out of the wreckage. They were transported to a bunker.

Will opened his eyes and found himself lying in a room with four other people. He didn't recognize three of them, but as he looked closer, he recognized the fourth: Fred. He was lying on a bed so close to the floor, at first, Will thought he was actually lying on the floor. Will sat up and took in his surroundings; he was lying on one of such beds, and so was everyone else in the room. The room was lit by a single suspended light from the ceiling; the low light barely lit the room. In a smaller room further inside, Will could see a toilet. He could smell the stench from where he was lying. The smaller room had no door, meaning he would be inhaling the stench of human waste for the remainder of his stay.

"Where am I?" Will asked no one in particular, not expecting an answer.

"We are in a place where one thing is sure: we are all going to die one way or the other," the man who was lying close to the toilet murmured.

"You were brought in two nights ago, and we all thought you dead until you lifted your head some minutes ago. You should check on your friend; you were both brought in together," the man continued.

Will worried over what might have possibly happened in those days he was out. He remembered the bomb blast they had attempted to stop; he remembered Sandy and how he hadn't heard from her since she left West Federation, which was strange. He bowed his head with self-contempt at the thought that he had failed his country, failed his family, failed his team, failed Sandy. The thought of Sandy broke his heart and made him shiver at the thought; she might be in danger without him, especially with the way things were at the moment. He dropped to his knees and crawled over to Fred, trying to wake him up. He was cold, and the only hope he was alive was his pulse, which was faint, and even his breathing was barely audible.

"He needs help, or he might die; I can't lose him; he's all I've got left," Will said, turning his head from left to right. Someone moved closer to him and began covering Fred with blankets. Then, he lit a fire with some cloth and papers, keeping the area around him warm. Will sat beside him, rubbing his palm as he sobbed silently.

Hours passed before Fred started responding to his environment; he lifted his fingers, then slowly opened his eyes. He looked faint and could use some serious medical attention, but all he could get was the fire around him. Minutes later, footsteps were heard coming up the hallway, and the food slot on the cell door was opened. Five dried-out bread slices were thrown into the cell, and a glass of water was placed beside it. The man who spoke to Will earlier moved to gather the bread and water to share it amongst the group.

Will placed Fred's portion beside the fire so it could get warm. He helped him drink some water and lie back down, tucking his bread into his pockets.

He didn't know how he was going to escape, but he knew he was going to plan an escape anyways; just, he wasn't going to be able to do it with Fred in that condition. So, he would wait for Fred to get better, and by then, he should have a plan. Then, when they were ready, they would just have to actualize the plan. He shut his eyes and began reminiscing about the good times—back when he was happy to be a secret agent, where he went about his assignments with pride and loved conquering enemies.

He thought about Sandy and how happy they would've been if they could have gone on a vacation together. Her black skin on his white skin reminded him of caramel; he shivered at the thought of their past escapades. He wanted to be there again, to see her face and watch her smile and laugh at his jokes. The little time they spent together had made him realize how just how alone he had always been outside his job. His thoughts were interrupted by metal scraping against concrete just outside the cell. Soon, there was banging against the cell door.

"All prisoners, get up and face the wall," a voice thundered from outside. They all got up and faced the wall, except Fred, who was deep asleep. There was a heavy clanking of chains, and the metal door swung open; two people stepped in, observing everyone. They had turned to leave when the taller one noticed Fred. He walked over to Fred and kicked him, hard, on the ribs; Fred didn't move, so he turned and left him alone. After closing the door, they locked up and went down the hall.

"You will have to make him wake up during the next inspection, or else he will be taken out to the garbage post. And that's an even scarier place to be," said one of the cellmates. Going back to his previous position on the bed, Will returned to his deep thoughts and regrets.

… … …

Power at Stake: Afrasia

The New Order is a combined force from different powers in different countries. It had one motive: to unify the nations and create a universal order.

This was what George Lay and the other top world's elite made their followers believe. They put spies and followers at different strategic points on the map. They controlled the affairs of the political societies and put only their trusted members in top government offices. Their main agenda was hidden, and bound to stay that way until they were sure all the weapons and tools they would need were in place.

George Lay had made numerous sacrifices, being that he was among the top command. He lost his wife, not via death, but by betraying her and making her a pawn in his dirty chess game. He had made her choose sides, and when she went against him, he made her pay dearly by sending her out into the open as bait. He intended to pull down two powerful nations: West Federation and Afrasia, with their most experienced agents, Will Burne and Sandy Krave, respectively.

He had it all carefully planned out, but his plans lost direction when the two agents overcame his craftiness. This singular event set the example to many as to the lengths the New Order would go, just to actualize its dream. This incited fear; where there is fear, the people do what they think is right. Special agents who had fled and went into hiding came forward to declare their stand with the New Order. They did this to avoid being an enemy of the majority.

… … …

It was a new day, as shown by the tiny rays of light shining into the cell through the barred windows. Fred was awake and had his back against the wall with his head bent, hands resting on his raised knees. He was still weak from the trauma he suffered when the plane crashed. He raised his head when he noticed a shadow over him.

Will was standing over him, looking lean, with bloodshot eyes—he looked like someone who had not slept in weeks. He walked away from Fred, over to the toilet to take a leak. When he returned, he lowered himself beside Fred. He didn't utter a word to Fred as he shut his eyes and reminisced the nightmare that plagued him and devoured him of sleep the entire night. First, his mother and siblings had been bound, hands and feet, to an electric chair. Then, they were electrocuted in turns by Will himself.

He watched them scream for help, begging him to come to their rescue. He couldn't move because he was glued to the machine controlling the chair. He would increase the voltage and watch his mother vibrate until her head fell back, and her eyes rolled to the back of her head, with her lips slightly parted, but she let out no sound.

He had the nightmare repeatedly, twice that night; it kept him awake until the early hours of the morning, when he fell asleep. And, he had another terrifying dream, where he was in Sandy's secret bunker. It was not as neat as the last time. Instead, it was scattered with books and other things all around.

He searched for her frantically and found her in the corner of her room, crying and shaking violently. He reached out to hold her as he used to, but she recoiled away from him. Then, she yelled at him, and when she turned her face to him, he saw *'Failure,'* written boldly on her forehead, in bloody print. He withdrew from her immediately and turned to leave when he heard her calmly call his name, imploring him to save her.

He was brought out of his thoughts by one of the cellmates. He sat in the centre of the room; he had used the ash from the previous day's fire and drew what turned out to be a map.

"You see, Will, you can't fight the enemy on uneven ground; you can't run in an open field with a sniper's crosshair on your back. It's the most stupid thing anyone could ever do," he started.

"Here comes another sermon on life survival from someone who is living on a short thread," the second cellmate teased, shocking Will. He had just spoken for the first time since Will got here.

"It's not about survival today. It's about something new: the New Order," replied the man who was talking previously. At the mention of the New Order, Fred jerked his head up and shot stares at the man.

"Aha, I see your friend here is interested and may know a thing or two. When I was on the outside, before being brought in here, I was tortured like a common thief. You see, I was working for a very influential man in Afrasia here. He was good to all of us until he went for a business meeting with someone from the Underworld. After he returned, things took a downward turn, and he began going out more at night and was shady about his business deals. He sent his family away to some safe place. He kept saying he was protecting them from the new world and from himself.

"We, his workers, were left to attend to his needs there. Then, people began leaving, each passing day. He had over fifty workers, but within two months, we dropped in number to about fifteen. Initially, I thought the workers had returned home to their family, but apparently, they never made it home."

By now, he had the attention of almost everyone in the room. He bowed his head and remained that way for some time. When he raised his head to continue his story, he had teary eyes, and his face looked as though he was about to cry.

"One of those days, a certain lady showed up at the gate with a three-year-old baby girl. She said she wanted to see her husband, that he hadn't sent home any letters, money; neither had he called in over two months. Her husband was among the first set of workers to go home. She said she and her daughter were starving and needed help urgently.

"We tried explaining to her that her husband had since stopped working there, and he had gone home, but she wouldn't listen; she started yelling and was causing a ruckus. This got my boss's attention; this singular act, she regretted, and may still be regretting—if she is alive. So he came out, and when he heard of her outburst and what it was all about, he asked her to be brought up to him.

"She was given a room and asked to bathe and go relax. He cancelled his plans for the rest of the day, saying he had suddenly taken ill and needed some rest. At about 1:00 a.m., I heard screams coming from the main house and went in to see what was happening. I shouldn't have—because to date, I'm still haunted by that event.

"When I got inside, I realized the screams were coming from her room, so I made my way there, and the door was slightly open. I peeped inside and saw the lady on all fours; my boss was behind her having his way with her anally. He had a whip in his hand, and when she tried to withdraw herself from him, he'd whip her, and that's why she was screaming.

"I returned to my room, shaken and confused over what to do. In the morning, I heard she was sent down to the dungeon. This dungeon was a place he kept women to pleasure him whenever he wanted. He kept them in chains, rarely bringing them out. He'd keep them there like that until he found them useless, and then they would never be seen again. Her daughter was separated from her and taken away." He stopped again and inhaled.

"This was one of many horror cases that happened around that house," he continued, "I was one of the workers that had access to his room and his study. One of those days, I was cleaning his table when I stumbled across a file that contained illustrations of plans, and it had detailed coordination of events. Most of the events had already taken place, whilst some were yet to happen. I put it back where I found it and left the room. For days, I was scared of my boss, of what he was capable of doing. He was a good man, so his sudden change amazed me," he stopped talking, lost in his thoughts.

"You haven't told us about the New Order yet," Fred said weakly.

"The New Order is like a new government; only this government will be far worse than the former. It's the harmonization of the different countries. You see, the elite are so power-hungry that they will do absolutely anything just to get what they want.

"My boss was friends with George Lay, so he trusts him, even though deep inside, he knows the path he's chosen could lead to his destruction. The New Order has already started its reign; that's why there is an increase in evil and mayhem lurking in the streets.

"There will be wars, and from what I saw and know, there is a new age of technology; even the present AIs can't beat this new technology. The plan was broad: they want control over everything and everyone, so they have decided to make people they can control. So much money and effort have been invested in this. That is why no matter how hard you try to stop them, they keep stopping you; because their followers are everywhere, and they are just waiting for a command to execute." He rose from his position to use the restroom, leaving everyone in the room completely dazed.

… … …

Sandy had spent the past twenty-four hours feeling confused. She was still with Will at the Sav Fehaen facility, and she still hadn't reconnected with Natalie. If she were honest with herself, she probably could have made an effort to find Natalie, but sadness had lodged in her chest, making her feel apathetic. What had gone wrong between her and Will? Things were not looking good between them, and she knew they had once had something—a connection. Had they not?

Will had taken her to a room to freshen up and get some rest after she had found him in the facility. She was careful to only allow Will into her room, as she was not ready to be discovered by the enemy. She just did not have the energy to fight right now. As she was lying on her bed, she heard the door beep, then click, signalling that someone was coming in. She jumped to her feet, running to take cover close by the door.

When it opened, a mini-robot rolled in, scanned the room, and went on to clean it. Then it promptly left, with the door locking behind it. Sandy stepped out from her hiding spot and went back to lying down. She'd had more robots with her since she got here than humans, except for Will, of course.

She began reminiscing about Will, how they shared so much in common, and how they had been through a lot together, having each other's back. The romantic trysts. She wished things could go back to how they used to be. That seemed a hopeless wish because since she got there, Will had been different, talking only about programming and other things that could make sense, only if he cared to explain better.

Will knocked and announced his arrival, and when she told him to come in, he walked into the room. He stared at her form on the bed and proceeded to sit on the chair. She stared back a few seconds before sitting up.

"Will, what happened back at San Mateo?" she asked.

"San Mateo is located in the West Federation, and it's amongst the first places to be conquered by the New Order," Will replied.

"What is the New Order?"

"The New Order is the rise of a new age. It's the peace, harmony, and absence of violence we've all been seeking. It's the era where the weak will not have to worry about being oppressed; they would have freedom, equal rights, and opportunities, same as the rich," he replied with much charisma.

"When did you become so interested in things that have to do with the other side? You were more concerned about justice and getting to the root of this matter, but right now, you sound… different," Sandy was getting agitated now. She felt like smacking some sense into him.

"I have always been on this side. I was made for this. It just took time to show it," he said, with damning finality.

"What do you stand to gain in all this? Why not go against the New Order and come with me? Let's leave this place."

At her words, Will suddenly rose to his feet and looked at her with distaste.

"I can never go against the New Order," he said firmly, then he returned to his previous position in the seat, "the New Order is part of me; it is part of who I am. I wouldn't hesitate to destroy anyone who dared to stand between me and my duty to the New Order. I take orders from my superiors only, and I will not go against them; my programming will not allow it," he finished and rose to leave the room.

Sandy finally realized that she was dealing with a different Will. She decided that she would find out what had happened to him and why he went against their mission.

… … …

Fred found the information he just heard from his cellmate useful, but there was still so much puzzle to solve, especially regarding the boss's identity. He would find that out, but first, he needed to talk to Will because he knew him too well. He was not the type who would remain idle in such a place for too long. He must have hatched a plan by now, and that plan, Fred needed to know. His cellmate returned, and he proceeded to ask him a few questions.

"How did you end up here?" Fred asked the man.

"I was given a relief letter, so I packed up and left. The last thing I remember was boarding a transport to take me home to my family. When I came to my senses, I found myself here. I've been here ever since," he told him.

At that, deciding not to press him any further and just let him be, Fred decided to talk with him privately some other time. Then, making a mental note, he decided to lay back on his bed and get some rest, figuring he would need it for the expected escape—if he knew Will like he thought he did.

… … …

Prisonbreak: Afrasia

Will and Fred decided to break out in the early hours of the morning; they would leave during the first round of morning inspections. They slept so they would have enough strength for the mission ahead of them. And they slept well since they had spent the previous night tearing their bedsheets into shreds to make them into long ropes, which Fred hid under his thin, flat mattress. They didn't know whether to involve the other members of their room because they were worried about how they might react, so they decided to do it alone, without them. As usual, they heard the scraping sound of metal against the floor and the clanking of chains, then the cell door opened.

"Face the wall; be good, so you don't bring trouble on yourself," sneered a guard before making his way in. Everyone stood facing the wall except Fred. He was seated on the floor with his head bowed. He looked as though he was nearly lifeless.

"I was told you would give us problems; that's why I beat the two of you senseless before locking you in here. But look at you now, all strong and wanting to fight," the second guard jeered. He was standing outside. He came in, making his way towards Fred, while the first guard walked around the room. The first guard was approaching Will, who was standing, nonchalantly, facing the wall. He walked past him, turning his back to Will. Will was ready. Just then, he turned and grabbed his head from the back, putting him in a chokehold.

The guard wasn't expecting it. He struggled against Will, but Will was taller and stronger and easily overpowered him. When the second guard saw what was happening, he ran over to help him but crashed face-first into the concrete. Fred, holding a rope, which was the cause of the guard's demise, grinned. As part of their plan, he had waited until just the right moment to yank on the pre-tied rope, sending the guard crashing to his face. Before he could gather his strength to get back up, his own baton made a painful impact to the back of his head, thanks to Fred.

By then, Will had finished off the first guard, so he joined Fred and the other cellmates in beating the other guard to his death. Will and Fred undressed the guards, then gave the clothes to two of the cellmates; that way, they could all escape unnoticed. The ex-cellmates/now guards bound the three remaining cellmates and led them out as though they were taking them somewhere. This kept the other guards off their backs and made their navigation through the long hallways easier.

They walked until they came into an open area. The building was built inwards, with all the corridors leading to one big open area and each opening facing the other. A large open square was in the centre. They immediately drew back into the long hallways and decided to try going out another exit. Fewer guards were there now, so they hurried their steps and soon made it through a fire exit to the back parking lot with no one and no cars. Fred volunteered to go look for a car, leaving the others behind.

He made it out into the parking area, where he saw a large gate and a few guards around. He saw a black van parked at the farthest end of the parking area, and he knew that was their ticket to freedom. He proceeded to walk briskly towards the van. He was paid no notice, which he found troubling. He made it to the van, and from previous knowledge, disabled the alarm and started the engine. He drove the van back to where he left the others but was surprised to find only Will and one of the cellmates still alive. The other two were lying on the ground, dead.

Will had taken the guard's clothing from one of the dead cellmates and slipped it on. He opened the back doors and got into the van, pulling the last cellmate along. Fred gunned the accelerator and drove towards the gate, but when they got there, they needed clearance, which they didn't have. Fred knew the gate couldn't be torn down with a mere van. So, he turned to Will for help. Will opened the doors of the van and climbed out, running over to the gatehouse.

The controls were upstairs, so he had to run upstairs. He met three guards, which was a fair number, and he was by himself. He had only the baton he had retrieved from the guard he took down in the cell. So, he walked up to the first guard and said something barely audible. When the guard walked up to him and asked him what he said, Will smashed him in the head with the baton; he hit him two more times, then hit him on the neck. It was so quick and unexpected; he pulled it off before the other two guards had time to respond.

The other two guards came at him, one on each side. Will attacked the one on the right because he looked more agile, so he figured he would first take out the better fighter. He gave him an uppercut and proceeded to hit him with the baton repeatedly; meanwhile, the other guard punched Will in the ribs. Will stumbled back, attempting to gather his footing. He soon regained his balance and started smashing the second guard as well. Soon, both guards were on their knees, sucking wind and trying to regain their feet. Finally, he left them and made his way to a large red button. On instinct, he didn't press it; rather, he looked for a lever, and when he found one, he pushed it towards the end that had "open" on it. On the screen, he saw the gates begin to open slowly.

The van began rolling towards it, and he knew it was time to go. The guards were trying to get up, so he hit them again before racing out the door, down the stairs, and towards the slow-moving van. He jumped into the van, and before he had even settled down, Fred jammed on the accelerator and raced out of there. To their surprise, they were being held at an abandoned prison that had been shut down years ago due to poor maintenance.

……………

Natalie had soon figured out that the laboratory had different sections for various tests and analyses. She had since learned a few things about the laboratory. She knew her way around and where to go in search of substances to use. What she couldn't understand was why all this testing was being carried out. She was still trying to figure some things out, although time was not on her side. She had occasionally gone out to search for Sandy, but it looked as though she had vanished since she got here. She became worried, hoping that Sandy was in one piece.

……………

Sandy eventually grew tired of hiding in her room with nothing to do but wonder about Will's changed personality and decided to go in search of Natalie. She believed Natalie had somehow found her way inside but was worried about her because of the guards and miniature robot that would instantly raise the alarm about an intruder. She rose from her bed and got dressed in something less alarming and attractive. She made her way to the door and was about to open it when she heard a knock. She peeped through the peephole and saw Will, so she opened the door to let him in. He observed her briefly before going to sit down.

"Going somewhere?" he asked.

"I was thinking of going out for a stroll, but now that you're here, I'll just forget about it," Sandy replied. She stared at him and remembered when his hands used to caress her in ways she couldn't explain, how he kissed her and made love to her passionately without either of them holding back or being reluctant. Finally, Sandy decided to make a move on him. Walking over to him, she stood in front of him and began to stroke his hair; he raised his head and stared at her as though she had lost her mind. She bent to his level and kissed his forehead. Then, she kissed the bridge of his nose and proceeded to place her lips on his. She ran her tongue across his lips before kissing him, but he responded coldly to her. He didn't return the kiss nor touch her; instead, he pushed her away gently and got up. He wiped his lips and stared past her, avoiding her eyes.

"My programming forbids me from involving in such activities and the likes. I was made to receive and carry out commands, not to express myself in such a manner," he said to Sandy. Sandy felt the heat of rejection burn low in her stomach as she stared at him, panting with want. She didn't understand what was going on anymore, and this singular act went to prove her point that Will must have undergone some major form of transformation to behave this way towards her.

"I will be taking my leave now," Will said, bringing Sandy back from her thoughts, "I am sorry if you feel downcast and disappointed, but I was made not to feel affectionate towards anyone so that it wouldn't interfere with my job. Like I have been saying, I was made to serve, not be served. So if you need anything else—something nonphysical—call me."

And with that, he left the room and shut the door with a soft *click*. Sandy swore gloriously as she returned to her bed; she wished he had slammed the door, wished he had shown some emotion. She sat fuming and swore to uncover whatever the hell was wrong with Will, but first, she needed to find Natalie.

… … …

"What happened back there when I left?" Fred asked Will.

"They were both members of the New Order, and they were going to rat us out, so I did what had to be done," Will replied.

"What next?" asked the remaining cellmate. He was the one who had told the story, and they soon learned his name was Steph.

"We are going to find a friend of ours; she is from Afrasia, but the problem is we don't yet know where we can find her," Will rumbled.

"We will leave the van with you, Steph; it will help you, but not for long, and as soon as there's trouble, ditch the van and continue your journey on foot. I hope you find your family," Fred said with a pot full of camaraderie. The journey continued until they connected to the major road, where they began to see minute settlements. Fred was focused on the road, although he had a lot on his mind regarding the person they sought. He knew who Will was talking about, and he decided to drop the topic because, at this rate, the only people he could trust right now were her, Will, and himself. He didn't want any more surprises, so he independently decided to leave the van for Steph, with the hope that Will would support him without asking any questions, and that's what happened. He also thought about people, forces, and other elements that must have been alerted to their escape, which meant the van would be on the radar.

Fred drove to the train station and parked the van away from public view. He and Will got out, leaving the van for Steph. They wished him well and parted ways. Fred led them from the train station towards the transport rank. Will followed him, hoping he was sure about what he was doing. When they got to the taxi rank, he led them across the street and made a sharp turn, which brought them onto the dirtiest of streets in Afrasia. Fred led them up a row of stairs and onto a dirty, creaky porch. He knocked once and said something quickly into the window. When the door opened, he stepped in, pulling Will along with him. The inside wasn't any better than the outside.

"You're not welcome here," said the young lady with an airy voice as she emerged from behind the counter. "What do you want?"

"A car. Something unattractive, but fast," replied Fred.

"We don't sell cars here or deal in car services. This is strictly a pawn shop," she replied defensively.

"I have information on your father's whereabouts," Fred said to her. She froze at the mention of her father and considered his words carefully before giving them the keys to a modern car parked two streets away. Fred rounded up business with her, giving her the information he knew, and they left her shop. Then they headed to the car, and it fit the description Fred had requested.

"What do you think Sandy's last location might be?" Fred asked, once inside the car.

"I have no idea; I seriously doubt she would be in her bunker," Will replied, his troubles rearing its head.

"Does she know of Sav Fehaen?" Fred asked.

"She does," Will confirmed. Fred turned the ignition and sped off towards Sav Fehaen in search of Sandy.

……………

New Technology: Afrasia

Sandy couldn't get over the ordeal with Will, so she decided to go see if she could figure out what was going on. She dressed like she had seen most of the workers were dressed. She opened the door of her room and made her way out to the hallway. She looked from left to right before deciding to go right. She walked for several minutes without seeing anyone and was almost upset with herself for going the wrong way when she found a room with the words *"Out of Bounds."* She knew from experience that only important stuff would be hidden behind a door marked as an out-of-bounds room. She used the card she had taken from Will to unlock the door.

She stepped into the room, seeing it had another door; this door needed a combination code to unlock it. She thought for a long while about what the passcode might be and remembered Fred was the one who told them to come here the last time he communicated with them. She punched in 242638, the code he gave them to memorize, and with a beep and flash of green light, the door unlocked and slid open. She walked into what looked like a factory.

Numerous robots were zooming around, fixing things. They seemed busy with making something. She moved slowly, staying close to the wall, when she saw a room with rows of robots—only they weren't exactly robots; they looked like humans. Each of them had unfinished faces, which you could see the inner workings. Sandy was wondering what was really going on in there when she saw a group of technologists standing around discussing in low tones. She tip-toed towards them, and when she got close, she hid behind a pillar and dropped to her knees, straining her ears as she listened hard.

"These humanoids are the latest generation, and they will do their jobs, accurately and efficiently, without question. Their programming is better optimized than the last group. This group is the successful group we have been striving to achieve," a man conversed, pride lacing his voice.

"Are there any differences in job duties from the last batch?" asked one of the men.

"Yes, actually. These are replicants because they are specifically programmed to replace dead secret agents. They will get rid of the stubborn agents and replace them with these humanoids to fool the public. We've had good results so far with the agents we've already replaced; no one can even tell the difference. And, this way, we're able to monitor the movement of any rebellion that would be rising too," he explained.

"But you can't just put them out there," said the third person.

"They undergo training to act, walk, speak, and do so much more, exactly as their predecessor," said the man to the others. "They will be released into society upon the death of their human," he replied.

Sandy watched as a replicant was brought out and powered on. It was asked a series of questions, and it replied just like a human would. It was given a task to perform, and it carried it out efficiently. Sandy felt her heart racing with shock and the dawn of realization at what she heard and saw; she had been talking to a fake all along. *That's why he kept talking about the New Order and the new program update!* She quietly sneaked out undetected and went to explore the facility. The replicants were innumerable; they looked like a whole army, just waiting for orders from their superiors. Sandy began to wonder what happened to Will and if he was truly dead because his replacement was active. After she saw enough, she decided to leave the facility to avoid getting captured.

She went back to her room and retrieved her satellite phone. Though the battery was low, she'd kept it and had been hiding it. She was glad she did, given the circumstances she found herself in. She hit the power button and waited for the beeping icon on the screen to settle down; then, she punched in Will's secret number. As she waited for the call to connect, she paced about, wondering what she would do if Will were indeed dead.

Her lips curled into the beginnings of a smile as the call went through, but then, no one answered. She growled painfully and tried again, hoping to get a response this time. When she couldn't get through to him, she felt dread spreading over her. She had heard about the bombing at his agency, and according to the news, no one got out alive. Could Will be dead, along with the others? There's no way he could have even been there when it happened, though. But if he wasn't in the building, then where could he possibly be that would warrant his replicant to be turned on? She became worried sick and decided to go in search of Natalie. It was about damn time to leave.

… … …

Natalie walked briskly on high alert as she made her way down the hall. She was on her way back from the storehouse after retrieving some chemicals. She had made herself a part of the team so she could try to find out why all those tests were being performed. Then, out of nowhere, a hand dragged her into a room. She spun around and was surprised at who she saw: a tensed-up Sandy.

"You shouldn't do that to people, disappear like that without any sign in all this time!" said Natalie.

"We need to leave as soon as possible, before we become references of the past," replied Sandy.

"I found something. You'd be surprised by what goes on in here, and I am sure if we searched further, we would find out more," Natalie confided.

"Could anything be more shocking and nerve-racking than what I just witnessed?" Sandy asked in disbelief.

"Well, there's only one way to find out. But before we leave, you need to see this," Natalie said as she walked out of the room, followed by Sandy. Natalie led her to the laboratory where she had been observing. They hid under a frame and waited for what Natalie called "an experiment." Soon, a box containing an albino rat was brought in. The rat was removed and placed in a glass compartment. A man came forward and began operating the machine. He took a large syringe that contained some greenish gas and inserted it into the machine, then he checked the tubes and stepped aside. Sandy couldn't quite shake the feeling that he seemed familiar as she narrowed her eyes at the only visible part of his face, and then recognition sank in. *It can't be*, she thought, *the one person that was responsible for this whole mess.*

"Kean!" Sandy yelled out, which caused an uproar as several guards rushed towards them, but Dr Kean stopped them. Dr Kean wanted Sandy to see what was going to happen to the rat in the glass compartment. He went to the machine and turned it on. Sandy watched as a green coloured gas flowed through the tube connecting the machine to the compartment.

It slowly began to fill the compartment while the rat ran around, trying to escape. But there was nowhere to go, as the compartment was sealed shut.

"That could be anyone someday, Miss Sandy," Dr Kean said. "You see, I have been working on this my entire life, and now that it's ready, all that is left, my darling, is testing it on a human subject—and you, my dear, seem to be the best candidate for this." He waved his hand towards the guards, who dragged a screaming Natalie and a shell-shocked Sandy away.

… … …

Dr Kean sat in his rolling chair at his workstation. It just happened to be one of his best days. A successful laboratory experiment and a surprise visit by the one person he had been trying so hard to get rid of all this time—Sandy Krave. He wondered where Will went and who the new girl was.

With Sandy here, it meant Will would be there soon. He had called his superiors, and plans to move Sandy to the Underworld were in the works. She had handed herself over to him on a silver platter. She became the missing piece in the large puzzle; she was going to be the reason why the New Order would possess what they had wanted for so long. Of course, he had more plans for Sandy and Will. But, more importantly, he knew Will would come for Sandy, and he would break him by using what mattered to him most—Sandy. It was glorious.

There was a knock on his door, and he told the staff outside to come in. He stepped in with "Sandy." He doubted any possibility of Will knowing about replicant technology, and even if he did, he wasn't going to think rationally when it came to Sandy's life at stake.

"Take her to the instructor; she has a lot of programming and kinks to iron out in a short period of time," Kean ordered. The guard led replicant Sandy away, leaving Dr Kean alone with his thoughts. Replicants could not be killed with the gas, but he could make it look good. So, he had a plan to shut her down, staging the whole encounter. He also planned to display it all on a big screen for Sandy to watch before she was shipped off to the Underworld. He wanted her to know Will thought she was dead, with no hope he'd come searching for her.

For him, that was the bonus part of his win, and Sandy's reaction would also be a win. He laughed at his plans and decided to celebrate with a glass of wine from his favourite bottle.

……… ……… ………

Will and Fred had tracked down Sav Fehaen, and they were driving towards it. Will stuck his hand out the window and felt the fast-moving wind against his hand. He thought of what it would be like to hold Sandy once more. He was sure she would be elated to see him. He longed to kiss her and hold her in his arms. Caress her face and touch her in places that made her drip only for him. But what if he didn't find her there; what if something bad had happened to her?

He shouldn't think like this, but with the way things were going, he couldn't help but think that way. He turned to Fred and watched him drive. He found his driving slow and wished he were the one driving instead.

"Couldn't we go any faster?" he asked Fred.

"Try to calm down. We're almost there, and hopefully, nothing has happened. Have you heard from the Fiery Eagle?"

"The last time we spoke, he sounded as though he never wanted to hear from me again, and now that things are the way they are, I think it's best not to call him to tell him more about how I'm not taking care of Sandy at the moment," he replied.

Fred nodded and concentrated on his driving, stepping harder on the accelerator.

They got to Sav Fehaen and parked out of public view. Then, like Sandy, they realized the pathways were a cover, and went off the beaten path. Once they found the huge compound, they approached the edge of the property and proceeded to enter the facility. They, too, realized it was loaded with landmines, and there were guards swarming the whole facility. They found that strange because the Sav Fehaen they had heard about wasn't what they discovered when they got there.

Will scaled through the mines leaving trails for Fred. They made it through and were faced with the task of going over the fence. They walked around the facility and uncovered a fresh break-in point, which gave Will and Fred hope for Sandy. They climbed through it carefully and decided to check out the main building.

… … …

Dr Kean sat in his office, smiling smugly as he watched Will and Fred from the CCTV as they promptly took his bait, proud of himself for leaving that opening in the fence. He was quite happy things were beginning to fall into place…

… … …

Will and Fred got in through the air vent and dropped out in the corridor. They had made their way into the corridor that led to the laboratory. And then a booming voice scared their wits away.

"Welcome to Sav Fehaen, gentlemen; your presence has been long-awaited, and I was beginning to fret that my predictions were wrong. Nevertheless, I will give you directions as to where you can find me—and her," he paused mockingly. "Surprised? Don't be. I know what, or rather, who you are here for." This voice came from the speakers mounted in the hallway.

Fred and Will were surprised their presence was expected. Of course, there would be more free passes, as it was clear the broken fence was there for a reason.

"Follow my directions, and you won't get lost; walk straight ahead." So they followed the directions given by the voice. It was obvious they couldn't go against him, as they were being watched. Will was hesitant, but Fred dragged him along.

"Agent Burne, you should be happy; I mean, you will get to see that one person you haven't seen in such a long time. The elevator has been unlocked for you; step in, and it will bring you right up to me. When you get there, turn left; you will know it's me when you get there." By now, they were standing in front of the elevator. With a ding and a whoosh, the elevator doors opened, and they stepped inside. After it closed, it took them up three floors. Stepping out of the elevator, they walked towards their right as directed until they came upon the laboratory. Will stopped in his tracks when he saw Dr Kean smiling at them through the transparent glass.

He was completely covered except for his head, which he covered with a helmet after smiling at them. Then, he walked over to the microphone and spoke into it.

"Bring in the subject," he said. A bound, hooded figure was brought in and placed in a chair inside a tall, glass compartment. She was cut free and injected with a substance; after a few seconds, she opened her eyes and rose from the chair, removing the hood.

Sandy! Will roared in hysterics at the sight of her and began searching for the door. Fred stood helplessly at one end, watching the drama unfolding before his eyes. Dr Kean was smiling from ear to ear while he was putting things in order. He was having fun as he watched Will going crazy with anger and fear. Sandy stood in the compartment and stared at Will with fear in her eyes.

"Say your goodbyes because this will be your last time seeing each other," Kean said as he tapped the eject button on the machine. A green gas steadily ran through the tubes and into the compartment, and Sandy started banging on the door and screaming. Seconds later, she was coughing and holding her chest. Then she just dropped to the floor with her eyes wide, frozen in death. Will sank to his knees, his heart fractured, as his hands drifted to his face in shock. Fred began urging him to leave, but Will couldn't hear anything over the ringing in his ears. He had zoned out completely, staring blankly in shock.

In the next room, Sandy sobbed as she watched Will going crazy with anger and fear, then kneeling brokenly on the floor. She understood his anger at Dr Kean, and his level of hatred for him mirrored all she felt.

She watched him on the screen as he descended into emotion. Fear and rage that he had let her down, thinking she was paying with her life. He was punching the transparent doors repeatedly, but his blows were of no consequence against those doors. He could not find a way inside, neither could he make one. She watched him let out a tortured scream, the scream of a broken, hopeless creature as he watched the fake Sandy lying dead. He wasn't calming down, neither was he listening to Fred. The last thing she saw before being blindfolded was Fred dragging the struggling, roaring Will away.

Sandy felt a sense of doom embrace her, like she had just heard Will's voice for the last time. A voice that brought back all the memories they had together. His breath on her neck, his pleasured moans making their way to her ears. She was so lost in her thoughts that she didn't even notice when she was bundled up and placed in a shipping container.

After the guards captured Natalie in the laboratory, they took her to a holding room where she was kept alone for some time. She was later tended to by a lady who claimed to know everything about her. After hours of painless interrogation by the lady, Dr Kean entered the room.

"I ensured that you were treated well, yet you are refusing to tell us who you are and why you are here," he said to her, "so I came with a friend who will make you talk by any means necessary." He stepped away from the door, and a man pushed a trolly into the room. It had all sorts of equipment on it. Soon, the room was transformed from a comfortable, normal holding room into a torture chamber.

She was moved from her chair into an electric chair. She was strapped in, and soon, wave after wave of electric current began flowing through her body. She screamed at the top of her voice as bolts and waves of wicked intensity flooded her very core, and when it was turned off, Kean asked her if she was willing to talk or ready to handle more of the current. The torture continued, and with each passing round, she assured herself that she would keep doing the right thing.

Natalie didn't want to die because if she did, her mission would be incomplete, which meant putting everyone in harm's way. So, she decided to do the needful. After the current had been turned off several rounds later, she began rambling with just the slightest touch of desperation.

"I don't know Sandy! We only met in a transport van. I have no one. I have nothing to lose, so I can help you with whatever you've planned for her. I am close to her now, and she will trust me if you put us back together. I could always get information for you; I can be your extra pair of eyes," she finished with convincing finality.

"Are you saying what I think you are?" Kean teased.

"I am, and much more. Make me a part of you, a part of the New Order. I don't know what you have against Sandy, but I can help you make your dreams come true," she promised.

"The New Order isn't a body you can joke with, dearest. If you turn against it, it will turn against you, in ways you can only imagine."

Natalie swallowed and nodded her understanding eagerly.

"You will need a whole lot of training before you can even go on missions. As for Sandy, she will be involved in a trade, and soon she will be leaving for the Underworld," Kean finished, pinning her with an intense stare.

"Put on that ship? What if things go wrong and you need someone to pull the trigger for you? Are you sure about the ones you put with her?" Natalie asked. It seemed the proper question, as Kean thought of what Natalie had said and realized she was right.

"I am doing this because you seem like a good little lap dog, but the moment you turn against me is the moment you die," Kean said to her before turning away. Then, to the guard, he gave specific orders concerning Natalie and left the room.

Natalie sighed raggedly; she had managed to convince him to spare her, but this, she determined—this was his mistake. He would not know what hit him.

… … …

Fred dragged a very enraged Will away while trying to figure out where an escape route might be. Will wasn't thinking straight, so he was of no use. Fred led them to the elevator, and luckily, it opened.

They got out on the ground floor that led to the parking lot. Fred broke the security system on a truck and shoved Will into it. Then, he drove at a very high rate of speed, and when they got to the gate, surprisingly, it opened right up for them. Fred and Will escaped from the facility, completely unaware that Natalie and Sandy were on a ship headed for the Underworld.

… … …

The Rebels' Base: Afrasia

The sky was dark, and the truck was getting slower by the minute. Will sat in a trance, unable to speak or respond to anything Fred said. The scene of Sandy falling dead, clutching her heart, filled his brain. He remembered the first time he saw her with Kean.

He thought of her tiptoeing into his room like a cute little kitten in a shimmering nightdress. Goosebumps rose on his body as he thought of their first embrace. He remembered the struggle in her eyes when she saw him through the glass doors.

Something was amiss. Sandy didn't seem to recognise him at all. Will shook his head at himself. Seriously, Will. What should a dying person do? Should they smile and wave at their lover when they are struggling with poison in their lungs? Will chastised himself for the millionth time, "if only I had gotten there a little sooner…"

He felt Fred shake him. "What?" he sneered.

"I need your help. We're being followed. That grey van is still behind us, for a long time now. The fuel won't last much longer." Fred was desperate to get Will's attention. Without warning, Will pressed the emergency "Halt" button in the truck.

"Will! What are you doing!?" Fred screeched as the truck came to a sudden stop with a massive jolt, and the vehicle following them hit their rear, throwing the men inside of it around. Will jumped out in a split second.

"What do you want, bastards?" Will thundered, approaching them like a hulk, picking up a piece of broken glass from the ground as he stormed towards them.

The people in the grey vehicle got out and raised their hands in surrender. "We come in peace. Please…" the scrawny man pleaded.

"Peace, you butchers… You want to know where we are headed next. Don't you?" Will kicked him hard in the ribs.

"Please believe us. We are on your side. Help us," the second, wounded man from the car pleaded. Will turned towards him and threw the glass shard at him like a spear. The man moved at the last minute to dodge the glass. Fred had gotten out by now. "Will, behind you!" he shouted.

But before he could turn, Will felt a sharp syringe pierce his nape, and the world around him went black yet again, for the umpteenth time. The man he kicked had drugged him in a split second.

… … …

Will tried to force his eyes open. Two blurry men peering over him was the first thing he saw. Will still couldn't move a muscle. But he could see various people being treated on a veranda on the floor above him. "Where am I? Is this a hospital?" Will asked.

The two men attending him moved away, and Fred's face appeared. He was gleaming with happiness. "Will, Sandy is alive."

Will let out a roar in ecstasy. Then, he heard someone say, "Let him rest for a while. The dosage in the sleeping syringe will last for another half an hour."

Fred reassuringly touched his arms and whispered again into his ears, "Will, Sandy is alive. She is being transported to an unknown destination. Although odds are against us, we can still save her." Will was drifting off again, but he heard Fred clearly. Will slept peacefully, feeling more relief than he'd felt in his entire life.

An hour later, Will, Fred, and three other people sat next to each other on a hospital bed, while Nyman, their leader, sat on a small desk used to store medicines in front of them.

Will now understood they were in a hidden facility run by the rebels. They had converted the underground parking lot of a hospital into a functioning base. The hospital on top had been bombed and turned into rubble. Nobody suspected the unaffected basement, and the group operated from there.

"This is not an ideal place to conduct meetings. But you know our situation. I'm Nyman. I was a cop here just over two weeks ago. My sister, Natalie, was training to become a cop. I came across some conspiracies. I sensed our chief was acting weird on some important issues. Then, I was assigned to wipe out a secret rebel group with my colleagues.

"We were given way more ammo and hi-tech weapons than needed. I suspected something fishy. The rebels were a group of three people: a man with a distorted face and two old scientists." Nyman let the idea sink into their heads.

"Where is my father?" one person shouted, losing patience.

"Yes. And where is Sandy?" Will pitched in.

"Is my brother still alive?" another person asked, frightened.

"Yes. Your father and your brother are both alive and safe. I was assigned to kill them. But they pleaded with me for their life in exchange for telling me some big secret. They told me about the New Order—it wants powerful people to do exactly as they say. Else they are eliminated, and their robot clones, called replicants, replace them."

"Clones?" everybody in the audience gasped except Fred.

"Yes. Clones. Or, more specifically, replicants. They look exactly like the human they are meant to replace. The third person we saved was a replicant. Nearly three defective replicants are produced for every functioning one. The defective ones have varying levels of artificial intelligence. They are designed to feel things physically like humans, too. But they are killed mercilessly. They are thrown into a furnace, alive," Nyman sighed.

"What sort of cannibalistic New Order is this?" the third person in the bed clenched his fist and shouted.

"You're the reason for all this technology. You created this monstrosity!" Nyman shouted as he lost his patience, lunged forward and struck him on the jaw. The man crumpled on the bed with a bleeding nose.

"Please stop it, Nyman!" Fred interrupted, pushing him back. The other two tended to the wounded man.

"You are acting as unscrupulous as Will here," Fred blamed, pointing at Nyman.

"Shut the fuck up, techie trash! I lost my whole family—my father, mother, dog, friends, every single one. The only one alive is my sister, Nat. And those bastards have her!" Nyman roared in anger, with bulging biceps and a reddening face.

"I understand how you both feel. I assure you, Nat and Sandy are both fine. Natalie placed a tracking device into Sandy's heel. We've started getting signals from it. They are both on the same ship," Fred clarified. Will heaved a sigh of relief.

"Don't be so happy. They are better off dead than on that ship. They are under the direct control of George Lay. And they're using Sandy to blackmail Adi Kalim. They want the nuclear codes from him. It will destroy all four capitals, in Afrasia, Oceania, West Federation, and the Underworld," Nyman spat, filled with bitterness.

"I did not mean for any of this to happen. I only perfected the cell mitosis technology to help people who lost their body parts. It will cure people suffering from brain-cell damage," the person who got hit spoke with fear now.

Fred interfered again, "It is not your fault. I understand. You shouldn't have sold it to George Lay."

"I didn't. The government sponsored my project. Shouldn't I work for my own country? President Morgan gave me a special medal for my achievement," the wounded man said pitiably.

"That is a clone. President Morgan, my chief, and many others were killed. The ones in the seat of power now are clone puppets controlled by that bastard George!" Nyman shouted again.

"Did you learn all this from the rebels?" Will questioned.

"Yes. Those rebels were scientists trying to escape from the base you saw earlier. Kean had their families under surveillance. They tried to save the replicants from being brutally killed. They escaped, saving one for proof, and asked me to save their families. Only these two remain. All the others died in the bombings," Nyman explained.

"And he is Mr Abdul Jamal, a great biologist who perfected the cell mitosis technology used to create humanoid replicants," Fred introduced the wounded man.

"And I'm Dr Hunter Springs. I am also a biologist and scientist. My brother worked with Mr Jamal," the other man said.

"I get it. Who is this?" Will questioned.

"He is in marketing. His name is Andrew Foster. Andrew is the other scientist's son," Fred introduced him. "We only saw Sandy's clone die that day. Sandy was deported on a ship. According to the scientists, that green gas doesn't kill the clones. It just puts them into a death-like trance. They can be revived from it," Fred explained.

"Why did you follow us?" Will asked Nyman.

"We came to save Natalie. We couldn't get into the facility. We saw you coming out of there and followed you to ask for help," Nyman explained.

"So, then, what's the plan?" Will asked.

"We should head to that damned ship and save my sister," Nyman said.

"And Sandy," Fred said.

"We asked Fred to guide us with technology. The rebels and I have amassed as much ammo as we could," Nyman explained.

"The rebels and Nyman's remaining colleagues should tour the city to bring the wounded and anyone who needs help back here," Fred added.

"Let's start immediately. I don't want to waste another minute," Will said, jumping up from the bed with enthusiasm. *These fools should have held this briefing while we were on the move. We could have saved lots of time,* he thought to himself. He smiled at himself for aching so severely for Sandy.

… … …

"You have no other choice Adi Kalim. You saw Sandy. Give me my wife and the nuclear codes. You have thirty minutes to reach this ship and activate them with your bio-signals." George Lay cut the video call.

He saw the badly bruised Sandy with Natalie holding her at gunpoint. "It is merely hours before I become the ruler of this world. I will destroy all four cities. The damage will be so massive, every continent will beg the New Order to save them from further attacks," he chuckled, thinking to himself.

"Did you finish planting that bomb in her brain?" George asked one of his henchmen. He nodded robotically and gave him the remote trigger. George waved it teasingly in front of Sandy.

"One more hour, dear. I will send you to heaven to meet your parents," he sniggered.

… … …

The luxury ship en route to the Underworld was brimming with humanoid workers diligently doing their jobs. Sandy had a broken arm—a gift she received from her replicant when she tried to escape. She remembered seeing Will break down, watching her robot clone die. Sandy knew Natalie was up to something, but she couldn't quite figure out what.

She was beaten badly to keep her immobile and was kept bound in a kneeling position. Secretly, Natalie had popped some pain pills in Sandy's mouth. Sandy's knees ached terribly; she had been in this kneeling position for so long. The pain in her broken arm was unbearable. Her head was throbbing from multiple blows. But the pain was somewhat bearable after the pills kicked in. She tried to guess how Will would perceive her if he saw her now?

"Battered" was the first word that came to mind. Then, out of the corner of her eye, Sandy could have sworn she saw someone landing on the deck of the ship, from out of nowhere… "Are they jumping in from a helicopter?" Sandy wondered.

Before she had even finished her thought, she saw Will rushing over to her. He kneeled before her, taking her face in both his palms. "Oh my God! You are beautiful," he said, panting, "Thank God you are alive."

Sandy opened her mouth to warn him, but before she could say anything, one of the humanoid henchmen had hit him on the neck with the butt of his gun. Will crumpled to the floor, unconscious beside her. "Will!" she cried out, her head pounding.

"What the hell is happening!?" George shouted at the top of his lungs. His fists started to shake, and drops of sweat appeared on his forehead, even amidst the cold ocean breeze.

"The rebels have hijacked your supply helicopter and infiltrated," Natalie explained.

"How did they know our coordinates?" Mr Lay questioned.

Natalie blinked for a minute. Her brother likely tracked the coordinates from the signal she sent. She, too, had a tracker in her heel.

"It must be Adi Kalim," she said before anyone could suspect her. "He won't give up without a fight. He probably gave the order to track the coordinates as soon as your call started, then gave them to Will. You know he was with Sandy on the last failed mission," she said confidently.

"But how did they get ahold of the supply copter?" one henchman asked, confused.

"Kalim has links everywhere. He would have dug up all the details about this ship by now. For all we know, an army could be on its way to attack us as we speak," Natalie tried to divert the topic.

"Like hell, it will. I have all the world leaders under my control. Nobody will give ears to an old bureaucrat. And get rid of him," he gestured at Will. "Check whether anybody else jumped in with him," George ordered.

Sandy felt something touch her hand. Looking down at Will, she smiled. He was okay. He slipped her a small, dot-like item, and she quickly put it behind her earlobe. She knew what it was. She smiled within herself, starting to understand the plan.

George approached Will and kicked him hard. "I've tried to kill this man more than ten times in just the past week! Some people just don't know how to die. Bring in Sandy's clone. If Kalim comes, she should be the one to treat him. That old fox will have some trick under his sleeve. He will not yield to my plan that easily.

"And for God's sake, someone just kill Will Burne for real this time!" George ordered in total frustration. As two of his henchmen started towards Will with guns drawn, Sandy screeched in terror, unable to move because of her injuries and bound position.

……………

In a Ship: Heading to Unknown Destination

"I've got it; I want to finish him off myself," Natalie said, levelling her piece at Will. Then, without hesitation, she shot Will squarely in the chest. Blood oozed from the hole in his jacket, and Will lay motionless with open eyes. Sandy screamed in agony, feeling her heart shatter into a million pieces. But she still felt Will's hand clutching her palm. She also felt warmth in his body.

"Is he dying? Is he dead? Why is he not blinking? What will I do if he dies?" Terror filled her heart in a microsecond. "Is that why he gave me the microdot? Did he intend for me to finish the mission?" Sandy's mind whirled with a dozen questions all at once.

"I always thought you were planning something. Kean was a fool to send you here. But you proved your worth. It's good you finished him off with a clean shot. And I trust you. But this son of a bitch won't even die in a plane crash! Pop him in the furnace with the clones. The facility is in the bottom part of the ship. I want him reduced to ashes before Kalim arrives," George said to Natalie.

She nodded and started dragging Will away. Sandy felt like part of her chest was being ripped out. She understood how dreadful Will must have felt watching her die. She took a deep breath and tried to calm herself, but she couldn't concentrate on anything, and her heart was thundering in her chest.

Will's body is still warm. Natalie will save him.

Sandy wondered how she got herself into this pitiable position. She cursed herself for not identifying the replicant Will sooner, wasting time in the base hiding, and for several other things. She dreaded what would happen if the New Order got the nuclear codes from Adha.

Think, Sandy, think. Now is no time to panic. There is still time to stop all this. Ugh, you can't do anything, at least not in this physical or emotional state. Visions of Will being beaten and shot filled her head again. Sandy closed her eyes and took some more deep breaths. She remembered a technique taught to her in her training.

"Think about gifts." She tried closing her eyes and thinking about good memories to soothe herself. Then she remembered Will's death stare again. She felt the same painful pull she knew all too well. She felt the same distress when she found out her parents died.

No. Concentrate. Think about gifts. The 40 Grade sex ritual trained agents to think about happy times to keep motivated in bad situations. It was useful to overcome stress when a friend or colleague dies. Sandy tried hard to bring back good memories with Will.

Sandy thought about her encounter with Will in the bathroom. They started scrubbing each other gently. Will filled the loofah with a lovely scented body wash, then rubbed it all across her lower belly. Sandy just put her arms around his shoulders like a garland and kept her body swinging with the move.

Will eventually ditched the loofah and started caressing her with his rough hands. Sandy felt elated. His hands glided liberally along with the foam all around her midsection. His finger peeked in and out of her belly button while the other hand rubbed her back gently.

His head was on her neck, licking her shoulder now and then. Will's hands caressed her buttocks lovingly while his lips pressed gently on hers. His other hand moved up under her breasts. Sandy moaned in ecstasy. Will moved down to her nipples and took turns taking them in his mouth while his other hand kept caressing her buttocks. Then, before she knew it, he was massaging the area between her thighs.

"Will, you sure know your around way down there," Sandy teased. Will did not answer…

…Sandy saw his wound bleeding a little. She felt emotion stab her gut like a searing hot knife…

…She let out a low yelp. Will had entered a finger into her while biting her ever so slightly on the nipple. He gave her ass a hard little squeeze at that exact moment. The triple-action drove Sandy wild. She pushed him aside and got under the hot shower.

Will followed with a gleeful smile. He extended the foreplay, turning her away from him, and pulled her back close to his chest. Will started kissing all over her back, starting from her nape. He licked behind her ear, flickered her ear lobes with his tongue, and planted numerous kisses over her neck. All the while, his fingers kept popping in and out of her most intimate parts, between the thighs. Will's other hand kept caressing her nipples and under her breasts.

Sandy was utterly lost in sensation as all her pleasure points were expertly taken care of by Will's capable hands and tongue. She wondered how long this would go on before she could climax. Just then, Will peeled her away from him and turned her towards him. He entered her with his enormous dick, and Sandy's eyes rolled back in her head as he gave her the best climax of her life.

Sandy's eyes rolled back now, too, as she saw Natalie coming back alone. "He's dead. I locked him in the furnace myself," she said to George. He still seemed grumpy and paced the room awkwardly. "What's wrong?" Natalie asked, "Can I help?"

"It's my wife. I'm not sure how to handle her just yet. She's a witness to all my crimes, and Kalim has her in some secret base, so I want to extract her. That foolish clone of Simons isn't much use. And Sandy knows where she is, but she won't open her mouth even after being beaten this bad," George said.

"Why don't you replace her with a clone?" Natalie asked, bringing him a coffee.

"It's not that easy. Most of the trust funds I use are in her name. It was all her father's property. She was managing them well. The replicant could sign and smile like her. But her cutthroat lawyers would spot the difference in no time."

"Why do you need her money anyway? Don't you have enough already?" Natalie asked, confused.

"You are just as naïve as most of the commoners. No person on this earth will ever have enough money. I made some grave mistakes funding Underworld terrorists. I wanted to become more powerful and earn more profit. So I exploited certain nations in the Underworld with my money, making the terrorists wreak havoc over there. Then, those bastards turned against me, blaming me for exploiting them," George sighed.

"I started targeting the more prosperous areas like West Federation and Oceania then. I invested everything I had into this war. If this move wins, I will be all-powerful. I will control it all and have an unlimited source of money, and everything will be mine. Else, I am left with nothing, and May will finish me off for misusing funds from her trust," George said.

"Sir, Adi Kalim is here," one of the humanoids announced as they all heard a chopper. Sandy tensed, fearing the death of millions.

"I need to free myself. I can't let Adha do such a hideous crime. The world will not forgive him if he does it for me," Sandy thought. At the same time, she wondered whether Adha would do it for her. He had known George murdered her parents. Yet, he hadn't taken any step against him until now. What are the odds he cares?

Why would he even come here if he doesn't intend to save me? Conflicting thoughts filled her mind while her eyes scanned a video continuously playing on a screen. The room had a huge monitor showing several parts of the ship. George watched every nook and corner from this monitor room, sitting comfortably in his lounge chair.

Scientists were working diligently in one part of the ship, creating vials and vials of purple liquid and green pills. From where she was bound close to the monitor, she noted the code the scientists punched in when they entered and left the lab. Sandy made a mental note to check the lab and retrieve some samples before she left.

The monitor went black momentarily as George switched cameras and brought up a video of the furnace below the ship. Sandy watched as George started a replay of Natalie dragging Will into the area and pushing his body into the furnace. Her heart skipped a beat. She couldn't stop her mind from running away with questions. Is Natalie a traitor? What is happening? Is Will Burne, the mighty spy of the West Federation, really dead? Is he no more?

The pain in Sandy's body seemed to multiply a hundred times now. Agony filled her as every inch started to ache unbearably. Just then, two henchmen brought Adha into the room at gunpoint.

Adha took one look at the struggling Sandy. Then, in one sweeping move, Adha used his knee to hit one man in the crotch. Adha's hands unfurled his belt at the same time. The second one's right eye got poked with the buckle pin in a nanosecond.

Natalie rushed to Sandy and placed a gun at her temple. "Don't you dare make another move," she shouted. At this, Adha relented, and several other humanoid henchmen surrounded him with great caution. Two of them held his hands in a vice grip.

"Can't you just cuff his hands?" George asked in the same irritated tone. "These damn robots are good for nothing. What a waste of money. I just wish I could hurry up and win this war and make everybody obey me with free will."

"I told you not to hurt Sandy. And this is how you treat her? You will never get the codes from me!" Adha yelled at George.

"This bitch is mourning the death of her last hook-up. I killed Will Burne, that spy from the West Federation. He acted like some big hero barging in here trying to save your daughter. See his fate." George simultaneously played the videos side-by-side of Natalie shooting Will, then dumping his body into the furnace.

Sandy cried uncontrollably. Looking over at her, Adha couldn't remember when she had last cried so hard. Always very aware, his mind was instantly abuzz with questions. *Why would he die for my daughter? And why is she hurting so much after losing someone she barely knew?* Adha started to guess some things. *Did they like each other? Were they in love? What a terrible time for them to meet. First her parents, and now her lover? Can Sandy never live in peace?*

George stood from his lounge chair and walked over to face Adha. "I wouldn't have beaten her so badly if she would've just told me where you hid my wife. She did not relent to any third-degree treatment."

"Did you put her through third-degree torture, you bastard!?" Adha used his head to bash George on the nose. He started bleeding profusely. Natalie rushed over to help him, holding a cloth to his nose.

"No! Stay with Sandy! You don't leave her. There is no more time to waste," George said, recovering quickly. "Adi Kalim, I want the codes, and I want them now!"

"I will not give them to you! I don't care if you kill me. Sandy will escape somehow. She is a well-trained agent," Adha refused, blatantly.

"Will Burne was the best agent in the West Federation. Didn't you just see him die not two minutes ago? The same fate will befall your daughter. Don't try me! Just give me the codes," George insisted.

Adha maintained his stoic silence, staring past George like he didn't exist, so George nodded to one of his humanoid henchmen. "Well, then, you've given me no other choice. Take him to the hypnotherapy chamber. And keep Sandy locked up. We need to do this smoothly," he said.

As Adha was led away, he kept twisting and turning to see Sandy. Then Natalie took Sandy to a chamber to lock her up. Inside, there were many glass closets just big enough for one person to stand. She put Sandy in one, locked it, and punched a code into the box on the door. Sandy immediately felt extremely dizzy. She still couldn't believe Will was dead.

A thick fog began to fill the chamber. Sandy didn't know whether she was dreaming or if everything was clouded from her watering eyes. Maybe it was the breath from her nostrils fogging the glass. The glass chamber was so close to her face, it was forming a mist. She used her hand to wipe away the fog and saw Will staring back at her.

Sandy was shocked. She also noticed she was using both her hands to wipe the quick-forming mist, again and again. Her broken arm was working fine. It was healing—fast. What is this chamber? Sandy looked around curiously and caught another glimpse of Will among the mist. Again, she wiped the fog, and this time he signalled for her to keep quiet by placing a finger over his lips.

Natalie was playing with the cameras on the far end of the room. Finally, realization dawned: a medical chamber. She had seen a similar model in the Afrasian training facility for treating people with grave injuries. But this one seemed far more advanced. Sandy felt like 90% of her wounds had healed instantly. The fogging stopped, and as the fog cleared, the chamber door popped open.

Sandy stumbled into the waiting arms of Will. Will kissed her eagerly. He looked better than she had ever seen him. He should have been in the chamber too. *Wait.* She pulled back. Was this was his replicant? Maybe they updated his programming to feel affection for her…

"No. I am not the clone," Will assured, picking up her hesitation. "Do you remember when you pinched me on my right hip, and it left a mark?" Will lifted his T-shirt to show the love mark. Sandy blushed, thinking about it.

It happened right after her climax in the shower. "Why did you bite me on the nipple?" Sandy asked playfully and pinched him on his hips again—gently this time. She ran her hand over the mark, and tears filled her eyes.

"Can someone just tell me what the hell is happening on this ship? Am I hallucinating, or am I going mad?" Sandy demanded.

Will chuckled. "It's simple. Natalie is a double agent. She is with us. I am with Nyman, her brother, and the rebel group. You are with me—safe, happy, and healthy," Will kissed her again on the forehead and hugged her hard.

Sandy pulled him into the medical chamber she had just came out of and locked it. Fog started covering the glass from their quickening breaths as she undressed Will like a fierce predator.

"I thought I lost you," Will said, cooperating with her eagerly and helping her undress.

"I thought the same too. First, I watched you see me die. Then I watched Natalie shoot you and put your body in a furnace," Sandy said.

She kissed the mostly undressed Will on his ear lobes and liberally let a finger probe his ass.

"I thought I was doomed, Sandy. I was not myself until I knew you were alive," Will said, holding her hips and positioning her to fit his dick. He kissed her again with passion for the umpteenth time.

"I felt the same. I swear I will never let you out of my sight, for even a single second, if we get out of this alive," Sandy broke their kiss briefly to say this. She continued to taste his freshly healed lips again. Her hands massaged his backside quickly yet gently, and she found the exact spot to finger him.

Their tongues swirled together, and they both closed their eyes in ecstasy as Will entered her with his swollen member. Sandy's slick 40-Grade-trained fingers entered his ass at the same time. Will started pounding her as hard as the compact space allowed, still not breaking the kiss.

Sandy's fingers proceeded to find the erotic male G-spot inside him. She pressed it at just the right moment, and he came in loads, deep inside her. As he came, she felt her world explode into shimmering rays of ecstasy, with his dick hitting every sensitive spot inside her golden triangle, stimulating all the right nerve endings.

… … …

"Guys, will you hurry up? The fake camera feed will only last five more minutes," Natalie called from her post. Will and Sandy were out of the chamber now, giggling like teenagers and exchanging knowing glances, trying to get dressed.

"Was it a fake blood packet on your chest? Did you talk with Natalie early? You knew she was going to shoot you, didn't you?" Sandy asked.

"No. I didn't talk to Burne. He was supposed to get into the ship stealthily and help us. I only transmitted the coordinates. I am under constant surveillance, too. Your idiot boyfriend blew his cover rushing to you once he saw you," Natalie said.

"Don't call him an idiot. It is love," Sandy giggled and took both his cheeks between her hands like Will had done to her earlier and said, "You look really handsome."

Will smiled in response. "By the way, it was a dummy wearing my clothes that she threw in the furnace. I activated the blood packet as soon she pointed the gun at me. I am wearing a bulletproof suit, too. We changed it in a corner while going to the furnace. It was one of the few blind spots on this ship," Will explained further.

"Let us get off this damned ship and get to that hospital base. I don't want to stay here," Sandy said.

"Noooo!" both Will and Natalie refused.

"We are still on a mission here. We have to save Adha and prevent that bomb blast, too," Will explained.

"Sandy, come on. We need to find your guardian," Natalie called.

"You both go ahead. I need to see what those notorious scientists are cooking up in the lab. I'll catch up to you soon," Sandy said, heading towards the lab. Will and Natalie proceeded towards the area where Adha was locked up.

… … …

Somewhere Between the Underworld and Afrasia

"Natalie is an excellent agent," Sandy thought to herself as she moved with her regained agility. The boost of endorphins from the treatment in the medical chamber had made her highly energetic and studious once again. She remembered Adha's explanation of why medical chambers were created in the first place.

About a century ago, the entire world was threatened in the wake of a vast viral pandemic. Doctors were afraid to touch patients directly to provide treatment, so medical chambers were created to scan their bodies, get their biological data, and prescribe the necessary treatment.

Over the decades, the medical chambers were embedded with fast-healing medications. The patient just needs to get inside. The advanced cell-regeneration technology releases a nanite-filled fog into the glass enclave. The damaged cell structures in the body are healed at hyper speed.

"Cell-regeneration technology," Sandy sighed. Humans always find a way to mess with everything extremely useful to them. And now they have perfected the technology to clone people with replicants and use it to make war with their humanoid armies. What next? Maybe, becoming immortals by regenerating the cells countless times, without allowing them to age?

"Those scientists are probably working on something sinister, like immortality," Sandy thought as she stealthily approached a scientist coming out of the lab. He sat down at a table to eat something. Sandy quickly put a nylon wire around his neck.

……… …

Back in his chamber, George saw one of his scientists being attacked. "Who escaped? Sandy or Kalim?" he wondered and pressed a red alarm button.

The whole ship came alive, buzzing with several flying nanorobots called Voladors. There were fifty of them, scanning every area. One entered the scientist being attacked. His brain was loaded with several types of defence moves—in a second.

He stopped struggling and balanced both his feet on the edge of the table. Then, he backflipped onto Sandy's shoulders.

Sandy pushed him away in a fraction of a second and stamped down on his crotch, hard while blowing continuous punches on his eyes. As he fell from her shoulders, he also took a good hit to the head. Sandy quickly pulled the table before them to shield herself from the camera.

She saw several other tiny bots flying in her direction. She used the small table as a shield to protect herself. She ran towards the lab, attacking as many Voladors as possible.

Natalie and Will were scanned by the Voladors too. Fortunately, Natalie had Will change into the special synthetic wear for replicants. The robots scanned them and deemed them unsuspecting. Will signalled for Natalie to see what was going on and continued the search for Adha.

Natalie entered George's chamber. "What took you so long?" George asked, bringing the lock-up section onto his screen. Luckily, Natalie had already loaded the fake footage of Sandy staying there. She had captured the original footage of Sandy when she was in the chamber earlier and played it on a loop to avoid suspicion.

"I'm sorry, I had to use the washroom," Natalie lied. George found the reason logical and acceptable. Besides, she had killed Will, the undefeatable, and Sandy was right before his eyes on the screen.

The robots had scanned all the other areas of the ship and found nothing potentially dangerous. All the remaining robots swarmed to the scientist Sandy had attacked. One Volador called for a humanoid to take the scientist to the medical chamber. The other Voladors joined together to form a colossal rod-like shape and entered the lab.

Several humanoid henchmen assembled before the lab. Sandy had managed to enter the lab using the code she saw the scientists punch in. She hid behind a water dispenser. She happened to know about Voladors, as Adha had briefed her about almost every advanced technology in the world. The Voladors sensed humans using the heat signals in their bodies.

The warm water dispenser was a great place to hide. The Voladors are extraordinarily tiny and have minimal sensors, which could be easily confused. They are programmed to identify intruders and infiltrate an area with micro cameras.

However, Sandy had only ever seen a Volador entering a person's body and empowering their brain, just now, on this ship. *George Lay had invested too much into advanced technology,* she thought. *He doesn't seem like such a brainy person who would execute such a coordinated plan,* Sandy mused. *Is there another boss controlling the New Order?*

The Volador rod was thoroughly scanning the lab, and all the scientists left. Sandy quietly reached into a corner and silently slipped into one of the protective suits the scientists were wearing. It was pretty easy as she just had to stand on the terminal and suit up in a second, her disguise completed by the ID she stole from the scientist.

She moved around the lab, mingling with the others as the protective suit covered her identity. She quickly slid some vials into her pocket as she moved out with the other scientists.

She couldn't even venture to guess what the purple and the green vials were for. But she saw they were mass-produced and stored by the ton inside protected chambers. "The suspect is a woman," one of the humanoid henchmen shouted, holding his earpiece. "A woman attacked the scientist." He went on to say she is young and Afrasian. "Probably that Sandy Krave," he said to others.

The henchmen ordered the scientists to remove their protective suits. Half of them had already released their face protection as soon as they were out of the lab. *Uh oh.* She thought fast to come up with a plan. She removed the bodysuit, first securing the vials, as the armed henchmen approached her suspiciously. She pulled the face protection in place and held the vial in her hand.

Sandy saw them backing up immediately once they saw the vial. *Interesting!* She waved it in front of them, and both the scientists and the henchmen screamed. "Shut up and don't shoot," she ordered. *It must be something deadly,* Sandy thought as she moved away from them, using the vial as a shield. She backed toward the door, making good her escape from the lab. She disappeared down the stairwell to reach the bottom chambers near the clone furnace. But she couldn't help but wonder why the humanoids didn't shoot her.

…… …… ……

Back in the monitor room, Natalie was watching the monitors with George when the scientists started coming out of the lab. She knew Sandy would appear on the screen at any moment. She turned to George.

"Shall we go check on Kalim's progress? There's no use watching the ship like a hawk. The rebels, government, or some other agent will keep trying to get on board. We should concentrate on getting the codes and executing the bombs now," Natalie said.

She was standing facing the monitor, and George turned to look at her with his back to the monitor just as Sandy came out of her protective suit.

"You are right. The replicants and the Voladors will take care of the intruders. Let us go," George said, turning to take one final look at the monitor.

Sandy had moved swiftly and disappeared into oblivion by then. Natalie silently praised Sandy for her fast, blitzkrieg movements.

"What's all the commotion about? Why are they screaming?" George asked, looking at the panicked scientists and the cloned henchman.

"The Voladors are checking the lab," Natalie said, walking out the door. She knew George would follow her. She had gained his trust. "Sir, please hurry. We should not let the intruder reach Adi Kalim at any cost. What if he kills him? We would never get the codes then," Natalie said in a grave tone.

Her persuasive talk did the trick, and George started walking in front of her, leading her right to Adha. George entered the control room in the central portion of the ship. It was a colossal, hexagon-shaped room with a large, centralised glass dome looming above to let in sunlight. It was the topmost part of the ship.

George tapped his feet in a rhythm five times and gave a voice command, "Dome reveal." The dome transformed immediately into a chamber. Natalie focused her thoughts on concealing her surprise; the whole dome effect was an illusion. It was a ceiling screen projecting the image of a 3D dome.

The screen stopped transmitting and rolled to one side. The platform above came down, filling the hexagon-shaped tile, revealing the actual skylight dome. Natalie sighed with exasperation. There's no way Will or any other person on this ship would guess this location. And even if they did, they wouldn't know how to reveal the chamber.

Adha was lying comfortably on the therapy chair in a sedated state. A scientist and two humanoids were near him on the platform. A screen above Adha's face showed Sandy pleading with him to give them the codes.

"Adha, don't you see how red-hot this sharp metal is? They inserted one into my vagina a short while ago. I can't bear the pain; I can't move, shout, or even cry. I rolled on the floor, trying to get it out of me. My thighs burned. My hands burned, trying to pull it out of me," the image of Sandy showed her with burned, blistered hands.

"I won't survive if they insert another one into me. Please give them the codes. We will find a way to stop the New Order, I promise. I will try to my last breath. But please save my life now. Don't let me die like my parents," Sandy pleaded again.

Don't give up, Adha! Resist, Adha, resist! Your daughter would never plead like this. She endured the third-degree treatment like it was nothing. Understand. Please! It is just an illusion. Wake up! Natalie screamed inside herself, terrified Adha would reveal the codes.

Where is that damn Will Burne? she wondered.

"Adha… Please…" Sandy's image on the screen above him pleaded once more. The video feed showed one of the henchmen gagging her and another one opening her thighs wide. Then, using a heat-proof glove, another one approached her holding a glowing-hot, sharp iron rod.

The camera showed the rod, and then Sandy's terrified face pleading with her eyes, shaking her head pitiably. "Stop. Stop it! Don't torture my baby. I don't care about this world or anything else. I will give you the codes. Please, just leave her alone! Take her to a doctor. She can't bear this much pain!" Adha screeched in his trance-like state.

The scientist near him took a retinal scan, collected Adha's blood, sweat, and fingerprints, along with the codes, and handed them to

George. "Each code should be activated with one bio-signal," he explained further.

Natalie quietly clenched her fist hard. "Dammit, Will Burne, if you are anything near a mediocre agent, please come and save the day, now." She started praying to all the gods she knew.

… … …

Back in the monitor room, Will was busy messing with the system. Sandy had managed to enter the furnace room by skilfully using the blind spots under the cameras. She saw scores of distorted humanoids lined up to be thrown into the blazing furnace. Her heart missed a beat. Though they were part-robot and only half-developed, they felt pain.

Sandy's brief time with Will's replicant had shown her they were programmed to behave in a certain way. But they had feelings too. She could see some were weeping, and some were shuddering in fear at their impending doom.

Only four cloned henchmen were there, ensuring each defective humanoid was pushed into the furnace. But by her count, there were over two hundred humanoid clones on this ship alone. So why didn't they just fight back? Maybe they didn't know they *could* fight back. The cloned henchmen were no different; they didn't seem to know any better.

All she had to do was find out how to program them, or rather, deprogram them. She couldn't do it. But maybe the scientists at the rebel base could. She just had to stop them from burning alive for now. Sandy searched frantically for a way to stop the murders, then noticed the gas lines to the furnace. She followed them to find their source. There might be a switch to turn them off.

The gas lines ended in a vast, locked wooden cubicle. Sandy went to kick it open but was pushed back brutally. "Ah, it's me. Hello, my twin. I'm glad you didn't die. I never expected to fight myself. Actually, I did once or twice in the tramach. But this will prove to be very interesting. I will get you, for my broken arm," Sandy said, coming back to her heels.

"You should not break this. It's the switch for the furnace," the replicant said.

"I guessed so. I want to break this and switch off the furnace. I don't want all the replicants to die for no reason," Sandy said.

"Really? Why?" her replicant asked innocently.

"Sandy, you died before, once. Did you like it?"

"No! It was horrible. I felt… choked. My eyes burned, and my chest hurt," the clone said with a wide-eyed expression.

"It hurts when you die. Those people there are going to die. And it will hurt if we don't stop this. Together, we can save them. If we work together," Sandy said.

"But I'm supposed to stop you from doing this. I want to help them. But I can't do as I wish. My programming prevents it," the replicant said pitiably.

"Don't whine, for God's sake," Sandy said, irritated.

"I am whining because it hurts—a lot. They put a hot iron rod into me to get some codes from an old man. I couldn't even stand," the humanoid confided, clutching between her thighs.

Sandy was speechless. She immediately understood what had happened to her and felt extremely sorry for her. She also felt anger rushing at her very core. Can't they even let her rest a while after torturing her so badly? She is still part-human, with all the biological features, not just a machine who doesn't feel pain.

"I promise I will not meddle with the switch. You take this elevator and go to the fourth floor. There is a medical chamber there. It looks more or less like the chamber in which you were killed. Get into it, and it will heal all your pain. Then you can come back here to continue your duty," Sandy said smoothly. The clone gave a gleeful smile and entered the elevator limping and whining.

"Thank God! She obeyed me," Sandy said aloud, thoughtlessly.

"We have to obey everyone with the chip." Sandy's replicant pointed to the ID Sandy had stolen from the scientist. "Oh! You saved my day," Sandy's clone waved from the closing elevator happily.

"So much for the New Order. It is the most barbaric order mankind will ever see," Sandy cursed within herself. She kicked open the closet and broke the furnace switch with her bare hands.

The ship was immediately filled with loud alarms blaring from all sides. The Voladors gathered again and started coming towards the furnace room.

Sandy moved quickly to the lines of replicants. She had already witnessed how the humanoids obeyed in the lab, as well as her own replicant when she told her to go to the healing chamber. "Listen, you cloned morons; I switched off that furnace to save you all from dying. Now, it is your turn to save me. Fifty Voladors are coming to attack me. I want you all to hit them with every flat thing you find," she ordered.

The humanoids looked confused. The henchmen came towards her confused, "We are replicants too. Do you want us to fight the Voladors too?" they asked.

"Yes, of course. Save me from the Voladors," Sandy ordered. She waved the ID she had stolen from the scientist in front of them. They joined hands with the distorted clones and fiercely started attacking the Voladors. Sandy rushed to the monitor room to prevent George from using the codes for the nuclear bomb.

… … …

"Will, did you cause the alarm?" Natalie murmured into her earpiece while George was distracted momentarily by the sound of the alarm.

"No, I'm in the monitor room," Will said.

"The infiltrators are messing with the furnace," George said as they were walking back to the monitor room.

"I'll go check it out. You can proceed to the monitor room. You have the codes. Don't wait any longer for that blast," Natalie moved under the pretence of finding the infiltrator. She wanted to save Adha.

… … …

PART 5 - The Four Reigns at Risk

THE NEW ORDER: WHO ARE THE ENEMIES?

Powers at Stake and Conspiracy Revealed...

Chapters Thirty-Nine through Forty-Four

"We know very little, and yet it is astonishing that we know so much, and still more astonishing that so little knowledge can give us so much power."

–Bertrand Russell

The Doom of the World… 2166, June 11

George Lay sat on his lounge chair like a king. The monitor before him showed the four capitals of the world in Afrasia, West Federation, Oceania Liberation, and the Underworld. He gave out an evil chortle thinking about the imminent fate of those cities.

He had the nuclear codes to turn them into mushrooms of ash at the press of a button. "What am I waiting for?" he wondered. The alarm had stopped. Only four humanoid henchmen stood guard in the monitor room.

Natalie should have captured the infiltrator by now, and she would finish him in the furnace room. Adi Kalim is still in a trance. I just need to give the order and kill these people to become the next almighty king. George's body shivered slightly at the impending doom of the world. He brushed aside his fears and punched some quick messages.

… … …

Natalie held her gun on the scientist handling Adha. "Wake him up, now," she ordered. The scientist complied out of fear. "Why are you waking him up?" a human henchman asked her.

"Our boss wants Kalim to see the destruction personally. After all, he is going to take all the blame for the bombings because only he knew the codes," she said sarcastically. She was shivering inside, fearing the bombings and the mass destruction.

Adha was transferred into one of the medical chambers on the platform, where he regained full control of himself. Natalie dismissed everyone else.

"Adha, the image you saw wasn't Sandy. She is alive and well, but George is ready to bomb the cities. You have to stop him. You have to change the codes!" Natalie hissed.

Just then, two human henchmen jumped her. She saw movement in her peripheral vision and moved aside in a split second, making them run into each other. Then she deftly turned and shot them both before they could get up. "There are only about twenty-five human henchmen; the others are humanoids. I can control them with my ID because they are programmed to obey this chip no matter what. We need to fight the humans, though. They are dressed in brown, and all the humanoids are dressed in dark-green synthetic material," Natalie said.

Adha had already picked up the fallen henchmens' guns and started shooting the enormous army of replicants coming in scores towards him. Natalie waved her ID in front of them and ordered them all to stand down and assemble on the dome platform. When it was full, she tapped her foot to send the dome back up, locking them inside.

Adha was fighting the humans like a machine. He shot with both hands, sliding in-between brown-shirted men. He hit them with his head, kicked out their legs from behind, then took out their kneecaps with swift sidekicks. Adha incapacitated them, then shot them before they could even hit the ground.

He killed four men in two minutes then moved towards the others like a tsunami clearing an island. Sandy popped out of the elevator on the top floor and saw him pointing his gun towards her. Adha's expression changed immediately. "My child, are you ok?" he asked, concerned.

"I am perfectly alright; it was my clone you saw being tortured. But we have to stop that monster from bombing the cities," Sandy said, panting.

"More men at three o'clock," Natalie warned, stopping as many cloned henchmen as she could.

"Order all of them to the furnace room to fight the Voladors. It will keep them occupied. Send them there!" Sandy shouted. She and Adha had already started shooting full force at the human henchmen approaching them.

Within the next two minutes, they had killed another four men. The remaining twelve men formed a circle around Sandy and Adha. "Adha, I'm out of ammo," Sandy whispered to him.

"Me too," he said, whipping one gun towards a man's head like a boomerang. It hit him square on the nose with a *thunk*, throwing his head back, and made him fall flat on his back. The others started to shoot at them blindly, and both Sandy and Adha threw themselves onto the floor while grasping at two men's legs, pulling them onto the floor with them.

They captured their guns, shot them, and took cover before the smoke cleared. Everything happened within thirty seconds. The remaining nine men looked confused about where they went. Sandy was hiding under a dead body; the henchman's massive frame was enough to cover her petite one.

Adha was hiding in plain sight. He was acting as if he were wounded, lying face down, just waiting for someone to approach him. "What just happened?" the men enquired of each other.

"Are they really going to bomb all the capitals? My cousin lives in Afrasia. I have to warn him," one said, panicking.

"This is not the time," their leader chastised them. "We need to find the traitors. We will all be killed if we miss them." They started to turn the bodies over, dividing into groups and found Adha first. "I think he's dead," one man said.

"We can't be sure. There is blood all over Kalim's body. But it might be someone else's blood. Is his body still warm?" another one asked.

At that, Adha pulled him down and kicked the other one in the gut. He then shot them both before they even knew what hit them. Sandy, from her side, fired off three shots, taking down three more men from her position. The remaining four had taken cover and started firing off random shots.

Just then, a grenade landed a few feet from them, and Sandy came out of her hiding position, fearing it would explode close to her. All four had started to shoot at her when the grenade exploded.

Sandy thought she was a dead duck at that point. But then she felt a very familiar warm embrace and looked up to see Will's smiling face. "Was that a dummy grenade?" she asked in disbelief. She saw Adha hiding on the far end, still firing away. Will and Sandy joined him, hiding at the opposite end.

"I only had enough time to replace the grenades with practice ones. Unfortunately, they took their weapons before I could replace the ammo," Will said sadly.

"Where have you been all my life, hero?" Sandy teased him. They shot a few more rounds then dodged a dagger by a hairline. Then Will threw a live grenade in their direction, and one man blew to pieces before them.

The other three men slowed down a mite at the brutal death of their colleague. Adha used the opportunity and took down another one. “He really is the Fiery Eagle. I am honoured to see him in action. Age hasn’t slowed your father down one bit,” Will gushed.

“He’s not my father. He is just my guardian,” Sandy said quietly. She couldn’t forgive Adha for lying to her all these years and letting that wicked George grow into such a devastating force. He could have used this talent to bring him to justice sooner.

Another gunshot whizzed past them. Will fired into oblivion without any aim, but one of his bullets hit the mark and seriously wounded one man. He fell from his sitting position.

“There is only one man left,” Sandy said.

“There are three others in the monitor room. The rest are humanoids,” Will said.

At the same time he spoke, shots started to rain down randomly from different directions in the room. “Dammit; an auto-firing setup-installed hall. That frustrated soldier must have activated it to kill us, even if it kills him, too,” Sandy gasped.

“I’m sure of it. Okay, I’ve been through many places set up like this. This hall is a semi-circle. Only specific spots will be targeted at a time, and in a pattern. So crawl, and stay behind the objects. Don’t look up. We will be home free if we can get behind that glass,” Will said, gesturing.

“Adha…” Sandy looked back. He signalled her to go on with Will. He was following the same technique Will just explained.

In a flash, Will stood up, jumping on a table, took a clean shot at the last enemy man alive, and dived back into the crawling position again.

“Why the hell did you just do that?” Sandy cursed.

“There will be a forty-five-second interval before the second round of firing starts. The system has to reload its ammo. I used that time to kill the man,” Will explained.

By now, Adha had crawled closer to them. "We should reach the monitor room. We will be safe there," he said.

"We have to wait until it finishes hitting this round and move in intervals," Will said.

Sandy called Natalie through her earpiece and asked her to switch off the auto-guns on the top floor. She responded by saying it could only be done from the control room.

"Then don't step foot on this floor," she warned Natalie.

They neared the monitor room inch by inch. Finally, they entered it, shooting all three of the men standing around George at once.

"No more humans. Only compliant robots," Will sighed.

George laughed heartily. "Isn't it ironic? I want to establish just the same. Humans are complicated, but robots are compliant. All hail the New Order," he said, pressing the trigger in his hand to activate the bomb blast.

Within a millisecond, the monitor showed all the cities turning into mushroom clouds, followed by close-up shots of fires and rubble. "Noooooo!" Adha screamed, running to the controls and pressing all the buttons in an attempt to stop the catastrophic event. But it was already too late.

The monitors showed footage of building after building crumbling to the ground in wreckage. Colossal mushroom clouds filled the skies. Human bodies piled high, flying in every possible direction as blood splattered the drone's cameras.

Camera after camera angle showed the worst possible footage of the massacre. One city's buildings crumbled, while the cameras in another city were filled with bloody images of gore showing a blurry view. A fire raged through another city, showing several explosions and the few remaining humans fleeing for their life. Audible screeches of agony filled every corner of the room, and streets littered with butchered human remains filled the screen as the smoke began to clear.

"This is not possible. This is not possible. What did you do? Why?" Adha sank to the floor and banged his head on the wall. Sandy kicked George in the head, as hard as she could, with one swift movement of her slender leg.

“You wicked moron! What do you get out of all this? Why did you kill so many innocent people? Can’t you just threaten them? Don’t you have enough money to enjoy everything in the world?” she held him by the collar and shouted, inches from his face.

“Careful, Sandy, I can make the same thing happen to you. I have a bomb planted inside your head. Here is the trigger,” George laughed in her face.

“No, don’t hurt her! We had a deal!” Adha screamed, trying to attack him. But, seeing the trigger in George’s hand caused him to think twice; with enormous effort, he got himself under control.

“I am asking you one last time, Kalim. Where is my wife? I will kill Sandy if you don’t answer me now,” he threatened.

“No, you won’t. You can’t,” Will chuckled.

“Will you never die?” George asked, irritated, reaching for his gun.

Will sprang forward and overpowered him within two seconds, then made him kneel down just as he had forced Sandy to do earlier.

“Natalie! Clones! Someone just come…!” George shouted at the top of his voice.

“Nobody will come. I have taken care of it. All of it,” Will laughed again.

“What did you take care of, Agent Burne? Our mission is established. Didn’t you see the mass destruction?” George said triumphantly. “You might take me out, but you’re too late to stop them. The New Order has risen.”

“No, it did not, you moron. Not while I am alive. Not while Sandy and Adi Kalim are alive.” Will kicked him, then did something with the monitor. The cities that were destroyed just moments ago were now operating peacefully, as if nothing had ever happened.

“What is this? Why did you change the footage? Those cities are gone. Wiped away. All my debts are gone, with the industrialists in them. All my criminal records are wiped away, with the headquarters turned to rubble,” George said, sweating.

“In your dreams, Lay. I am arresting you on my continent’s behalf for the attempted bombing of the West Federation. You saw the altered footage I planted. I unplugged all the system connections when you were out of the room with Natalie. None of the codes you entered worked. You trusted the clones much more than humans. They were obliged to obey any human with the ID chip," Will laughed again, sitting like a king in George's lounge chair.

"Will, are you telling the truth? Are the cities safe?" Adha asked, still shaken.

"They are as safe as they will ever be. Go ahead, call your contacts and confirm," Will said. Adha started calling his colleagues from the satellite phone on the ship. Sandy was standing behind him, eagerly keeping an eye on George.

"You did not win, you pig. I still have the brain bomb trigger!" George pulled it out of his sleeve and pressed it.

"Sandy!" Adha screeched. Sandy looked at him unaffected.

"I gave her a dampener to place on her ears. The bomb won't work while the dampener is there," Will said in a calm and aloof manner.

"You monster. What have you done? You angered the supreme almighty. This is the end of my life. I am finished if the cities don't burn as I promised!" George shouted again, enraged.

He suddenly clutched his head and fell to the floor. Then, as they watched, his head exploded into pieces.

"How the hell did you do that?" Sandy asked Will, amazed.

"I promise, I didn't do it. There must be a bigger fish in the sea than George. Perhaps the New Order has a central control, or another boss that was controlling him," Will said thoughtfully.

"I suspected as much," Sandy agreed.

"We have won this battle, children. But we still don't know with whom we are fighting. There is still so much work to do. But, we can rest assured, no more mass destruction, for now. Only I had access to such devastating codes," Adha said.

"I agree, sir. You should lead us in this revolution against the New Order. We can make this ship our new base. We will reprogram the clones to fight for us and bring Fred, Nyman, and the rebel scientists here. Then we can scourge this area completely for any small clues," Will stated.

Sandy talked to Natalie through the com, explaining the situation, who then contacted Nyman, Fred, and the team, passing on the message. Adha looked at the fast-approaching Afrasian shores with a relaxed heart. Will held Sandy's hand tightly in his and smiled. "I want to say this before I see you die again. I love you, Sandy. My life is nothing without you," Will said, sitting beside her.

"I love you too, Will. Don't you dare die before me." Sandy leaned on his shoulder, blissfully watching the ocean.

… … …

Being Chased by Killer Bombing Drones…

Fred, Nyman, and the rebel scientists entered the ship through the same supply chopper that brought Will. Adha, Sandy, and Natalie were waiting to greet them. Mr Abdul Jamal was also with them.

"Nat!" Nyman rushed to hug his sister. The scientists gave Will an admiring look of appreciation. "They never thought you would be able to make this mission successful single-handedly. But I know you," Fred said, beaming.

"Indeed," Adha nodded in approval. "Agent Burne saved the day and lots of lives," he said.

Nyman and the other scientists bowed to Adha in respect. "Nyman broke into the facility where Sandy was imprisoned and captured all the replicants there. Kean escaped. But we managed to save hundreds of humanoids from being murdered," Fred explained further, "but, then, the facility blew up."

At that, the chopper that dropped them off blew up mid-air. The group ducked and covered their heads as burning pieces and parts started littering the ship's surface. They ran inside to take cover.

"There's an awful lot of things mysteriously blowing up without cause, Fred. This ship might be rigged, so we need to act fast. Someone is watching us. They might be waiting to kill us all together after you land," Sandy shouted, narrowly escaping a fiery seat that nearly fell on top of her.

"Quick, Burne, install this jammer in the central part of the ship. It will dampen all the explosives, microphones, everything. No signals whatsoever will get out of the ship." Fred handed him an object that looked like a tennis ball. Will snatched it from him and ran with Sandy towards the middle of the ship.

"Locate it on the central portion. It will emit enough interference to cut off all signals being transmitted from the ship," Fred shouted after them.

Natalie caught a glimpse from her peripheral vision as a burning, flying rod dropped from the chopper, right over Fred, and pulled him aside at the very last millisecond. Fred scraped his knees and fell, hitting his face hard on the ground. He stood up, bleeding profusely from his lips and forehead.

"Will, Sandy, place it on top of the skylight dome where Adha was kept. It is the central portion of the ship on the very top floor," Natalie spoke through her earpiece.

"Are you Natalie?" Fred asked. Natalie nodded her response while leading him safely into a cargo hold below deck.

Nyman and Adha were leading the scientists right behind them. Natalie rushed to Nyman as soon as they reached safety, "Are mom and dad ok? Did you find them?" she asked, panting from all the quick running.

"No, Nat. They did not make it. None of them, except us, made it," Nyman said, trying hard to control his emotions. Natalie sank to the floor and curled into a ball, trying to digest the information. Nyman patted her helplessly.

"We need to scan the ship for secret explosives. Nyman, get the scientists to the clones. They should start reprogramming them right away," Adha tried to bring them back to the present situation.

"Don't worry. The ship won't blow as long as the main jammer is installed and working. Also, I brought an advanced scanner from the West Federation base that we use to find hidden bombs. We can use it to find bombs and deactivate them," Fred said.

"Give it to me. I will set the replicants to work using it," Natalie told him, regaining her feet. Fred saw her properly for the first time. He was amazed at how quickly she composed herself.

"You played well transmitting the signals from here. By the way, I am Fred, Will's friend," he said, stretching his hand in front of her for a handshake.

"I wondered whether anybody would even see it. You saw it and deciphered it precisely. Thank you for all your help. Fred, come with me. We have some bombs to deactivate. We don't want this ship to blow like George Lay's head," Natalie led him away, holding his outstretched hand. Adha led the scientists and Nyman to reprogram the clones.

……………

Sandy and Will were left alone in the dome. They installed the jammer successfully.

"What's bothering you? You seem disturbed," Will asked Sandy.

"I hate being so formal with Adha. I just want to scream, 'did you know who killed my parents all these years?' at him," Sandy said and clenched her fist.

Will leaned closer to her and rubbed in-between her thighs gently. He planted a soft kiss on her neck.

"Sandy, be careful. Choose your words wisely. We need his leadership now. Besides, he loves you a lot. He gave away the nuclear codes to save you. And did you see how he controlled the Voladors, rendering them useless with just a few swipes of the computer? That man is an asset to the world," Will said. His fingers were now entirely inside her trousers, and Sandy did not oppose.

"I always thought he was. I trusted him like a puppy. I have asked him what happened to my parents at least a million times. He never answered properly. It was always, train harder or after you complete this stage or when you shoot better… it hurts to know he knew all along…" Sandy sighed.

"Maybe he was blackmailed. Or…"

"Come on, Will. You saw him in action. He is one of the most influential men in the world. Who could blackmail him…?" Sandy scoffed.

"Well, George Lay was no ordinary man, either. So who is even more powerful than him? Any guesses?" Will asked thoughtfully.

"I would guess better if you stopped kneading me like this. I'm not a dough to make bread," Sandy simpered.

"You don't seem quite to dislike it…" Will teased.

Sandy's face glowed instantly. "What did you just say?"

"Don't you like me doing this?" Will gave another gentle yet firm squeeze to her plump vagina, pushing a part of his finger inside it.

"No, Will. You said 'dislike.' Who dislikes our system the most? I was thinking, George Lay doesn't seem like the mastermind of such a coordinated plan," Sandy said.

"We need to discuss this with Adha. Let's make a list. Okay, someone powerful enough to pull such a stunt, someone who dislikes the current system, and someone who will profit enormously from all this," Will listed. He pushed Sandy back on the same therapy bed where Adha had been earlier, then mounted her, kissing her deeply.

He pulled down her trousers and aimed for a quickie. "This bed is mighty comfortable for a therapy bed," Sandy said. She felt Will enter her, with his hands grasping her hips. She felt her trousers on her knees.

She felt herself drifting to a far-off land. She could see children, and as she watched, they were being home-schooled through online classes.

Then the school bell rang, like usual. She came running out of her childhood bedroom. She heard a thunderous sound, and everything went black.

"Noooo…! Leave the child," she distinctly heard Adha's pleading voice. "Do whatever you want. I will never open my mouth, and I'll move away from Oceania. I will never interfere in your matters again. It's a deal. Just spare the child…" Sandy kicked and screamed like a maniac as a strong arm swooped her away from the blinding smoke.

Sandy felt strong hands pulling her away from her comfortable position. Will pushed a lever, turning the bed back into a chair. Will slapped her cheeks hard. "Sandy, wake up. What happened to you?" he asked. "Nat, something is wrong with Sandy," he spoke to Natalie through his earpiece.

"It's the chair. It emits weird, invisible frequencies that induce a trance-like state," Natalie said.

Will pulled her out of the chair and sat down with Sandy's head on his lap. Sandy came to her senses. Her body was still shivering. "Did you grab me up? Were you there when my parents died?" she asked, confused.

"No. I pulled you out of this witchcraft chair. I thought you were screaming because of… me. But you seemed out of it," Will said.

"I saw Adha, begging for my life when I was a child. It was so real. It was like I was really there. We need to save this chair. It's going to be very handy in the future," Sandy said. Will tried to get up by pushing her aside. But Sandy just nestled deeper and more comfortably on his lap. "This is also quite comfortable. It's a little rough and hard. But I will adjust," she said, winking at him.

"It's all yours, agent Sandy. But I have a ship full of people to save," Will smiled back.

"I do not know how that quickie ended. Let's do it one more time. Two minutes," Sandy pleaded, pouting her lips.

"It did end quite well. See, how wet you are…" Will pointed between her thighs. Sandy got up from his lap and pushed him back. She pulled down his trousers in a flash and started riding him.

Then she scooted down and kneeled in-between his thighs and pulled out his semi-erect dick. She started flickering the tip of his dick with her thumb and index finger. She cupped his balls, caressing them gently, and bent down to lick the crevices of his thigh.

Will moaned in ecstasy. He was used to nerve-racking action and having limitless fun. But sex with Sandy was always special. The ever-lurking danger made it much more enjoyable. Everything she did seemed unique. "I am in love with this brave woman," Will thought, smiling to himself.

Meanwhile, Sandy was showing her expertise with her tongue on all Will's erogenous zones. She licked his thigh crevices and moved to his balls. She licked them and blew on them alternatively, cupping them with her hand and caressing them gently, letting his skin brush against her cheeks.

She positioned herself in a kneeling position and slid his member directly into her. She started riding him up and down, shaking like a bobblehead. Will put both his hands behind his head and just enjoyed being served. He imagined how her nipples would bounce if they were naked. But Sandy was fully clothed, aside from her shorts.

Nevertheless, she did not disappoint. She rode him like an expert. The 40 Grade ritual had trained her well on how to please a partner. She was deploying all her skills with expertise now. Though it was only two minutes, Will captured it in his mind for all eternity.

"Ohhh… oouch… I am… that is…" Will's eyes closed in pleasure as Sandy's hands started to caress his nipples. Both had quick but intense climaxes. "I did hit the back wall there," he smiled, laughing as he felt the familiar wet goo when he pulled out.

"There's no back wall there. Only a cylinder leading up to my throat," Sandy laughed, wiggling on his now limp dick. She took it into her mouth again and started deep throating it with gusto. Will thoroughly enjoyed the sensations her lips created on his body.

Will felt relieved and ecstatic. His Sandy was with him safe and healthy and, he had saved her. Will felt an extraordinarily proud and uncontrollable love for Sandy. Both were lying side by side under the dome, relaxed and content. Will rolled on top of her and kissed her lips, ears, and neck. He moved down to kiss her vagina.

Will felt pretty exhilarated after their two quickies. Sandy and Will linked hands together and lay quietly, viewing the clear blue sky. They felt calm and peaceful. Both wanted to cherish the moment as long as they could.

Sandy saw the warm, bright sun through the dome. Then she saw a swarm of drones hovering over it. "Is that what I think it is?" Sandy screeched.

"I bet yes. An army of flying drones is here to attack the ship! Those are bombing drones. I know them well. They'll turn this ship into a shipwreck within minutes." Will was already on his feet and warning the others through his earpiece.

… … …

Hidden Submarine on the Ship…

Natalie and her crew also saw the swarm of drones through the porthole. Surprisingly, several drones seemed to cross the area without identifying the ship.

"Don't worry. The drones did not detect the ship. The signal jammer did its work," Fred assured them.

"The drones did not pick up any signal. But I am damn sure some humans will be following them. We cannot hide the ship completely from the human eye," Adha said.

The scientists were already working on reprogramming the clones. "We are working on their central nervous system. After that, they will have free will, but it will take another fifteen to twenty minutes to get them all finished," Mr Jamal said.

"They would have tracked the ship's last known location. The enemy is sending drones to check all the ocean paths to Afrasia from that location," Nyman said.

"You're right. We steered clear of the Afrasian path and diverted the ship's course towards an unknown island. We will be completely out of view in another ten minutes," Natalie said.

"We have to prevent humans from spotting us within that timeframe. Alright, everybody, assemble on the surface of the ship. We have some mighty big shooting to do," Adha ordered.

"Nyman, Mr Kalim, come down to the armoury on the second floor. There are enough weapons on this ship to fight half an army," Will called through his earpiece.

Will and Sandy were already in the armoury. He noticed something fishy about this part of the ship. He pointed it out to Sandy.

"This part of the ship is quite different, Sandy. It is not made of steel alloy. I think it's titanium. And, it's shaped like a bullet," Will said thoughtfully.

"It's more or less like a submarine. I think this part detaches completely with all the weapons if the ship is bombed or damaged. See, there are hinges everywhere," Sandy pointed out.

Adha and Nyman came inside. "Mr Kalim, are you familiar with this type of technology? I haven't seen this anywhere."

"Neither have I. But this seems like a submarine that can be detached. A well-loaded lifeboat, to be precise. Nyman, check whether you can activate it. We could escape in this if we are brutally attacked on deck," Adha ordered, examining the surroundings closely.

"Look, we have enough food and water stores for everybody on the ship here," Sandy pointed out. There were numerous emergency bags with basic essentials.

… … …

Nyman, Will, Natalie, Sandy, and Adha were on the ship's top deck, each equipped with a telescope that could sense choppers or other boats up to five miles away. They were wearing UV400 sunglasses to overcome the blinding sunlight. The automatic missile launchers, which could fly nearly fifteen miles into the sky to hit their target, were set and ready on deck.

Fred was in the monitor room, meddling with the radar to identify any camouflaged choppers or submarines approaching them in stealth mode.

Sandy walked onto the deck behind Nyman, beaming with a new glow. "What are you doing here? Aren't you supposed to be on the starboard side of the ship?" he asked.

"Human Sandy is over there. I am her replicant," she said.

Nyman looked at her in disbelief as she looked exactly like the real Sandy. He liked her instantly. "Go to the scientist's lab floor. They will reprogram you to have free will," he guided her.

"She looks stunning," Nyman thought.

"Alert, positions everybody," Adha shouted before replicant Sandy could depart the deck.

Nyman just pulled her close to him. "There is a rifle on my hip. Unlock it and start fighting anything incoming," he ordered the humanoid Sandy, showing his stolen ID card. She obeyed, instantly running her hands across his hips.

Nyman felt a chill run through his spine. *This is not the time for romance. She is just fucking pulling out the rifle*, he thought.

They spotted incoming choppers. Through their telescopes, they could see humans on board, scanning the area for the ship. The humans also had powerful binocular-type equipment and watched the area carefully. One soldier spotted the ship.

He was about to alert his companions when a sleeping dart stuck him. He fell into the ocean, unconscious.

"They will know we are nearby if we shoot down the choppers. I just used a sleeping dart, as we used on Will. It will be useful if we can capture the choppers and trace who is controlling them," Nyman said.

"Agreed. I see three choppers," Will said.

"Guys, one of you, go get into the chopper and do as I say. I will be able to trace their control frequency. I will also be able to morph the signals the choppers send," Fred said from the lab.

"Let's send Sandy's replicant. They won't suspect her," Will suggested.

Nyman clearly did not like the idea. He'd only just met her a few minutes ago, but Nyman hated the idea of endangering her life. However, he had already eliminated two others in the chopper.

"Sandy, use this jetpack and fly to that chopper. Take this earpiece. Follow Fred's instructions," Adha instructed her rapidly. After he finished, she was gone, flying towards the chopper. She quickly ducked some bullets, dodged a missile aimed at her, and landed in the helicopter with ease.

"I am humanoid. I am on your side," Sandy's replicant said to the enemies in the chopper, as instructed. Then, she shot them with round after round of sleeping darts before they knew what hit them. She started meddling with the controls, following Fred's commands.

"What is happening? Did you lose men? Requesting pilot to report now," the intercom in the chopper loudly announced.

Sandy was scanning the pilot's voice with a device attached to the jetpack. She played it and talked fluently. "We are safe—no trace of the ship on this side. No men lost," she said. The message sounded in the pilot's voice to the other side.

"I suspect something fishy. Show me the live footage of your chopper. I want to confirm whether everything is ok inside," the other side demanded.

The clone Sandy had already taken a shot from camera footage inside the chopper. Cleverly, she played it on loop, masking her presence and showing only the soldiers as previously unharmed inside the helicopter.

"Confirmed, pilot. We are turning east to check the other routes to Afrasia. Follow us," the command voice said.

"She can't do that," Nyman said to the team. "She will be caught if any of the soldiers wake up!"

"They will spot her in the chopper if she gets closer," Will said thoughtfully.

"I need access to that chopper for another ten minutes. I can't trace where the signals are originating from," Fred said, panicking.

"She can't go back. She has to come here. But she can't let the chopper cameras pick up the ship's location," Adha sighed.

"What do I do?" the humanoid Sandy thought for a moment. "Permission requested to fly a few more miles closer, take a better look, and then follow you," she said, using the pilot's voice.

"Permission granted," the other side said. Sandy's replicant triumphantly turned the chopper towards the ship.

"She is as brilliant as Sandy," Adha said proudly.

"Yes. Now, the clone will keep flying as long as Fred needs her. She won't bring the chopper camera into the vicinity of the ship," Will shook his head, satisfied at her idea.

Nyman looked at the chopper flying above them with amazement.

"Guys, is it just me, or do you hear it too?" Natalie asked from the other side of the ship.

"What's wrong, Nat?" Sandy asked.

"I don't know. I pick up a lot of commotion from the lower deck. There is crazy yelling and shouting down here," Natalie said, keeping her face close to the floor of the deck.

"I feel it too," Will agreed. Then they saw it. The Voladors had formed a tremendous bird-like shape, complete with wings. They were carrying the huge glass containers with the purple and green vials inside. They broke open the dome and began flying up into the sky.

"It's not possible. There are absolutely no signals being transmitted from the ship. In or out. How are the Voladors doing it!?" Fred screamed from the monitor room.

"Does that mean some sort of secret signal is being emitted from the ship? Will the bombing drones detect us?" Sandy asked, frightened.

"Look! The bombing drones are coming back!" Nyman shouted, terrified.

"Will…" Sandy suddenly clutched her head and slumped to the floor. Adha and Will both came rushing over to her. Sandy was writhing in pain.

"The Voladors knocked out the jammer! I think the enemy forces are trying to activate the brain bomb in her head while the jammer is down. The only reason it's not working is because of the dampener," Adha said. Sandy's face was twisted in enormous pain.

"The dampener will lose its power soon," Will said, worried.

"Will, go save Sandy," Adha ordered, preparing to shoot down the drones.

"I will take her to the scientists," Will said, dragging her downstairs.

… … …

Instead of bombing the ship, the drones joined together to support the Voladors in their bird formation. The heavy glass containers of vials weighing more than a ton were carried away safely into the blue sky. As the rest of the group stood, dumbfounded, there was nothing they could do but watch as the containers disappeared into the distance as a faraway dot.

"What the hell just happened?" Nyman asked, confused.

"Sandy said the scientists were working on something deadly in the lab. She even risked her life to get a sample of the vials. Let's go interrogate them," Natalie said.

"'The jammer is broken. We are exposed. We need to get everyone to safety," Adha said, moving towards the lifeboat submarine.

"We should amass as many weapons as we can. Natalie, get all the scientists and clones into the armoury," Nyman ordered and rushed downstairs.

The clone Sandy saw everything that happened from the chopper. As soon as the jammer was off, the helicopter started to get signals about the ship's location.

"Hit my chopper with a missile launcher. I will jump out," the clone Sandy said to Adha via her earpiece. She set the chopper's course on autopilot and jumped out, using her jetpack. He shot the chopper with one clean shot and rushed down to the submarine deck. The helicopter exploded mid-air, damaging another chopper approaching it.

The third pilot approached with caution, shocked at the previous exploding helicopters' plight before them. Cautiously, Sandy flew up underneath the chopper and attached a hand grenade to it. Then, she pressed the propel 10x button on her jetpack and flew full-speed ahead as far as she could get from the third chopper.

The crew in the ship saw all three choppers exploding in the sky. After the chopper attacks, more hi-tech robots would swarm in, searching for them.

Will and Nyman were busy packing people and humanoids into the submarine. Will had left Sandy in the hands of Mr Abdul Jamal.

"Nyman set the course of the submarine to Oceania. This ship is certainly going to blow. But the enemies believe we are heading towards Afrasia. So, go to Oceania and stay safe there," Adha said.

"Aren't you coming with us?" Will questioned.

"No. I'm going to fetch May. I will get you the coordinates of her secret bunker in the hillside estate. Nobody will raid George Lay's place that soon. The world doesn't know he's dead yet," Adha said, loading another jetpack.

Most of the people had entered the submarine, which was half detached now.

"You make sure this thing is explosive-free and not rigged," Natalie nudged Fred.

"How did the Voladors escape, Fred?" Will questioned.

"I seriously have no idea," Fred surrendered, throwing his hand in the air.

"Perhaps you could rip this one open and check it out," Will said. "Sandy picked one up when the humanoids were smashing them in the base of the ship."

Sandy handed the vials to the scientists. "Do you know what this is? Is it some sort of deadly disease? A bio-bomb?" she asked.

"We helped create it. Unfortunately, it is much deadlier than that," one of the rebel scientists said.

"What is it?" Nyman and Adha both questioned in unison.

"It is an itching bomb. Once it is deployed, people in its vicinity will start itching terribly. They will scratch their scalp, skin, and even their eyes until they bleed. The itching won't stop until they have the antidote. People will literally scratch themselves to death without it," one scientist explained.

"Perfect. A person cannot handle a gun while they are itching all over. What a clever way to render human armies useless," Nyman said, irritated.

"It doesn't just affect humans. It's also designed to rust machine's metal parts in a fraction of a second. It will build rust a thousand times faster when reacting with oxygen," the scientist continued.

"Is that why they aimed in retrieving the precious cargo from the ship rather than attacking us?" Will questioned.

"Yes. The Voladors will not have the strength to fly carrying such heavy glass containers. So the drones supported them in deporting the cargo," Sandy said.

The replicant Sandy returned and jumped on the deck of the ship. "I saw flying robots coming towards us," she said.

"Get inside the submarine now," Adha ordered. He took one look at Sandy and gave her a warrior salute. He turned to Will, "Keep me updated about our girl." He pressed the propel button and flew away.

Sandy saw it from the table on which she was being examined and felt terrible. She hadn't spoken anything to him. What if something happened to him? Will he reach May safely? What if she never sees him again?

She felt Will hugging her, and she leaned on him for support. The submarine had detached completely and started sailing towards Oceania before the robots bombed George Lay's empty ship into oblivion.

… … …

Who is the Enemy?

"Sandy did a good job saving one of these. Pretty smart thinking. These Voladors are not like the normal ones we use in training. These are more highly advanced," Fred said, examining the parts.

The whole crew was watching him with awe. "They are auto-programmed to fetch the vial containers if they do not receive constant signals for a certain period of time," Fred explained.

"Did the Voladors sense something was wrong when we cut off all the signals from the ship?" Will asked.

"Yes, exactly. The Voladors auto-programming judged they were cut off from the normal signals, so their preprogramming kicked in to work together and retrieve the vials. It became their top priority mission. They are tungsten and graphene. They can bear ten times more weight than steel," Fred explained further.

"Most of them were badly damaged by the robot clones. Did they transmit a distress signal for the drones to respond?" Sandy's replicant asked.

"They did, and they have something like a super-brain, which is programmed to protect the vials at any cost," Fred explained, pointing to a tiny chip with his magnifying glass.

"Can you find out where the vials were taken?" Nyman asked.

"They were taken to another base like the one Natalie and Sandy were kept. I need to find out who is behind all this. I can trace the origins of where this super-brain chip was made. It will take a few hours," Fred said.

"Great, Fred. You carry on," Will patted him on the back and turned to the scientists.

"Can you create more antidotes for the itching bomb, using the supplies in this submarine?" he questioned them.

"We can create it. We can set the crew of scientists working on them to do the same ASAP," they agreed.

"Create as many antidotes as possible until the raw materials run out," Will ordered and turned to Nyman.

"We need to figure out who is with us and who is against us, Nyman. I am sure there are other rebel groups like us. We need to establish a connection between us before we reach Oceania," he said.

"Nyman, let's monitor the messages in all the contact channels—Cloudnet, cyberspace, Wireframe—everywhere possible. We will respond to every distress call and let them know what is happening," Will said.

"We have a ton of humanoids. We can use them to monitor and track the messages asking for help and declaring revolution," Nyman said.

"How will we know if they are real messages? What if the messages are a trap?" Natalie asked.

"We have to risk it. We can send Sandy's replicant with Natalie in the opposite direction of the submarine, with a false signal originator," Will said.

"How will that help?" the clone Sandy asked.

"If the enemy transmits the messages we respond to, they will try to locate and attack us. The false transmitter will lead them to us instead of the submarine," Natalie explained.

"It is a good plan. We will be able to find out who sends false messages and convey it to others, warning them," Natalie said.

"But how will we know who attacks us and who doesn't?" the clone Sandy asked again.

"There is a facility in the submarine to turn on a satellite camera. We can check the base to see where the transmissions come from. If we see weapons coming up from certain bases towards us, they are the enemy," Nyman explained.

"I know what you are thinking, Sandy. You'll be risking your life as there are high chances of being attacked frequently," Natalie said to clone Sandy.

"I am sending you both precisely because you are well-trained. You both know how to defend yourself from such types of attacks," Will said.

"Let me go with clone Sandy, Will. Let Natalie stay here. You might need her help here in tracking the messages and transmitting data. Fred is already busy. I can handle the missile attacks," Nyman said.

Will thought for a moment and agreed. Nyman's reason was quite logical. "Natalie studied communication technology," Nyman said, preparing to leave with the humanoid Sandy.

He stopped for a moment, looking at Sandy's replicant, and asked, "Sandy, are you willing to do this? If not, I will take Natalie with me. You can stay and help Fred," he said.

Will and Natalie looked at each other meaningfully. Clone Sandy seemed perplexed for a moment.

Then she answered, "I don't know. The scientists reprogrammed my mind for free will only ten minutes ago. I was always ordered to do things. No one ever asked me whether I wanted to do anything," she shrugged her shoulders.

"It seemed like you enjoyed your rendezvous in the sky. Are you up for some more action?" Will asked her.

"Of course, I did. I have been pumped with energy since I came out of the medical chamber. I don't want to miss the thrill of action at any cost," the humanoid responded, beaming with enthusiasm.

"Spoken like a true Sandy. There is nothing to worry about then. Off you go with Nyman. Have fun," Will said, laughing.

……………

"Why can't you deactivate the brain bomb, Jamal?" Will asked, shocked.

"The brain bomb in Sandy's head was placed by Dr Kean himself. It is very advanced. There are two parts to it," another scientist offered.

"The explosive is in the brain. So if we pull it out, the second tech-piece in the heart will be activated," Mr Jamal explained.

"Will it crush her heart?" Natalie asked, terrified.

"No, it won't kill her. Instead, it will transform her into a mindless robot," Mr Jamal said.

"What? I don't understand..." Will blinked.

"You see, the latest technological advances of humanoids are true clones, meaning they are full-blown human beings. Not robots. All the body parts are grown in the lab, including the brain, heart, lungs, etc. The New Order places a chip on their head and heart. It synchronizes the brain signals and makes them obey their commands by programming the chip," one scientist explained.

"We were able to give free will to the distorted clones, only by deactivating the chip, so they could think on their own," he continued.

"Just do the same now!" Will shouted, losing patience. His face grew red, and he clenched his fists. He had just saved Sandy, and she was already in danger again.

"We cannot access a brain chip this advanced. Only Dr Kean and the head of the New Order have access to override it. If we deactivate the brain bomb, Sandy will be transformed into an enemy clone," Mr Jamal said helplessly.

"I already tried. We cannot override this program. It is quite complex. It is designed to be foolproof," Fred agreed.

Will clutched his head and sat down. "Can't we just keep using the dampeners?" Natalie asked.

"Dampeners won't work for long. Without the jammer, they get weaker by the minute. It works by interrupting the neural signals. Sandy might go into a coma if the dampener is used more than a day," Mr Jamal explained.

"What is the solution for this? We either let her die or turn into our enemy?" Will asked, frustrated.

"That is the only option now, Agent Burne. Let us remove the bomb and send Sandy to the enemy. We will find Dr Kean and make him deactivate the chip in her head," the rebel scientist said.

Will went to Sandy, who was half-conscious, "You are going to have a hell of a time fighting me, Agent Burne. Don't kill me," she smiled like a goddess.

Full of emotion, Will clutched her hand and kissed it passionately. "I swear I will make Kean run naked on top of a volcano, roasting himself alive," he said with immense anger.

"Will, do what needs to be done. Find out who the enemy is. I love you. I want a life with you. I don't want to die like this. We will win this and get back together," Sandy kissed Will's hands, which clutched her palms.

"Take care of Adha. I am still his daughter," she said, drifting off to deep sleep. The scientists pushed the stretcher away from Will. He felt like his heart was stabbed.

"We have a real Will and a clone Sandy with us. Our enemies now have the real Sandy and the clone Will," Natalie said.

"Do you know who the greatest enemy is? It's you two. I bet the leader of the New Order will have you both as his chief security guards. You will have to fight yourself and Sandy," Fred said.

Will nodded with a heavy heart. "I will track down that bastard, whoever he is. Let's start tracking the rebel messages," he said, briskly getting back to work.

… … …

Sandy woke up with a heavy head and looked around in dismay. She was in the middle of the ocean on a lifeboat. She could not judge where she was. There was an emergency bag near her with food, water, a light rod, and some other essential items. She loaded the bag on her shoulder.

She saw a jetpack resting on the end of the lifeboat. She wondered where she was and what she must do next. A distinct voice in her head said, "Obey the New Order." Sandy complied immediately as her head filled with instructions.

She secured the jetpack in place and pressed the propel button, flying towards a nearby enemy base without losing any time. Will sighed, watching the scene unfolding through the satellite camera.

"She landed in an enemy base in Afrasia," Natalie said. The reprogrammed Volador placed inside Sandy's bag silently crept out from behind her and stealthily entered the base when she stopped at the checkpoint.

It quickly moved past the security cameras, entered the mainframe area, and attached itself to the central Cloudnet node. Then, it activated its camouflage, blending excellently with the surroundings.

"Good job, Natalie and Fred. Now we will find out who the culprit is behind all this New Order shit," Will said, barely controlling his fuming anger.

… … …

Robots, Clones Everywhere…

Adi Kalim entered his base in Afrasia like a lion, and his associates swarmed him with various questions. There were over fifty of his trusted men. Adha questioned whom to trust after losing Simons and Walker. He wondered who among them is a clone and wished the scientists would come up with an easy way to judge it.

Adha remembered the ID chip the scientists used to make the clones obey the humans instantly. He ordered all his men to assemble in the hall and waved the chip in front of them.

"All the clones, raise both your hands in the air and come forward," he ordered.

Three of them came forward, as controlled by the chip. The other agents looked on in disbelief as Adha ordered the clones to disclose everything from the minute they entered the base.

He waited patiently, only to hear them say they were searching for May and were transmitting signals regarding the location to the enemy group.

Adha had installed a jammer, similar to Fred's in the base, which had prevented the clone's signals from getting out. He ordered his men to guard them and moved inside.

He entered his private chamber and then used a device to scan for microphones, explosives, and any electronic or magnetic items. Once he was satisfied that he found no extra spy items, he pressed a floral pattern on his desk, and the wall behind the desk automatically moved aside.

Adha saw May Lay seated inside. The secret room contained some of his most confidential files and enough supplies for one person to stay alive for two weeks.

May gave a disgusted look at Adha. "I know you are a traitor. You knew my husband was such a villain and did nothing to stop him. He killed Sandy's parents—brutally!" May shouted in agitation, throwing a file at Adha.

"Did you do something foolish? Did you try to contact anyone about this?" Adha asked, tensed.

"Yes! I used your system when you let me out the last time, and I messaged Sandy!" May said.

Adha was taken aback. He imagined how terrible Sandy must have felt when she read that message. Yet, neither Sandy nor Will had questioned him and still trusted him to lead the rebellion. His love for Sandy grew enormously at that moment.

At the very same time the thought ran through his head, Sandy accessed her personal mobile through Cloudnet backup. She had apparently wondered where her mobile was and used the enemy's systems to retrieve the information. Adha's mobile alarm beeped, indicating Sandy was accessing her device remotely.

As he watched, Sandy opened the message from May. Although he could do nothing to stop it, he watched as she sent the blitzmail to her new superiors.

"I got a message from May. We can track the base's location where she is by using the message," she reported promptly to the New Order.

Adha turned to May. "You should not have contacted Sandy. Things have changed," Adha said. He had received a message about Sandy's condition from Will just before he entered the base to check on May. He rushed out, pulling May out of the room.

"Save yourselves. We might be attacked at any minute. Code red!" he thundered to everyone within earshot and pressed the alarm button, which warned everyone by emitting a loud siren.

Adha pressed another symbol below his desk and retrieved a bag. He thrust it at May and ran to the other side of the base. Then, without warning, a massive earthquake-like jolt came out of nowhere, and May hit the floor, unable to keep her balance.

Adha came to her with his own bag and helped her stand up. Every person in the base was rushing out. "Give me the location of your estate bunker. I know you have an entire island near Bequia in the Caribbean region," he said.

May complied, and Adha transmitted the details she gave to his entire team. "Head there. Stay safe. We have to fight the New Order. Take all you can from here!" he bellowed through the intercom. Another colossal bomb fell on the base, and the roof shattered.

"You scoundrel, you are sending them right to my husband, the leader of the New Order. How can you betray your own men!?" May screamed.

"Your husband is dead!" Adha shouted. May did not believe him, so he had no choice but to pull the footage up on his mobile device of George's gruesome death.

Adha then showed her the footage of George Lay's head exploding. "We don't know who did it. But we have to find out," he said, transmitting the same video to all his men. Bullets started raining on the building from all sides now.

They took cover behind a broken steel desk. "Wear this," Adha shoved a bulletproof suit at May and stuffed himself into one. The bag he brought had weapons too. He handed May a rifle.

"I am sorry for your husband's death Mrs Lay. I thought he was the leader of the New Order too. But we were deceived," Adha said.

He led May away from the bullets and into an underground chamber. Most of the men from the base were already hurrying through the tunnel.

"Don't get out in plain sight. We will use the underground water tunnel to escape through the sea. We are too exposed on land," Adha warned them as he moved forward with May.

"Why are we going up?" May asked, perplexed.

"We need to create a distraction. If nobody comes out of the base, they will start digging deeper and come in after us," Adha said. Some of his men followed him. Adha saw they had brought the clones out, dressed in bulletproof suits. He ordered the clones to run in three different directions.

The enemy's automatic robots chased the three running clones while his men used the distraction to escape on the other side. They loaded a vehicle and gunned it, driving away at top speed. The vehicle engaged its active holographic camouflage and transformed itself to look like an enemy autobot, driving out right under the other enemy robots' noses.

"How did this van transform itself?" May asked, surprised.

"We have advanced weapons too. George isn't the only one," one of Adha's men said in a stern tone. May realized most of them hated her for being George's wife. Maybe that's why Adha had kept her so well-hidden on the base.

She was silent as the van passed through the thick jungle. Its camouflage changed to match the surroundings every ten minutes.

"Who killed him?" she asked Adha softly after a few minutes.

"We don't know yet. Mr Lay's head exploded after we sabotaged his plan to bomb all the continent's capitals. Who are his closest associates?" Adha asked.

"Why should I tell you? I strongly doubt you killed my husband," May sneered.

"That monster put a red-hot rod inside Sandy's vagina. Well, it was her clone. But it is still not human to do such barbaric acts. I would have definitely killed him if he didn't die through that brain blast," Adha said firmly.

"I don't trust you. You knew he killed Sandy's parents. Yet, you did nothing about it all these years. See how dangerous the world is now. You could have stopped all this. It is not the mistakes of great men that cause harm. It is their inaction that causes disaster," May blamed Adha.

"It is your husband who tried to bomb the cities. Not Adha," one of the men spoke in his defence.

"How did they track the base if Adha was the only one who knew where it was? Even you people in the bunker did not know I was hidden there," May questioned.

"It's Sandy. She is on their side now," Adha took a few minutes to explain everything quickly. "We are all at a standstill. We can only fight further if we know who our real enemy is. Can you tell me who was close with your husband?" Adha asked again.

"President Morgan, West Federation chief industrialist Mr Evangelic Mathew…" May said.

"They both are clones. Can you think of anybody else? Anybody whom George showed great respect or fear?" Adha pressed further.

"There is Benedict Henderson, Henry Adams, Marshall Cartier… they were all his friends. George had great respect for each of them," May said. Adha turned to his men.

"Guys, this is the frequency of a cyberspace secret node network Fred set up. Use it to check all the details about the names May gives. Then, transmit the message to Will if you find anything useful," Adha said, jumping out of the now slowing vehicle.

He pulled May out, too, before she could protest. "What the hell is wrong with you? What did you do that for?" she protested vehemently.

"They will spot us getting out if the vehicle stops," Adha explained.

They were in the middle of a busy rural street. Adha led her into a dingy motel room and locked the door behind them. "Dress yourself quickly. All the essential items are in your bag," he said.

They heard another thunderous bomb exploding nearby. "Just as I feared. The New Order is searching for your face everywhere. Their satellites would have traced your face when we walked through the street," Adha said.

They heard numerous crashing sounds and took cover behind an overturned wooden table. Adha handed her a pair of goggles and wore some himself.

Once she put on the goggles, May could see through the wooden table and concrete walls. The green-coloured images were superimposed, but she could see the thermal outlines of humans and objects.

She saw a robot breaking open each wall, stretching its wired head inside and scanning in all directions for May.

Adha pressed the bag, signalling her to use it. He jumped out of hiding and took one clean shot at the robot. It was dismantled into pieces in no time. He rushed out, fighting the other robotic vehicles.

May wondered whether to trust him or not while digging into the bag's supplies. She found a rubber mask inside the bag and a wig made of human hair. The disguise concealed her identity quickly, and when she put on the pumps, it made her look much taller.

She came out of the building, which was now in rubbles. A man casually approached her and walked along, whispering to her. "It's me, Adha," he said, showing her the goggles he had been wearing previously. He, too, was disguised in a rubber mask and looked much different.

They moved stealthily, mingling with the frightened crowd. Chaos ensued, and people were running without aim. They moved steadily, without touching anyone, and took shelter behind a large garbage bin.

There was already a mass of people hidden behind the garbage bin. It was a huge one for facilities to recycle plastic packaging. The bin started to beep loudly as soon as Adha and May approached it. Others hiding behind the bin immediately scattered in fear.

Adha wondered how a mere dustbin detected them within a split second. He pushed May further away and mingled deeper within the crowd. Three street dogs approached the area, and within seconds, they had transformed into small robots and blew the recycling bin to bits.

A crowd of people had gathered around at this point, watching the fiasco in extreme fear and curiosity. "How the hell did it know we were hiding there? We are safe if we stay mingled with other people," Adha said.

He wondered what had given up their identity. Some cops approached the area, trying to protect the public. The street dog robots came alive again and shot them like a sieve. The crowd panicked and ran away in all directions.

May and Adha kept running with them. "It is not us. It's the weapons the New Order is detecting. They are killing everybody with weapons to create fear among the public," Adha said.

He transmitted the message to his and Will's teams through his wrist communicating device.

"How the hell did the street dogs and dustbins turn robotic?" May asked, panting as she ran.

A female passerby heard her and answered in disgust, "I knew this shit would happen when the IC people set up the new garbage bins. I warned them anything this techy would be used to monitor and control us!"

"The IC," Adha gasped, "The Inter-Continental Federation. Didn't you say Benedict Henderson was close with your husband?" Adha asked.

May nodded a terrified "Yes."

… … …

Beginning of the New Order…

Fred approached Will with heaps of paper. "It is Benedict Henderson," he confirmed in disbelief.

"The Volador we spied with gave us access to the mainframe in Sandy's base. We analysed all the messages received through an advanced AI. The core messages coming from the IC head office came directly from Benedict Henderson," Natalie explained.

"We also traced the manufacturing unit of the advanced auto-programmed super-brain in the Voladors. It is manufactured in a direct IC-controlled factory used to make memory units for them," Fred elaborated.

"Will, we were attacked after you contacted the last rebel base that asked for help. They are an enemy base. We are safe now. Check it out," a call from Nyman said.

"That base is situated directly under the Alps. It operates from an IC facility used to aid underdeveloped countries," a clone interpreting the base location satellite feeds reported.

"Mr Burne, Adi Kalim's men used iSuspct, an advanced AI system to scan various suspect names they collected from May. They strongly suspect Benedict Henderson—the head of the Inter-Continental Federation. He supplied numerous advanced garbage and recycling bins to the underdeveloped Afrasian and Underworld countries. They are killing every cop or person with a weapon now," another clone relayed the message as it was received.

"Benedict Henderson," Will clutched his head, "the head of the Inter-Continental Federation. He is powerful, influential, has enough contacts, and can easily manipulate world leaders. But why? Why is he doing it?" he wondered out loud.

"Power, Will. Control," Natalie said, "In my history lessons growing up, I used to read about an organisation similar to the IC before the pandemics, called the NU. IC does not have any actual, major power. Mr Henderson is an ambitious man who couldn't do much with his seemingly powerless position as head of the IC. He likely dreamed of having absolute world domination," Natalie said.

"I was thinking about several people. But I never suspected him because he has enormous charisma. I have worked close to him on countless missions, protecting him from Underworld terrorists. He was my hero," Will said, sounding disappointed.

"Mine too," Fred agreed. "Do you see the irony? The masses will consider him their hero, now, too. Anything he says or does in such a chaotic situation will be accepted, without opposition," Fred said.

Will contacted Adha, "It is the perfect plan, and he has the motive, Will. He is threatening the rural areas by taking out the cops. It will create major issues with law and order. He is using the dustbins and the street dog robots as a ruse, instead of the major city bombings," Adha explained.

Will and his team understood the gravity of the situation. They had successfully sabotaged his plan to kill millions and unite the people together in the name of a single UniContinent. Making every street unsafe will create the same amount of panic, even though the death rate is relatively low.

Most people will look for a trustworthy leader to save them. Benedict Henderson had already won their heart with the pretence of giving them numerous goodies to make the planet better.

Even well-trained agents like Will Burne will be ready to follow him. All the opposition had already been replaced with puppeteer clones. Benedict had probably planned this for more than a decade. How did all the world governments miss the intel?

"I seriously did not suspect him one bit. Mr Henderson is a very manipulative man. Even the Maharaj I work for will say nobody can beat him in an argument. The world leaders made him the head of the IC, hoping it would prevent him from growing as a leader in their opposition. President Morgan was very close to him," Adha said.

"Adha, what if he starts talking to the public? What if he reaches them directly?" Will asked, petrified.

"He is planning precisely that, Will," Fred said, "The head of the IC, Benedict Henderson, will address the public in five minutes. All the media is showing his face. Even the unaffected cities in the Oceania and West Federation are scared by the sudden bombings and chaos. The whole world will start looking up to him in two minutes," Fred said.

Just as he was talking, the ship's monitors started showing the face of a compassionate Benedict Henderson on the screens. The room listened on high alert. Adha stopped at a stadium with mega screens showing Mr Henderson's face.

"Adha, I signed a document giving him unlimited access to my wealth. He persuaded me to give a power of attorney to him under the guise of helping the Underworld nations. George also supported it," May whispered into Adha's ears.

"How much money?" Adha asked, shocked.

"It was over a decade ago. You know my father was the richest man in Oceania, and I am his only child. That is quite a lot of money. Hundreds of billions," May said.

"That explains the clones and the street dog robots. Mr Henderson used every penny wisely," Adha clenched his teeth helplessly. Then, the speech of Benedict Henderson began.

……… ………

"My dear, beloved people," Benedict Henderson started his speech with all the frills, "we are under attack. Your governments have failed to keep you safe. Major cities are under attack on every continent. Lives are lost, and families are separated. Nobody knows what is happening. We have to band together, to fight together, with everything we have to survive. I plead with you to help me. Let us unite everyone together as one UniContinent, so that we may overcome these attacks together, as one."

Adha saw the masses cheering wildly. People were crying and smiling in relief. Some were bowing to him in respect; others looked frightened. He knew every scared face around him trusted this charming personality wholeheartedly.

"Fred, do you have the footage of George Lay's head exploding and his confession to Natalie recorded?" Will asked.

"Yes. I do. Why are you asking, Will?"

"Hack the telecast and play those footages; play all the proof we have, with prompts pointing to Henderson as the culprit, without any doubt left to wonder. This speech should be his last," Will said, brimming with anger. "Let this be the end of him."

Will still couldn't believe one man could cause such devastating damage, all for the greed of power—especially Benedict Henderson. He felt like he was stabbed in the back by a trusted friend. He dreaded how easily Mr Henderson deceived him and other high officials. Even Adha did not suspect Mr Henderson, one iota.

Benedict Henderson's speech continued as Fred worked his skills, hacking the system. "My trusted citizens, most of the world's leaders are dead. The surviving ones are not ready to accept their failure. This is not the time for the blame game. Now is the time for uniting together to find out who caused such massive chaos. We should not make the same mistake our governments did in failing to protect the people, in failing to protect us. Unite with me to fight against the invisible forces hunting us down. I call every cop, every military personnel, every spy, and every man and woman with a backbone to support me in this quest. Unite with me to create one UniContinent—a safe haven for all of us who have escaped these dreadful weeks with our lives."

The monitor blurred for a moment. The footage of George Lay confessing about his financial mistakes to Natalie played. It was followed by the footage of him trying to blow down the cities, failing desperately, then getting his head blown out.

Then, the footage showed the proof of the bombs being made in IC headquarters and videos of the IC-supplied dustbins targeting and murdering government police officers and military officials. Finally, it ended with the following words in big, bold lettering:

ALL FOR WHAT?

TO MAKE HIM THE LEADER OF THE WORLD?

HE IS THE CULPRIT.

BENEDICT HENDERSON IS THE VILLAIN!

Adha gave a grateful sigh. The team had saved the day. Benedict Henderson was finally finished, once and for all.

The team in Will's cabin, scientists and all, clapped for joy as they saw the hacked message blinking in, repeating itself, again and again.

Will, too, let out a great sigh of relief. They had finally defeated the leader of the New Order.

The screen changed again, and a seemingly unaffected Benedict Henderson appeared on the screen. He spoke with the same poise as before. "Benedict Henderson is the villain," he repeated, "Benedict Henderson is the villain because he believed his friends. Benedict Henderson is the villain because he trusted his associates, who created bombs right under his nose. Benedict Henderson is the villain because he agreed to whatever the world leaders like President Morgan said without question. I am the villain responsible for all this devastation because I did not use my power to stop them at the right time. I trusted them to give a peaceful life to my fellow citizens. I did not oppose when my position in the IC was diplomatic, and I had no power to stop these atrocious acts of violence.

"Now, I call upon you, my fellow sufferers, my fellow people of the world. I need your help. I am going to stand up and rage a full-fledged fight against all these governments. I am not fighting because I want to change the world. I am not fighting because I want to make the world a better place. I am fighting because I am lucky to be alive, and I want to stay alive for a few more years. I am fighting to help everyone still alive to survive a little longer against these evil forces. Who is with me? Will you support me? Will you help me to build a UniContinent!?" he ended his speech with a shout.

The applauding masses erupted in a ferocious cheer and began chanting, "Yes, we will! Yes, we will!" over and over again. Adha looked at the people around him, stunned at the development. Will and his team were equally stunned, unable to conjure how to proceed next.

Benedict Henderson had faced the gravest accusation of his life and turned it into his favour. He had declared war, single-handedly, against all the four continents. Will and Adha knew Mr Henderson had the technology to take on all the world's military. Now, he also had the immense support of the people, which will make him the leader of the world forever.

The screen again showed George Lay's attempt to bomb the cities and Will and Sandy sabotaging it effectively. The footage was now edited to show Sandy and Will's faces in a closeup. Benedict Henderson appeared on the screen again. Sandy and replicant Will were with him now. He joined hands with both of them and raised their hands, "Will Burne, the best special agent of the West Federation. Sandy Krave, the best agent in Afrasia—the beloved daughter of Adi Kalim the Great."

"They are the unsung heroes who have saved our cities from George Lay. They are with me. Are you with me? These talented young people risked their lives to save you, and I will do the same in the blink of an eye. They trust me. Do you trust me? Will you fight against your government to create a safer UniContinent for us all?" Benedict Henderson asked.

The crowd surrounding Adha broke out in loud cheers. Then, someone started chanting "New Order" as the words "UniContinent – the New Order" appeared on the screen. The group began to chant in a hypnotized state.

Adha knew that people around the world were likely doing the same.

"What do we do now?" May asked, perplexed.

"We do what we are trained to do. We fight against all odds," Adha said, leading her away to safety.

… … …

Nyman and the clone Sandy watched the telecast from their isolated, hidden position on an island in the middle of the ocean.

"What just happened?" the clone Sandy asked, confused.

"The barbaric and extremely dangerous New Order is beginning its reign," Nyman said.

"Does that mean we failed?" the clone Sandy asked innocently.

"No, Sandy. We did not fail. In fact, we saved millions of lives. We are just starting the war. This is the first day…" Nyman said, looking at the star-filled skies.

… … …

Will and his team stood, stunned, watching the telecast.

"What do we do now?" Natalie asked Will.

"Just what we always do, Natalie; we fight. We have to fight to protect the masses from the New Order, fight to stay alive, and fight to keep those who are alive safe…." Will said in his base, collecting his weapon and getting ready to face the real enemy.

… … …

Sandy settled in at the base she entered, looking at the various clones, humanoids, and replicants, and examined all the advanced weapons. Next, she went through an orientation process that thoroughly checked her spy tech and took her on a clone facility tour.

Sandy sat in a room beside Will's replicant. He was busy uploading instructions regarding weapons handling into a clone's brain. "Will is an expert," Sandy thought. "But why is he teaching his techniques to the entire army?" her instincts wondered.

Suddenly, she felt compelled to do the same. Will's clone moved further over, making way for her to pull up another holographic monitor. "It's not right," Sandy thought. She knew something was amiss.

"Every soldier has a special move. Don't share your best moves with others. It's what makes you unique," the 40 Grades training had stressed several times. She wondered why they were breaking the rules now.

She felt intense pain in her head when she resisted uploading the information regarding her special move. "This is not right," Sandy mumbled, clutching her head. Then, a sudden electric jolt passed through her body, making her crumble to the floor in pain.

"Don't resist the New Order, Sandy. You should obey instantly," Will's clone stated with a blank expression. Deep down, Sandy knew something was off.

She felt anger rushing through her every nerve when she saw Dr Kean. But Sandy could do nothing to act on it as the voice in her head kept compelling her to obey him.

"I told you we should kill her. She is definitely a threat. Just look at her brain signals. She is trying so hard to fight the programming chip inside her," Dr Kean's assistant said, looking at the monitor. They were in a lab monitoring Sandy's brain activity.

"You think I didn't try? Mr Henderson is furious after the attempt to bomb the cities got sabotaged. Adha is a greater threat, and she is the only bait we have to keep him docile," he said.

Sandy wanted to blast open the laboratory doors and kick Dr Kean squarely in the face. But, just then, someone else walked into the room. Sandy froze, recognizing him instantly. It was the leader of the New Order…

End of Book One

BOOK TWO

PART I - A Secret Island; Close to Oceania

AN EXTRAORDINARY PHENOMENON

Is the World Ready For Sandy Krave?

"Start by doing what's necessary; then do what's possible; and suddenly you are doing the impossible."

–Francis of Assisi

Chapter One

Sandy was deep in the water, trying to focus on not drowning. The 40 Grade Code training sometimes puts the trainees in precarious situations for several reasons. First, they wanted to see their ability to adapt. Second, they wanted to see if pressure could unlock the secret powers they had. Sandy was special, and her trainers knew she was going to break a new record.

One by one, other trainees swam right back to the surface, gasping for breath. But not Sandy. She continued holding her breath, hoping she could go another minute longer than she thought she could. Sandy grasped the weights that kept her underwater and renewed her focus. Her lungs were burning, and her eyes were starting to hurt. But that wasn't her biggest worry. She just wanted to go another minute.

"Do you think she'll make it? I think we should pull her out!"

"No," Adha Long shouted, "if Sandy wants to stay in there another minute, we should let her!"

The readings on her vitals showed she was still alive, but it was putting major stress on her organs. It could kill her. But if Adha Long knew what Sandy was capable of, no one would dare doubt him, let alone challenge him.

As Sandy continued holding her breath, her green eyes started glowing. Panic engulfed her since she had never experienced anything like that before. Her first instinct was to kick off the riverbed and start swimming to the surface. But after a moment, she began to realize she was breathing underwater, so Sandy hesitated. Did she have superpowers? Had she unlocked another level of the 40 Grade Code training?

It was the sudden sound of steady footsteps that pulled Sandy back to reality. She opened her eyes and what she saw brought her a sudden shock—her jaw almost hit the floorboards.

Sandy Krave's first instinct was to launch herself forward and punch Mr Henderson in the throat, as she'd been trained for years to do. But no matter how hard she tried, the alien programming in her brain wouldn't allow it. She remained transfixed on her knees despite her best efforts to make a move. Powerless, Sandy remained in that submissive position, helplessly watching as the group of men, robots, and clones stared right back at her as though she were a lab rat.

"Still having trouble with this one, I see," Mr Henderson scoffed as he strode across the polished laboratory floor. He wore an evil smile on his face, which looked somewhat odd for a man known for his charisma. However, Benedict Henderson didn't have to carry around the Mr Nice Guy demeanour any longer. He was on the verge of winning.

"She's tough, as was expected. She was one of Mr Kalim's first trainees and, more importantly, his daughter. But with the new tech, I think we can break her," Dr Kean said timidly.

"And when will that be? We are at war, in case you didn't get the memo. We may be on the verge of victory, but that shouldn't blind us. The world's governments are coming for us. Also, Kalim and his team are still out there. Every moment we waste is another they take to recover, to regroup. So, we should strike while we still have the upper hand."

"Yes, sir."

That was all the reassurance Mr Henderson needed. He knew Dr Kean was a man of his word. If he said he'd get the job done, he was most certainly going to do it. Dr Kean was also too smart to try anything that would undermine their plans. Exhausted from his hour-long speech, Benedict Henderson made a beeline to the comfortable seat at the furthest end of the state-of-the-art lab and sunk lazily into it. From there, he could watch everything unfolding without batting an eye.

Three robots and four clones immediately surrounded the chair. So, naturally, keeping the leader of the New Order safe was a high priority, especially in such trying times. Henderson was soon to be crowned the first leader of UniContinent. Unfortunately, such a coveted position had a way of attracting old and new enemies from out of the woodwork, and Benedict Henderson knew better than to take any chances.

He'd already created enemies within the governments. Thankfully, he had already dealt with most of the high-ranking officials and replaced them with clones. The only threat that would prove an uphill task to annihilate was Adi Kalim and his team. *The sooner, the better*, Mr Henderson sighed.

Every fibre of his being told him to take a moment to bask in the glory of it all, but he just couldn't. Mr Henderson never thought for a moment that his plan was going to succeed as smoothly as it did. But for him to be truly happy, he had to see it through.

Maybe the takeover was too smooth to be accurate? Perhaps I'm playing into one of their traps. He couldn't savour the moment. His conscience wasn't at peace. But, since Mr Henderson never got to where Mr Kalim was, he sprung back to action by forcing himself to ignore his sixth sense. He was torn between wondering if he was playing into a trap and wanting to celebrate coming this far. *I can always kick back and celebrate when the work is done,* he reassured himself a second time before taking his coat off and rolling his sleeves all the way up.

Mr Henderson activated his super smartwatch with a slight tap, which he pressed almost immediately, confirming his thumbprint and DNA, which was analysed from his sweat. A green light shot from the watch onto his face, scanning his retina before an AI voice uttered, "*Granted.*"

A hologram screen rose from the watch, and Mr Henderson scooped it and put it in front of him. Doing so allowed him complete access to all major news outlets. He'd used much of May Lay's inheritance to either buy or bribe all the news networks. Now they did his bidding. As expected, they were applauding him for taking full responsibility for the attacks and standing up to the powers and governments.

Besides buying the media, the Inter-Continental Federation, or the IC for short, had secretly designed and launched six satellites into orbit. These high-tech satellites allowed Mr Henderson to spy on everyone without raising suspicion. The latter explained how he always found himself in the middle of world-changing events. He could access all his spy satellites from his super smartwatch. That's how he decided to use it to double-zero-down on Kalim and his team of assassins.

… … …

Nyman squeezed the last of their water from the bottle before pounding it into the sand. He was never a fan of sitting out a good fight. He knew his sister, Natalie, and the rest of the team were fighting for their lives, and he wanted in on the action. But if he and Sandy's clone were to get off this island, they needed to find some form of transport.

Sandy's clone returned from bathing and was naked. She walked directly in front of Nyman, who was sitting at the entrance of the trend, causing him to blush a little. Sandy's clone took notice and started to giggle.

"Are you blushing?" she asked as she stood in front of him, her hands akimbo.

"No, I'm not," Nyman replied, still looking away.

"Then what's wrong?"

"Nothing."

Sandy's clone walked into the tent to put on some clothes, leaving Nyman plagued with impure thoughts. What Nyman didn't tell anyone was that he was attracted to Sandy. But since they were at war, he thought it best not to be vocal about his feelings. Besides, it did seem as though Sandy had a thing with Will Burne. Nyman let out another sigh before raising the bottle back to his mouth. He frowned upon realizing it was empty. *Damn!*

"You know, we aren't going to live in hiding forever. At some point, we'll have to find a way off this island and help in the fight. Benedict Henderson is coming to power, and when he does, we won't be safe, not even in hiding," Sandy's clone said as she appeared from inside the makeshift tent.

"I know. But how are we supposed to do that? This island's got nothing. Look around."

"Yes, so it appears, but that's why we have to go take a good look around. You may be surprised at what we might find. Come on," Sandy's clone said, offering Nyman a hand, "Don't worry, I'm not naked. Besides, my vagina doesn't bite."

Weird, Nyman thought. *A clone with a dark sense of humour.*

… … …

While Benedict Henderson was engrossed in browsing through virtual screens, Dr Kean and his team of distraught scientists did their best to retrieve information from Sandy's brain. They were all shocked at how well she managed to resist them for as long as she did. At one point, Dr Kean wanted to talk to Mr Henderson about more severe options but decided against the idea after glancing over his shoulder to catch a glimpse of his boss working.

Mr Henderson loathed being interrupted. That's when something strange happened.

"Do you think we should continue?" asked one of his assistants.

Dr Kean didn't answer. He was thinking the same. But then again, the doctor wasn't moving forward without the leader of the New Order's consent. If it were up to Dr Kean, he would have already killed Sandy and cut her brain from her skull. But, on the other hand, he knew ways to extract information from the brain as long as he kept those neurons firing.

"Sir?"

Dr Kean had been in a trance for a while without realizing it.

"I've been calling you for almost a minute. Are you ok?"

"Yeah, I am. What?"

I'm losing my mind. What is happening to me? Dr Kean thought. One moment he was fine, and the next, he was off in his own little world. His team looked at him without uttering a word. They seemed just as confused as Dr Kean was.

"There's no change. We've tried everything ethical to get information from her brain, but it's virtually impossible," said the intern.

"What do you mean 'virtually impossible?'" Dr Kean asked, trying to appear unshaken about his momentary trance.

"The subject seems to have formed an electromagnetic field around her brain. We've never seen anything like this."

"What? That's impossible!"

……………

"We're picking up some interference from an unidentified satellite," Fred said as he kicked back and rolled across the room on his wheeled chair. He'd been cooped up in the secret control room for eighteen straight hours while Adha, Will, and what remained of their assault team trained in the adjacent room.

While the others trained with the simulations, Adha stayed busy on the sidelines crafting plans to rescue Sandy. The only problem was finding the secret IC hideout where the doctor and his team of evil scientists were holding her. That's the riddle Fred was tasked with unravelling.

Adha knew it was only a matter of time before Mr Henderson's private army came knocking. Even though he'd done a great job of turning his most devastating loss into a win, there's no way Mr Henderson was gifting them the opportunity to catch him off guard again. That's just how careful he was as a man.

"Benedict Henderson is going to come down on us hard. So we need to prepare and be ready for when that happens. If anything, we should strike first," Adha had told the team as a way to motivate them to train harder.

"I agree. Mr Henderson thinks we are too fragile to pull a frontal attack at the moment. Well, he's in for the biggest surprise of his life," Will growled.

"I don't think that's the case. If Mr Henderson managed to fool everyone for all these years without even trying, the last thing we'd want to do is underestimate him. So, let's assume he's covered on all fronts. That way, we can come up with an airtight plan that covers the worst-case scenarios."

"And how do you suggest we do that?" Natalie asked. She was still cuddling her vast, fully-charged laser gun like it was an overgrown baby.

"By keeping our eyes peeled on his eyes if you know what I mean."

No one understood when Adha chose to speak in parables, but they nodded nonetheless. The team of assassins was too tired to raise questions. Thankfully, they trusted that Adha knew what he was doing. After the briefing, everyone was dismissed. They'd gone almost eighteen hours without sleep, and the fatigue was starting to get the better of them. The last thing Adha wanted was a bunch of tired soldiers fending off a group of robots and motivated, well-rested savages.

After seeing everyone off, Adha joined Fred in the control room. The badass geek was so focused on the screens he didn't notice the intrusion for a moment. At first, Adha didn't want to interrupt. Instead, he hovered around like a ghost, choosing to observe in silence. Fred adjusted his glasses with his middle finger before the rattling on his keyboard resumed. This went on for another minute before Fred broke the deafening silence.

"I know you have something to say, boss. Lurking in the shadows like that gives me the creeps," Fred said amid the rattling.

"I didn't want to interrupt the process."

"Too late for that." There was a smile curving at the corners of Fred's mouth as soon as he replied.

"Apologies," Adha said before continuing, "So, where are we with the tracking?"

"I was wondering when you were going to ask. When you told me to worry when the New Order stopped dropping bombs on our heads, I haven't been thinking straight. Honestly, I haven't been thinking straight ever since the hack. So, I took the liberty to cover our digital footprints, then ensured our signal was untraceable. So, we're officially off the grid in every sense of the term.

"Afterward, I piggybacked most satellites to keep an eye on every kind of interference, especially with electromagnetic fields. That's when I noticed something fishy. There's an area where there aren't any electromagnetic fields. Or maybe there are, but they're suppressed. I don't know. What I'm saying is, I've never seen anything like it before, boss.

"Here, look at this area over this region," Fred said while pointing the area with his index finger, "You told me to inform you if I find anything weird. Well, that's weird."

Adha edged a bit closer and squinted his eyes before they widened right back. A flash of determination burned bright in his eyes, leaving Fred a little confused. *What was the old man thinking?* Before Fred could ask, Adha pressed the red button below the desk, and an alarm went off immediately. *CODE RED! CODE RED!* sounded the AI in a female voice. It took about a minute and a half for the entire assault team to rush into the control room, laser guns cocked and ready to fire.

"We've located Sandy. We're going in!"

… … …

Mr Henderson was about to throw in the proverbial towel when something on the screen blipped, catching his attention almost immediately. One of the satellites, linked to the automated garbage bins, had picked something up and sent it back to the control room. Henderson quickly swiped across the virtual screens, zooming in on one area of the aerial map.

The software had automatically notified his entire assault team, which was now surrounding the president of the New Order, watching closely as they awaited his instruction. The facial recognition software brought up three familiar faces.

"We got them! They're in a hideout somewhere nearby. I think they didn't go far after our last attack. Clever. But now we crush them before they make it to George Lay's Island."

The soon-to-be president of UniContinent gave the word, and it was time for his minions, both human and machine, to make him proud. The human followers were promised riches beyond measure once Mr Henderson's UniContinent dreams came to fruition. That's how Mr Henderson managed to win their loyalty, besides his hypnotizing charisma.

Moments after Mr Henderson issued his decree, a battalion of soldiers spurted out of the underground base like high-pressure water from a broken pipe, flooding the parking area where fully-fuelled combat autobots awaited them. The alarm was still sounding in the background, adding to the level of urgency that floated around them like a restless ghost.

Mr Henderson didn't join them. *Generals never mingle with pawns*, he thought as he watched men who had no stake in the war head out to die for his cause. An evil smile plastered across his face as the autobots clinked amid transforming into fighter jets before heading out, one after the other.

"What's your status?" Mr Henderson asked one of his generals with whom he'd tasked with the mission.

"T-minus ten minutes. That doesn't give them enough time to escape."

"So?" replied a voice from the other end of the intercom. But, of course, it was a secure line, so Henderson wasn't worried about the information falling on unwanted ears.

"Good. We're getting them this time around. Kalim's and Burne's respective deaths will make my ascension to power smoother than I'd ever anticipated."

"That's good news, sir," Dr Kean responded. Unlike Mr Henderson, the doctor had a worried look on his face.

He'd just realized he was in a trance for almost four minutes and had no idea what he was up to during that time. *As soon as Mr Henderson's mission is concluded successfully, I'll go and watch the surveillance*, Dr Kean told himself as they silently watched as the autobots-turned-jets switch into stealth mode momentarily before disappearing into the sky.

"Drop a few missiles and level that area. Kill everything that moves. Send in the drones to finish off the survivors."

"What if word gets around that we were behind the attacks?"

"We'll find a way to spin this. Remember, we own the media. Whatever we say is the gospel truth. Can you believe people two hundred years ago used to believe that shit? The gospel?" Mr Henderson chortled as he walked off majestically, "It's ridiculous."

Sandy lay peacefully on the table while the world around her burned. She looked unconscious; at least, that's what she made everyone around her think.

What they didn't know was Sandy had somehow accessed Dr Kean's brain for a few minutes, making him do her bidding. First, Sandy made the evil doctor send a signal to Fred. Sandy knew Fred would be watching. They didn't call him "eye in the sky" for nothing. Sandy also deactivated the electromagnetic field around the area, creating an abnormality, just in case Fred didn't connect the dots with the first hint. After that, all that was left was Adha mobilizing a team to come rescue her.

As soon as the soldiers were out of range, the door to the lab exploded, catching everyone by surprise. Before Mr Henderson's security detail could react, bullets began flying, taking them out one after another. Dr Kean and Mr Henderson took cover, ducking the bullets that rained over their heads.

The robots shielded the bullets as the two rushed towards the substantial room situated a couple of yards away. Dr Kean pressed his smartwatch and punched in the password when they got to the reinforced door. The adjacent wall moved to the side and immediately closed as soon as the two got in. That was a close shave. The robots turned around to guard the entrance.

"Save your ammo. Take out their eyes!" Adha shouted.

Adha had trained his team well. Half of his assault team took a knee and focused on the shootout with their human enemies while the sharpshooters took out the robot eyes. Without their eyes, the robots couldn't tell the hostiles from the friendlies. So, they shut down as they'd been programmed to do. The latter made it easy for Adha's team to take out the humans and clones. Thankfully, most of Mr Henderson's force had been dispatched for the decoy mission.

Mr Henderson and Dr Kean were right to worry about Adha Long's combat abilities. He was a veteran who'd fought and won countless battles, many of which he was at a disadvantage. However, Adha's skill as a tactician was also unmatched. That's why they wanted to neutralize him as quickly as possible.

"We don't have much time! Henderson's generals will realize the images their satellites picked up were doctored when they get to the wastelands. So, we better hurry! First, take the hard drives and set everything else ablaze. Then, shoot up everything else that moves!"

While Adha was busy shouting instructions to his assault team, Will and Natalie went straight to Sandy and began cutting the straps that held her down to the computerized bed. Sandy looked out of it, but at least she was still breathing. Will checked her pulse and was relieved to discover that Sandy was still alive.

He still had feelings for her, despite it going against his military training. Not having something to lose was what made great soldiers great. Sandy opened her eyes half-mast and managed a feeble smile as soon as she saw Will holding her in his strong arms.

"Took you long enough," Sandy joked feebly.

"We had to cause a diversion. Getting here wasn't easy."

"I'm glad you came. Something strange is happening to me, and I need to find out why."

Adha wanted Mr Henderson and Dr Kean dead, but they got away. He figured he'd catch them next time. The only thing that mattered at that moment was taking Sandy and escaping before the tide turned against them. But before Adha could mobilize his team to force their way out, the large screen in the control deck glitched, and in front of them appeared the image of the very man they hated most—Benedict Henderson.

"I have to admit, Kalim, you did well. Very few men in my life managed to deceive me the way you did. Congrats. I'll give you a second or two to celebrate that rare feat. But just like the few who managed to dupe me, you're about to meet your end. So, savour this victory because it'll most certainly be your last."

The image disappeared before Adha had the chance to respond. The reinforced doors and windows were shut before the ventilation began spraying a poisonous gas into the lab. Adha and his team began coughing and gasping for breath as they tried to find a way out. Will, who was struggling to stay conscious, held on to Sandy, who was slipping in and out.

"I love you," Will managed to say in between coughs before passing out completely.

It was at this point Sandy opened her eyes, and they were glowing green. She stared at the control centre situated at the furthest end of the lab and joined her consciousness with the motherboard. *This is the strangest feeling,* Sandy thought. Sandy could feel her mind connected to the AI software, which seemed not only to understand but execute her commands.

It took a few seconds, but the settings began reversing. Both Dr Kean and Mr Henderson couldn't believe what was happening. The New Order leader picked up his glass tablet and began pressing buttons on the screen repeatedly, but nothing worked.

"Have we been hacked?" he growled angrily, throwing his tablet into the floor.

"No, sir. I don't think so," Dr Kean said calmly as he pointed at the screen right in front of them. "I think Sandy Krave is doing that!"

……………

Chapter Two

"That's impossible!" Mr Henderson roared, "call back the forces. We need to end this here and now!" Dr Kean fumbled with his com device before giving the order.

"We're on our way, sir. The intel we intercepted…"

"What about it?"

"A smokescreen, sir."

"Yes, we're aware of that! Kalim and his men are here! How long until you get here? We're under attack!"

"We're approximately ten minutes out, sir. So, we'll try and speed things up."

The harmful gas cleared out of the lab, and Adha's men slowly regained consciousness. Most of them had no idea where they were. But after taking a moment to examine their surroundings and gather their thoughts, reality dawned pretty quickly.

"Pick up the guns and get into battle formation!" Adha growled; the rawness of his baritone was proof of his readiness to shed enemy blood.

The assault team followed his orders, grabbed their guns, and got into formation. They overturned the steel tables facing both entrances and took cover behind them. They were ready for the worst.

Sandy was kneeling next to Will with two pistols pointing in opposite directions. She still wasn't operating at a hundred per cent, though her current condition was more than most of her enemies could manage. Nevertheless, Sandy was Adha's best recruit, and he was always proud of her accomplishments.

She had many unanswered questions, and the only person she was sure had the answers was Adha. But, her mission at the moment was to get her team out of there as quickly as possible.

"Can you re-access the mainframe? We need the schematics of the building if we're to find a way out!" Adha shouted.

"I… I think I can," Sandy stuttered. *How could he even know I could do that?* She closed her eyes and tried to focus, and just like before, her consciousness linked with the AI that ran Mr Henderson's secret base.

It took a few seconds before Sandy opened her eyes and pointed to the left with a pistol nozzle.

"We need to blow a hole in that wall using C4. It'll lead us directly to the underground parking lot. From there, we can fight our way out through the driveway."

"You heard her. Let's move!" Will shouted.

Two of the soldiers ran towards the wall, stuck the C4 in place, and connected the necessary wires. From the looks of it, one could tell the soldiers had done that several times before. The rest of the assault team took cover behind overturned tables and waited for the blast. It took less than a minute to get everything in order before they set the fuse.

But before they could activate the C4 on the wall, a massive explosion went off behind them, sending everyone flying in all directions. Mr Henderson's team breached the steel doors using an RPG projectile, catching Adha and his assault team off guard. Sandy had successfully shut Dr Kean and Mr Henderson out of the controls. That's why they chose to go old-school.

Sandy woke up to an ear-splitting headache. The ringing in her ear took a moment to clear up. Then, though her eyes were blurry, Sandy could see robots coming in through the rubble with their laser guns blazing. She immediately got up and began shooting wildly while screaming blue murder. On that fateful afternoon, many of Mr Henderson's foot soldiers died by Sandy's hand.

Since she'd been practising, her shots were perfect. Sometimes a single bullet could kill more than three soldiers as it ricocheted and bounced on the steel walls. Sandy's violence provided cover for all her people to set the C4 and only stopped to take cover outside when she heard, "Fire in the hole!" The C4 exploded, and it was the enemy's turn to get thrown off their feet.

"MOVE!" Adha shouted amid firing several rounds a minute. He hit his mark every time he squeezed the trigger. They were outnumbered ten to one. But even with such a disadvantage, they still managed to do some severe damage.

As soon as Adha's assault team escaped into the underground parking lot, the motion-sensor lights began flickering up, revealing another battalion of hardened soldiers waiting for them. The enemy in the parking lot began firing electric-charged rubber bullets as soon as they saw movement.

Two of their devastating rounds found a home in two of Adha's men, taking them out immediately. The two fell to the ground and immediately began convulsing with jolts of electricity running through them.

"Fuck! Take cover!" Will shouted as he pressed against the nearest armoured autobot.

… … …

"What did I tell you?" Sandy's clone said with a smile on her cute face. "You never know what we would find in this Godforsaken island."

"Hell yes, you were right."

Nyman and Sandy's clone had been walking for almost half a day before they got to a secret military base. From the looks of it, it was one of the many secret IC bases that Mr Henderson liked to have. But, for some reason, it was abandoned. So Nyman figured that maybe they'd been recalled by Mr Henderson to act as reinforcements.

"Is that an autobot?"

"I think so," said Nyman.

"Can you fly one of those?"

"My sister and I are the best pilots in the four continents. We just don't like to brag."

"Ok, if you insist. In that case, let's commandeer the autobot and fly out."

"Fly out to where?"

"We are flying out to the hot zone. I am Sandy's clone. I can sense where she's being held. If we fly there on time, we can get them."

Nyman didn't wait another second. They took out their guns and cautiously walked to the autobot. A few minutes later, Nyman and Sandy's clone were up in the air.

… … …

Attacks from both fronts made it hard for Adha's assault team to move. The only option was staying put and grinding it out to the bitter end. All they could do was hope they didn't run out of ammunition. From where Will was standing, he could see more troops pouring into the underground parking lot. So, he switched his tactic and started firing at the entrance, making it hard for more to come in.

Adha was on the other side of the parking lot doing what he did best—taking names and kicking ass. He ran as fast as he could towards the first human soldier and kicked him in the belly. As the victim bent over, retching his insides in pain, Adha grabbed his head and planted it into the concrete, killing him instantly. The three soldiers who bore down in his direction met the same gruesome fate. Adha took their guns and began shooting as a man possessed.

Sandy, who was watching Adha's six, did the same. She put down everyone and everything in her path: soldiers, clones, and robots. Simply put, Sandy just wasn't in the mood to discriminate. So instead, she did precisely what Adha did when he ran out of ammo—overwhelm her next victim, take their piece, then simply carry on with the carnage.

The shootout lasted for almost an hour. That was when it became clear that the New Order was losing. Even though Adha and his team of assassins were outnumbered, they proved to be way more effective. That and the fact that Sandy, Will, and Adha were on the same team, Mr Henderson's small army simply had no chance.

"Sir, I think we should recall our forces from the borders," Dr Kean suggested.

Mr Henderson didn't have an immediate answer, as was his norm. If his body language was anything to go by, he needed more time to think. His ego wanted his men to keep pushing until they overwhelmed Adha's men. His mettle, on the other hand, told him to retreat and live to fight another day.

Recalling his forces from the borders will weaken his defences, exposing them to the neighbouring enemies they just created. For a moment, Mr Henderson regretted having created so many enemies.

But there are no great rewards that come without taking significant risks. Besides, the one thing that made him so successful was his ability to put his ego aside, acknowledge defeat, then turn that defeat into a win.

If anyone would pull such a stunt and do so successfully, then it would be him. *Besides, losing a battle doesn't mean I can't win the war*, Mr Henderson told himself. If he allowed his ego to take over, Adha and his assault team would quickly kill the rest of his forces before the reinforcements came. There was no telling if Adha would go for him next.

"Tell the men in the parking lot to fall back. Give Adha and his men leeway to escape, then tag their autobot with a tracker. After that, we will regroup and go after them."

"Well, you heard the man!" Dr Kean shouted, leaving the IT personnel dodging missiles of his spittle as they looked for a secure line to connect the intercom.

Adha noticed Mr Henderson's men falling back and urged his own to march forward, guns blazing. The left side of his face was red with blood that almost blocked his eye. But that wasn't enough to make him less effective. Adha wielded a blood-soaked machete in one hand and a pistol in the other, doing the most damage.

As soon as they were all gone, an autobot appeared from thin air and began firing at the retreating troops. Adha and his men pointed their guns and almost fired at the autobot, only for them to catch a glimpse of Nyman.

"Don't shoot! Don't shoot! It's me!" Nyman shouted as soon as he landed the autobot. "We don't have time. The enemy is coming in droves. We need to get the hell out of here!" Sandy noticed her clone and raised her gun to shoot her, only for Nyman to stop her. "I know it's weird, but I wouldn't be here without her help. I'll explain later, but for now, we need to get moving."

No one trusted the clones, but they trusted Nyman. So, they put their guns away and began evacuating as quickly as they could.

Sandy and Will were tending to their wounded, patching them up and quickly loading them into Nyman's autobot. Sandy could tell Will had many questions to ask her, but the timing was wrong. Heck, Sandy also had a lot of questions she needed answered.

For instance, Sandy wanted to know how she managed to read Will's mind. *Maybe Adha had the answers. That crafty old man always has answers for everything!* But, the most important thing at the time was getting out of there alive. Even in the face of victory, the odds were still stacked against them. No one in their right mind would dare underestimate Mr Henderson, especially his ability to catch his opponents off guard.

"Is everyone in?" Adha asked as he pulled a blade that he'd buried into a dying clone's chest. His bloodied face was covered in disgust as he stared at the clone taking its last breath. Adha hated clones, especially after the Sandy-clone debacle.

"I think so, sir. But, first, we need to collect the dead…"

"We don't have time for that! If we don't leave now, we'll be joining them in the afterlife."

Adha was the last one to get in after ensuring no one was left behind. Natalie took the controls and began following the protocols to fire up the engines. Out of twenty, only seven were left. The idea of leaving their dead brothers- and sisters-in-arms behind was against the 40 Grade Code. But a lot had happened, and a lot was still at stake.

The world was about to be taken over by a maniac, and Adha Long's team was the only hope for salvation. They couldn't afford to get their spark fizzled out. Everyone let out a sigh of relief as soon as they heard the engines roaring. Even though it only took Natalie a few minutes to get it started, it felt like hours.

For the first time, Will sat back and took a good look at Sandy's bloodied-up face. Despite the mess, Sandy looked as beautiful as ever, especially her bewitching green eyes. Their eyes met moments later, and Sandy blushed. She could read his mind, so she knew whatever dirty thoughts Will entertained about what he was planning on doing to her later on.

Then out of the hole emerged a clone—Sandy's other clone. She had a gun in her hand, took an aim, and squeezed the trigger. Will, who spotted the clone, knew precisely who the bullet was intended for. He quickly pushed Sandy to the side and began firing rapidly at the clone before falling on the ground lifeless. The bullet that was meant for Sandy hit him in the head, killing him instantly.

"NOOOOOO!" Sandy screamed as the autobot doors slammed shut before it converted into a fighter jet.

Adha and his men held Sandy down as she fought against them for her freedom. She wanted to jump from the fighter jet and kill her other clone. Sandy kicked and punched, but the team held her down. A sudden surge of power exploded from Sandy, passing through everyone like a wave and knocking out all electromagnetic waves for a few seconds. Thankfully since the plane was getting ready to take off, the built-in solar cells power reserves kept it from being completely dead in the water. Natalie struggled to repower the engines to full power as Sandy's eyes rolled back in her head. The raw energy was too much for Sandy, and she passed out. As the engines roared back to life, Sandy's eyes fluttered back open. Confusion, then recognition of what had just happened, passed across her gaze.

Adha and his men continued holding Sandy down, making sure she wasn't endangering herself or anyone else as Natalie manoeuvred the plane into the air. But she just lay there, not knowing how to react. She couldn't believe what she had just witnessed. Everyone was shocked. The last thing they ever expected was to lose Will, at least not at that moment. He was instrumental in the war, and now that he was gone, Adha and his assault team knew they had their work cut out for them.

Painful tears blurred Sandy's green eyes as she looked over to Will's lifeless body. His eyes were still open as he lay motionless in a pool of his own blood. Sandy reached over and grabbed his hand, squeezing it as gently as she could. "I'm so sorry I couldn't save you," Sandy told Will silently as she cried.

Sandy Krave had lost many friends in battle, but it never hurt her as much as it did now. Will Burne was special. He made her love working with other people. He was a superb soldier, and most importantly, he was her lover. Will's hand continued to grow colder as they flew higher and higher into the stratosphere.

The feeling of sadness was immediately replaced with the feeling of anger. Sandy could feel her entire body trembling. The last time she had that feeling was when she found out how her parents were killed when she was just a baby. The only difference was that now, Sandy was old enough to do something about it. It was then that she swore to kill Benedict Henderson and everyone that stood by him.

Adha Long and the remnants of his assault team flew safely out of Benedict Henderson's secret base and out of range. They were down but not out. Yet again, the rest of them had lived to fight another day.

……………

Acknowledgements

To my wife for always going on the journey with me.
To my son for his invaluable interest in everything I do.

To my close friends for keeping me reasonably sane and encouraging me to continue believing in myself.

To Jeannie Culbertson, The Noteworthy Mom, for her contributions to this book.

ABOUT THE AUTHOR

Robert De Vinn is a fresh new author of military science fiction with a spark of intimate romance and subtle amusement.

Projected in a new era, he will take you through a journey into a world of potential cataclysm and drastic change, not far from today's apocalyptic realism of skeptical experts who do not see future technology and the thirst for power as a good sign for mankind.

In the 22nd century, the super-rich and evil underworld are ready to establish power and control over the Four Reigns.

What they didn't realize was that our rising hero, Special Agent Sandy Krave, graduate of the mystic 40 Grade Military Elite, was about to unleash a hidden force from deep within.

Will our gorgeous superhero protect humanity and restore peace and democracy before it's too late? You won't want to miss Book 2.

Thank You for Reading My Book!

I really appreciate all of your feedback, and I love hearing what you have to say. I need your input to make my future books better.

Please leave me an honest review on Amazon to let me know your thoughts and where you think Sandy Krave might end up next!

Thanks so much!

–Robert de Vinn

www.robertdevinn.com

Printed in Poland
by Amazon Fulfillment
Poland Sp. z o.o., Wrocław

79425848R00209